THE TWISTED CROWN

ANITA BUNKLEY

RINARD PUBLISHING

ALSO BY ANITA RICHMOND BUNKLEY

Fiction

A Thousand Steps

Starlight Passage

Wild Embers

Black Gold

Emily, the Yellow Rose

Between Goodbyes

You Only Get Better

Silent Wager

Relative Interest

Mirrored Life

Girlfriends

Balancing Act

Romance

Boardroom Seduction

First Class Seduction

Vote for Love

Spotlight on Desire

Suite Embrace

Non-Fiction

Stepping Out With Attitude: Sister, Sell Your Dream

To My Family
Another link is broken
In our household band
But a chain is forming
In a better land

PART I

"Babies was snatched from deir mother's breast and sold to speculators. Chillens was separated from sisters and brothers and never saw each other again. 'Course dey cry. You think they not cry when dey was sold like cattle? I could tell you about it all day, but even den you couldn't guess the awfulness of it."

Delia Garlic, enslaved in Virginia. Interviewed in Fruithurst, Alabama at age 100. *Voices from Slavery*
(New York: Holt, Rinehart and Winston, 1970)

PROLOGUE

MAYREE

1846 St. John's Berkeley, South Carolina

A flat white disk settled high into an inky black sky created a wide swath of moonlight over the dark waters of the Cooper River. The luminous glow, broken intermittently by shadows of a fleeting cloud, lingered over the landscape in a shimmering veil of silver.

Mayree studied the river, so quiet, dark, and full of promise, fearing she had come too late, terrified that her plan would fail. From deep within the curtain of darkness that offered a welcome, but false, sense of safety, came the tart smell of burning pine pitch, most likely, she thought, from the camp of Indians living in the abandoned plantation on the east side of the river.

Mayree squeezed Eva's small hand, then squatted down to level her eyes with those of her daughter. Placing a finger to her lips, she shook her head, praying that the four-year-old understood the desperate need to remain quiet, calm, and brave. Placing her hand on the child's tousled black curls, she studied Eva's round cheeks and inquisitive dark eyes, knowing that a child as sweet and trusting as Eva could not possibly understand what Mayree was about to do.

While lying on the blood-soaked straw that had been her birthing bed, Mayree had vowed to protect the only girl-child she had ever brought into the world from the future she would endure as a woman on Stillwater Plantation. And now the time had come to do the unthinkable: Mayree was going to give her daughter away.

The night air was restless. Agitated by a damp wind sweeping off the river, declaring a threat of rain, heightening the acrid scent of rotting palmetto leaves that carpeted the forest floor. After placing a firm kiss on Eva's forehead, Mayree stood, took the child's hand, and walked closer to the water's edge to scan the length of the river with concern. Her gaze moved slowly as she carefully assessed the shadowy edges of the muted landscape, shifting from the oak-shaded clearing on the opposite shore where the Indians had made camp to the bend in the river where a thick drape of Spanish moss floated down from the limbs of a massive cypress tree, blocking her downriver view.

A coil of fear tightened inside Mayree as she stood there, waiting, worrying, and watching. Clasping the folds of her brown cotton skirt in a tight fist she lifted it high, knowing she had to keep her dress dry, keep her hair free of twigs, and make sure her hands and arms showed no sign that she'd pushed her way through brambles and brush to reach the riverbank. If the mistress of Stillwater spied water stains on the hem of Mayree's dress when she served the Cantrell family their morning meal of corncake, ham, and warm sweet milk, what excuse could Mayree possibly give for a sullied appearance, or the absence of Eva at her side?

Cautiously, she tucked the hem of her dress into her waistband, lifted Eva into her arms, and stepped into the water, her bare feet sinking into the marshy shoreline as mud inched up around her ankles. She stood like a sentry on watch, the night sounds of the forest filling her head and sending her heart racing. Clutching her child, eyes unblinking, every muscle frozen, she waited.

It was not until the shadowy image of a crude dugout sitting low in the water came into view that Mayree sucked in a sharp breath, her relief tinged with heartbreak.

Desperate to calm her child, as well as herself, Mayree began to whisper-sing softly into her daughter's ear.

Ka a fo, ka a fo,Kaa a fo no mo ko kwa-da
Ji ka ke kpo, You daa, kaa foni, ma ko, kusto dan.

The gentle African lullaby was nearly all that Mayree remembered of her own mother, who had sung it to her while they were chained together in the belly of a roiling ship packed with others from their village. Eight-years-old at the time, Mayree had allowed the soothing sound of her mother's voice to replace the fear that gripped her as they made their way to the strange new land where they were split apart forever.

Now, as Eva's small body grew limp in her arms, Mayree gripped her daughter more fiercely, willing herself to be brave. And when Eva snuggled her head against her mother's breast Mayree began to whisper-sing the song once more, this time in the language that Eva understood.

Don't cry, don't cry, don't cry and let anyone see your mouth. There is gold in your mouth. Don't cry and let anyone see your mouth.

Suddenly, the boat was near, so close that Mayree could see the woman sitting in the bow of the vessel; a plain lady with a wood-brown face, dressed in the rough clothing of a river man. It was Tully Simson. The free black woman Mayree had met just six days earlier: The woman who was keeping her promise to take Eva away from the slave-breeding plantation that even the locals referred to as a prison rather than a place where indigo and cotton were grown.

Mayree had heard about Tully Simson, whose talent with a needle and thread made her the most sought-after seamstress in St. Johns Berkeley. The white ladies living along the river paid Tully a handsome wage to sew their dresses, as well as draperies and bed linens for their low country mansions. After accumulating sufficient money to purchase her freedom Tully had approached her master, who agreed to set her free. And now that she was leaving South Carolina, as the law required she do, she had offered to take Eva with her when she started her journey north.

Now, the crude vessel made a slow half-turn in the middle of the

Cooper River and headed directly to the spot where Mayree and Eva waited. Taking careful steps deeper into the water, Mayree leaned forward, lifted a hand, and waved a scrap of white cloth in the air. Tully raised her arm as well, sending Mayree the signal she had been praying to see. In spite of the swirl of fear, the weight of her grief, and the press of guilt that flooded Mayree, she gave in to a quiet sense of joy. She had to do this. She had no choice.

When the boat had drawn close enough for Mayree to make eye contact with Tully, she nodded at the woman but dared not speak, having decided not to utter any words of parting. When Tully stood and motioned for Mayree to pass the child to her, it took all of Mayree's emotional strength to deliver her daughter into the hands of this woman who, hopefully, would be a comfort to her child.

Tully quickly wrapped a tattered bed quilt around Eva, binding her arms to her sides, turning her into a miniature mummy with only her small brown face peering out. When suddenly, Eva screamed for her mother, her tiny voice cracking the still night air, Mayree broke her vow of silence and comforted her daughter in the loudest whisper she dared to use.

"*Ka a fo, ka a fo*. Don't cry, don't cry," she sang with a hand over her heart while stepping back onto land. She leaned against the rough bark of the cypress tree, shaking her head in sorrow as Tully tied a kerchief over Eva's mouth to stifle what Mayree knew would have been a desperate, chilling plea filled with anger and fright.

'*Course she gonna cry,* Mayree silently lamented. *Wouldn't any chile torn from her mother's arms cry out?*

When the boat pushed out toward the middle of the river, Mayree covered her ears with her hands in an effort to block out Tully's voice as she urged Eva not to be afraid, not to struggle or call out for her mother, who was not coming with them.

The dull throbbing that had been hammering inside Mayree's chest for the past six days swelled into an acute pain that held her in place. Her daughter was going out of her life forever, and the realization brought a deep sense of loss that was piercingly painful, but still, oddly comforting. Mayree had already lost five sons to the

Slave Market in Charleston. She would not lose her only daughter. And even though she knew that once the master of Stillwater discovered what she had done, she too, would surely find herself on the auction block or punished so severely she might wish she had been sold. But Mayree didn't care what happened to her. Eva now had a chance to live her life far from the degradation and evil into which she had been born.

Silent tears flowed from Mayree's eyes as she watched the boat slip into the purposeful flow of the Cooper River and disappear from sight. She did not move until the sound of Jacob Cantrell's barking dogs, peppered with her master's shouts to move faster, shattered the quiet night air and sent her mind whirling back to the day she overheard Cantrell boasting to a neighboring landowner that he fed stillborn babies to the dogs to make them hungry for black flesh. Mayree steeled herself for capture, a wry smile of satisfaction on her lips. Eva was safely around the bend in the river, sweeping southward toward Charleston Harbor, and hopefully, into the life of a free woman with a real chance at happiness.

The captain of the ship assured Tully that as long as she and Eva remained hidden among the crates and barrels of cotton and rice headed to market in Boston, Massachusetts they would be safe. He'd been kind enough to place a jug of water, an overripe peach, and a chunk of dried pork on the floor of the cramped space they would occupy for the next ten days.

With a great sense of relief, but without a loss of fear, Tully removed the quilt from around Eva's small body and spread it on the splintered wood floor. "We are safe now," she said, holding the jug of water to Eva's mouth to let her drink her fill. "You eat that peach," she urged Eva, pointing at the piece of fruit. "Take it. It's all right."

Eva's large brown eyes moved slowly from Tully's face to the fragrant peach, her tiny fingers hovering above it as if seeking reassurance that no punishment would come from accepting the first real food she'd seen in days.

"Go on. Take it," Tully urged, understanding the child's fear and confusion. The only food they had eaten since starting their journey had been wild berries pulled from thorny bushes and crumbs of dry bread she carried in her skirt pocket. However, the journey so far, had been trouble-free. Travelling after the sun disappeared below the horizon, they drifted southward on a slow-moving current that pulled them toward the outskirts of Charleston. After arriving at the city, Tully had successfully located the house of the white woman she had been told would help her on the next leg of her journey. The woman quickly hid the newly arrived fugitives in the back of her wagon and took them directly to the wharf, to be handed over to the captain of the *Marbelle*, with whom she often arranged passage for runaways. When the ship's captain saw that Tully had brought a child with her who was dressed in rough slave clothing, and shaking with fear, he'd asked no questions, but had gruffly ordered, "Get on below and stay there."

Now, Tully tilted her head toward Eva and wagged a finger. "If you don't want the peach, I will eat it. I'm just as hungry as you are," she said in an authoritative tone, taking control of the situation. The child was her responsibility now, both a blessing and a burden, and Tully knew she had to act like a mother, had to put the little girl on notice that she'd be wise to do as she was told.

Tully's lips curved slightly when Eva grabbed the peach and eagerly bit into it, the sticky juice dripping between her small fingers and running down her chin. It was clear to Tully why Mayree had been so desperate to get her daughter away from Still-water, where possessing a beautiful female child brought more pain than joy to a mother. Eva's skin was the color of gingerbread, a rich brown hue harboring a deeper shade of red, and when she turned her small round face up to Tully, the sight made her catch her breath. Once they arrived in Boston, she knew she'd have to shield Eva from the view of strangers as they walked the cobbled streets, where curious people might walk right up to the pretty little girl and place admiring hands on her head or run curious fingers through her thick black curls, drawing unwanted attention.

Would Jacob Cantrell send bounty hunters to rip the girl from Tully's arms and return her to a life of horror? Eva's beauty was rare, and the uncertainty of their future brought a cascade of worry to Tully. Who would help them once they left the protection of the ship's captain and entered the world of free black people? Where would she and Eva find shelter in a place she had heard was teeming with people from places far beyond the great sea? The thoughts that whirled around in Tully's head twisted and turned, making her dizzy. Scooting deeper into a corner, she closed her eyes and tried to ignore the aches and pains that gripped her soul.

She had nearly drifted off to sleep when, with a jolt, the ship began to creak and groan as it started out to sea, startling Eva, who dropped her half-eaten peach and crawled onto Tully's lap. The child burrowed her head against Tully's breast and exhaled a sigh that seemed to deflate her tiny body, making her even smaller. Firming her lips, determined to stay brave, Tully dragged the ragged quilt from the floor and covered Eva's quivering shoulders.

CHAPTER 1

EVA

Boston
November 1862

He didn't look like the usual merchant who came into *Fitzgerald's Signs and Maps* seeking a sign-maker to create a placard to hang outside his establishment. First of all, he was not white, and he was wearing a well-tailored shirt with a collar, a tan twill jacket, trousers with a decent crease, and brown leather boots that had been polished to an impressive shine. Neat, clean, and not at all shabby, he presented a competent, clean appearance. He was youthful, with a mature set to his features, and Eva, who was approaching twenty-one years of age, calculated that the man could not have been more than a year or two older than she.

Eva set aside the thin piece of pinewood she had been studiously transforming into a colorful window sign for the local baker's shop, featuring her rendition of the establishment's specialty: blueberry pie. Cleaning her paintbrush with a piece of cloth, she smiled at the stranger standing in front of her and said, "Hello. May I help you?"

Leaning over the worktable stationed between them, the young man slid his gaze across Eva's face, removed his hat, and nodded. After a pause slight enough to indicate his obvious pleasure in looking at Eva, he cleared his throat with a muffled cough and said, "Yes. I'm here to see the mapmaker, Mr. Fitzgerald."

Eva suppressed a smile while matching his inspection of her with one of her own, noting that his mahogany features were pleasantly arranged in a kind of harmony that struck her as nearly perfect. He had a high forehead that was boldly domed, broad, and free of worry lines. His expression radiated an impression of studious intelligence, coupled with a cockiness that added sparkle to keen eyes that were sharp and deliberate, as if he were accustomed to searching for things not readily visible but certain he would find them. His nose had a slightly stubby shape to the end, softening the sharp crest of cheekbones that stood out like tiny brown apples, polished and smooth. He was of medium height, rather stocky in stature, implying strength that might have come from engaging in some type of manual labor. However, Eva suspected this young man had moved beyond work that made him sweat, even though so many of the black men living in Boston earned their living as longshoremen or day laborers on the wharf.

"Oh, I'm sorry." Eva tilted her head to the side, an apologetic expression tightening her lips. "Mr. Fitzgerald is not here."

The young man stepped back from the table, pausing as he considered this news. However, impatience did not color his words when he asked Eva, "How long before Mr. Fitzgerald returns?"

"He has left for the day ... and I was preparing to close the shop." When he did not speak, she quickly added, "But perhaps I might be able to help you, Mr. ...?"

"Phillips," he promptly supplied. "Chester Phillips. I'm here to pick up the map that Mr. Fitzgerald completed for my employer, Lawyer Daniels. He said it would be ready today."

As Chester spoke, Eva noticed that his inquisitive eyes were flitting about the room, scanning the tables, desks, and shelves along the walls, all stacked with books and papers that had accumulated during the twenty-plus years that Mr. Fitzgerald had been in business. In addition to providing street maps of the city and property descriptions for local residents, Fitzgerald's mapmaking skills were sought out by professors, explorers, farmers, and seamen from all across the country.

The fact that Mr. Fitzgerald had left Eva alone, and in charge of the closing the shop for the day, proved that he felt she was perfectly capable of tending the establishment in his absence. When she first came to the mapmaker's place of business three years ago and politely requested he consider her as an apprentice, he had smiled indulgently and shrugged off her inquiry with a wave of his ink-stained hand. However, after examining the samples of her artwork that she boldly placed upon his desk, he immediately took notice of her potential and agreed to accept her as his assistant. Never one to shy away from a challenge or refuse to step into a situation that might hold another, more modest and careful, young lady back, Eva had greeted her position with relish, determined to prove, not only to herself but also to those who doubted her, that she had what it took to do the job.

Now, she adopted her most professional tone as she told Chester Phillips, "Oh yes. Mr. Fitzgerald did tell me that Mr. Daniels would be sending someone to pick up his map today." She drew in a short breath, then added in a lighthearted tone, "So, you're the *someone*?"

Chester's reaction to her teasing clearly amused him. He grinned broadly and raised his chin. "Yes. I'm that someone. I pick up and deliver Lawyer Daniels' important papers." Then, he added, with inquisitive brown eyes steady with hers, "I do appreciate your help, Miss…..?" obviously fishing for her name.

"Miss Simson. Eva Simson," she told him, pleased that he had asked.

"Pleased to meet you," he replied.

Assuming the role of the person in charge, she stood. Adopting the business-like tone that she'd heard Mr. Fitzgerald use with his clients, she told Chester, "I know the piece you want. Wait here. I'll get it for you." Turning from him, she walked into an alcove off the main room where a tall cabinet fit with narrow drawers stood between two windows. Opening a middle drawer, she removed a piece of parchment the size of a large handbill and placed it on a nearby table. Looking back at Chester, she motioned him over. "Would you like to see this before I wrap it?"

Without answering, Chester moved closer to Eva, entering the alcove and standing at her side. He picked up the map and studied it closely. "Very nice," he remarked, scrutinizing the maze of streets and alleyways and buildings marked on the map in sharp black ink. However, his attention quickly shifted to Eva as he inquired, "Did you draw this?"

"Oh, no," she rushed to reply, straightening her shoulders with a bit of pride that the good-looking man standing with her might think so. After completing her education at Boston's Abiel Smith School for Negroes, she had welcomed the opportunity to apprentice with the local sign-maker, who believed her artistic talent and excellent penmanship made her well suited to the work. "But ..." she continued, "as Mr. Fitzgerald's assistant, I was allowed to complete the lettering along the borders."

"Most impressive. So, you plan to be a mapmaker, too?" he asked, placing the map back down on the table.

"I'd like to think so. Drawing fruits and flowers and shoes and hats for merchants' signs is enjoyable, but I'd much prefer to map city streets or country roads. Mr. Fitzgerald allowed me to complete the lettering on Mr. Daniels' map because he thinks my penmanship is neater than his."

"And I would have to agree with him, though I've never seen his work." Chester lowered his eyes to the map again, giving the drawing an appreciative lift of his eyebrows as he pointed to a spot where two streets came together. "Mount Vernon and Joy," he said, tapping the paper. "That's where I live.... with Lawyer Daniels."

"Oh?" Eva leaned closer, appreciating the sweet scent of laundry soap that came to her from Chester's clothing. "That's directly across the street from the courthouse," she remarked.

"Yes, it is," he agreed, then added, "I stay right there, with him."

"Well, I'd say that's a proper location for a lawyer and his assistant."

"Exactly," Chester replied.

Eva took up the map and reached for a sheet of brown paper. "Would you like me to roll it or do you want me to wrap it flat?" she inquired, having heard Mr. Fitzgerald ask his customers the same question.

"You can roll it. Lawyer Daniels keeps all his maps rolled."

"Fine." She tore off a square of brown paper from a hefty roll. "Do you know what this map will be used for?" she inquired, making conversation while her fingers held onto the corners of the map as she created a tight, cylindrical package.

"It's for a case Lawyer Daniels is presenting in court tomorrow. … somethin' about a fight over a fence between two houses. You know, he's a right smart man… the only colored lawyer I ever met."

"I know. I've seen him around the city," Eva remarked. "I hear he does a lot of good, helping our people with legal matters." She kept her eyes on the task at hand, aware that Chester had moved forward and was standing closer, watching her, and she wondered if he could sense how tense he made her feel.

After she had carefully rolled and tied the map with a generous length of twine, she wrote Mr. Daniels's name on the outside of the package and handed it to Chester.

"Here you are. I hope your employer will be pleased."

"Lawyer Daniels said for Mr. Fitzgerald to send him the bill," Chester informed Eva, extending his hand, which she quickly shook.

"I'll make sure he gets the message," she replied, stepping away from the table and moving toward the door, indicating their exchange was over. However, Chester did not move. He simply gazed at her as if he had more to say. "Is there anything else I can help you with?" she prompted. "I have to close the shop now."

Shaking his head, he finally walked toward the entry. "Oh…no. Nothing else. Thank you for your help, Miss Simson," he stated, clearly enjoying saying her name. However, instead of reaching for the doorknob, Chester clasped his hands together and remained rooted where he stood, biting his bottom lip, hesitant to go. After a pause, he asked, in a rush of words that tumbled from his mouth like pebbles falling over a ledge, "If you're about to close the shop … would you like me to wait?"

"Wait?" she repeated.

"Yes, ma'am. It gets dark real fast these days ..."

The quizzical expression that Eva shot Chester pushed him to clarify, "I mean … I'd be happy to walk you home. That's if …"

"If I would like the company?" she finished, unable to disguise her pleasure.

"Yes. That's exactly what I mean."

After giving the offer a moment of thought, Eva answered, "That would be very nice of you, Mr. Phillips."

Eva hurriedly cleared her workstation of the pots of paint and array of brushes she used in her work, extinguished the oil lamps burning throughout the shop, and then removed her shawl from the hook beside the door to wrap it around her shoulders.

"I'm ready to go," she told Chester, and after locking the shop door behind her, they started down Beacon Street, fighting a brisk November wind that was sending a shower of colorful leaves whirling along the cobblestone walk.

"Now, which way do we go?" Chester asked.

When Eva looked over at him, he smiled, holding her eyes with his long enough for her heart to turn over and settle in her stomach. She exhaled, gathering her composure. "I live on Russell Street."

"You live with your ma and pa?" he tentatively probed.

"No, I live with my aunt. Her name is Tully Simson. We're not far from the African Meeting House … I'm sure you know where that is."

"I do. I heard Frederick Douglass speak there … a week past … he had a lot to say about the war."

"I wish I'd seen him," Eva murmured, still regretting she had taken her aunt's advice and stayed away from the abolitionists' meeting. Too dangerous, Tully had decided. Too political. Too risky, even for a girl who had lived in the city as a free black woman most all of her life.

The anti-slavery issue was an extremely volatile topic, drawing orators and activists to Boston where they spoke to large crowds in meeting halls and churches to inform and inspire Northern blacks and whites alike to speak out against the institution of slavery.

"What did Mr. Douglass talk about?" Eva asked, turning her thoughts back to Chester.

"He said black men oughta be allowed to fight for the Union … for the freedom of their enslaved brothers and sisters. He said there's black men in the South actually fighting for the *Confederates*."

"Really?"

"Yeah. Mostly free blacks who got it in their heads they have to defend their homeland. But they don't carry guns. They just serve their masters and do the hard work in the soldiers' camps. You can bet southerners not lettin' their slaves really fight … well … not like real soldiers with muskets on their shoulders and bullets in their pockets." Chester grunted in disgust. "Mr. Douglass said black Union soldiers need to be in the field, with guns, fighting right alongside the white men. Let 'em fight, he said. Sacrifices gotta be made."

Chester stepped forward to walk slightly in front of Eva to clear her path through a knot of white men who were standing on the sidewalk, talking in an animated manner. As Eva followed him, she heard one of the men utter a derogatory comment that caused her to stare directly into his face. He made a motion, as if spitting on the ground, but his eyes never left hers. Straightening her back, Eva broke the connection and looked straight ahead, quickening her steps to catch up with Chester.

"Enough talk about the war," Chester decided as they matched their strides and continued up the street, shoulders nearly touching. "It's not a suitable subject to talk about with a lady, anyway."

"But I think it is," Eva insisted, eager to hear more of Chester's thoughts on a war that would determine the fate of thousands of enslaved people. People like her mother, whom Eva hoped was still alive—the mother who might be thinking of the daughter she gave away.

"Would you join up and fight if you could?" she asked.

"Of course," Chester was quick to answer. "It'd be my duty as a black man."

"Yes, I agree ... I guess it would," Eva murmured, impressed with the ring of certainty in his words.

"Well ... gettin' off the subject of war," he started, "what do you do when you're not workin' for the mapmaker?"

Before responding, Eva hurried over to the milliner's shop window to peruse the display of ladies' hats, and while admiring the decorative feathers and ribbons that adorned the hats, she considered Chester's question. Working for Mr. Fitzgerald four days a week and helping her aunt with chores on her free days had been the pattern of Eva's life for the last three years. There was nothing particularly exciting about how she spent her time; she was as content as she felt she deserved to be and had settled into a rhythm that suited her and her aunt. Turning slightly to face Chester, who had stepped up behind her, she settled on an answer. "I go to church."

"Church?" he repeated, head tilted to the side as he sucked his teeth and sighed. "Truth be told, been a long while since I been in a church."

Eva widened her eyes and grinned. "I'm going next Sunday."

"Where do you go?" he wanted to know.

"The AME church on Grove Street."

"What time?" he cautiously probed.

She lifted a shoulder, then returned to her examination of the hats in the window. "Service starts at nine o'clock...," she said, keeping her back to Chester. "And ... our Fall Potluck Dinner is next Sunday, directly after service. It'll be outside on the church grounds if the weather holds. There'll be food, and music too." An uncertain moment passed before she turned around to face him. "You should come." Then, Eva raised her chin and searched

Chester's face, wondering if she was inviting him to church because she wanted to see him again, or if she were simply making polite conversation. Either way, she hoped he would accept the invitation.

"Maybe I will come to your church next Sunday ... but only if I can sit with you."

"You can sit anywhere you want," she teased.

"Oh, all right. I'm gonna be there, looking for you," he jumped to say, rewarding Eva with a self-satisfied expression that clarified everything.

As they continued up the street, Chester lowered his head and counted the bricks in the pavement, consumed with thoughts of Eva Simson. The attractive young woman with burnished brown skin, inquisitive dark eyes, and thick black hair had set his heart racing. He was twenty-three-years-old. Had never had feelings one way or another about any woman, at least not in a romantic way.

Nearly three months had passed since he fled the tobacco plantation in Virginia where he had been born. He'd left no family behind, and as far as he knew, no one, not even frail old Master O'Donal, who was nearly blind and dead broke, or the scrawny overseer who was too lazy to go looking for him, cared that Chester had run off.

Consumed with making it to a place where he could find refuge, Chester had fought stray dogs for scraps of food and hidden from patrollers by sleeping in trees. He had trusted no one, especially not the suspicious free blacks he encountered on the road, who were quick to run him off, fearing he might bring his troubles to them or rob them of the few possessions they had.

By the time Chester entered the city of Boston he was ragged, exhausted, and desperate for food and shelter. When he stopped to rest in the alley behind the home of Jeremiah Daniels, he had prayed he would be safe. And when the lawyer opened the back door of his Joy Street law office, where he also lived, preparing to toss trash into the alley, Chester's circumstances improved. Daniels handed Chester a scrawny chicken leg and invited the starving fugitive inside. He gave him a bowl of broth and led him to an empty back room where he told Chester he could sleep. And for the first time in weeks, Chester slept without fear or hunger.

The encounter with the lawyer led Chester to believe that perhaps all men weren't to be feared. Maybe everyone did not want to see him dead, or punished, or at the least, invisible and out of their sight. However, Chester soon learned that Jeremiah Daniels was not the magnanimous, sympathetic savior of the unfortunate as he had first thought. The rotund man bluntly informed Chester, "Don't think I hold to the ways of the raging abolitionists that preach freedom on street corners and in meeting halls. I don't like them. I don't like slavery, but I keep my thoughts about the messy situation to myself. I don't care about what you been through and I don't want to hear about your troubles. If you want to stay, I can use a young man like you, if you're willing to do as I say."

Chester placed his trust in the lawyer, an obese, arthritic, penny-pinching man who was only consumed with making and hoarding money. Advanced in age, his physical ailments prevented him from walking much farther than the one-hundred-fifty steps from the front door of his law office to the courthouse across the street, where he represented Negro clients who paid him whatever they could afford for his knowledge of matters related to buying and selling real property. Keeping Chester around cost the lawyer very little. He provided the boy meager sustenance, a decent amount of clothing, and protection from the slave catchers who roamed the city with "Wanted" fliers in their hands. Chester's strong legs and bright disposition became the lawyer's salvation.

Now, continuing on, Chester walked with Eva to the intersection where Spruce's Bakery and Harold's Feed Store faced each other across a narrow street. He helped Eva sidestep a puddle of dirty water lingering in the gutter and tucked Lawyer Daniel's map more securely under his arm. He expelled a long breath to release the familiar tightness in his chest that kept him tautly wired and prepared for the dangers all black men walking the streets of Boston faced on a daily basis. But, with Eva at his side, he felt lighter, even oddly optimistic, an unfamiliar sensation that he attributed to having been lucky enough to meet this pretty girl.

As they threaded through the throng of people walking along the street, he mentally chanted, *Eva Simson, Eva Simson. She will be at church on Sunday. She will be there. I will be there too.* However, Chester's thoughts of Eva were completely shattered when he absently stepped off the sidewalk and into the path of a horse drawn carriage moving briskly down the street.

Instinctively, Eva jumped in front of Chester and pulled him to safety, forcing the large gray bay to skitter to the side and clamor away.

"Are you okay?" she asked, her hands firmly clamped around his arm.

"Yes. I think so," he told her, feeling ashamed of his inattention, but making no move to disentangle himself from the taut hold she had on his jacket. In fact, Chester deliberately held still, savoring her closeness, entranced by the clean, citrusy smell of her clothing and her hair. "That coulda been bad," he finally conceded, loosening himself from her grip.

Eva let go, breaking their connection. "Yes, but at least, you didn't get hurt." Smiling in a satisfied manner, she allowed him to cup her elbow as they started up the hill toward the North Slope of the city.

After walking in silence for a few minutes, Chester halted and pointed toward a knot of people gathered at the upcoming intersection. It was evident that something of importance was going on. "Look, up there. I wonder what's happening."

"Let's go see," Eva advised, curious to find out what the people, both black and white, were doing.

Approaching the gathering, Eva could hear the people talking among themselves in a variety of tones. Some seemed to infer approval of whatever they were watching, while others grunted in disgusted, subdued anger. Drawing closer, she saw a tall black man wearing a Lincoln-esque stovepipe hat. He was standing on an overturned crate and delivering an impassioned speech while clutching a crumpled copy of *The North Star* in a hardened fist as he decried the evil, unpopular Fugitive Slave Act.

Cautiously, Chester guided Eva to the outer fringes of the onlookers, anxious to get a better view of the man.

"Why, it's Minister Pennworth," Eva whispered to Chester. "He's the preacher from my church. He's delivering another one of his fiery speeches about liberating the slaves."

The fact that the outspoken religious leader had taken to the streets of Boston and was actively recruiting sympathetic souls to the anti-slavery movement did not surprise Eva at all. Even though Bostonians had actively created a haven in their city for slaves fleeing from their masters, there still remained a large number of northern citizens who sympathized with Southerners and believed in the right for southern men to hold onto their "property".

The city was a hotbed of activity for abolitionists eager to further their cause, even though men who hunted other men to put them back in chains still roamed the streets with warrants in their hands.

With both arms raised and his narrow, ebony jaw jutting forward, Minister Pennworth addressed his audience in an urgent tone. "As Frederick Douglass said, 'We cannot have a republic or a genuine democracy without African-Americans who are full and equal citizens in every aspect of their lives'." His authoritative tone shushed the restless audience, providing space for him to continue. "People of Boston, you must realize that the intention of the abolition movement is not simply to end slavery, but to further the goal of black citizenship and equality while ridding society of all claims of racial inferiority."

Murmurs of support, along with grunts of opposition, filtered through the crowd. A white woman wearing a bright blue bonnet raised a flowered handkerchief and waved it in the air. The man standing beside her quickly grabbed her arm and sharply pulled it down.

Caught up in the minister's message, Chester tugged Eva forward, putting them at the very front of the crowd, directly facing the minister.

"How can we, as a rational people, feeling the blessings of a God who loves us, form a valid, welcoming Union? How? Through the grace and blessings of one God, a Savior who is revered. Do not trust the words of a man who says slaves are held as chattel for their own good. Or that liberty is a curse to the free people of color, their circumstances no better than that of slaves. Do not fall for such falsehoods and words of evil trickery! There can be no true Union without freedom for all people. Citizens of Boston! Stand up! Demand the unfettered emancipation of all slaves. Now!"

His charge to action elicited shouts of approval that brought a wide grin to Minister Pennworth's mouth, which was still gaping open, exposing a great number of his square white teeth, when a white man wearing rough seaman's clothing and carrying a large metal pail, sprang from the crowd. Heaving the pail high, he splashed its contents into the preacher's face, releasing the putrid smell of horse manure into the crowd. The slimy mass splattered the brim of the preacher's tall hat, slid across his stunned expression, and darkened the man's light shirt. It also stained the sleeve of Chester's tan jacket and dripped onto the toes of his polished brown boots.

As the agitated crowd, which immediately turned loud and angry, erupted in a frenzy of outrage, men began pushing and shoving one another, anxious to escape the commotion. Women and children squealed in horror, covering their noses with handkerchiefs and gloved hands to fend off the offensive odor.

"Oh, no!" Chester wailed, kicking at the foul mass that landed on his foot. Frowning, he glanced at Eva and shook his head, then looked around to find the man who had caused the awful mess. However, when Chester's eyes met those of the attacker, he immediately sensed trouble. The man sprinted toward Chester with tightened lips and a lowered chin, as if zeroing in on a target he'd long been searching for.

Acting quickly, Chester yanked Eva by the arm and pulled her toward a narrow side street. Holding her firmly, he shouted, "I gotta run! I gotta run! You go home!" Dropping Lawyer Daniels's map in the street, Chester fled, racing away from Eva and the man who had attacked the preacher.

Eva hesitated only a second before chasing after Chester, shouting at him to wait for her. But he continued on, his boots slapping the cobblestones as he raced down one alley, then another before slipping into a slim passageway that separated the fish market from the local beer tavern. Eva remained right behind him, their footsteps bouncing off the walls of the red brick buildings, echoing those of their pursuer, who rushed to gain on them. When Eva finally caught up with Chester, he stopped running, turned, gripped her by the shoulders and shook her sternly, his face hard in anger.

"Go home! Now! Do not follow me!" he ordered.

But before Eva could utter a word of protest, the man tackled Chester and brought him down, face first, to the ground. After jamming a booted foot in the middle of Chester's back, the attacker reached out and grabbed Eva by the arm. When she struggled to get free, he slapped her so hard she collapsed next to Chester, the taste of blood in her mouth. Chester looked over at Eva and moved his head back and forth, as if to tell her he was sorry for what was happening.

The man yanked a piece of paper from inside his shirt, bent down, and waved it in front of Chester's face. "Charlie O'Donal!" he growled. "You goin' back home to Virginny."

Eva struggled to sit up, angry, and not about to back down from whatever misery this encounter might bring. She had been a fighter all her life, fighting to be looked upon and accepted as a person who deserved to be treated fairly. Her aunt had raised her to demand respect without being insolent, to express herself while tempering her words in order not to be thought of as rude. Early on, she had learned to accept the fact that she might be punished for speaking her mind or allowing her curiosity to lead her into a situation others might avoid, but in her opinion, not doing so, was a far worse attitude to adopt.

Now, every fiber in her petite body was taut with rage and on alert. Clearly, the man had made a mistake, and she was not about to let him get away with whatever evil he was about to inflict.

"His name is *Chester Phillips*," she protested in a most indignant tone. However, her protest was rewarded with another hard smack to her head, which hurt, but did not prevent her from continuing to express her outrage. "You've got the wrong man!" she snapped, silently daring the man to hit her again. "I told you! His name is Chester Phillips."

The man laughed at Eva as he ripped off Chester's jacket and tore away the sleeve of his shirt. Grabbing Chester by the elbow, he smiled in satisfaction and leered at Eva with an expression of triumph on his face. "So what's he doing with *this* on his arm?"

Eva scooted closer to Chester and looked at his forearm, where the letter "O" had been branded into the soft skin just inside his elbow. The raised scar, all dark brown and puckered told Eva all she needed to know about the life Chester had lived before he walked into hers. Her eyes shifted to his, and he whispered, "I'm sorry."

She stood, then whispered, "I'm sorry, too."

The bounty hunter placed heavy metal cuffs on Chester's wrists, gave him a hard kick to his side. "You're goin' back to Virginny where your name is Charlie O'Donal. Mr. Tom wants his property back."

"Leave him be!" Eva shouted, deciding there was little to lose by continuing her protest. She yanked on the man's dirty jacket, desperate to make him listen.

Turning his attention to Eva, he wrapped one arm around her shoulders and brought her face close to his. "Not a chance, missy," he sneered as he clasped both her wrists in his large grip. "He's not getting' away from me. And neither are you."

"Let her go!" Chester yelled. "You're right! I *am* Charlie O'Donal, but you gotta let her go!" Chester shot to his feet. "She's a free woman…you've got no right to hold her!"

The man laughed in a sinister gruffness that seemed to come naturally. "She's with you ain't she?"

"So what?"

"Then she's an accomplice. That's against the law, she knows that."

"She does not know anything about me! I just met her! Let her go!"

"Too bad for her. She oughta be more careful 'bout who she takes company with 'cause she'll be goin' back to Virginny with you."

CHAPTER 2

Tully Simson closed her Bible, rested her right hand on its cracked leather cover, and then settled back in her seat in the pulpit, viewing the congregation with dread in her heart. While assessing the expressions on the faces of the people filling the pews of Grove Street AME Church, she wondered if she had made a huge mistake by agreeing to tell her story. On the first Tuesday of each month, Minister Pennworth invited testimony from members who had managed to escape enslavement in the South, requesting that he or she relate the tale of their flight to freedom. When the pastor asked Tully if she would agree to speak, she'd asked him what she could possibly say that the people who came to his Tuesday night meetings hadn't heard before. He knew Tully hadn't fled from her master with dogs at her heels. That she had been owned by a master who had granted her great liberties, even allowing her to purchase her freedom. However, he had insisted her experience was worthy of sharing, and so, she had agreed.

Now, Tully watched as Minister Pennworth walked up the center aisle of the church and strode to the podium, where he stood waiting until a hush came over the congregation. He smoothed the lapels of his greenish-gray jacket before settling a pair of wire-rim spectacles onto his prominent nose. "I apologize for arriving late to evening service but I had to take the time to wash filth from my body and don clean clothing. Even though I stand before you now, smelling of lye soap and free of the stench of horse manure, the filth I washed from my body does not compare with the filth that remains in the minds of those who fight to keep human beings enslaved. No amount of scrubbing will cleanse their minds, but with your help we may be able to cleanse their souls of the evil that makes them perpetuate such horrors on our fellow mankind."

He gave the congregation space to mummer their agreement before turning toward Tully to give her a vigorous nod. "Come on up to the podium, Miss Simson." Then, looking back at the congregation, he added, "She's a bit reluctant to speak tonight, but I told her....don't you worry none 'bout what the people sitting in the pews listening to you want to hear. Worry 'bout those still in bondage. President Lincoln's already declared that the slaves will be freed, but many a master is still fighting to hold onto what he calls his *property*. Miss Simson, you are speaking for all those men, women, and children still suffering in the rebel states."

Tully stood, gave her long black skirt a shake to ease the wrinkles, and then replaced the minister at the podium, sending him to his high-back, red velvet chair behind the altar. Her eyes roamed the sanctuary from the front of the room to the back and up to the balcony where every seat was taken. Whites, blacks. Young people, old people. Some wealthy, some poor. Those well dressed and those in rags. All waiting to hear what she had to tell them. Oddly, her mind was not on what she planned to say. She was wondering why Eva hadn't come home from work at her regular time, why she hadn't sent word that she would miss the meeting this evening. Was Mr. Fitzgerald making her work late again? But even if that were the case, Eva always managed to get home in time for evening service on Tuesdays.

A flicker of uneasiness rippled through Tully. Eva could be a bit too adventurous, she knew. And the girl had always been very outspoken as well. When Eva was younger, Tully had encouraged the child's inquisitive nature while reinforcing an awareness of the dangers that, unfortunately, would always be present. These were unsettling times. The country and its citizens were divided. Simply a cross word, a sideways glance, or a gesture made at the wrong time or place could change a person's life forever.

Pressing her concern about Eva's absence to the back of her mind, Tully forced herself to concentrate on what she had agreed to do. Her nerves settled a bit when the soft beam of light from a gas lamp outside the church radiated through a stained glass window and illuminated an image of Jesus holding a lamb.

If it wasn't for Pastor's prodding, I wouldn't be doing this, Tully silently grumbled. Her eyes were tired, a dull ache plagued her lower back, and her feet had begun to swell. She'd had an exhausting day, cooking and cleaning for the Andersons, the white family that hired her to take care of their fashionable house on Charles Street. She knew her employer's wealth came from the sale of cloth made from cotton grown and harvested by slaves in the South. And even though, in public, Mr. Anderson confessed to supporting the abolitionist movement, he did not shield his reservations over the turmoil created by freedom-seekers when he spoke to the blacks to whom he paid minimal wages to clean, cook, and serve in his home. However, Tully felt no urge to complain. Like so many of her friends and neighbors, she was a domestic who managed quite well on what she earned, while the influx of runaways who were flooding into the city thinking they'd find work and live as well as whites most often died in the streets … poor, diseased, and alone.

Today, Tully's workload had been doubly hard because Mrs. Anderson had told her to care for the newborn baby boy because the regular nanny was in bed with a cold. But to be fair, Mrs. Anderson had handed Tully an extra dollar for the day, which she spent on the plumpest chicken the butcher had to offer. At least the apples for the pie Tully planned to bake for the church potluck dinner wouldn't cost more than half-an-hour of picking from the tree behind her neighbor's house.

"Go ahead, Miss Simson. You can start talking now," Minister Pennworth urged. Tully glanced at him, lowered her chin, took a deep breath, and then faced her audience.

"I was born a slave on Tall Palms Plantation, a rice growing plantation on the Santee Canal, north of a place called Moncks Corner, in South Carolina. I wasn't ever hungry, I wasn't ever beat with a lash, and I never slept on a dirt floor in a slave cabin in the quarters. I lived in the main house in a proper, but tiny, room off the mistress's bedroom. I sewed her dresses and made most o' the clothes for the family. So, you all must think I'm sayin' I was more content than others in bondage at Tall Palms. You might consider I felt safe because I was treated a bit better than the others. Well, let me tell you ... No, that was not the case, not at all. I wasn't content because I wasn't free. I wasn't safe because I didn't belong to myself.

"But I lernt early on how ta use my talent with a needle and thread ta earn enough ta buy myself, and when I got ta be about thirty-years-old, that's what I did. Maybe I *was* lucky in some way. Master was a fair-minded man who seemed caught up in the middle of things. When his daddy died and passed the plantation and the slaves on to him, he didn't much want the burden or the bother. So after I bought my freedom, the sheriff come 'round and said I had to leave the state. That was the way of things. Still is. I couldn't stay there any longer. One day I met a slave named Mayree ... a young mother from Stillwater, the plantation right next to where I was living. She came up to me at the river and asked me to take her baby girl with me when I left for the North. I was shocked at first, then I looked at the girl and knew I had to say yes, I would take the child as far as the good Lord would let us get. I had my free papers, but that didn't mean a thing, 'specially since I'd be takin' a white man's property with me.

"For me...slavery days weren't the worse days of my life. The worse day of my life was when I took that little girl away from her mamma in the middle of the night, leaving the poor woman standing on the riverbank, crying. Dogs barking. The girl hollering for her mamma, not knowing where she was going. That was the first of many sad, sad days. Me and the girl travelled downriver in a leaky old dugout I bartered from some Indians. I gave 'em five yards of calico for that boat. We made it to Charleston where a white lady, what was part of the underground railroad, took us in, put us in the belly of a ship, and sent us on to Boston."

Tully drew in a long breath and paused to study the rapt faces peering back at her. Some were as still as a nun in prayer. Others were contorted in concern. "Guess that's not much of a story," Tully apologized, "but that's what happened to me. Many of you know me, and you know the baby girl I brought out of slavery is my niece, Eva. I gave her my last name. I raised her to be a fine young lady. She's got a good head on her shoulders and a good job working for Mr. Fitzgerald. She means the world to me," Tully said, sniffing back tears as she took a moment to gather her emotions. Speaking about her love for, and pride in, Eva often made her heart swell to the point where she couldn't help but cry. "I told Eva the truth about her mother when she got old enough to understand, and I told her every day that her mother loved her enough to give her away. Mayree didn't toss that chile to me because she didn't want her…. and now, that's all I got to say."

Tears glistened in Tully's eyes as she stepped down from the pulpit and went to sit in the third pew from the front of the church, where she and Eva sat and prayed every Sunday. She swiped at the tears, relieved to have told her story, overcome with a sense of contentment. She would never have a child of her own, but she did have Eva, and if God ever saw fit to bless Eva with a child, Tully's family would be complete.

The Tuesday evening service droned as others gave their testimonials, finally ending with a stirring rendition of *How Great Thou Art*, sung by Hattie Harris, the talented soloist from the regular church choir whose voice brought all in attendance to their feet. Eager to get home and check on Eva, whom Tully hoped must be there by now, she rose from her seat and turned toward the exit, anxious to learn what had prevented her niece from attending service.

~

Jeremiah Daniels glared at the mud-covered parcel that the boy was holding out to him and turned up his nose in disgust. He didn't know which was more off-putting, the filthy package or the dirty-faced urchin whose shirt and trousers were little more than strips of tattered rags. He recognized the ragamuffin everyone called Tippy, who ran through the alleyways, begging from merchants and scavenging for discarded items to use as barter for food or coin. He was a scrappy street-wise kid, a familiar sight on the streets around Beacon Hill, but Daniels had never had occasion to interact with him. "What is that? Where'd you get it?" Daniels demanded, refusing to take the filthy item.

"Found it in the gutter, sir," Tippy replied in a self-satisfied manner, gracing the lawyer with a grin that stretched the brown skin of his mud-stained cheeks. "I lernt enough letters to see it got your name on it. Thought you might want it back," he stated, assessing Daniels with expectation, clearly angling for a reward.

With a squint of his eyes, the lawyer ruminated on what the boy had said, the heat of his fury steadily building. The ragamuffin was holding the map that Daniels had told Chester to pick up from the mapmaker, the document he needed to present in court the next day. Gingerly, he took the parcel from the boy and unfurled it, verifying his suspicion. Luckily, the brown paper wrapping had protected the map, which was not as badly damaged as he had suspected. Other than the loss of some lettering along the border where water had seeped into the package, it was fine.

"How did you come to find this?" Daniels asked. "Did you see who threw it away?"

"Oh, yes sir," Tippy jumped to answer. "I was there. Saw it all."

"Where? Saw what?" Daniels snapped, his curiosity and his impatience heightened.

"Up on Beacon Street, near Spruce. That's where a white man threw horse poop on everybody and chased the man that dropped your package. Chased him into the alley behind ole Mick's tavern. There was a woman with him, too. A real pretty gal."

"A girl? What'd she look like?"

"Brown skin ... kinda red like ... maybe, ya know ... like ginger-bread? Had long black curly hair all twisted up in the back."

"Did you hear the young man say anything?"

"Naw...he just kept hollering at the gal. Called her Eva. She called him Chester but the white man said that wasn't his name. Said his real name is Charlie."

"Chester....Eva," Daniels repeated, certain Tippy was referring to Eva Simson, the young lady who worked at the mapmaker's shop, who lived with Tully Simson. Daniels had known Tully Simson for many years, having sold her the narrow, three-room house on Russell Street where she still lived. He recalled his surprise when she handed him the cash money to purchase the little house that had two rooms down and one upstairs, thinking it was a lot of space just for herself and a little girl. "What happened to the girl and the young man?"

"The white man took both of 'em away. Took 'em down to a shack at the wharf. I followed 'em, just to see what was goin' on." Tippy stopped long enough to swallow the spittle that had begun foaming on his lips, then plunged ahead. "The man said he's gonna take the two of 'em back to Virginny. Runaways, I reckon."

A slow nod of understanding came to Jeremiah Daniels, as it was not difficult to decipher what had most likely happened. Chester *was* a runaway after all, and for all the fiery talk that the abolitionists were doing around the city, slave catchers still came, looking to secure reward money for the return of property to their clients. But the girl named Eva had been taken as well. That did surprise Daniels. He had not known that Chester was keeping female company and did not know why Tully Simson's niece would be caught in the streets with a runaway slave. Daniels reached into the pocket of his black broadcloth vest and took out a silver nickel, which he held in front of the boy and said, "I'll give you this coin if you go down to the wharf and find the man holding the girl and the boy. Tell the white man not to take them away, to wait until I get there. I'll be right along as soon as I arrange for a carriage." He steadied himself with a cane in each hand to maintain his balance as he peered down at the tiny messenger. "You understand what I'm asking you to do"

"Yes sir!"

"All right. The young man's name *is* Chester." He paused, his breathing labored and rapid as he assessed the street urchin's face. "You remember that name? Chester."

"Chester," the boy repeated.

"Tell the man who is holding them that Lawyer Daniels will be there soon to settle all of this. Go on, now." Then he handed the coin to Tippy and turned his attention back to his map, adding in a softer tone, "I do thank you, Tippy, for bringing this to me."

When Chester's fingers found Eva's, she gripped his hand and held it fast, anxious to maintain contact with him. The dim shed where they were imprisoned was not much bigger than the storage closet at Mr. Fitzgerald's shop, and the smell of rotted fish, wet earth, and moldy wood hung heavy in the air. Eva sat on the damp dirt floor with her legs stretched out next to Chester's, their shoulders braced against a splintered wall that was riddled with holes where chinks of dried mud plaster had crumbled and fallen away. Pinpoints of light from campfires that the sailors and dockworkers lit along the shore cut into the darkness and created inky shadows.

"I'm sorry," Chester started, his voice low and unsteady. "I never shoulda asked permission to walk you home. I had no right to get you all mixed up in my troubles." He let out a shudder of a sigh and pressed his back more firmly against the wall. "Forgive me, Eva. Please."

Sensing his shame, Eva turned in the dark and pushed her face closer to his, wishing she could look into his eyes. "Nothing to forgive….you didn't do anything wrong," she consoled in a suffocated whisper. "I agreed to let you walk me home because I wanted to spend more time with you."

"You, you did?" Chester sputtered, a trace of relief coloring his words.

"Yes, I did," Eva replied with assurance.

"I'm glad to know that 'cause I knew as soon as I met you that I wanted to be around you, too. But now just look at the mess I got you in." He released Eva's hand and touched her on the shoulder, drawing her nearer, speaking into her ear. "I stopped being Charlie O'Donal so long ago guess I got to believin' I was really Chester Phillips. A free man. Guess I thought I deserved to be with a girl like you. I should of never got it into my head that I could keep company with someone as pretty and smart as you."

"Hush," Eva interrupted, wishing she could make him understand that she did not blame him for what had happened. "Isn't your fault."

"But it is," Chester protested. "I should have told you I was a runaway."

"Hump. That's not important. A runaway?" Eva grunted. "You're no different than a whole lot of others. There're plenty of colored men just like you, come to Boston on the run."

Chester sucked in an audible breath, but did not respond.

Eva scooter closer, slid her hand up to his shoulder, and let it rest there in a gesture of comfort. "At least we're together," she offered, attempting to push her own fears aside. She had no idea what was going to happen to her, but it was a comfort to know that she was not alone. Folding her body into Chester's arms when he reached out, she let him wrap her in a warm embrace.

"Being with you …. that's about the only good thing come from all of this," Chester whispered against her hair.

They remained silent for a long while, holding onto each other, listening to the sound of water lapping against the pier as it hit the sides of a vessel tied up at the wharf. In the distance, they could hear the drunken voice of the bounty hunter as he yelled obscenities at the seamen who frequented the tavern at the dock. Having captured his prey, he was celebrating his catch by swigging rum with the rowdy sailors who lived aboard the ships in port.

Sitting in the dark, Eva felt surprisingly calm, though she was well aware of the danger she was in. The situation was dire: No one knew where she was. No one knew that she had been in the company of a fugitive slave tonight. Though Aunt Tully must be wondering why Eva missed evening service at church, her aunt would never think to come looking for her at the harbor. Eva was a punctual, reliable young woman who was never this late getting home from work. She knew Aunt Tully must be worried sick. And what if this slave catcher really did take her to Virginia with Chester? Would she be trapped on a plantation somewhere in the South? Separated from her aunt, stripped of the life of freedom her mother had sacrificed to send her to? The thought sent a tremor of fear through Eva, pushing a lump of trepidation high into her throat. When she felt tears rising in her eyes, she fiercely blinked them back.

No need to feel sad, she silently admonished. *Ka a fo, ka a fo, don't cry, don't cry,* she mentally chanted in the language that her mother had sung to her on the riverbank so long ago. That simple song, just a few words sung in a language Eva knew nothing about was a chant that often came to her when she needed to be strong. The memory of her mother's voice and the dim image of a brown-skinned woman with braided hair were seared into Eva's memory as well as her heart. That was all she possessed that kept her tethered to the mother she had never forgotten.

"We'll get out of this," Chester broke the silence, as if reading Eva's thoughts, using words to push aside any concern of failure. "I got away once before, and I'll do it again, Eva. Just place your faith in me." He stroked her cheek, his gentle touch reinforcing his words. "I promise you, I'm not going back to Virginia and neither are you. Trust me. I don't know how, but I'm gonna get us away from this man."

The strength of Chester's words buoyed Eva's hope for escape. Impulsively, she reached out and cupped his chin in her palm, as if he were a child that needed her reassurance. "I believe in you, Chester, but if things don't turn out so well, I pray we can stay together, no matter what happens."

"Yes… together," he murmured, pulling her even closer, as if fueled by her confidence in him.

Having decided to trust his assessment of the situation, Eva clenched her hands into hard fists and forced calm to her quivering limbs. And in an effort to ease the tension of the moment, she gave Chester a playful shove and teasingly said, "You could of told me your real name was *Charlie*."

A grunt of a chuckle slipped from Chester's throat. "Oh, no … I stopped being Charlie O'Donal the day I ran away. Charlie is dead. Chester is the only one who's living now."

His voice, though wavering slightly, was deep and clear, prompting Eva to sense that he wanted to say more. "Tell me who Chester used to be," she urged, eager to know this man who was holding her so close.

In words that seemed, at first, difficult for Chester to speak, he told Eva about his life on the O'Donal plantation, of how impoverished his master had been, of how lonely a life Chester had led. He described the hard journey north and how his loyalty to Lawyer Daniels had been born. And when he finished his tale, he listened as Eva told him about her and her Aunt Tully's escape from South Carolina, as well as how much Eva missed her mother.

"When the war is over, I'm going back to Stillwater and find her," she said.

"That might be real hard to do," Chester countered.

"I don't care, I have to try," Eva said, the ever-present desire to reunite with her mother rising anew. The fuzzy memories that she coveted had grown more difficult to summon with each passing year, receding into a blur of fog and trees and streams of Spanish moss. She remembered standing on the riverbank, watching a boat approach, and then slipping out of her mother's arms into those of a stranger. A four-year-old remembered. A grown woman still heard a song in her head and the snarling bark of dogs in the night.

Suddenly, an explosion of loud voices laced with curses and threats shook Chester and Eva alert. Scrambling to their knees, they turned to face the wall and peered through the cracks as a volley of foul language erupted.

"I see the slave catcher is back," Eva said. "And it looks like he's arguing with a drunken sailor."

"I hope that dirty slave hunter is stinking, falling down drunk," Chester added, sinking back down to the floor beside Eva. And after a few moments, when he touched her arm, he whispered, "All right. The sailor is walking away. We gotta be real quiet now and let the slave catcher think we're asleep. If he's as drunk as I think he is, he'll open the door to check on us, and when he does, you stand back and let me jump him. I know I can take him down, and then we can get away."

"All right," Eva agreed, praying Chester's plan would work. She was about to ask him which way they should run once they got outside, when the rumble of carriage wheels on the oyster shell road stopped her. Quickly, Chester pushed to his feet and crept to the door to listen. Using a splinter of wood, he dislodged a large chunk of flaky mud-plaster to create a hole wide enough to better see outside. "Why, that's Lawyer Daniels," he whisper-spoke to Eva, motioning for her to come to the door. She slid next to Chester, bent down, and together they watched as Jeremiah Daniels struggled to get out of his carriage, using two canes to support himself. After successfully maneuvering away from the coach, the lawyer made his way toward the front of the shack, turned, and shouted at the bounty hunter, who was now staggering along the water's edge while gripping a bottle of rum.

"You! I need to speak with you!" Lawyer Daniels shouted at the man.

The bounty hunter's head jerked up and he squinted into the darkness. After tossing his now-empty bottle into the water, he staggered toward the lawyer.

"What do you want with me, old man?" the slave-catcher demanded as he jerkily approached.

"I'm Jeremiah Daniels, Esquire. I sent word that I was coming!"

"Yeah… and I told that damned pickininny you sent down here that I don't take orders from nobody!"

"I demand the release of the young man and the girl you have abducted," Daniels stated in an authoritarian tone while bracing his bulky body with two canes. He lifted his jaw and glared at the bounty hunter in a taunting, come-hither stance.

"And why should I do that?" the drunken man sneered, stepping so close to Daniels that their noses nearly touched.

Without making a reply, Daniels filled his lungs with air, raised the cane in his right hand, and smacked the slave catcher across the top of his head, sending the man, howling, to the ground. Using all of his three-hundred-plus pounds of flesh for leverage, Daniels jammed a heavy foot into the center of the man's chest, pinning him down, holding him fast.

Chester gasped, turned to look at Eva, and grinned. Digging away more of the mud-plaster, he created an even larger hole for them to watch and listen to the heated exchange.

"How much bounty are you to be paid for the boy?" Daniels demanded to know.

"One hundred dollars," the man managed to choke out.

"I'm giving you fifty," Daniels decided, pressing his foot down so hard on the man's chest that Eva thought she heard bones cracking. "And I'm ordering you to get out of town. Tonight. I suggest you head West instead of South, if you want to stay alive."

"And why should I do as you want?" the struggling man growled, squirming as he tried to sit up, yet quickly forced back by Daniels's foot.

"Because, if you don't take my fifty dollars and leave town, you're going to find yourself in court tomorrow… facing assault charges."

"Says who?"

"Says me. I am a lawyer."

"A nigger lawyer?" came the scoffed retort. He spit a bloody gob onto the ground, barely missing Daniels's foot.

"I am a certified officer of the court, and I will see to it that you are charged with battery and assault."

"Assault? Battery? Who would dare charge me with crimes like that?" he snarled.

"All those decent white folks who were standing in the street. The ones you threw horse shit on."

Chester slapped a hand over his mouth to keep from laughing. Whispering to Eva, he said, "Lawyer Daniels has really got that bounty hunter in a bind, don't he? Offering him money to keep white folks off his back. He's gonna get us out."

"I hope so," Eva replied in amazement, not shifting her eyes from the scene outside.

"I tell you, he's a real good lawyer. You should see him in court. I swear he makes those white lawyers sit up and take notice. Just like he's makin' that man do now."

The argument outside the shack intensified, before suddenly falling into a long stretch of silence. When the door was abruptly wrenched open, Chester and Eva stumbled out into the darkness, gasping for fresh air.

"You just cost me fifty dollars!" Jeremiah spewed at Chester, poking him in the ribs with the tip of his gnarled-wood cane. "I'll be taking it out of your pay, young man. I don't know why I bothered with saving you from going back to wherever you came from, other than the fact that I need you with me in court tomorrow. And *you*, young lady ..." he started, addressing Eva before Chester could say a word or try to explain what had happened. "I know you ... you're Tully Simson's niece aren't you?"

Eva nodded glumly, but did not dare speak.

"How foolish of you to get involved with my assistant. You get on home. Now!" he spat. "The slave catcher had no warrant for you, so be glad he let you go. A pretty gal looking like you do ... that man coulda sold you into bondage in less time than it takes to light a candle. Nobody's after you. So, if you know what's good for you, you'll go on home and leave Chester Phillips alone."

Tully was in a state of heightened worry when Eva finally arrived home, well after dark, accompanied by a young man she introduced as her new friend, Chester Phillips. After hearing what had happened to them, and knowing how close Eva had come to disappearing forever, Tully collapsed into a chair and sobbed aloud, crying in front of Eva for the first time in her life.

CHAPTER 3

Disregarding her aunt's and the lawyer's warning to stay away from Chester, Eva dedicated herself to getting to know everything she could about her new friend. She discovered he was intelligent, kind-hearted, and lonely, with an empty place in his soul that she longed to fill. He was making his way in the world all alone, as was she, without a single blood relative to claim as his own, and their mutual craving to belong, to be loved, to have someone with whom to share a life drew them into a bond that quickly shifted into love.

As the blustery Massachusetts fall turned into a bleak winter and snow piled up in the streets of Boston, Eva and Chester attended church together, went to lecture halls to hear the abolitionists speak, took long walks along the frozen ponds, and huddled in front of the fire that Tully kept burning in the downstairs hearth of her house. Many of their conversations revolved around the war, and how the bloody conflict interfered with their ability to envision a clear picture of the future. When Christmas Day arrived, Chester began to speak of marriage. Together, they went to see Minister Pennworth and requested that he officiate at their wedding on the first day of the New Year to launch 1863 in a festive, hopeful manner.

Once the wedding plans were underway, Tully purchased eight

yards of white silk from the dressmaker's shop and created a bridal dress for Eva that rivaled the creations imported from Paris that were draped on mannequins in the shop owner's window. She offered Chester and Eva the extra room upstairs where they could live rent-free and save money to, eventually, get a place of their own. However, Chester staunchly refused Tully's offer, declaring with pride that he was able to support his wife and was unwilling to be a burden to the woman who had raised his fiancée. His protests continued until he and Tully finally agreed that a small payment for rent would be an acceptable compromise.

Jeremiah Daniels, who now saw Eva as the best thing that had ever happened to Chester, gave the couple his blessing and agreed to stand with Chester at the service.

During the ceremony on the first day of January, Tully watched as Eva and Chester stood side by side with their hands clasped together and exchanged their marriage vows. She smiled to think of how easily Chester had come into Eva's life, of how easily Eva had brought him into hers. His short courtship of her niece had been more than enough time for Tully to see that the young man was exactly the kind of husband Eva deserved: An honorable, hard-working man with a good head on his shoulders and dreams enough for them both. Though he could be a bit over-zealous when it came to discussing matters of war and the work of the abolitionists, she was relieved to see that he knew enough to stay out of trouble, and knew when to keep his mouth shut.

Lawyer Daniels' wedding gift for the newlyweds was a beautifully illustrated World Atlas that he personally inscribed to them. Chester's wedding present to Eva was the frilly, lace-trimmed bonnet she had admired in the window of the milliner's shop on the day he first met her. Made of dark red velvet with white rosebuds set into deep ruffles around the brim and a white satin ribbon to tie under her chin, she told him it was the loveliest hat she had ever owned and she planned to wear it forever.

It was long past midnight when the celebratory wedding meal was complete and the friends, neighbors, and church members who had crowded into Tully's modest home departed. Eva and Chester retired to their room upstairs where the bride had put her own decorative touches on the cozy, yet adequate space that now sported delicate lace curtains at the high square windows and a colorful rag rug on the scarred wooden floor.

Without any show of embarrassment, Chester promptly shed his black wedding suit, hung it on a peg by the door, and then stripped away the remainder of his clothing, providing Eva with her first glimpse of his muscular frame, his smooth brown skin, and what she realized was a most impressive male member. The sight of his manhood, stiff and eager to welcome her, did not frighten her in the least. In fact, she savored the feeling of anticipation that shivered over her skin and welcomed the tightening sensation that heightened her desire to embrace her new role as lover and wife to the man she had married.

Without hesitating, Eva followed Chester's lead and stepped out of her wedding dress, which she placed, along with her undergarments, on a side chair. Then, slipping beneath the quilt she had made for her wedding night, she curled her body up against Chester's side, seeking his warmth, her heart filled with longing to be at last, fully, completely his. Her heart did a flip that nearly made her gasp when his hand came down to possess a throbbing breast, which he wholly embraced, spreading his fingers far apart, firmly thumbing her nipple.

With a moan of pleasure, Eva shifted even closer and reached out to him, her trembling fingers seeking places to pleasure Chester's naked skin, which felt soft in places, coarse in others, where Eva knew the sting of a lash or the blow of a stick had left their marks on his body. When he groaned in response to her gentle ministrations and pulled her down to lie beneath him, she kissed him fiercely, aching for the fulfillment he proposed. She was relieved that he didn't fumble, hesitate, or hold back from letting her know how much he wanted her. She relaxed and let him stroke and kiss and touch her in places that sent jolts of need to her womanly core, engulfing her in the startling crescendo that was building inside her body.

A cold winter rain was pounding the roof, slashing at the windows, and tamping down the sounds of their lovemaking as their pleasure-filled union unfolded. And in the dim lamplight of a golden glow that caressed the room, Eva opened her eyes and gazed at Chester, her heart turning over as her love for him soared, almost painfully, to new heights.

Chester smiled at her, as if to acknowledge her silent devotion, and then slid his hand up her spine to grasp the ends of her unbraided tresses. Eva arched her naked torso, tilted back her head, and lifted her swollen breasts to his lips, which he lovingly kissed, his tongue circling her hardened nipples, pushing her desire for him to the brink of exploding.

Sliding down onto her back, Eva murmured in contentment and opened herself completely, making space for Chester to settle between her welcoming legs. She knew that Chester was aware that this would be her first time with a man and she sensed his patience, felt his concern for her comfort. The fire that coursed through Eva burst into flame when he fingered her throbbing bud and sent jolts of pleasure rocketing through her body. Drawing in a deep breath to calm her own desire, she brushed her palms down his back, across his hard buttocks, and urged him to enter her sweet, welcoming path to ecstasy as they settled into a rhythm that took them to an explosive climax that shattered their innocence and made them one.

CHAPTER 4

Three days into her marriage, on a bone-chilling evening in January, Eva smoothed out the crumpled newspaper that Mr. Fitzgerald had given to her when she arrived at his shop that day. Aware that Chester's skill at reading was at a lower level than hers, Eva placed the paper on Tully's white cotton tablecloth and traced a finger over the fine print on the page. Leaning closer to the tall oil lamp, she began to read President Abraham Lincoln's Emancipation Proclamation aloud:

"That on the first day of January, in the year of our Lord one thousand eight hundred and sixty-three, all persons held as slaves within any State or designated part of a State, the people whereof shall then be in rebellion against the United States, shall be then, thenceforward, and forever free; and the Executive Government of the United States, including the military and naval authority thereof, will recognize and maintain the freedom of such persons, and will do no act or acts to repress such persons, or any of them, in any efforts they may make for their actual freedom)...

"What's it all mean?" Tully asked, tilting across her empty dinner plate to peer at the water-stained newspaper that Eva lifted from the table.

"I think the President is sayin' the war is over," Chester decided, setting down his fork, scowling as he pondered the recently released declaration from the President of the United States. "The rebels in the South have to turn their slaves out. Right, Eva? They gotta let 'em go free?"

Eva puckered her lips, a perplexed expression tightening her features as she sat back in her chair and studied the scraps of ham remaining on the blue china platter in the center of the table. Chester's question was exactly what she had asked Mr. Fitzgerald when he read President Lincoln's proclamation to her. She would try to explain it all to Tully and Chester just as the mapmaker had interpreted it for her.

"No ... Mr. Fitzgerald said this means that the President told the rebel states they had until the first day in January to stop fighting and come back into the Union. They didn't do that, so now the war will continue."

"Oh," Tully remarked, her voice faint and deflated. She rubbed two fingers across her chin and shook her head, clearly puzzled. "So why is he sayin' the slaves are free?"

"The proclamation only frees slaves in the states that didn't leave the Union. Let's see ..." Eva paused to search the article for more information. "Here is it. It says, slaves will be freed in Kentucky, Maryland, Delaware, Missouri ... and some parts of Louisiana. Mr. Fitzgerald says he's sure nothing is going to change for the slaves in the rebel states."

Chester shook his head in disgust. "Oh. So, the fightin' goes on." His remark was gruff with disappointment, tinged with a trace of anger. "Guess this means just a few more black men can call themselves free." He focused on Eva, his brown eyes steady on hers as he frowned, then told her, "Go on, Eva, read some more."

Eva continued. *"And I hereby enjoin upon the people so declared to be free to abstain from all violence, unless in necessary self-defense; and I recommend to them that, in all cases when allowed, they labor faithfully for reasonable wages. And I further declare and make known, that such persons of suitable condition, will be received into the armed service of the*

United States to garrison forts, positions, stations, and other places, and to
man vessels of all sorts in said service."

"President Lincoln wants black men to sign up to fight for the Union," Eva interpreted before Chester could ask her to decipher the president's message.

"That's good!" he called out with a whoop, rising from his chair to go stand at the hearth. Facing the two women, his back to the crackling fire, he told them, "I knew Negroes were gonna get put in the fight one day, and now, it's happening!" He slapped a hand against his thigh and grinned. "Just like Mr. Douglass said it would."

Eva's attention shifted from the newspaper up to meet Chester's excited expression. A wave of apprehension crept up her back; his reaction contained much more enthusiasm than suited her, initiating a silent prayer for strength to accept what she sensed he was going to say. The first day she met him, he'd told her he wanted to fight for the Union, and at that time, she had admired his patriotic stand. But now, as his wife, she wasn't so sure about this joyful eagerness he was displaying, and wished she felt less fearful about the prospect of her husband going off to war. She knew he would make a good and faithful soldier. He would follow orders and give his all for the Union for as long as they needed him. But she needed him too. He'd been her husband for a scant matter of days, not even long enough for them to plan much of a future. Didn't he have to think of what would become of her, and Tully, before deciding to rush off to war?

"Yes, that is what Frederick Douglass predicted," she finally agreed with Chester. "The president wants black men to sign up to fight for the Union."

"And that's just what I plan on doin'," Chester interrupted, giving Eva a smile that sent a searing pain of worry straight into her heart.

Later that evening, after Tully had retired, Eva and Chester sat on the bed in their room as they spoke in low tones, trying not to disturb Tully. For the first time since their wedding, they exchanged blunt words that pulled them in two different directions. As Chester talked about his desire to embrace the rugged life of a soldier, his eyes gleamed with an intensity that conveyed determination. His longing to join other black men in the fight against slavery validated his male-driven need to merge with the mass of able-bodied recruits who were marching off to war. Eva loved Chester for loving her, and respected him for wanting to do his part in ending the South's rebellion, but she also hated the idea of waking up one morning to find him gone. His adventurous attitude toward serving in the Army seemed oddly naïve as far as Eva was concerned. But when she pointed out all of the dangers he would face, the horror of battle and the loss of life, he dismissed her concerns with his assurance that he planned to be among those who marched home to celebrate when all the fighting was done.

In early March of 1863, before spring flowers had even shown their colorful blooms, word spread through the city of Boston that Governor John Andrew, the abolitionist governor of Massachusetts, had authorized the formation of an all colored regiment.

Black men who wanted to volunteer showed up in the city in droves, eager to join, ready to serve, excited about fighting for their country. They came from all over the land. Some were dressed in suits, others in work clothes or rags, and a large number of them arrived barefoot, their feet bloodied and bruised from their journey. They were common laborers as well as educated men of social standing, in all shades of brown and black. Some were small in stature, others large, but all were eager to wear the uniform of their country. More than 1,000 men responded to the news, including Chester Phillips, who enlisted as a member of the 54th Massachusetts Infantry Regiment, one of the first black regiments to be raised in the North.

Training for the 54th regiment began at Camp Meigs in Readville, just outside of Boston. All of the faithful abolitionist organizations contributed moral, material, and financial support to this radical and welcome expansion of the Union Army. Ladies sewed warm blankets, created battle flags, and made clothing for the black soldiers. Anti-slave activists raised funds to purchase musical instruments for a regimental band and helped spread the word near and far in order to recruit as many Negro men as were willing to serve.

"He says the Army doctor gave him a most complete medical examination, poking and prodding every inch of his body," Eva read from the first letter she'd received from Chester since he left for training a month earlier. "The men are living four to a tent with barely enough room to turn over in their sleep. He says the black soldiers are getting paid ten dollars a month. White soldiers get three dollars more."

"Hump," Tully grunted. "Ain't close by a long shot to what the lawyer was paying him, but I guess he'll get by alright."

Eva gave her aunt a soft murmur of irritation. "Ten dollars a month? How can he possibly manage on that? The government deducts three dollars for uniforms, shoes, and under-clothing. Leaving Chester what? Only seven dollars. He sent me five dollars this month. Now he has two dollars to his name. What can he do with that?" She set the letter aside and bit her bottom lip in concern. "I'm so worried about him, Aunt Tully. But what can I do?"

"Stay strong," Tully calmly replied. She sipped from her cup of tea, then held it suspended in front of her lips as she studied Eva. Before speaking, she firmly set the cup back down in its saucer. "Now, don't you be lookin' so sad," she admonished Eva. "Chester's training is almost finished. He said he wants you not to fuss about him. He's exactly where he wants to be. And just think... he'll be parading through town any day now. Don't get yourself all upset, Eva. He'll be fine. Nothin' you can do anyway. You have to accept his decision to join the Army. That's what he wanted and he's gonna be a good soldier. The government will give him all what he needs."

"I hope so," Eva murmured, filled with a muddled sense of dread and pride that seemed to be waging a war of its own inside of her.

~

Three weeks later, after learning that the 54th Infantry was scheduled to march through Boston on its way to the ships that would carry them south, Eva sat in the shimmering glow of a squat oil lamp with a sheet of paper set out on the table. After she dipped her quill pen into the pewter inkwell, she began her letter to Chester.

May 1, 1863

My dearest husband,

To simply say I will miss you after you go South to fight would not express the depths of my feelings for your absence. I am desperate to have you here with me, to share my days and nights. Our time together was far too short, and I long for your return. Even so, I want you to know how proud I am of your decision to fight for the Union. You are doing the right thing, even though it means that we must be separated for some time.

I promise you, my dear husband, my love will not lessen as the days and nights pass us by, but will only grow stronger. There are no more shadows creeping across my heart, as my love for you has banished all thoughts of despair. We will be together again, when the war is over, when those less fortunate than us will be free to love and live as we will once were are reunited.

Though tears of loneliness often threaten to overtake me, I shove them aside with words sung to me by my mother in the language of her homeland, Ka a fo, ka a fo. Don't cry, don't cry. And then I swallow my tears and resolve to stay strong until I see you again. Keep my letter close. You take my love and my heart with you,

Your loving wife, Eva.

A newly awakened sense of strength came to Eva as she sat back and re-read her words. She drew comfort from the knowledge that no matter the outcome of the war, her love for Chester would never die. How could it? It was as deeply ingrained in her heart as was her love for her mother, even though her maternal love only came to Eva through the words of a song that filtered into her dreams.

Instead of preparing the letter for posting, she folded it into a small square, tied it with a red ribbon, and placed it into her reticule.

On May 13, when the air was warm and all traces of winter had vanished, the black soldiers of the 54th Infantry, led by Colonel Robert Shaw, paraded through the streets of Boston to great applause and celebration. Wearing her red velvet hat, Eva waved a small American flag and saluted the troops while shouting her goodbyes to the men as they marched by, eyes front, looking very handsome in their dark blue uniforms and smart Army caps.

"Stay safe!" she shouted at them, wringing her hands in worry.

"Hurry home! All of you, hurry home!" Tully yelled, adding her cries of support to the riotous mix of pride, sadness, and joyous patriotism.

"We love you all!" Eva called out above the noisy crowd as the lively music of the fifes and drums crackled in the air. Stirred by the sight of the brave black men who were so obviously proud of their achievement, Eva blinked back tears of joy and apprehension. A part of her reveled in the soldiers' display of courage and patriotism, while another part of her dissolved into a hollow sense of dread as she heard the click of their heels on the cobblestone street, the musical shrill of the fife, and the loud thump of the drums that filled her head and momentarily erased her fears.

Eva's breathing stopped and her lips tightened when she saw Chester approaching. Quickly, she removed the letter from her purse and held it tightly between two fingers, grinning with relief to see that he was marching at the end of his row, placing him close to her. When he drew near, she easily shoved the beribboned square piece of paper beneath the cuff of his uniform sleeve, and then shouted, "I love you! Hurry home!"

Unable to speak, Chester cut his eyes at Eva as he passed her by, but then turned his head back toward her, winked, and blew a kiss her way, melting the fear that had gripped her heart since the day he first went away.

By the time Eva arrived home after the parade, she knew that Chester had already boarded a ship bound for Beaufort, South Carolina where his training would be put to the test. She removed her red bonnet, placed it in the hatbox, and wiped away her tears. Feeling deflated, yet excited, she sucked in a long breath and sank down into a chair. The 54th was headed into the Deep South, preparing to enter the fight. There would be no turning back now. Clutching the arms of the rocking chair, she recalled the promise that Chester had made in his last letter to her: *Once I get to South Carolina, I will do what I can to find news about your mother.*

And now that he was on his way, Eva knew that he would not let her down.

CHAPTER 5

After many months of training and preparation for battle, the 54th Massachusetts Infantry Regiment finally saw action when they took to the battlefield in a skirmish with Confederate troops on James Island, South Carolina on July 16, 1863. The all-black regiment fought valiantly and successfully, repelling the enemy while making Colonel Robert Shaw both grateful and proud of the men he commanded.

Two days later, the supreme test of the courage and valor of the black soldiers was upon them once more when they were ordered to lead the assault on Battery Wagner, a South Carolina Confederate fort erected on Morris Island, an 840 acre uninhabited isle accessible only by boat. The sandy mass of land, situated in the outer reaches of Charleston Harbor, was a strategic location sought by the Union. In addressing his soldiers before leading them in the charge across the deserted beach, Colonel Shaw told his men, "I want you to prove yourselves. The eyes of thousands will look on what you do tonight."

On July 18, 1863, the 54th Massachusetts Infantry Regiment advanced across the sandy beach and stormed Battery Wagner, encountering strong opposition from the Confederates.

As ammunition exploded in a deafening hail of cannon blasts and gunfire, Chester gritted his teeth and pressed forward, his long rifle pointed directly at the enemy. His steely determination to crush the Confederates tamped down the raging fear that ate at his insides and honed his resolve. The wind whipped grit into his eyes and his boots sank into the shifting sands. Each step forward was a labored attempt to maintain the posture of a soldier on a mission to kill. He could hardly keep in step with the drummer's cadence as the tap-tap of the drumbeat steadily propelled his jerky gait. Step-by-step he labored to advance toward the shadowy image of the heavily fortified fort in the distance, its walls growing taller, its embankment more ominous with each blast of gunfire that erupted from within.

When Colonel Shaw barked, "Charge! Company advance!" Chester lifted his rifle and leapt forward, running hard across the beach, his bayonet pointed at the invisible faces of the enemy behind the fortified walls. When he arrived at the foot of the mountain of sand that the Confederates had packed around the fort for protection, he stumbled across the bodies of fallen soldiers that were scattered in a mishmash of the dead and the wounded. The screams of the injured assaulted his ears, the smell of blood coiled in his gut. He wished he could stop to help the men he had grown to respect and trust, wished he could turn back time to the nightly campfire jokes and endless complaints they had shared, which now seemed of such inconsequence. But there was nothing to do at the moment but press on. He was a Union soldier, trained and dedicated to do his job, and he could not allow himself to panic. Nothing, he kept telling himself, was going to stop him from completing the mission of the 54th.

Hours later, when sunlight bathed the bloody battlefield and illuminated the results of the horrific conflict, Chester's eyes fluttered open. He awakened to find himself lying face down in the sand, his mouth filled with grit, his stomach boiling as if set afire. Shifting onto his side, he screamed, then bit down hard, grinding his teeth as a shocking flash of pain tore through the midsection of his body. Groping at his abdomen, he slid his fingers into the slick pool of blood that was seeping through his uniform. Immediately he knew he was seriously wounded. Slowly, Chester swiveled his head to the side and assessed his situation. Devastation lay piled all around him. The carnage was nearly impossible to comprehend, and he gaped in despair at the bodies of his comrades, scattered helter-skelter across the sandy battlefield, their flesh as shredded and torn as the tattered blue uniforms they wore. The six hundred men of the 54th had known that they were outgunned and outnumbered. However, they had not dared to believe they would not prevail.

The horrific screams of the wounded that echoed across the beach made Chester go limp, filling him with an odd sense of perverse satisfaction. He had survived. He was among those who would live to tell the tale of the proud black men of the 54th as they faced the enemy with steely resistance. He would tell his children what it had been like to fight alongside a loyal leader like Colonel Robert Shaw and how the valiant white man had sacrificed all for his men.

Closing his eyes, Chester eased his fingers beneath the buttons on the front of his uniform jacket and touched the letter Eva had given to him when he last saw her at the parade in Boston. Just the feel of the paper summoned an image of her wearing her red bonnet, smiling as she waved the American flag. He cherished her reaction when he winked at her after she blew a kiss his way. His vision of Eva grew sharp and brilliant, like the glitter of a sword or a forked flash of lightning.

When another excruciating pain tore through Chester, he screamed aloud, his voice fearful and shrill; the voice of a man fully aware that the end was near. He had been foolish to believe he would come out of this alive, that the blood steadily draining into the sand would not eventually empty him of life. Giving in to the inevitable darkness that he prayed would bring a final relief, he relaxed, sighing as he allowed himself to slip quietly into Eva's open arms.

CHAPTER 6

The United States Department of War
Washington, D.C.

September 1, 1863
   Dear Mrs. Phillips:
   It is with much regret that we inform you that your husband, Private Chester Phillips was killed in battle during the Union forces' assault on Fort Wagner at Morris Island, South Carolina on July 18, 1863. The 54th Massachusetts Infantry Regiment fought valiantly, and the United States Army is grateful for your husband's service. Private Phillips was buried on Morris Island along with those in his unit who fought and died during the engagement with the Confederate Army. The regiment's commander, Colonel Robert Gould Shaw was placed to rest in the grave with his men. As the widow of a US serviceman, you are eligible to receive any back pay that was due to Private Phillips at the time of his death, as well as a widow's pension of $25.00 per annum.
   Sincerely,
   E.D. Townsend
   Secretary of War

Eva passed the letter to Tully, who had been watching Eva with a worried stare ever since the uniformed man showed up at their door with an envelope in his hand. Without speaking to her aunt, Eva got up and left the room, climbed the stairs, and went into the bedroom she had shared with her husband for such a short time. During the six weeks since the 54th Regiment assaulted the Confederates at Fort Wagner, newspaper reports about the stunning defeat of the Union forces had been described in great detail. Eva had read that of the six-hundred men who charged up the beach, more than a third had been killed, wounded, or captured by the enemy. She had been praying every day that Chester might be among those who had survived, but now she knew he was not. Their souls were now forever separated, their love scattered like straw blown away on a gust of wind. Slowly, she removed her yellow and blue striped housedress and stripped down to her plain muslin chemise and bloomers. Reaching into the trunk at the foot of her bed, she pulled out the only black dress that she owned. As she slipped it over her head and adjusted its high lace collar, she vowed not to wear any color but black until the day the war ended and all the slaves were free.

PART II

I know, as my life grows older,
And mine eyes have clearer sight,
That under each rank wrong somewhere
There lies the root of Right.

Ella Wheeler Wilcox, poet

CHAPTER 7

TRENT

While the US Army was removing the Winnebago Indians from Green Bay, Wisconsin to the safety of Fort Atkinson in the1850's, they established the "Old Mission Road" as a military wagon route. During the move, the soldiers made camp near Jessup's Spring, deep within a stand of timber abundant with wild strawberries, and marked the campsite with a wooden stake inscribed with the name, "Strawberry Point."

Among those early settlers of Strawberry Point was Paul Hartwell, a farmer from Vermont who had been looking for a place where he could settle with his bride and start a family. When he stopped to water his horse at Jessup's Spring, he knew he had found the piece of land upon which he would stake his claim. He bought five hundred acres of rich black Iowa soil for sixty dollars, planted fields of corn and wheat, raised hogs and cows, became a wealthy man, and produced two sons, Robert and Trent.

Twenty years after Paul's sons were born, his wife died of pneumonia, sending the farmer into a downward spiral that ended when, while in a drunken state, he slipped on a mossy rock, fell into the spring, and drowned.

Strawberry Point, Iowa
September 1863

Trent Hartwell stared at his reflection in the oak-frame mirror hanging on his bedroom wall, satisfied with the image he saw. Honey brown eyes, dark brown hair with a hint of curl, and a clean-shaven jaw as pronounced and square as his deceased father's had been. His trim, youthful, physique, made taut and muscular from manual labor as he worked the family farm, gave little hint that Trent was two months shy of thirty, or that within a week's time he would become a married man. The golden wedding band he'd bought for his fiancée Rebecca was safely tucked away in a desk drawer in the downstairs parlor, where their intimate family ceremony was going to be held. The short guest list included Rebecca's widowed mother, her younger sister, Ivy, and two cousins who had already arrived from Chicago. Trent's family would be represented by his brother, Robert, and a handful of longtime neighbors who had known the Hartwell boys all their lives.

With no mother or father to turn to for assistance with planning such a festive occasion, Trent was depending on his longtime house-keeper, Polly, to make all the celebratory arrangements.

Now, Trent mentally reviewed the list of things Polly had told him she would be more than happy to take care of for him: bake a three-tier wedding cake decorated with candy roses, prepare a generous meal for the guests, and place large vases of flowers cut from the garden throughout the ten-room house. Polly, a fugitive slave that his parents had taken into their home when she was a girl, was only two years older than Trent, but had already garnered the reputation as one of the best cooks in Clayton County.

Looking around his bedroom, Trent saw that Polly had already pressed his Sunday-suit-of-clothes and hung them on the hook next to his bed, the bed he looked forward to sharing with the woman he had loved since childhood. Just thinking of his approaching wedding to Rebecca Wilkenson made Trent begin to blush, with little shame and much anticipation. In his opinion, she was the prettiest girl in Strawberry Point, the girl with whom Trent had played hide-and-seek when he was a boy, gone fishing with in the nearby spring, and exchanged letters when he went off to the university in Des Moines to study law. He had not been surprised to find, when he finished his studies and returned to the farm, that his connection to Rebecca had shifted from friendship into love. Spending the rest of his life with her while creating a family and working the Hartwell farm was exactly how he envisioned his future to unfold.

After the death of their father, Trent and his brother, Robert, vowed never to sell the spacious, two-story wood-frame house or the five-hundred-acre farm that they managed with the help of half-a-dozen seasonal workers. Due to their father's careful attention to financial matters, he had left each of his sons a handsome amount of money to maintain and improve the property. And even though Trent possessed the credentials to join the ranks of men who worked in the legal profession, he was content to live on the family farm that he loved and spend his days tilling the soil instead of reading heavy law books and arguing cases in front of a judge.

Now, he buttoned his plaid cotton shirt with quick fingers, tucked his shirttail into his denim work pants, and then sat on the edge of the bed and pulled on a scuffed pair of ankle jacks, still splattered with mud from his work in the field the previous day. Surveying his bedroom, Trent realized that he had a lot of rearranging and cleaning up to do before he brought a wife into the room. In fact, the entire house had been without a woman's touch for far too long. His bedroom was sparsely furnished, outfitted with a mahogany sleigh bed, a highboy chest of drawers, a fireplace, and two side chairs upholstered in dark blue twill. It was a shabbily comfortable room that suited him fine, but would most likely not appeal to Rebecca. He'd never bothered with putting a rug on the rough pine floor or hanging window coverings to block out the sunlight. He awoke before dawn and went to bed long after dark, and so, had never considered addressing such things, until now.

The strong aroma of coffee wafted up from the kitchen, interrupting his thoughts. Trent hurried down the narrow staircase and went directly to the stove, where Polly's ham and eggs sat waiting for him.

"Think we oughta spruce up the place a bit before Rebecca moves in?" he asked the woman who kept the house in order. He took his plate and went to sit at the table near the window that provided a view of the fields of corn and wheat beyond the open yard where late September roses still bloomed.

Silently considering Trent's remark, Polly took her time pouring his cup of coffee before she spoke. "Might be best to let Miss Rebecca decide what she wants changed. No need in worrying about that now. She been in this house enough times over the years to know what she's gettin'."

"Ummm," Trent murmured, nodding in agreement as he bit into a piece of ham. "You got a point there, Polly. Whatever she wants to do with the house is fine with me." He gulped a swallow of coffee, then asked, "Robert already gone?"

"Um, hum. Left out real early. Took the wagon down to the springs. Said he was goin' fishin', hopin' to catch some trout for dinner."

"Right," Trent replied, recalling Robert's earlier remark that he wanted to get in some fishing early in the day. Trent finished off his eggs and ham, gulped the last of his coffee, then removed his black broad-brimmed hat from a hook by the door. With a tug, he settled it over his deep brown hair and opened the back door. "Guess I'll walk on down and catch up with him ... see what he's got so far."

Taking the secluded path that wound its way through a generous stand of sycamore and elm trees bordered by wood ferns, Trent made his way toward Jessup's Spring. He savored the feel of the warm September air of an Indian summer he hoped would hold until his wedding day. The sight of fat brown squirrels scurrying across the path and the back-and-forth calls of redbirds in the trees filled Trent with an overwhelming sense of optimism and joy, increasing his awareness of how lucky he was: He had good land to farm, a brother to help him, and Rebecca to love. Only a few more days, and she would be his wife, the mother of the children he hoped they would be blessed to have.

Emerging from the path, Trent scanned the rocky spring for Robert, who was usually standing knee-deep in their favorite fishing spot. He saw that the wagon had been parked farther away, off the path, with the horse hitched to the knobby elm tree that he, Robert, and Rebecca had loved to climb when they were young.

Trent increased his pace, searching for Robert, anxious to see how many fish his brother had already caught. He swung his gaze up and down the rocky bank, and was about to call out his brother's name when he noticed him sitting in the bed of the wagon.

"Oh, there you are!" Trent shouted, walking toward Robert, whose head snapped around in surprise. His eyes remained riveted on Trent as he approached. "Having much luck?" Trent asked.

Robert didn't answer. Instead, he stood, slowly climbed down from the wagon, then reached back into the bed of the low-sided cart and offered his hand to Rebecca, who accepted his assistance and rose, cautiously, easing to her feet. Glancing away from Trent, she hurriedly brushed straw from her shockingly bare shoulders and out of her tousled blonde hair.

Trent froze. His mouth ajar as he watched his fiancée descend from the wagon to stand beside his brother. Surely, that wasn't *his* Rebecca staring at him with only a hint of shame on her face, her rosy nipples barely covered, her pantaloons exposed. Surely, he wasn't witnessing what appeared to be the most horrible betrayal that could happen to any man. Trent's breath caught in his throat. He'd never even seen Rebecca's naked breasts, had never placed his lips any place on her body other than her lips, her cheek, and along the side of her neck. Protecting her purity until their wedding night had been a vow they'd made together, and as difficult as it had been for Trent to keep his lips from her bosom and his manhood in his pants, he had never considered breaking his promise to her.

"My God, Rebecca! Robert! What is going on?" Trent swung

wide eyes from his fiancée to his brother and back again, feeling Polly's ham and eggs threatening to rise in his stomach.

"Just a minute, now, Trent," Robert stammered, heaving in a deep breath, as if preparing for a showdown.

"Damn you, Robert! What is this?" Trent demanded, realizing that Robert had ruined everything! He'd torn Trent's and Rebecca's lives apart as if uprooting a beautiful tree. Questions swirled in his head but he could not speak. How could his brother be involved in such a despicable encounter? And how much of a fool had Trent been not to know?

Lifting her chin with a touch of defiance, Rebecca smiled weakly at Trent, then shook out her rumpled skirt and fumbled with the buttons on her half-open bodice as she tried to cover her nakedness.

The moment Robert took a step forward, Trent yanked off his hat, threw it to the ground, and using all the strength he could muster, launched at his brother and landed a punch to the side of his head. Trent was too angry to gain satisfaction from the fact that his unexpected assault sent Robert reeling, stumbling backward, an expression of pure shock contorting his face. "You dirty bastard!" Trent shouted. "You low down dog of a man. How could you do this to me?"

Robert quickly regained his footing and bounded forward, landing a violent jab to the middle of Trent's chest, forcing him to his knees. "Rebecca never loved you," he yelled at Trent. "It was me ... me, she always wanted. I was the one who kept her company while you went off to the university to study law, playing big man in the big city." Robert spat at the ground, his top lip curling up at the corner as he narrowed his eyes at Trent. "*Law.*" He spat again. "You fool. A farmer doesn't need to know more than when to plant and when to harvest. You deserted Rebecca so you could make yourself think you were better than me. Well, you're not. Rebecca turned to me and I was glad to fill the void you left."

"You liar!" Trent shot back, scrambling to his feet. "You've always been jealous of me because I was accepted to the university. Not my fault you failed the entrance exams. You think taking

Rebecca from me makes you look big? Smart?" Trent grunted in disgust. "No, it makes you the fool, a foolish man chasing after a woman he does not deserve." Lowering his head, Trent rushed at Robert like an angry bull and head-butted him in the stomach. The brothers tumbled to the ground in a jumble of flailing arms, kicking feet, and fiery fists, engaging in a tangle of pounding blows that continued until blood ran from both their noses and dark bruises covered their cheeks. When Trent finally disengaged, he scooted away from Robert and sat back on his heels, his chest heaving as he struggled to pull air into his lungs.

"You can have her," Trent wheezed, swinging his gaze to Rebecca, looking into her blue eyes for the first time. He was disgusted to see her standing there, her clothing hastily rearranged. "In fact, Robert, you can have my share of the farm as well, but you're gonna pay me a fair price for it."

Robert lowered his head in silent agreement as he wiped his bloody nose with the sleeve of his shirt. "Fine with me."

Clinching his teeth to maintain a modicum of composure, Trent got up from the ground, bent down to snatch up his hat, and slapped it against his thigh. "Wire my money to me at the Regal Hotel in Chicago. I'll be leaving in the morning."

CHAPTER 8

Chicago
April 1865

Trent Hartwell's law office on Polk Street was only a few yards away from the jail that Chicagoans referred to as the Bridewell, the facility's name having been derived from an old English term for a place designed to house low-level offenders. Those who were arrested and detained for public drunkenness, fighting, or minor issues like disturbing the peace were held at the Bridewell until they paid their fines or engaged a lawyer such as Trent, who might manage to secure their release. By establishing his law office near the city's jail at the edge of the local vice district, Trent had guaranteed himself a continuous supply of desperate clients who kept him busy representing a revolving door of oft-repeating criminals who rarely remained incarcerated for more than a few weeks. In addition to assisting petty criminals, he also drafted legal papers to end failed marriages or settle small estates.

For nearly two years, Trent had buried himself in his work, which paid very little and consumed most of his time, preventing him from dwelling on Robert, Rebecca, or their gut-wrenching betrayal. Soon after arriving in Chicago, in addition to opening his law practice, he made a wise investment in a local ammunitions factory that fabricated pistols, bullets, and cannonballs for the Union Army. His investment had been paying off handsomely, adding cash to his bank account, which already held his inheritance from his father and the settlement from Robert for the sale of his share of the farm.

A man as wealthy as Trent Hartwell might have purchased a grand house in an exclusive neighborhood and socialized with Chicago's fashionable set, hob-knobbing with the moneyed men who made their fortunes in railroads, commodities, and the booming business of mercantile trade. However, Trent shunned the ostentatious lifestyle of the mega-rich, preferring to live rather modestly in a three-room flat ten minutes from his office where he enjoyed the sense of anonymity that his low social profile afforded.

Though he shunned fancy parties and avoided expensive restaurants, he did enjoy going out for a drink now and then, frequenting a pub called Red Ruby's, a watering hole where men who worked in the nearby ammunition factory went to pass the time. There, he found comfort in listening to the men's rough banter and blunt talk about politics and war. Their lively discussions, which ranged from debates on the success of the abolitionist movement to the high cost of wheat and cattle were stimulating and interesting to Trent. The men who flocked to Red Ruby's were Negro and white, foreign born and home grown; it was a boisterous melting pot of humanity that fascinated Trent and gave him a larger sense of the world. Having lived all of his life in Iowa, Trent was eager to enlarge his worldview, to expose himself to people from places beyond his Midwestern upbringing. Polly, who had been with his family since he was a boy, was the only person of color he had actually come close to calling a friend.

At the boisterous pub, Trent was often approached for free legal advice, which he didn't mind providing to men who wanted to discuss their broken marriages, dangerous jobs, unfair bosses, and a variety of challenges that made getting ahead in life so difficult.

They confessed their misfortunes, grumbled about their wages, bragged about their sexual conquests, and exuded a spirit of adventure that for some reason, made Trent a bit envious. Thus far, his life had been rather tame. He saw himself as a farmer who had managed to become a lawyer, almost against his will. Not a day went by when he did not think of Strawberry Point, of the farm where he had been born, the land he had worked with devotion. In a desperately aching way, he still yearned for the sight of fields flush with corn, of clear streams of water flowing freely through the forests where patches of red strawberries grew wild in the woods. Residing in a dreary furnished flat, eating meals alone or with strangers who often did not speak his language, was not how he had envisioned spending the best years of his life. But for now, he had no choice but to call Chicago home.

On a rainy evening in early April, after spending the day ensconced in his office, Trent set aside the case files he had been reviewing, which were due to the court the next day. He'd stuck with the task until his eyes grew tired, and now he was ready to abandon the papers for a tall cool beer. Leaving his office, he made his way to Red Ruby's Pub, hoping to arrive before the beer ran out, as it often did on Friday nights. When he entered the establishment, he was surprised by the boisterous crowd he encountered. Men were yelling, shouting, and shoving one another, but not in an angry or pugilistic manner. Friday nights usually brought out a decent number of patrons, but tonight every table was taken, the bar was three-deep, and customers lined the walls with mugs of beer in their hands.

He squeezed into a space between two colored men standing at the bar who were dressed in rough brown suits with black bowlers on their heads. He signaled to Ruby for a drink as he placed a coin on the bar.

"Comin' right up," Ruby called out, giving Trent a wink that made him smile. "I was thinkin' you'd be comin' in. This is quite a night, don't you think? So, where you been?"

Trent grinned, then said, "Been busy getting drunks out of jail and settling marital disputes."

Ruby laughed as the poured his beer into a fat mug. "Don't blame any of that on me," she chided. "I just sell the beer ... not my job to tell a man how much to drink." With a chuckle, Trent inclined his head in agreement. He enjoyed engaging in flirtatious banter with Ruby, who could have easily passed for white if it had not been for her tightly curled red hair, worn in an explosion of tiny braids held back from her face by a scarlet ribbon. She was friendly with all the customers, but with Trent, it was different. He knew her flirtation with him was genuine, often stirring thoughts of Rebecca, of how much he had planned on a life with her, and how much he longed for a woman's embrace. Ruby was a pretty woman. Trent was a lonely man. It took a lot of strength for him to turn away from her obvious invitations to her bed.

"Awful tight in here," Trent remarked to the man on his left, as if to apologize for rubbing shoulders with him as he squeezed closer to pick up his mug of beer. "What's brought everyone out?"

The man's head swiveled around in surprise. He widened his eyes, blinked, and threw an astonished look at Trent, nailing him with an expression of astonishment. "You don't know?" he shouted above the din of voices rising inside the pub. "You ain't heard?"

"Heard what?" Trent shouted back, acknowledging Ruby with a tilt of his head and a tad-too-long stare into her large dark eyes. "What's happened?"

"Lee surrendered to Grant at Appomattox. The Civil War's over. The fightin's finally finished," Ruby interjected with a grin.

"Damn right! The Yankees done whipped the rebels," the brown-skinned man in the bowler hat tossed out.

"Well, that's damn sure worth celebrating!" Trent agreed, clinking glasses with the stranger as he joined in the celebrating.

Toward midnight the beer ran out, having lasted longer than it usually did on Friday nights. However, instead of sending everyone home and closing the pub, Ruby told her brother, David, who helped out around the pub, to roll out a barrel of her finest whiskey: The end of the long and bloody war was reason to keep the party going.

The clock above the bar struck two when Ruby finally walked away from the bar and sat down at a table at the rear of the pub. Looking over at Trent, she nodded, and when she waved at him, asking him to join her, he did.

"What's all this end-of-the-war gonna mean for you?" Ruby asked Trent, taking a long draw on her cup of whiskey.

Trent thought for a moment, then shrugged. "Well, for sure, the Union won't be needing so many rifles and bullets, so work at the ammunition factory will most likely decline."

"But … for *you*… you're a lawyer…what does it mean for you?" she pressed.

"Not sure. I don't plan to leave Chicago, if that's what you're asking," he offered, leaning across the beer-sticky table, placing his face level with hers.

"Yeah, I guess I'm askin'. Good to know you're not leavin'," Ruby admitted, giving Trent a smile.

"When the soldiers come home, many will need a lawyer's advice, some may have legal matters to settle. Circumstances here at home will have changed while they were off fighting. So, the end of the war might be good for a lawyer like me." With a thoughtful expression, he glanced upward, noticing that the gas light overhead cast a star-shaped shadow across Ruby's face. "There'll be other business opportunities, too. Markets in the South have collapsed. People there need food … corn, wheat, meat, all kinds of goods that the North will be pressed to supply. Trade will boom between the North and the South now that the country is united."

"That sounds like good news. More jobs for everyone, right?" Ruby offered.

"Could be," Trent agreed. Leaning back in his chair, he took a moment let his eyes drift over Ruby, struck once again by how pretty she was, how easy it was to talk with her, and how obvious her attraction to him had become. "And what about you, Ruby? Didn't you once tell me you came to Chicago from some place in the South?"

"Moncks Corner, South Carolina. A fair size town north of Charleston. Born and raised there. But I been in Chicago close to fifteen years."

"Do you still have family there?"

"Nobody I know about, and I got no desire to go back."

"So, your parents are deceased?"

"Yeah, my father was an Irishman … named Jonathan Ruby. He …"

"Ruby?" Trent interrupted, clearly puzzled. "You mean *Ruby* is your last name?"

"It is," Ruby nodded. "My real name is Josephine Ruby, but ever since I was a little girl, everyone's called me Ruby. I like it much better than Josephine anyway."

"Oh… Josephine," Trent repeated. "Well, I think you're right. I prefer Ruby as well." Trent chuckled, then said, "Now, what were you saying about your father?"

"He supervised men working the locks on the Santee Canal. My mother was a mulatto. She cooked for the men who worked the Santee. One day my father fell into the locks and was killed. She ran off, left me to fend for myself."

"Oh," Trent murmured. "How old were you when all that happened?"

"Oh, about twelve I guess."

"What did you do?"

"Scrapped around and tried to survive. Then one day a white man named Elmer Ashford, who knew my father, asked me if I would go with him and his wife when they left for Chicago. He needed a girl to take care of their baby. I grabbed the chance and left. Mr. Ashford let me stay on with his family until I got old enough to work here at his pub. When the men started callin' his place Red Ruby's he liked it, and let it stick." She paused in thought, then added, "Go back to South Carolina? Nope." Ruby continued, "I don't ever want to set foot on South Carolina soil again. Ain't nothing there for me."

Trent could understand Ruby's reluctance to return to the town below the Mason-Dixon line where she had been born. After all, she had created a good life for herself in Chicago.

When she reached out and placed her hand on Trent's wrist, and said, "I like it fine right here," her long fingernails sent signals of desire through Trent.

"It's real nice sitting here, talking with you like this," she said. "But we don't have to stay here, you know. I've got a little place just a few blocks away. It'd be nice if you could..."

Trent removed his hand from beneath Ruby's touch, swallowed the last of his whiskey, and fell quiet for a moment, trying to clear his head. The beer and the whiskey and Ruby's pretty face were coming together in a dizzy blur that made him feel warm all over. He was not used to drinking hard liquor, did not usually stay up so late, and certainly had not felt such a strong urge to make love to a woman in his adult life. When she pushed back from the table and stood looking down at him, he found himself agreeing with Ruby when she asked him if he would like to walk her home.

Ruby's bedroom was just as exotic and enticing as Trent had imagined it to be: a cozy cocoon of bright floral pillows scattered over stark white sheets that were neatly tucked on a white iron bed draped with gauzy netting. The sight moved him to a strange exhilaration that heightened his anticipation of what he knew was to come. Rose-colored oil lamps on a low oak chest created a hazy veil of dim yellow light, sufficient for Trent to admire Ruby's well-endowed body when she easily slipped out of her green dress and, with unhurried moves, removed her chemisette and white cotton underwear. Trent felt himself harden at the sight of her cream-colored skin, bathed in pale milky light that was beckoning his touch. He made no move to hide the growing evidence of his desire, allowing the bulge in his trousers to remain on display, smiling slightly to see Ruby's eyes travel downward in admiration. Clinching a fist at his side, he narrowed his gaze when she turned aside, walked to the bed, and pulled back the sheets.

"You gonna just stand there, watching me?" she taunted, urging him to make a move. "I been watchin' you for a long time. Never seen you with a woman. Never heard you speak a woman's name. So, don't be actin' like you don't want me. I know you do." She sat on the edge of the bed and spread her legs wide, exposing the deep red tangle of hair between her thighs, inviting Trent to touch her, to taste her, to pleasure himself as he pleased. Placing both hands at her sides, she leaned back and thrust her rosy nipples at him, presenting her swollen breasts to Trent as if they were a gift.

Trent ran his tongue over his lips and continued to stare at Ruby, calculating his options. He'd been struck with a shocking bolt of eager anticipation when she asked him to walk her home, and now that he faced what he had hoped for, uncertainty held him in place. He could walk out the door, hurry down two flights of stairs, and return to the solitude of his three-room flat. But her appeal was devastatingly overwhelming. The throbbing urge for release that pulsed hotly in his groin pushed his lust for Ruby to the edge of surrender. When he took a step toward her, she lifted a hand and crooked a finger at him, inviting him to obey her command. Unable to resist, he strode closer, unloosening his shirt, then his trousers as he approached. Standing between her open legs, he tossed clothing aside until all of it lay in a pile on the floor. Almost brusquely, he took her by the shoulders and pushed her back on the bed. Lying atop her, he savored the feel of her skin, warm and smooth, fused against his as he rubbed his manhood back and forth in the curly patch of red hair surrounding the wet lips of her womanhood. A strange inner excitement coursed through Trent as his heart hammered faster in his chest. But when he tried to kiss Ruby's lips, she turned her head to the side, presenting her cheek to him instead. Surprised by this rebuff, he leaned back and studied her profile, curiously intrigued by this lovely woman who was willingly offering her body to him but did not want to be kissed.

"You invite me to your bed, yet refuse my kiss?" he queried with the slightest hint of amusement.

"This ain't about love, you know," she flatly stated, her face still turned from his.

Trent sucked in a silent breath, knowing she spoke the truth.

Ruby shifted, her gaze now meeting Trent's. "Save your kisses for the woman you plan to marry. Don't waste them on a passing fancy like me."

Trent opened his mouth to reject the assignation that she was just a passing fancy, but closed it after a moment of reflection. Instead of kissing her lips, he slid his tongue along the curve of her ear, down the slope of her jaw, across the hollow of her neck. He bent to capture a hardened nipple between his lips and suckled its sweetness until she sighed aloud in pleasure and melted deeper into the sheets.

Nibbling and licking his way across her chest, he realized that he did have feelings for Ruby. But she was right. He did not have feelings of love, not like the love he'd felt for Rebecca. *But what*, he mentally wondered, *had my love and kisses for Rebecca brought me, other than heartache and anger*? His attraction to Ruby swung between a strong desire to have her in his bed and a kind of respect that he could not name. She had always been more than friendly with him, and he had daydreamed more than once of putting his shaft inside her creamy core. And now that he was with her, he would do as she wanted and not ask for more than what she was willing to offer. Without speaking, he nudged his swollen member into her sweet, moist tunnel and pushed deeply into the heart of her pleasure. With a moan, Ruby wrapped her legs around his waist and locked her hands behind his neck, pressing her body to his skin, digging her heels into his buttocks as she held his stiff erection in place.

Blood pounding in his brain, Trent clutched Ruby about the waist and pulled her flush against his torso, rocking back and forth, greeting her like a flower that had opened just for him, gifting him with its sweet fragrance, his for the taking. Thrusting more forcefully than he had intended, he shuddered, unable to control the flash of heat that shot through him and seared his need for her and exposed his delight in having her. Her womanly warmth brought him to the brink of exploding as he felt her passion engulfing him, and falling completely into her spell, he tumbled into a cascade of rapture, losing himself in a pool of slick release that banished all thoughts of the past.

CHAPTER 9

Five days after the much-celebrated end of the Civil War, the nation's joyous observance came to an abrupt end when, on April 14, 1865, devastating news silenced the jubilant citizens: President Abraham Lincoln had been shot by John Wilkes Booth at Ford's Theater in Washington, D.C. and died early that morning.

Trent Hartwell sipped his morning coffee and continued reading the newspaper article about the president's assassination. *What an outrage,* he silently grieved. *For the president to have worked so diligently to free the slaves and reunite the country, to die before the results of his devotion to the nation were fully realized. Such a tragedy.*

As Trent continued reading the paper, he was drawn to an article that detailed the disastrous effects of the conflict on the rebel states. The Civil War had left the Confederacy in shambles. Railroad lines had been blown up, cities burned to the ground, thousands of acres of farmland either abandoned or decimated by ransacking troops. With no functioning, recognized government in place, the U.S. Congress had divided the Confederacy into five military districts, placing Union soldiers in each one to provide security and a sketchy political structure for the citizenry. There was no legal tender: Confederate money had been declared worthless, creating a financial crisis of great magnitude. And the newly freed slaves were totally abandoned, left to wander the roads as they searched for family and tried to survive without food, clothing, or shelter. The irony of the situation was not lost on Trent, who grumbled aloud in frustration: The former slaves were now referred to as freedmen and freed women, but what had freedom brought them? They owned nothing – no land, no money, no homes, no food, not even shoes to wear as they walked the roads. Surely, they deserved a hell of a lot better from the U.S. government.

Trent slowly set the newspaper aside. He placed his hands on the table and sat quietly, fully and deeply considering what he had just read. He had been with Ruby every night since their first encounter, and he enjoyed every moment he spent in her bed. It was true, he did not love her as he had loved Rebecca, but he had to admit that, so far, her companionship had partially assuaged his loneliness. He had never been with a woman of color before, and he'd come to realize how little skin color meant to him. The revelation was infinitely pleasing and refreshing. A woman was a woman, a man was a man. A person's race meant nothing to him at all. He could not see it any other way, and now, with the war at an end, he prayed that the people of the rebel states would come to the same conclusion.

A vague thought, as elusive and sheer as a curl of smoke, began to rise in Trent's mind as he pondered the newspaper article he had just read. Life in Chicago was not for him. He was tired of trying to fit himself into a situation that was not advancing his search for meaning and joy in his life.

Perhaps it's time to leave Chicago. I could travel into the South, where land is cheap and hard cash is scarce. He pressed the thought with more intensity. *I would be a much happier man farming land that I owned instead of processing legal papers for petty criminals. But where would I go? Where would be the best place for me to start fresh, to create a new, more satisfying life?*

Reaching for the world globe that was sitting on his desk, he gave it a spin, then stopped it to scrutinize the cluster of rebel states lining the Atlantic coast. He stared at South Carolina. Ruby's home state. During their time together, she had told him quite a bit about the state where she had been born. He could picture the landscape in his mind: Fields of fertile land that once supplied world markets with cotton, indigo, and rice. Tall stands of pine trees that went on for miles and provided ample lumber for construction of homes, barns, and warehouses. There were streams, rivers, and canals that made for ease of travel from Charleston Harbor to places deep within the state, allowing a man to fully explore and utilize large tracts of land.

With a jolt, his thoughts returned to Ruby's soft, warm body, to the smell of her perfumed bedroom as its scent rose in his head and sent his pulse racing. South Carolina had produced a woman who had brought him a deeper sense of understanding of who he was, of what would bring him peace of mind. He had money enough to buy as much land as he desired, and he wanted nothing more than to start over from scratch. Why not go to South Carolina and find out what might be waiting there for him?

CHAPTER 10

Charleston, South Carolina
October 1865

Located at the corner of Broad and State Streets, The Bank of Charleston was a two-story masonry building accentuated with a series of tall rectangular windows facing a flank of slender palmetto trees. A gold-leaf eagle looked down upon the busy street from above the arched entrance to the building, as it had since 1817, according to the eye-level plaque that greeted every customer.

Trent gripped the ornate wrought-iron handle, pulled back the heavy oak door, and entered the cavernous lobby, where he was immediately enveloped in a much cooler temperature, the result of tall louvered shutters that blocked the relentless low country sunshine wilting the people outside. Glancing around, his eyes gradually adjusted to the bank's dim interior, allowing him to admire the elaborately carved fretwork above the tellers' cages and the detailed plasterwork atop Corinthian capitals rising to a decorated ceiling. Impressed with the grandeur of the stately structure, he felt reassured that he had chosen well: This was a bank with stability and authority; a safe place to deposit the carpetbag of cash he had protectively held onto during his journey from Chicago.

It had taken six months, longer than Trent had anticipated, to settle his affairs with the court system and liquidate his holdings in order to secure the cash required for the investments he hoped to make. And after finally arriving in Charleston, he was anxious to put his money in a secure bank vault, having been informed by a fellow traveler with whom he'd shared a compartment on the Silver Line Limited, that The Bank of Charleston was a regional power with affiliates in Georgia, Alabama, Florida, and Louisiana. His travelling companion had also told Trent that the bank had managed to survive financially during the Civil War despite a $1.5 million loan to the Confederacy.

Trent walked over to the first free clerk he saw, introduced himself and asked to speak to the bank manager. After a very short wait, a slim man with a bushy black beard and an equally wiry mustache approached, an expression of curiosity and anticipation on his pale visage.

"Good morning. I'm Mansard York, the bank manager," he said with a touch of arrogance, his eyes travelling pointedly to the soft-sided, brown and green fabric valise that Trent was holding at his side. Before extending his hand, York stiffly inquired, "And how may I be of assistance, Mr. ...?"

"Hartwell. Trent Hartwell. I'd like to open an account, please. I wish to make a deposit and transact some business." Trent stated his business in his most official tone while locking eyes with Mansard York, as if to let him know that he'd come to discuss a serious matter and expected to be treated with the kind of respect that hard cash bought.

"Ah, Mr. Hartwell... you're not a Charleston resident, I assume?" York cautiously inquired.

"I've just recently arrived in your city and I hope to settle here, if certain expectations are met."

"I see. And, where are you from?"

"Iowa, by way of Chicago."

"Iowa? Chicago? Of course, of course," York stuttered, offering a long-fingered hand to Trent's outstretched one. Pulling back his shoulders, he nodded, then said, "Why don't we talk in my office. Come with me, please."

Trent followed Mr. York into a spacious room off the lobby that was furnished with a rather plain mahogany desk with matching side chairs upholstered in dark purple brocade, a rectangular meeting table that looked as if it could seat twenty people, and windows hung with purple silk drapes that swept in folds from the ceiling to the floor. After York retrieved a pen and paper from his desk, the men took seats across from each other in the middle of the conference table, where Trent deposited his bulging bag of cash.

"Well, now, let's see what we can do for you, Mr. Hartwell," York started, his attention trained on the bag that Trent had begun to unpack.

As Trent placed stack after stack of crisp American dollars in the space between them, York's mouth opened wider and wider. Lifting his chin, the banker narrowed his eyes and drew in an audible breath, either enjoying the smell of new money or calming his nerves at the sight of so much hard cold cash about to enter his financial institution.

"That's seventy-eight thousand dollars, Mr. York," Trent informed the bank manager, looking at the man from beneath lowered lashes. "All in valid American money, not useless Confederate dollars. If I put my money in your bank, I expect you to not only protect my deposit but to help me make it grow."

"The Bank of Charleston is at your service," York quickly enthused, his voice inflected with a near-giggle of approval.

"I've come to Charleston to make real estate investments," Trent clarified, eager to state his position clearly and determine how well it would be received. He was well aware of the fact that many people in the defeated south resented the intrusion of Northerners looking to cash in on the troubles facing their state, and he had no desire to falsely represent himself or disguise his motives for arriving. "I plan to settle here and participate fully in the reconstruction of South Carolina. I feel I can do a lot for the state, and most point-edly for the people of Charleston. I hope it can do as much for me. However, I am not naïve. Since I arrived four days ago, I've been called a Yankee Carpetbagger, a dirty traitor, a stinking predator, and a thief. I have no illusions that my settling here is going to be easy, but with time, I am hopeful that the men and women of your beautiful city will see that I'm here to help, not hurt, and that I am a fair man looking for a fair deal."

"Understood," York snapped with a gush of sincerity, his bushy beard moving up and down as he shook his head in admiration of Trent's honest and forthright statement. "Mr. Hartwell, I am in the business of protecting investments, making money, and helping investors' securities grow. I am pleased that you have decided to give my bank an opportunity to demonstrate our ability to provide prompt and thorough customer service. You've come to the right place. I can confidently say that The Bank of Charleston will meet your every expectation."

"Good," Trent replied, placing a hand, palm down, on his tall stack of cash. "I'm ready to get down to business. What do you need to know?"

It took Mr. York close to two hours to finalize Trent's deposits and set up his various accounts. When everything was signed and settled, Trent made a final request. "I would like to know more about a piece of property ... a house I saw for sale on Wentworth Street. Number 51. A lovely house."

"Ah, yes," York agreed.

Trent nodded his approval, and then informed Mr. York, "I am extremely interested in the Wentworth property, and I understand this bank is the owner. Do you know the property I speak of?"

York pressed an index finger to his lips and thought for a moment, then said, "Yes. I do. A lovely two-story red brick with beautiful double balconies. Eight-foot windows facing the garden and some of the most intricate ironwork fencing in Charleston. Yes, yes. At the corner of Wentworth and Meeting. Belonged to the Sawyer family... they abandoned the house back in '62 after the war broke out. Just ran away. Let the bank take it over. Left all the furnishings behind too."

"How much do you want for the property?" Trent asked, fingering his brand new deposit slips.

"We're asking four thousand. A steal. Fully furnished and in such a prime location..."

"I'll pay two," Trent curtly interrupted. "In cash. Today."

"Two thousand...hum. I don't think that will do..." York hedged, testing his new client. "Perhaps we could go as low as ..."

"Perhaps you'd prefer I withdraw my deposits," Trent cut him off. "You are welcome to sit on the property and wait for someone else to come along with a similar cash infusion for your financial institution?"

"Two thousand two-hundred?" York meekly prompted, and then rushed to add, "That would include any costs related to refurbishing the interior and bringing the gardens back to their former beauty. The house has fallen into a bit of disrepair, being empty so long, and all."

Trent retrieved his empty soft-sided bag, snapped it closed, and said, "All right. You have a deal. Please prepare the necessary papers as quickly as you can. I'd like to move in as soon as possible. Hotel living is not for me."

Mansard York's expression of apprehension immediately dissolved into one of relief. He reached across the table and tapped an index finger on Trent's coat sleeve, as if their recent business transaction now allowed for such an intimate gesture. "Please excuse my lapse of manners. I meant to ask, is there a Mrs. Hartwell who will be arriving to join you?" he inquired, lips pursed in question.

"No, I'm a single man."

York made a small coughing sound, smoothed his beard, and smiled. "I thought as much. Well, then, you'll be needing household help. A housekeeper, a cook, a carriage driver and of course a gardener. The property's grounds used to be so enchanting. I can help you bring the entire place back to life."

With a nod, Trent agreed. "Yes, of course. Could you recommend workers to help me with these matters?"

"Leave everything to me." York shifted closer to the table, tilted toward Trent, and spoke in a low tone as if divulging a secret. "With the slaves now free, there're plenty of blacks needing work. They are just wandering the roads begging for food, looking for shelter, desperate for even a pair of shoes. They'll take any wage you offer. I can find very reliable workers for you, and ... at very good price."

With a scrape of his chair, Trent pushed back from the table and crossed his arms at his chest, as if to put both physical and emotional distance between himself and Mr. York's comment. With a lift of his chin, he countered in a blunt tone, "I have no intention of taking advantage of anyone, black or white. I'm sure I have much to learn about the way things are done here in Charleston, but I have always paid a decent wage for anyone who worked for me. That will not change simply because I'm now living in the South."

Blinking back a jolt of surprise, York coughed softly into a fisted hand. "I understand. I would expect no less from you, Mr. Hartwell. You strike me as a very competent businessman." Pausing, he slid his gaze over Trent, taking his time, as if appraising him anew before he said, "If you would allow me, I'd like to assist in your introduction to the prominent families in Charleston. Men with whom I think you will be able to do a considerable amount of business."

"That would be most kind of you, Mr. York."

"Fine. Fine. My wife and I will be attending a small dinner party next Thursday at the home of Judge Rowland Turner. He's a most important man to know in our city. I would like to suggest that you attend as my guest."

"I'd be honored, if your host approves," Trent replied, anxious for the opportunity to launch his entry into Charleston's coveted society circles.

"Oh, he will be fine. Judge Rowland encourages new faces at his table and I feel certain he will be most interested in getting to know you. The Turner family can trace their Charleston roots back to the

Revolution. His son served in the Confederate Army, fought bravely, got wounded, but made it home alive thank God. True, the judge supported the Confederacy, but he is a fair man... much like yourself. He has embraced the reality that the South must change and he is changing with it. A most sagacious man, the judge is. Has a lovely daughter, too.... I'll send a note around to him to expect you."

"I appreciate the invitation," Trent replied without hesitation. "What time will we dine?"

CHAPTER 11

The red brick house on Elizabeth Street surpassed Trent's expectations. The old time Charleston mansion was surrounded by brick half walls topped with decorative iron rails that rose to pointed arches topped with diamond-shaped finials. When Trent's new carriage driver, Gus, stopped beneath the wide cobblestone portico, Trent was taken aback, not only by the size of Judge Turner's home, but also by its solid, stately character. The three-story house was surrounded on all four sides with protective verandas designed to take advantage of the cool breeze blowing in off the Cooper River. Having survived intact through the Civil War, the house retained its sturdy brick walls, its solid slate roof, and the grandeur that was a reminder of a way of life that the Confederacy had fought to preserve.

Stepping out of the carriage, Trent told Gus that he was free to leave and to come back for him at eleven o'clock. Then Trent strode up to the polished cedar-wood door, lifted the handle of a diamond-shaped brass knocker, and let it fall. A solemn-faced Negro man opened the door, nodded consent to enter, and accepted the hat and gloves that Trent offered to him. Looking around, Trent knew he had never been inside a more beautiful home. A glittering crystal chandelier set with dozens of burning candles was the showpiece of the huge foyer. It provided visual access to a vaulted, double-staircase that dominated the entry and ascended to the upper floors. Tall ceramic vases filled with lush floral arrangements sprang up on every polished surface. For Trent, gliding across the glistening marble floor, which reflected the hot blaze of generous candlelight, was like walking on a wide expanse of crystal clear water.

Trent followed the servant to the entrance of a spacious room where a group of people had gathered among the oversized brocade couches and chairs that stood proudly around the perimeter. He paused to take in the elegant surroundings. A fire blazed in a stone fireplace nearly as tall as Trent, and to his left, he could see a regal dining room where a beautifully set table awaited the guests. A sideboard fit with lions' claw feet was loaded with a generous display of food. Across the room, a set of tall French doors stood open onto a flower-filled garden anchored by a burnished copper fountain spilling water into a sculpted base.

When the servant announced Trent's arrival, the assembled dinner guests stopped talking and turned to look at him, the audible ticks of a stately grandfather clock filling the awkward silence. Trent inclined his head at Mansard York, acknowledging the banker who was standing with his arm around a woman whom Trent assumed might be his wife. Standing across the room were two other women and two men, stationed near the huge fireplace. Trent inhaled and pulled back his shoulders, gauging their readiness to accept this Yankee stranger who dared enter their domain.

Trent crossed the thick red and cream Audubon carpet and moved to shake Mr. York's hand.

"Thank you once more for the invitation. It's good to see you again," Trent said, releasing York's hand.

"Please meet my wife, Martha," York said, turning to the attractive, sandy-haired woman wearing a billowing blue dress who was standing at his side.

After Trent had appropriately greeted Mrs. York, her husband surveyed the room, his gaze eventually landing on a white-haired man who was smoking a cigar.

"Now, come with me, I want you to meet our host, Judge Turner," York said, stepping toward the man with deeply wrinkled, parchment-white skin, a barrel of a tummy, and a mane of white hair that brushed his shoulders.

"So gracious of you to allow me to be a guest in your home," Trent stated, pleased by the firmness of the judge's handshake.

"I absolutely had to meet you after Mansard told me all about you," the judge replied while waving over a slim, blonde, young woman who was dressed in a stylish pink and purple flowered dress that exposed a great deal of cleavage. "Please, meet my daughter, Sage," the judge announced, beaming with pride as he made the introductions. "She's the one who puts these little dinner parties together for me. So, if the food does not agree with you, blame her," he joked, laughing under his breath as he urged Sage to step closer to Trent.

"My pleasure, Ma'am," Trent stated, making a short bow at the waist. Looking up, he was certain he noticed a rather cynical smile flit over the young lady's lips. "I'm delighted to be in your beautiful home," he added, feeling a bit off kilter.

"Thank you, Mr. Hartwell, and welcome to Charleston. We hope you will feel at home here," Sage replied.

"I appreciate your most gracious hospitality," Trent replied, hoping his remarks were settling well with the strict mores of southern conversation. He'd been raised on a farm in Iowa, had recently resided two blocks from a city jail, and had included factory workers, Negroes, foreigners, and even petty criminals in his Chicago social circle. Getting accustomed to the polite, rigid, social niceties of South Carolina was going take some getting used to.

Mr. York eased Trent away from Sage and turned him toward the other guests, a man and a woman who were looking at Trent with impassive expressions. "And finally," Mr. York began, "I'd like you to meet my cousins ... second removed," he chuckled, "Coretta Gallard Saveneau and her brother, Dixon Gallard."

Trent shook their hands and made an admiring remark about Coretta's elegant emerald necklace.

"My dear departed mother's," Coretta informed with great exaggeration while gently touching the bright green stones. "This is one of the few items I was able to save from the …. well, from the invading *soldiers* … before fleeing my home when the war broke out."

Deciding not to comment, Trent simply nodded his understanding.

"Coretta and Dixon are third generation Charlestonians," the judge added. "The Gallards came here from England in the early 80's … settled in St. John's Berkeley and created Bryan Tract, one of the largest rice plantations in the state. More than five-thousand acres at its prime."

"South Carolina royalty," Sage Turner teasingly interjected, walking up to place a hand on Coretta's arm. "The Gallards once hosted Princess Alice, daughter of Queen Victoria, at their home. Charleston's most revered families came out for the event."

"Those days are long gone," Coretta replied, an air of nostalgia in her voice. "In fact, Dixon and I have decided it's time to sell what's left of Bryan Tract. Neither of us is interested in running the plantation and it's just sitting out there, decaying, in the country."

"We're hoping to get a decent price," Dixon added. "Seeing strangers grab land for a dollar an acre doesn't sit well with me. I plan to hold out for a fair market deal."

"I've been told you are from Chicago," the judge interjected, rescuing Trent from addressing Dixon's uncomfortable remark.

"Yes, I did reside there for a time, but my childhood home is in Iowa," Trent clarified, as if it made a difference. Iowa and Chicago were all the same to a southerner: places up north among enemies of the South.

"I have a confession to make," the judge went on, a mischievous smile on his lips. "I once lived in Illinois for a short time as well."

"Oh?' Trent remarked. "How did that come about?"

"Well, while I was studying at Augusta College in Kentucky, I met Randolf Foster. We became fast friends. Years later, when he became president of Northwestern University, he invited me to Evanston for a visit. Wanted me to see his new university. I went, planning to stay a few weeks, but I wound up staying almost a year after he talked me into doing a series of lectures. Kept me there until the weather took a turn. A most enlightening experience, it was."

"Good school, Northwestern," Trent supplied, and then joked, "But I guess you wanted to escape the Illinois winter, I suggest?"

"My Lord yes," Judge Turner laughed. "I didn't look forward to freezing to death. Couldn't wait to get back to a warm South Carolina winter, and my wife's Southern cooking. But I must say I did appreciate the experience of living in the North, and I so admired the caliber of the students I met while I was there."

"What Daddy hasn't told you is that he also met my mother while he was studying at Augusta College," Sage eagerly contributed to the story. "And once she met Daddy, she turned her back on Kentucky for good and came back to Charleston with him. They married two weeks later, at Bethel United Methodist Church."

"The big church at Calhoun and Pitt?" Trent asked.

"Yes," Sage said.

"I know exactly where it is. I've walked past it many times," Trent added, pleased to let everyone know he was becoming oriented to the city.

"It's a very old church," Sage continued. "The first to serve both white and black members even though lots of folks in Charleston were horrified back then, and some still are today. Anyway, we're building a new sanctuary, and we're going to donate the old building to the black congregation so they'll have their very own church."

"How admirable," Trent murmured, biting his tongue to keep from saying more.

"Bethel is a most pleasant place of worship. You'll have to join us for service one Sunday," Sage rattled on. "Though I do admit that it harbors a sad memory for me as well. You see Momma was funeralized there ... just two years ago."

"My sympathies," Trent remarked, locking eyes with Sage, who lowered hers beneath a lilac-hued fan while looking up at him. Trent was immediately struck by her resemblance to Rebecca. She had the same silky blonde hair, finely chiseled jawline, eyes the exact shade of blue. Her nose was a little more rounded than Rebecca's, but her rosy cheeks were much the same. Although two years had passed, during which he had struggled to harden his heart against Rebecca, he could not deny the flutter of memories that rose to the surface in a flood of regret as his gaze traveled over Sage Turner's face. How long would it take for him to get over the loss of the woman he had expected to marry? Why did he even let his thoughts stray to her now? Giving himself a mental shake, he re-focused on what Sage was saying.

"How are you enjoying our city?" she asked.

"I haven't been here long enough to do much more than try to get settled. Mr. York may have told you I've bought the Sawyer house on Wentworth Street."

"He did. I think that's an ideal house for a single man. Not too large, and in a very fashionable area." She chuckled softly beneath her fan. "Did you know that it is referred to as a Charleston *Single-House*?"

Trent raised both brows in question, noting her emphasis on the word single, which was not lost on him. "No, please explain. I am intrigued with the way the houses in the area do not face the street, but face the garden, as if presenting their shoulders to the world."

"You are correct. Many houses in the city are built that way, with a small entry at the street that leads into a shady courtyard or a garden. This assures privacy while minimizing the harsh glare of sunlight and the heat of the day. The width of the house is that of a *single* room, long and narrow, allowing all of the rooms to catch the breeze that blows up from the harbor."

"Very ingenious and well-planned," Trent commented, impressed with Sage's desire to impart information about Charleston's architectural treasures.

"I agree," Judge Turner interjected. "The house is a wise investment, Hartwell, all around."

When the solemn-faced servant arrived to announce that dinner was served, the Gallard siblings, along with Mansard York and his wife paired off and headed into the dining room. Sage quickly hooked her arm with Trent's and walked him in, leaving her father to enter alone. He took a seat at the head of the table and scowled at the empty chair on his right. The judge leaned over his plate and informed his guests, "I'm so sorry my son, Leon, won't be dining with us tonight. Unsettling our seating arrangements and all."

"Oh, don't concern yourself, Judge," Martha York interjected. "We will dine with seven and think no more about it. I know how unpredictable young men can be. I'm just glad Mr. Hartwell could be here."

With a snap of his fingers, the judge summoned a serving girl who quickly removed the extra place setting.

With everyone seated, the servants began passing the food around while conversation turned to the impact that the federal government was having on the city.

Trent calmly listened as Coretta Saveneau resumed a conversation she must have been engaged in before she entered the dining room.

"Well, anyway," she addressed her brother, "what I was saying was … he should not have been so rude. Where did he come from? I've never seen *him* around here before."

Dixon Gallard twisted the ends of his jet-black mustache while considering his response to his sister's complaint. "Coretta," Dixon finally answered, a tone of exasperation in his voice, "I told you he's the new officer under General Scott, assigned to Charleston. He was sent here from Washington."

"Why in the world does President Johnson think we need soldiers to run our city?" she tossed back, huffing her question to all seated at the table. "Those damned uniformed Yankees …" She stopped in mid-sentence, eyes wide, fingertips to her lips as she glanced at Trent.

"Oh my, excuse me, Mr. Hartwell," she stuttered, then exhaled aloud. "But that soldier had the nerve to tell me to sit out on the porch of my own house, in the damp, to wait while he checked *my* credentials. I was so upset. How dare he tell me I can't go inside my own house? Making me feel like a criminal on the door step of my home!"

"Well, Coretta," Dixon continued in a placating tone, "you know your town house was confiscated for the Army's use when they took over. The soldier just wanted to make sure you were the rightful owner before he turned it back over to you."

"It wasn't my fault I had to live in the country for four years. I stayed away all through the war, never dreaming my house in town would be taken over by Yankees! My husband died fighting to protect our property. If my dear departed husband had been here things wouldn't have happened like this," Coretta fumed with an upward tilt of her nose, as if checking the wind to see if any strange odors were blowing her way.

"You are right about one thing, Coretta," Judge Rowland entered the conversation. "The soldiers should not make our citizens feel afraid or uncomfortable." He slowly shifted his gaze from Coretta to Trent, as if sizing up the stranger he had invited into his home. "The Army's presence is meant to keep the peace in our city and help us recover. So, until we form a new government, the Reconstructionists are in charge."

"You're quite right," Trent agreed, prepared to declare his position on the government's reconstruction plan. "It is my understanding that Congress created the Committee on Reconstruction to ease the post-war burdens of the citizens of the South and help in the formation of a stable government."

"Well, the sooner we re-gain control of our state, the better," Mr. York added. "Cash flow is stagnant. Confederate money is still floating around. The economy of South Carolina will not grow without sufficient trade, and that requires a stable currency."

"It's coming," Judge Rowland advised as he took a piece of chicken from a platter being passed around. "Once we select our delegates to the Constitutional Convention and draft a new constitution we'll be on our way to rebuilding our city and our state."

As the dinner progressed, the topic of conversation veered away from politics and moved on to a discussion of the sad state of the Dock Street Theater, which suffered great damage during the war. When the last piece of rhubarb pie had been consumed, Sage stood and said, "If you all will excuse us, I want to show Mr. Hartwell the garden." And taking Trent by the arm, she led him away from the table and through the open French doors while the others retired to the parlor for coffee.

Though somewhat surprised at her move, Trent was grateful for the escape, knowing how easily something mentioned in a political conversation could go wrong, how quickly what he might have said, though intended as a perfectly innocent remark, could morph into an insult with disastrous results.

Standing next to the sparkling water flowing through the fountain, Sage dipped a finger into the cool water and tilted her head to one side. "Best to leave Coretta and Dixon to spill their fighting words in the parlor."

"I do understand their anger. They've been through a very difficult time," Trent offered.

"Don't worry about them. They'll settle down. They know the South will never be the same and that in the end, fighting change is of no use." Sage firmed her pink-tinted lips. "Coretta and her brother are always quarreling about something. Been at it all their lives. They own quite a bit of property up around the Santee Canal, and since their father's death and Coretta's husband's as well, they've been bickering over how to split it all up. Dixon is a heavy drinker, and I am sure he has squandered most of his inheritance. I heard he moved into a rented house near the Luckey Star Hotel, where he spends quite a bit of time. That's why he is so anxious for the sale of the family land. He's cash poor."

Trent nodded, then said, "I'm sure the war years have taken their toll on most of the families in the South."

"Especially on the number of eligible young men left here in

Charleston," Sage coyly added with a wide-eyed expression as she ran a hand over her forehead to push back a lock of her luminous yellow hair. "It's not that I don't feel sorry for Coretta and her brother, but most everybody in these parts suffered just as much as they did. A great number of our men came home in pine coffins. Or were left to rot on a bloody battlefield. Some were old, some so very young. My brother Leon fought with McKewn's Cavalry during the conflict, but thank God, he came home in one piece. Be patient with us, Mr. Hartwell. Once you get to know Charlestonians, you'll see that we are real decent people." She made a gesture of a salute toward those who remained in animated conversation while seated on couches in front of the stone fireplace. "Here's to mending deep wounds. To finding some kind of peace now that this damned war is over."

"Here, here," Trent repeated, his words reverberating against the stone walls of the garden as he focused on the room filled with people who had once been considered his country's enemies.

"Come along. Let me show you the rest of the house," Sage suggested, linking her arm through Trent's to guide him through a side parlor, into the foyer, and up the grand staircase.

At the second floor landing, Sage paused and swept her arm around the L-shaped loft where tall transom-topped doors with shiny brass knobs stood open, giving way to four handsome bedroom suites off an open second-floor sitting area.

"According to stories passed down through our family, this house once served as a boarding house for British soldiers passing through Charleston on their way to Florida," Sage told Trent while moving to stand in the doorway of the room closest to her.

Trent peeked inside to see an interior that was starkly bare and painted gray. It contained only a bed, a nightstand, and a large Confederate flag hanging from a drapery rod, blocking out a window. Next to the window, a sheathed Infantry sword was propped against a straight-back wooden chair that served as a valet stand for a Confederate soldier's jacket.

"As you may guess, this is my brother Leon's room. When he left for the war, it was filled with a hodgepodge of paraphernalia that he'd collected as a boy. Father left it as it was until Leon came home, thinking he would want to see it just as he'd left it. But as soon as my brother got home, he stripped everything away and painted the walls gray." Sage shook her head in disgust. "And ... well, I think it looks terrible, but it's *his* room."

"Are you and Leon close?" Trent asked.

Sage replied with a muffled laugh. "Close? I rarely see him. He prefers to spend his time with his war buddies, especially Hatch Ambrose. You see, Hatch saved Leon's life ... carried him ten miles on his back to the army doctor after Leon was wounded at the siege of Petersburg."

"Badly wounded?" Trent prompted.

"A bullet to the thigh," Sage clarified. "More than just a flesh wound. Leon recovered, but he carries a limp, as well as quite a bit of resentment over being referred to as a cripple. But, he was lucky. He would have bled to death if Hatch hadn't carried him off the battlefield." She stepped just inside Leon's bedroom and pointed to an oval rug in shades of brown and blue placed at the foot of the bed. "See that burnt spot there? Leon's experiment with bomb making during the height of the fighting. For some reason he refuses to let it go."

"Well, at least your brother didn't burn the house down," Trent laughed, trying to lighten the mood while wondering just what kind of a brother Sage had. "Perhaps I'll be able to meet Leon one day soon. He sounds like a most interesting young man."

"Interesting?" Sage repeated with a hint of surprise. "I guess you could say that, but I think he's far too intense. Angry at the world. And he takes everything so seriously. Maybe the war did that to him, made him think everyone is out to harm him. His hatred of Negroes and his resistance to accepting the fact that the war is over, that the South lost, makes Father feel so guilty."

Making no comment, Trent allowed Sage to lead him back into the dim hallway where she commented on the portraits of her ancestors that lined the walls. After a peek inside her father's handsome study, she took him to the far end of the hallway and turned the brass knob on the door. The first thing Trent saw was a four-poster bed stationed beneath a bower of fake violets. *Sage's room*, he thought right away. It looked just like her, with its soft purple coverlet and gauzy pink curtains. As light and airy as her personality. However, before he could comment on her attractive boudoir, Sage pulled him inside the room and shut the door behind them. He was even more surprised when she stepped right up to him and put her arms around his neck.

Trent stiffened in her embrace. "Are you sure I should be in here? Isn't this your bedroom, Miss Turner?" Trent managed, his voice rough with a sudden desire to kiss the young woman's inviting lips.

"You may call me Sage," she offered with a toss of her head, leaning against the closed bedroom door to study Trent through curious eyes. "I'm a grown woman, Mr. Hartwell. I never do things I am not sure of."

"However, I doubt *this* is what we should be doing."

"Why not?" she taunted. "As I mentioned earlier, there is a dearth of fine gentlemen like yourself in our city now. I feel most fortunate to have made your acquaintance."

"And I, yours," Trent countered, slipping his arm around her tiny waist to bring her lips closer to his.

PART III

Be you to others kind and true,
As you'd have others be to you;
And neither do nor say to them,
Whate'er you would not take again.

The Slave's Friend, 1839, author unknown

CHAPTER 12

STILLWATER

Boston, Massachusetts
November 1866

"My name is Arnold Jenkins. I bring you tidings from your esteemed senator, Mr. Charles Sumner, a passionate leader of the antislavery forces and an avid supporter of the Radical Republicans."

As the words of the senator's representative echoed throughout the grand chamber of Faneuil Hall, Eva leaned forward in her seat, paying close attention to Mr. Jenkins's speech. The death of Abraham Lincoln had been a devastating event, and now the newly elected president, Andrew Johnson, was actively promoting his plans to reconstruct the South. She tuned her ear more sharply to Mr. Jenkins's words, eager for news about what was happening in the recently defeated rebel states.

"Your senator has sent me here tonight to inform you that he is fighting to weaken the grip of the ex-Confederates. As you know, Congress has already passed the Civil Rights Bill giving black men the vote, giving them equal rights before the law. And now, the

Committee on Reconstruction is asking Congress to pass the 14th Amendment, so that anyone born or naturalized in the United States will be a citizen. We must block all ex-Confederates from holding power and undermining the gains achieved by the Union's victory."

Talk about the country's future was on everyone's lips, discussing the repair of roads, bridges, and railroad tracks, as well as the creation of political and financial systems to bring stability to the Confederate states. However, Eva was entirely consumed with her fierce determination to return to South Carolina and search for the woman who gave her away. Every day, she thought about the liberated slaves traipsing across the country, trying to put their lives back together. Was Mayree among the mass of newly freed souls who wanted nothing more than the right to live in peace and security? She tried to imagine how her life might have unfolded if Mayree had not been brave enough to hand her daughter to a stranger. Would she even be thinking of going to South Carolina if Chester hadn't gone off to war and been slaughtered on a strip of sandy beach hundreds of miles away?

Widowhood did not sit well with twenty-five-year-old Eva. Most days she was angry, depressed, and resentful to have lost the husband she'd barely had time to love. On good days, her pride in Chester's part in liberating the slaves pushed such feelings aside, though her heartache at losing him remained ever-present, even though three years had passed since the uniformed man with the letter in his hand turned her world upside down. In an effort to keep from dwelling on the past, she continued to work at the mapmaker's shop, perfecting her skill at creating maps to the point that Mr. Fitzgerald now allowed her to take on small projects by herself. She spent two evenings a week attending church with her aunt and volunteered at the Mercy Resettlement House where she distributed food, clothing, and medical supplies to the freedmen and women who flooded the city by the hundreds. It was only when she looked into the faces of the liberated slaves and absorbed their sense of hope and gratitude that her own self-centered pity eased to the back of her mind and lightened the weight of her sorrow.

Now, Eva shifted her gaze away from Mr. Jenkins. Scanning the light-filled rotunda of Faneuil Hall, she admired the intricate plasterwork, the tall stately columns, and the crush of people filling the galleries facing the stage. She counted the number of ladies dressed in black mourning clothes, and realized; I *am not alone. So many of us lost loved ones in the war. I wonder if they feel as lost and alone as I?*

"The federal government's plan to assist in the reconstruction of the South will be carried out through The Bureau of Refugees, Freedman, and Abandoned Lands," Mr. Jenkins was stating when Eva turned her attention back to him. "We call it The Freedman's Bureau." He paused, stepped to the side, and lifted a drape of cloth from a chart that had been placed on an artist's easel.

"The Freedman's Bureau has been charged to do the following," he began, pointing to words neatly printed on the tall canvas board. "Provide rations of food, clothing, and supplies for destitute people, both black and white. Provide transportation for those trying to relocate or unite with family members. Establish hospitals and schools for ex-slaves. Oversee Freedmen courts to settle legal disputes between blacks and whites. Supervise and manage matters relating to lands abandoned or seized during the Civil War. Supervise labor contracts between planters and freedmen, administer fair justice, and finally, help black soldiers, sailors, and their widows collect pensions and back pay."

Mr. Jenkins's final statement immediately caught Eva's attention. She shifted forward and narrowed her eyes in thought. Pensions for widows? Back pay? She squinted at the chart, then at Mr. Jenkins, who seemed to look a bit weary, as if he'd given this talk hundreds of times and was trying to get through with it as quickly as possible. Eva watched the man's freckled hands fan down the list on the board as he amplified his discourse on the government's plan to divide the rebel states into five districts controlled by Union soldiers.

Eva was relieved when Mr. Jenkins finally concluded his presentation by informing the audience that he would be happy to provide additional details and assistance to anyone who had questions or wished to file a claim for government benefits.

A small brass band struck up a spritely rendition of *Battle Cry of Freedom* as the meeting broke up and the audience began to stream out of the building. Eva remained seated until Mr. Jenkins had finished speaking with the last of those who had approached him, and when he stood, preparing to pack up his charts and his papers, she started down the side-aisle toward the stage.

"Mr. Jenkins," she started, walking up to him.

"Yes?" he remarked, turning to face Eva. "Can I help you?" he asked, stopping his attempt to take down his chart.

"I'm a widow," Eva started, going on to tell him about Chester Phillip's service with the Massachusetts 54th Infantry.

"Oh, the 54th!" Jenkins remarked, eyebrows raised, a broad smile on his lips. "A brave regiment they were... but so many young men perished at Battery Wagner. You should be proud of your husband, Mrs. Phillips. For his service to his country."

"Oh, I am," Eva replied sincerely. "But I want to inquire about the widow's pension, and the back pay, you mentioned..." she let her words die off, hoping he would know what she wanted to ask.

"Well, payments to widows of black Union soldiers *will* be processed." He grinned and straightened his tie. "However," he stated in a most official-sounding voice, "the government must validate all eligible recipients. First, you will need to fill out this form," he stated, digging a paper from the stack on the podium, which he offered to her. "Can you read?"

"Yes," Eva replied.

"Write, too?"

"Yes."

"Fine. Answer all of the questions on the form. And you must provide your marriage certificate, your husband's death certificate ... or the letter from the war department declaring him killed in action. And of course, proof of your residency." He lowered his chin and peered over the top of his wire-rim glasses at Eva. "And, please be patient," he finished. "All of it will take time."

"I understand," Eva said, accepting the paper, which she folded into her handbag. "May I ask you another question?"

"Most assuredly." He busied himself with collapsing the portable artist's easel while Eva began to talk.

"How would I go about locating a relative who was enslaved in South Carolina? A woman who was … you see…I was born there… in Saint John's Berkeley. My mother is still there…at least I hope she is," Eva stammered, wondering if she was crazy to even think her mother might still be alive.

"Saint John's Berkeley? Well, let me think…. General Saxton is in command of South Carolina…. Oh, yes …the district you refer to would be under the supervision of Captain Liedtke, stationed in Moncks Corner. He would be the one in charge of the Freedman's Bureau there."

"But, how do I contact him?"

Again, Mr. Jenkins dug into his pile of papers and handed a sheet of paper to Eva. "His address is on this list. Write him a letter. Perhaps your mother has requested assistance from the government. If so, the captain will surely have a record of her presence in the area." He pointed a finger at Eva and added with pride, "The government is taking great care to maintain complete and accurate records of every freed slave we assist. But, as I stated before… be patient. The climate in the former rebel states remains very unsettled, and somewhat dangerous, I must add. There is still a lot of anger and resentment over their defeat in the war, you know. It will take a lot of compassion and charity for the South to become whole again." Then he gave up an exasperated sigh and began to pack his papers into a large valise. "So very much to do."

"What if I wanted to go there? To Saint John's Berkeley. If I could speak to Captain Liedtke in person, perhaps I could find …"

"No, no, Mrs. Phillips," Mr. Jenkins quickly interrupted. "Don't even think of going off searching for family. The defeated South is not a safe place to go wandering around. I strongly advise you not to travel there. The Freedman's Bureau is working hard to bring order to the situation and assist the freedmen, but resources are scarce and lawlessness abounds."

"Oh...I'm sure you're right," Eva murmured, deflated by his strong rebuff of her idea.

"Just write Captain Liedtke a letter. You'll get a response," he advised.

"Yes, of course," Eva replied, nodding her thanks as she turned to leave.

Exiting the building, she stood under the light of an overhead lamp outside of Faneuil Hall and studied the papers Mr. Jenkins had given her. The lamplight illuminated the words on the page, as well as the fronts of the shops along the square. A soft glow had descended over the bustling neighborhood, and when the brisk November wind tossed a flurry of colorful leaves along the cobblestone street, she was jolted back to the day she met Chester, to the first walk they took together.

A wave of emptiness cascaded through Eva, leaving her feeling hollow. Losing Chester had shattered her, dimmed her love for the city where she had wandered the streets holding his hand as they laughed and planned their future. They had been swept up in the idea of their own grand adventure, but now Boston was simply a place where she lived, not a place where she would ever be happy. And even though Aunt Tully had been very supportive to Eva since Chester's death, Eva no longer felt as if she had the right to remain in her aunt's home. Eva was now a grown woman of twenty-five. She should be living with a husband, raising a family, not existing like a shadow in someone else's home. Taking a deep breath, she pulled in a draft of cool Autumn air and then started down Market Street, her heart racing, her mind churning, her future suddenly decided.

That evening after dinner, Eva sat across from Tully at the table by the hearth and told her aunt about her plans. After listening to what Eva had to say, Tully stared down into her yellow china plate for a moment before lifting her head to speak.

"I know it's been hard on you, Eva, losing Chester like you did. I understand how you feel. I can see you're disappointed, lonely, and impatient to get on with life, whatever it's supposed to bring. But going off into South Carolina? I don't rightly know if that's a good idea."

"But what choice do I have?" Eva asked, desperate for her aunt's support. "I don't want to simply write a letter to that captain and sit around waiting for an answer."

With a shake of her head, Tully said, "Goin' into South Carolina could be dangerous. A black woman, alone, traipsing across the country? I don't know, Eva. Might be a big mistake."

"I'm not afraid," Eva replied, a tinge of indignation threading her words. "It may not be an easy journey to undertake, but remember, Aunt Tully, you did the same thing when you brought me here. How dangerous was it for you to smuggle *me* ... a black slave child ... off a white man's plantation, huh?"

"Most dangerous thing a person could do."

"Right," Eva snapped, and then pressed, "Were *you* afraid?"

"I was terrified."

"But you did it anyway, didn't you?"

"Yes, I did, and I don't regret it, Eva. I just ... I guess ..." She stopped, pressed her lips together, and shuddered, trying to hold her emotions in check. "I'm afraid of losing you."

Eva kept her eyes on her aunt's face, pondering Tully's admission. "You won't ever lose me," she whispered. Then, pushing closer, she forced Tully's eyes to meet hers. "I have to go. I want to see Stillwater for myself. I want to see the place where I was born. I want to be on the land where my mother was a slave, and if she is still alive, I want to find her. If she isn't alive, I will know that as well. And, if I go to South Carolina, I plan to visit the island where Chester is buried. I want to know where he is!" A catch in her throat made her pause. "Aunt Tully, you understand, don't you? What peace will I ever have unless I visit Chester's grave and tell him goodbye? If I can do that, at least I'll know where he is resting. Where he'll be until we're together again, holding hands in Heaven."

Tully reached out and placed a hand on Eva's arm, smoothing her fingers across her niece's skin. "I love you like you are my own daughter, you know that don't you?"

"Of course," Eva murmured, gripping Tully's hand. "And I love you like a mother, but ..."

"But, I'm not your mother," Tully finished. "I understand what's driving you to go away, Eva. It's more than loneliness and heartache. You're young, you have no children, no family of your own. And deep inside... you're always gonna feel abandoned by your mama. I did the best I could to take her place, but there's a lost, restless feeling consuming you and it won't ever go away unless you find out for yourself what happened to Mayree. You were born in South Carolina on the Stillwater Plantation, and for all its evilness, it *was* once your home. Well, the big war is over. The slaves are free, so, Eva, if you think your mama is still alive, you go ahead and try to find her."

Eva thinned her lips as a tear slipped from her eye, sensing a finality in Tully's voice, aware that separating from her was going to be the most difficult thing she had ever experienced. "Do you think my mother could be out on the road, trying to make her way north? Maybe she's looking for me," Eva calculated, beginning to test the logic of leaving home.

"Could be she *is* tryin' to find you. Who knows what's goin' on?" Tully agreed. "But I'll be right here. You write to me, tell me where you are. And if Mayree somehow makes it to Boston and comes looking for you, I'll hear about it and I'll let you know."

"Tell me again what she looked like," Eva pled.

Tully raised her chin and focused on the ceiling, as if pulling old memories from the recesses of her mind. "When I first met her, she was gathering small stones along the riverbank. You were there, standing right up under her, holding onto her skirt. I remember how pretty your mother was. Her skin was several shades darker than yours. More like tree bark than gingerbread. Had a flat round face and big brown eyes that seemed to be able to see everything at once. She wasn't short, but not too tall, either. Kinda strong and sturdy looking. But what struck me strange was that her head was uncovered ... not a regular sight for a Cantrell slave. All the women on Stillwater had to bind their hair with white cloth. But Mayree was different; she was bold. Not defiant or angry, just real sure of herself. She wore her hair tangled up in a lot of thick braids springing from the top of her head."

"That's what I remember too," Eva added with excitement. "Her hair. She used to let me stick dandelion flowers in her braids when we were out in the fields."

"I reckon, if you see her, you'd know her by that hair, if she still has any to braid."

Eva stood from the table and began to clear the dinner dishes, which she piled into a tin tub full of water. As she began to clean the plates, she calculated the particulars of traveling into the South. Nearly two years had passed since the end of the Civil War, but most railroads and bridges that had been destroyed still had not been rebuilt. Overland transportation could be arduous and lengthy, limited to crude carts and rickety overland wagons. Travel by sea would be her best option, she mentally decided. She had saved $400 from her work with Mr. Fitzgerald, which she hoped would be sufficient for passage on a ship from Boston to Charleston Harbor. But she would need additional funds to live on while she was there. *If my money runs out, I'll find work*, she decided, suddenly filled with anxious energy, eager to make plans.

When she heard Tully call out, "Will you please stay here through winter and start your journey when the weather's warm? I'd be worried sick about you being stuck on a ship out in the ocean, in the cold. All miserable and drenched with rain when those storms roll in. At least do that for me."

Eva turned to face her aunt. Smiling, she said, "Of course, I'll wait for good weather. Besides, I must give Mr. Fitzgerald time to find a new assistant, and the longer I work the more money I'll be able to save." Moving to stand behind Tully, Eva leaned down and wrapped her arms around her aunt's shoulders, resting her chin atop her aunt's head. "Don't fret, Aunt Tully, I might be gone for a while, but I *will* see you again."

CHAPTER 13

May 1867
Charleston Harbor

The eight-hundred mile journey by sea from Boston to Charleston Harbor on an aging packet ship took fifteen days. In addition to carrying mail and a variety of cargo, the packet steamer also transported twenty-two passengers to numerous ports along the Virginia and Carolina coastlines. Eva's accommodations aboard the vessel were marginal, but clean, and she did not complain about the cramped, dark cabin for which she paid a nominal price to occupy.

Eva was thankful that Aunt Tully had insisted she take only a soft valise and a small traveling trunk, to which Eva had attached a strong leather strap to pull it along, eliminating the need for assistance as she moved about. She had packed frugally—three dresses, two skirts with accompanying blouses, her undergarments, and two pair of Chester's trousers. Though wearing men's pants was not socially acceptable, she was certain they would prove practical if worn underneath her skirt while traveling across the war-torn landscape. She also packed her Bible and the World Atlas that Lawyer Daniels had given to her as a wedding gift, a pair of sturdy boots, an adequate supply of personal toiletries, and the tattered old quilt that Tully had wrapped around Eva when she was a child.

Standing at the ship's rail, she admired the view of Charleston spread out before her. She was surprised to see fine residential homes lining the Battery of the eastern waterfront instead of warehouses and storage facilities, as she had seen at other coastal ports. Clearly, the houses had been constructed to adapt to the southern climate, with raised first floors to provide coolness as well as protection from damaging floods.

By the time the ship finally docked, a colorful sunrise was streaking across the horizon. Placing a hand at her waist, Eva took a deep breath to steady her nerves and seek reassurance that the money-pocket corset that Tully had sewn for her was still in place. Along with the cash she had tucked inside, she also carried a letter of reference from Mr. Fitzgerald and a map of Saint John's Berkeley drawn from Tully's recollection.

Eva took hold of the leather strap attached to her small trunk and pulled it along as she descended the gangplank. Stepping onto the Public Landing, she faced a jumble of pubs, merchants' shops, vendor stalls, and warehouses that hugged the wharf like weathered sentries standing guard over the city. Seamen's shouts and the braying of mules blended with the clop-clop of horses' hooves, the agitated cacophony seeming to physically assault Eva, initiating a nervous tremor that gave her pause. However, as disturbing as the scene was, it also invigorated her sense of adventure.

Sidestepping a pile of refuse, she kept walking, increasing her pace, dragging her small trunk, refusing to acknowledge the throngs of unfortunate ex-slaves who crowded the wharf, their hands extended for a spare coin or a scrap of food from anyone charitable enough to take pity on them. Under different circumstances, Eva would have reached into her reticle for a coin, but now, she knew she had to be careful with her money and make it last as long as possible.

Averting her eyes from the sorrowful dark faces of the newly freed throng, she continued along the waterfront, past ex-Confederate soldiers still wearing rebel uniforms, US soldiers with long rifles in their hands, and shirtless black men unloading cargo from the press of recently arrived ships anchored in the harbor. Open fires burned along the cobblestone lane, sending billows of black smoke above the heads of men who were gathered around the sooty fires, drinking, gambling, and cursing loudly at one another. Outside of the Tobacco Exchange building, in the middle of the street, a fistfight suddenly erupted. Eva watched in horror as two men pelted each other with hard, closed fists and shouted in a patois she did not understand. Agitated onlookers stood around the men, eager to yell at the fighters and urge them on.

The chaotic atmosphere struck Eva as very dangerous and extremely rowdy, pushing her thoughts back to Mr. Jenkins's warning against travelling into the post-war South. Squeezing through the pulsing crush of soldiers, ex-slaves, Indians, Creoles, and dockworkers, Eva silently urged herself to remain calm. She was in South Carolina now, there was no turning back, and there was no recourse but to press on with her mission. She had only just arrived, had a long way to go, and who knew what lay ahead.

Tully had advised Eva to look for a white clapboard house with blue shutters at the corner of East Bay and Pinckney, just north of the wharf. This was the house where she and Eva had taken refuge so many years before. Though Tully had no idea if the house or the woman would still be there, at least Eva had a destination in mind, knowing she would have to depend on the kindness of strangers to find a place to stay the night.

While assessing street signs and placards hanging over the entryways of various establishments, her attention landed on a hand-lettered notice tacked on the door of a narrow red brick building. It read, *Freedmen and Refugees Assistance and Transportation. Captain Peter George, 2nd Military District.*

Dodging a mule-drawn cart loaded with hay, she hurried across the street, entered the building, and took her place at the end of a line that snaked around a stifling hot room packed with anxious people. It was difficult for Eva not to stare at the desperate souls waiting to speak to the young soldier sitting in a straight-back chair at a long wooden table at the front of the room. A placard on his desk read: Captain Peter George, US Army.

Wounded soldiers, many of them missing an arm or a leg, their wounds wrapped in dirty bandages in desperate need of changing, stood alongside destitute black men and women who looked as worn and crushed as the impoverished white farmers standing with them. Everyone was glumly silent, their desperation evident in the set of their worried faces.

Easing forward, Eva focused her attention on a white man wearing a flat straw hat who was accompanied by a heavy-set woman dressed in a brown velvet cloak. She listened as the couple approached the soldier to make their issues known.

"We would like to leave Charleston today," the man stated.

"What are the names of those requiring transportation?" Captain George firmly inquired.

"Henry Van Ryan, and my wife, Mary Van Ryan," the man replied with a nod to the woman at his side.

"Proposed destination?"

"Nashville. I want to go to my brother's home in Nashville."

"Purpose?"

"*Purpose*?" came his indignant retort. "Because Sherman burned my crops, stole my livestock, and destroyed my farm! I don't have the money or the heart to re-build. My wife and I must start over in Nashville, where we have family to help us get on."

Without comment, the captain quickly wrote a few lines in his ledger, and then made a note on a piece of paper. Glancing up, he told the man, "The next transport train out of Charleston will leave tomorrow. It will take you as far as Atlanta. From there, you'll have to check with the Bureau to see what other transportation is available." He handed the note to Mr. Van Ryan, who grabbed it and stuck it into his coat pocket. "Thank you, Sir. Thank you," he repeated, taking his wife by the arm as they headed to the exit.

"Don't miss the train," Captain George cautioned. "Won't be another for at least a week."

"We won't miss it," Van Ryan assured the soldier as he led his wife out the door.

While waiting in line, Eva listened to the pleas of other distressed souls as they related their heartbreaking tales of property loss, near-starvation, total ruin, and gripping fear. So many of the recently freed slaves wanted transportation to search for family members who had been sold away to plantations all over the South. Some asked for medicine, or a piece of paper on which to write a note, or assistance in writing the note itself, as so many of them were illiterate. Others were desperate for shoes, clothing, or a scrap of cloth to use as a blanket to ward off the hordes of mosquitos plaguing them at night. Ration slips for food were freely distributed to anyone who proved to be destitute, including a great number of former Confederate soldiers.

Nearly two hours passed before Eva finally stepped up to the young officer in charge. "I'd like transportation to Fort Wagner on Morris Island," she stated in her most respectful tone.

The officer's head snapped up from his ledger and he fluttered his small blue eyes at Eva, as if she were asking for a pot of gold. "Why would you want to go there?" he quipped, obviously annoyed by her request.

"Because my husband is buried on the island. He fought with the Massachusetts 54th Infantry. Died in the assault on Fort Wagner. I'd like to see his grave."

"Ma'am," Captain George started in a voice laced with sarcasm, "there is no grave site or even a marker on the island. It's been close to four years since the assault on the fort." He blew out a long breath and sat back in his seat. "I am sorry your husband died in battle, but there's nothing there to see. All the dead were just covered with sand. No use for you to go there at all."

"But I want to see where he died. Where his body is buried."

"I understand, but Battery Wagner is off limits for Army transport." Shaking his head, he turned his attention back to his ledger, clearly dismissing Eva as he lifted a hand to motion for the next person in line.

However, Eva stopped him with another question. "Could you help me with this?" And pulling out the paper that Mr. Jenkins had given to her, she placed it on the officer's desk. "I want to speak to Captain Liedtke. How can I get to Moncks Corner?"

Giving Eva a frown of frustration, Officer George took up the paper, scanned it, and handed it back to Eva. "So, do you wish transportation to Moncks Corner?" he asked, eyebrows raised.

"Yes, I do," Eva was quick to reply.

"Very well. I can arrange that. What's your name?" He put his pen to a page of his open ledger.

"Eva Phillips."

He wrote her name in the book with a flourish. "The purpose of the transport request?"

"I am searching for my mother."

"Slave or free?"

"A slave."

"Her name?"

"Mayree."

"What plantation was she on?"

"Stillwater."

"Oh... one of Joseph Cantrell's slaves, huh?" Captain George murmured in a rather disparaging tone.

"So I have been told," Eva stated, feeling a bit uneasy with his remark. "Do you know anything about Stillwater? Have you registered any slaves from there?" she added, pressing the soldier for any information that might prove helpful.

"A few slaves off the Cantrell place did come through here some time ago. Far as I know, Stillwater burned during the war. Folks say nothing much is left of the place."

"Oh," Eva sighed, disappointed to start her search with such disheartening news.

"But Captain Liedtke would know more about that area, than me. That's his district, not mine," the soldier added, and after reviewing what he had written in his book, he waved a piece of paper at a black man wearing a rumpled dark blue jacket, a US soldier's cap, and knee-high black leather boots. "Zack," the officer called out, "you take Mrs. Phillips to Moncks Corner when you deliver the next load of supplies to the Bureau. No trains heading that way right now. Day after tomorrow, will do fine."

"Yes sir, Captain George," Zack replied, walking up to take the pass from the soldier. Then turning to Eva he said, "My name's Zack Foster and I'd be pleased to drive you up to Moncks Corner, Ma'am. We'll be leaving day after tomorrow. If you'd like, I can take that trunk you been draggin' along and hold onto it for you 'til we leave."

"Yes, yes, that would be fine," Eva agreed, deciding she had no option other than to trust him.

"Good. Day after tomorrow, you come to Zack's Livery Stable on Beaufain Street." He lifted her trunk onto his shoulder. "Just a few blocks west from here. I'll meet you there."

"Thank you," Eva told Zack, swept with a sense of relief when she looked into his kind dark eyes. He was a fairly young man, but his soft round chin and chubby mahogany cheeks were framed with a short curly beard that gave him a more mature appearance. His rumpled jacket was in need of a good pressing, but his boots were clean and the Union Army cap sat at a jaunty angle on his head, tempering his serious expression. Instantly, Eva felt that Zack Foster was a man she could depend on to be kind, and helpful, as she found her way around.

"Is there a place where I might buy some fruit? A biscuit? Anything to eat would do."

"Yes, ma'am. Just go right on up to Market Street … you'll see folks set up, selling what they have to offer."

"Thank you," Eva said, and after exiting the building, she walked a short distance along the wharf until she came to Market Street, a wide cobblestone avenue lined on both sides with vendor stalls. The area was crammed with people actively bargaining for everything from dried corn, to fried sausage, to bolts of cloth. Not having eaten since the previous day, Eva approached a fruit stand where a woman dressed in a bright yellow dress was fanning flies off her wares. She purchased two apples, tucked one away for later, and savored the other as she browsed the marketplace, momentarily taking her mind off her most pressing problem: Where would she spend the night?

"Enjoying the market?" a voice came from behind her.

Eva turned, surprised, yet greatly relieved to see a face she recognized. Zack, who must have stowed her trunk and then followed her from the Freedman's Bureau, gave her a toothy grin.

"Oh, hello, Mr. Foster. Well, yes, I am," Eva admitted. "After so much time aboard ship, I do enjoy just walking around."

Zack removed his hat and stepped closer to Eva, eyes lowered as he spoke. "I was a bit worried when I left you at the Bureau, Mrs. Phillips. You new to Charleston. Don't know nobody, ain't that right?"

"Yes, I just arrived from Boston this morning."

"Thought you come from up North. Well, you be careful, ma'am. This place can get to be awful rowdy come nightfall. You got a place to stay the night, Mrs. Phillips?"

Eva shook her head and sighed. "No. I was hoping to locate the home of a woman my aunt knew....years ago, before the war. I ... I..." she stammered, pausing, aware of how foolish it was of her to assume that a white woman who'd helped slaves escape almost twenty years ago might still be living in Charleston. "I really haven't figured out what I'll do, as of yet," she admitted. "Do you know where I could get a room?"

Zack shifted his eyes to the side and tilted his head. "Ain't no place round here for black folks, but maybe ..." he stopped and pointed toward the river, lips pursed in consideration. "Miss Luvena Nesbit's my cousin. Lives on Judith Street, farther down the street, right near the river. I think she be fine with you stayin' at her place for the night."

"Are you sure?"

"Oh, yes ma'am. Luvena's a sweet lady. You can trust her. I can take you over. She got room. Got herself a real nice house."

"She owns her own home?"

"Sure does. Nobody knows for sure how she got that house, but I think she probably won it at the tables."

"The tables?"

"Yep. She deals cards at the Luckey Star Hotel most nights. Gamblers wager all kinds of things when the cards don't go their way, and she's right there to get 'em," he laughed with a shrug.

"I'm so grateful for your help," Eva decided, allowing herself to depend on this man she had just met. After all, the Army paid him to deliver valuable supplies to the Freedman's Bureau, he knew how to get around, and she could learn a lot from him.

"You're quite welcome, Mrs. Phillips," Zack replied. He fingered his hat and tucked his bottom lip between his teeth, his eyes on Eva's face as if not quite prepared to leave. "I don't mean to pry none, ma'am, but I heard what you said to Captain George back there."

Curious, Eva considered Zack's remark for a moment before clarifying, "You mean what I said about looking for my mother?"

"Yes, but no... well, mostly what you said about your husband being in the fight at Battery Wagner."

"Oh....yes, that is true," Eva said. "My husband was killed during the assault."

A somber hint of a smile touched Zack's lips before he said, "I was there, too. With the 2nd Regiment, South Carolina Volunteer Infantry. My unit came right up behind the 54th."

"Oh my," Eva softly groaned. "Truly? You were there?"

"Yes, we did our best to beat them rebel jacks, but it wasn't meant to be. A terrible thing to witness that day. Hell on Earth it was."

"Then you understand why I want so much to see where my husband is buried?"

"I do," Zack agreed. "But Captain George is right. Ain't nothin' much there to see."

"I still want to go."

"All right. If you want, I can take you."

"You can? To Morris Island?"

"Yep. I got a boat. Just a small slip, but it'll get us there." He touched his cap and added, "I got a team of horses and three wagons too. Been in the livery business, hiring out as a driver around here for years. After the war, I got me a government contract to deliver for the Army. I take supplies and mail out to the soldiers on the island. The guards know me. Just pass me right on through. I can get you on the island, but you can't stay long."

Impulsively, Eva touched Zack's arm and wrapped nervous fingers around his elbow. "Oh yes, please. Do take me. When can we go?"

"Right now, be best. I got no more loads to deliver today. Tomorrow I gotta report to Captain George by ten."

"I'm ready to leave," Eva said, beginning to feel better about her decision to come to South Carolina.

A short walk along East Bay took Eva and Zack to Central Wharf. Eva climbed into Zack's boat, a crude shallow boat packed with barrels and parcels of supplies for the soldiers with scarcely enough room for two passengers. She pulled a cotton shawl from her valise and wrapped it around her shoulders as a shield against the brisk spray of water whipped up by gusts of wind. Zack pushed out from the dock and rowed in silence, eyes straining into the distance as he guided his vessel away from the wharf.

As they passed through the harbor and slipped out toward the ocean, Eva took notice of a horseshoe shaped building with tall chimneystacks sitting in the middle of a small piece of land less than a mile from shore. The red brick structure appeared deserted, presenting a formidable façade to those passing by. It had rows of square holes cut into its rounded walls, an ominous arched entry that resembled a gaping mouth, and a yawning expanse of crushed rock and sand that hugged the walls and covered the grounds leading down to the water's edge.

"Castle Pinckney," Zack informed Eva before she had time to inquire about the oddly shaped structure in the middle of the harbor. "Was a prison for Union soldiers after Bull Run in '61," he explained. "The Johnny rebs put heavy cannon in those ramparts and pushed all that earth up against the walls during the fightin'. The place got hit three times but never fell. Been empty since the end of the war. Confederates just ran off and left it to ruin, like a lot of things 'round here."

The eerily desolate image of the castle-prison sent a chill of despair through Eva despite the warm press of the muggy sea air. She could imagine how dark, foul smelling, and foreboding the interior must be, and how awful it would have been for soldiers imprisoned in such a place.

After a final look at the abandoned castle, she turned away and focused on the horizon as Zack urged his boat into the Atlantic waters. The wind whipped Eva's shawl around her body and sea gulls cawed and soared overhead. Leaning forward, she lifted her face to the wind and thought of Chester. What had he been thinking about when he crossed this very same water? Had he feared the upcoming battle? Or had he been anxious to get into the fight? Had he thought of her? Had he been prepared to give his life for his country, as he ultimately had done? Allowing her thoughts of him to sink into her soul, she relaxed, wanting to absorb his presence, to feel as if he were taking the journey with her now.

When Zack pointed out Fort Sumter, Eva was startled from her reverie. As they slid past the fort where the opening shot of the war had been fired, she studied the structure with interest. Once a flashpoint of the eventual conflict, it now appeared serene and peaceful, simply a mound of grassy land surrounded by choppy water.

Sweeping westward, Zack steered the boat close to a pile of rocks and twisted metal rising from the sea.

"What's that?" Eva asked, then added, "I guess I should ask what *was* that?"

"The old lighthouse," Zack commented as they drifted past the rubble. "The enemy destroyed it so it'd be no use to us as a lookout tower. A real shame. The lighthouse been standing there for close to a hundred years. Now just look at what's left."

Making no comment, Eva remained silent, absorbing the evidence of the loss and destruction the area had suffered. Though she had heard about the devastation wrought upon the South, and had read newspaper stories about the damage that the Union had delivered to the enemy, none of it had seemed real to her, until now.

When the sandy shores of Morris Island came into view, a jolt of apprehension tightened in her stomach. The fort was a desolate, grim-looking place; a boxy shadow in the distance that loomed over the water like a foreboding mountain of sand and rock topped by an American flag.

As Zack had told Eva to expect, a rifle-toting soldier patrolling the area waved Zack to a stop. They exchanged a few words, and then the soldier passed them through the Army checkpoint and directed Zack toward a boat landing a few yards down the beach. After docking, Zack helped Eva out, then pointed toward a steep sand dune piled high on their right

"Over there. That's where the men were buried," he told her. "Those of us strong enough to hold a shovel dug a long trench and put the dead in it. Covered 'em with sand. I saw Captain Shaw lying amongst his men ... so young he was ... a kind man, too, so I heard."

"Yes," Eva agreed. "My husband often commented in his letters that Captain Shaw treated his men with true respect." Eva's words caught in her throat as she spoke through the tears she was struggling to hold in check.

"Well, I've got my deliveries to make. You go on, I'll be back shortly."

After Zack left, Eva walked to the edge of the burial dune and stared at the sand-covered gravesite stretching far along the shore. And as she stood there remembering Chester, she prayed that he had died quickly, that he had not lingered in pain or suffered much before closing his eyes and drifting away. Their time together had been too short, yet filled with tender moments and joyous laughter that she vowed never to forget. He'd been her first love, her best friend, the man she had vowed to remain with until death parted them. Now, she prayed for the strength to carry on alone, to navigate life as his widow. A sob rose in her throat and trapped her breath in her lungs as she pictured Chester lying beneath that pile of sand, dressed as she'd last seen him in his snappy blue uniform and jaunty Army cap. The depth of her pain thrummed through her body, tore at her heart, and coursed like hot liquid through her veins. Slowly, she reached into the brim of her red velvet hat and removed a white rosebud, which she pressed into the sandy grave as her final good-bye to Chester.

CHAPTER 14

During the ride back to Charleston Harbor Zack was much more talkative than he had been during their trip to the island. He seemed eager to tell Eva all about himself. She learned that he was married, had two young sons, and was originally from Columbia, the state capital, where his family was currently residing.

"I don't get to see my wife and chil'ren much. But at least I know they safe," he said.

"How far away is Columbia?"

"Oh, it's quite a ways north of Charleston. A good three day-ride."

"I'm sure you miss your family very much," Eva commented.

"Yes I do, but that's okay by me. I got to work."

"You say your family is safe in Columbia. Safe from what?" Eva probed, indulging her growing interest in learning all she could from Zack.

"From all them mean ole Democrats tryin' to scare us colored off from votin'. One day the Army gonna pull out, then how we supposed to be safe? I'm tryin' ta get all the freedmen to vote, but it's a hard mountain ta climb. Too dangerous, they keep sayin'"

"So, there's a lot of fear about freedmen voting?" Eva commented, eager to hear more about the political climate.

"Oh, yeah, sure is. But in times like these, we gotta stay strong. Them evil Democrats be callin' the colored Republicans scalawags. And the whites from up north, well they call them carpetbaggers. The Democrats not too happy 'bout black men stepping up to the ballot box, but we gonna be there come election day."

"When is the election?" Eva asked.

"A while off … but there's much to do before then." Zack stopped rowing and pushed back his cap, as if needing a break from talking about such serious matters. "So, you looking for your ma, huh?" he stated, moving the discussion on to Eva's situation.

"Yes, I am. That's why I want to go to Saint John's Berkeley," Eva confirmed, going on to tell Zack how she escaped growing up in slavery because her mother gave her away. "I just hope Captain Liedtke will have some record of her, so I can find her."

"The Freedman's Bureau in Moncks Corner stays real busy. There's folks always crowded around the captain, beggin' for help. A real shame, so many folks doing so poorly. You'll see what I mean when you get there."

"How far is Moncks Corner from Charleston?" she asked, trying to get her bearings.

"A short ways north. There's a train from Charleston to Moncks Corner, but it's mostly for the Army. We gonna take my wagon up the road runnin' along the Cooper River. With a empty wagon I kin make it in half a day's ride, but with you ridin' along and a full wagon too, we'll get there right 'fore dark."

"Where do you stay when you're there?" she asked, worried once again about finding accommodations.

"I got a friend. Name's Benton. He's livin' up that way. He takes in colored travelling folks now and then. I'll take you to meet him. Might wanna stay at his place while you get yourself squared away."

"You seem to know *everyone*," Eva said in a joking manner, relieved and thankful to have met Zack, who was turning out to be her savior. If she had not met him, where might she be? Wandering around, lost, and afraid?

"I been deliverin' goods all through these parts for years. A travelling man can make a lot of friends when he's on the road as much as I am."

"I'm so grateful for your help."

"Well, a woman, 'specially, gotta be careful who she take up with, Ma'am. Mighty dangerous times, these days. Don't mean to frighten you, Mrs. Phillips, but for some folks, the war ain't over."

After settling their arrangements for their trip to Moncks Corner, Zack took Eva to his cousin's house and then headed back to work at his busy livery stable.

Luvena Nesbit greeted Eva with a sincere smile and a genuine hug, banishing any apprehension Eva might have had about spending the night in a stranger's home. Luvena's house was a modest, yet tasteful, two-story frame house on a secluded riverside street—an eclectic mix of fine Charleston style and rustic, country charm. The parlor's stone fireplace with its semi-circular iron grate and polished pine mantle was the centerpiece of the room. An array of silver-framed photos and tiny porcelain figurines lined the mantel's top. Two richly upholstered barrel-shaped chairs with fringe and beaded roping around their bases faced each other across a round table covered in white cotton lace. A tall wire birdcage stood in front of the main parlor window, where a vibrant yellow canary flitted about, as if excited to have a visitor enter its domain.

While getting acquainted, the two ladies took tea, nibbling on teacakes as they fell into easy conversation. After Eva told Luvena about her reasons for coming to South Carolina, they chatted about family, the effects of the war, and the alarming scarcity of necessities, their talk flowing as if they had known each other for ages.

Eva was impressed with Luvena's positive attitude and her adventurous spirt, as well as the woman's voluptuous figure, glossy dark skin, and the whirl of fine brown hair worn swept up in a cascade of loose curls that framed her striking features. Eva silently admired Luvena's fashion-current black and white striped dress of finely spun cotton that was tucked and draped to accentuate her hourglass figure. And Eva had no doubt that the ruffled lace at Luvena's throat and wrists had been created by a lace-maker in some village far away, imported for sale at a fine milliner's shop. Luvena was bright, ambitious, and fiercely independent, making it clear to Eva that she knew how to take care of herself.

When Eva gently probed into Luvena past, curious to know more about this exotic woman, Luvena welcomed the opportunity to talk about her life.

"I was born free…. my father was a free black man who spent his life gambling on riverboats and working on paddle-wheelers. I never knew my mother. Pa took me with him wherever he traveled … all up and down the rivers around here. He taught me how to cook, how to roll dice, and how to shoot a pistol, too. He gave me a gun for my tenth birthday and made sure I was fast, accurate, and not afraid to use it. He also taught me how to deal a winning hand at cards. That's why I decided to entertain the risky life of a professional gambler, following Pa's example." She chuckled, leaned back in her seat, and sighed. "I guess you could say I enjoyed a rather carefree childhood."

Luvena went on to tell Eva that, at seventeen, she fell in love with a handsome gentleman gambler from Ohio who stole her heart as well as her virginity. She had hoped her much-older suitor would marry her and take her North to live in style, but he squandered his bankroll in a three-day poker session and fled the riverboat without her.

"That taught me a lot," Luvena said. "I learned how to survive on my own, and not be afraid of anything. You know, Eva, I never feared for my life, but I always feared being poor. I never wanted to be at the mercy of anybody who could have money-power over me. So I started dealing cards to earn a living. Damn respectability! It ain't that important, but possessing hard cash is."

Luvena told Eva that she went to work at the Luckey Star Hotel in Charleston each night, accepting the hand she'd been dealt in life and knowing how to play it. There, she served drinks and dealt cards in the gaming hall for all types of men; black, white, Creole, and Indian … any man who wanted to try his luck at getting his hands on real money because the Confederate dollars stuffed in his pockets were as worthless as blank paper.

"Speaking of money," Luvena finished, "I guess you brought some with you?"

Eva nodded. "I did."

"Well …it'd be wise not to let too many people know about it."

Eva placed her hand to her waist as she commented, "I keep it in a safe place."

A look of skepticism flitted over Luvena's features as she eyed Eva's midsection in question. "A pocket-corset, I presume?"

Eva nodded again.

Making a tisk-tisk sound with her tongue, Luvena said, "Hard cash is about as scarce as a decent bottle of champagne in Charleston right now. Be careful. A bank is a much safer place to put your money than inside your bodice."

Moving fingertips to her lips, Eva considered Luvena's suggestion. "You are probably right," she conceded. "I just arrived this morning. Where do you suggest I go to take care of financial affairs?"

"Any place other than the Freedman's Bank," Luvena warned. "I don't trust it. All the Negroes are rushing to hand their money over to the government. I don't understand why. Putting money in that bank for blacks is just like handing it over to the politicians. Who knows where it will end up? No, you go to the white bank, Eva. The Bank of Charleston."

"A white bank? Will I have trouble opening an account?" Eva queried, beginning to understand more fully how segregated everything remained in the South.

"Well, a few blacks who own property or have established themselves in business have accounts there. With you being from Boston …. You may not have a problem. I feel sure the bank manager, Mr.

York, will be happy to accept your money. Just keep a small amount on your person and put the rest in the bank. I can't stress enough how hard it is to come by real money nowadays." Luvena paused for a moment, then asked, "Do you have proof that you earned the money? A letter from someone back home?"

"Yes, I do. From Mr. Fitzgerald, the mapmaker I worked for in Boston. He gave me a letter of reference if I should need to seek employment."

"Fine. That will do fine. Tomorrow, you take my buggy into town and open an account at The Bank of Charleston. Use my address as your residence. Thirty-seven Judith Street. " Moving to the edge of her seat, she reached over and took Eva's hand. "Please, consider my house your home. You are welcome here whenever you need a place to stay."

"Thank you… I'm so very grateful for your help, and for your advice, as well," Eva conceded. "There's so much I don't know about how things are done in your part of the country."

"You'll learn soon enough," Luvena murmured with a grunt. "You're going to see and hear things that will surprise you, even frighten you. My advice …keep your eyes open, your mouth shut, and stay out of other folks' affairs. You'll be all right."

Setting her teacup aside, suddenly weary after such a long day, Eva slumped back in her chair. "I sincerely hope so, because I don't plan to leave here until I find out what has happened to my mother."

"You're very brave to come this far by yourself, to take on what you have," Luvena stated.

"I don't know about that. I'm not particularly brave," Eva protested. "I just want to know the truth."

"I hope you find it," Luvena commented, and seeing Eva shield her lips with her palm to stifle a yawn, she stood and waved a ring-laden hand toward the staircase as she motioned for Eva to follow her. "Come along. I can see you are tired. Let me show you to your room."

As she climbed the stairs, she turned her head to the side and told Eva, "I'm so pleased cousin Zack thought to bring you here. I've enjoyed your company immensely." Moving on to the top of the stairs, she stopped and motioned toward a closed door at the end of a short hallway. "I've prepared the spare room for you. It faces the river so you should get a decent breeze ... I hope you'll be comfortable."

The attic room was clean and attractively decorated with blue and white checkered curtains at its three dormer windows and a matching coverlet on the shiny brass bed. A porcelain bowl and a pitcher filled with water sat on the bedside nightstand. A delicate ladies' writing desk was tucked into a corner, where pen, ink, and paper had been laid out for Eva's use.

Though terribly tired, Eva sat at the desk and dipped the pen into the inkwell, anxious to write her first letter to Aunt Tully. As her pen moved across the paper, she smiled, feeling pleased at how well her first day in Charleston had gone. Her careful handwriting, boldly drawn in slanted loops, covered two pages as she described her progress: She had secured transportation to meet with Captain Liedtke in Moncks Corner. She had visited Chester's grave and made peace with his death. And now she had two new friends in Zack and Luvena. Hopefully, the days ahead would unfold just as smoothly and bring her closer to completing her mission.

Wearing her best gray cotton dress, her red velvet hat, and a paisley shawl of Luvena's that her host had insisted she borrow, Eva walked into The Bank of Charleston at exactly nine o'clock the next day. She approached the young man standing at the teller's cage and placed her money, folded within a sheaf of paper, on the counter.

"I'd like to open an account," she told him, making a confident connection with his deep blue eyes.

"Oh? Well, I'm very sorry. I am not permitted to accept your money," he sniffed, eyebrows moving upward. "You'll have to go to the Freedman's Bank."

"Oh? Why is that?" Eva asked, her tone slightly more indignant than curious.

"Negroes are not permitted to have accounts here," the teller stated in a tone intended to convey his authority.

"I guess I must have been misinformed," she remarked, feigning surprise and disappointment. "Are you sure not one person of color has an account at The Bank of Charleston?"

"Well… we may have a few tradesmen who are depositors, local business people with whom the bank has dealings. But without a business reference…well… I'm sorry we can't permit you to open an account."

"I do have a business reference," Eva insisted, removing an envelope from her purse. She placed it on the counter it in front of the man. "I have a letter of reference from Mr. Jonas Fitzgerald of Fitzgerald's Maps and Signs in Boston. I worked for him for many years."

The teller made no move to touch the letter, as if it might contaminate him. "I have never heard of that company," he smugly flung back at Eva, tightening lips that nearly disappeared. "Anyway, a *local* reference is required."

Frustrated, and knowing better than to press the issue and make a scene, she straightened her shoulders, picked up the letter, and took her packet of cash. She was preparing to place them into her purse when a man and a woman who had been standing behind her moved forward, as if desiring to take her place. Thinking they were eager for her to move out of their way so they could approach the teller, she turned to look at them. The man was tall, good-looking, with wavy brown hair and clear brown eyes. He was wearing an elegantly cut tan suit of clothes, a white pleated-front shirt, a navy silk cravat, and a tall beaver hat. The woman was a yellow-haired beauty who was dressed in a lovely pale blue cloak with matching gloves and a feathered hat.

Nodding at them, Eva moved away from the teller's cage to give them space, but instead of approaching the window to transact his business, the man walked toward Eva and made a slight bow. His female companion stood back, her gloved hands folded at her waist, her inquisitive eyes trained on the man.

"I don't mean to intrude," he said, "and I do apologize ... but I overheard your conversation with the teller." He paused, as if giving Eva space to grant him permission to continue. When she did not reply, he went on. "Allow me to introduce myself," he said, while reaching into his vest pocket to remove a white business card that he handed to her. "My name is Trent Hartwell. If I may be of assistance, Miss...?"

"*Mrs.* Phillips," Eva stiffly clarified while examining the rich vellum card scripted in bold black letters: *Trent Hartwell, Attorney at Law, Real Estate Investments.* She inclined her head in acknowledgement. "What kind of assistance could you offer? I don't need a lawyer. I just want to open a bank account," she stated, appreciative of the man's respectful demeanor.

"Mrs. Phillips," Trent repeated. "Yes, I am a lawyer, recently arrived here from Chicago. I recall utilizing Mr. Fitzgerald's maps while I was studying property law at the university. Mr. Fitzgerald's maps were always very well done. Most helpful. I met him when he personally delivered a lecture at the university."

This news made Eva feel a great deal better.

"May I inquire after Jonas Fitzgerald?" Trent asked.

"Mr. Fitzgerald was well when I left him in Boston," she informed, curious of this stranger's intent. He was stylishly dressed, had been most polite, and she felt he was telling her the truth because he knew Mr. Fitzgerald's first name and the quality of his maps.

Trent glanced at the document in Eva's hand. "So, you require assistance with your business here?"

Taking a deep breath, Eva decided to consent. "Yes, Mr. Hartwell, I do believe you may be able to help me." Having made her decision to trust him, she handed him her letter.

"Trent," his female companion interrupted before Trent could open the letter. She quickly moved to stand facing Eva as she spoke to Trent. "Please. Don't get involved. It's not the way things are done here." With a lift of her jaw, she peered down her nose at Eva, staring directly into Eva's eyes. "Negroes cannot do business here."

Trent glanced at his companion and lifted his eyebrows, as if to question her right to question him, and then told her, "Oh, Sage. Don't be like that. All this lady needs is a reference, and I am familiar with her employer."

Eva watched the couple's exchange with fear, dreading a scene that would cause more problems.

"Let's see," Trent murmured as he unfolded the piece of paper and began to read in a low tone:

"The bearer of this letter, Mrs. Eva Phillips worked in my shop for six years, most recently as my assistant mapmaker for the past three years. She is a trustworthy, competent young woman who will be an asset to any tradesman or firm. I highly recommend her for any position that you may deem appropriate.

Most appreciatively, Jonas Fitzgerald.

Fitzgerald's Maps & Signs.

361 Beacon Street, Boston, Massachusetts."

"Well, Mrs. Phillips, I think this should do well enough for you to open an account," Trent decided as he returned the letter to Eva. "Let me see what I can ..."

Before he could finish, Sage took Trent by the arm and tugged his sleeve, eager to move away. However, he placed his hand over her gloved fingers and said, "Just a moment, Sage. I want to speak to Mr. York. I'm certain he will be able to assist Mrs. Phillips in transacting her business." And without waiting for Sage to continue her objections, Trent motioned for Eva to follow him.

He led her into a room off the lobby where a slim man with a thick black beard and a wiry mustache was sitting behind a desk. When Trent Hartwell spoke, the man jumped to his feet. When Trent

Hartwell introduced Eva to Mr. Mansard York and explained to him that she wanted to open an account, Mr. York rushed around his desk and offered her a seat at his spacious conference table. When Trent Hartwell said goodbye to Eva, she felt his eyes lingering on her face for a moment too long.

CHAPTER 15

Trent knew that Sage was not at all pleased with his intervention at the bank, but he had no regrets about helping the Negro lady. He had simply offered his assistance to a woman who needed it and he was pleased that Mansard York had accommodated her. Now, Trent lifted his elbow to allow Sage's gloved fingers to grip his arm as they exited the bank and stepped outside. Though he had planned to take his carriage to his house, Sage rejected the idea, insisting they enjoy the lovely spring weather by walking the short six blocks to his home.

"Take the carriage on to the house, Gus. We'll walk," Trent told his driver, giving in to Sage's suggestion.

As they strolled past shops and residences along the street, Sage made imperceptible acknowledgements to those whose attention she openly sought. She inclined her head with a tilt of her lips and a flutter of her eyelashes each time she encountered a friend or an acquaintance, openly demonstrating that she and the wealthy Yankee, who was creating quite a stir among the local businessmen and planters, had grown extremely close since their introduction more than a year ago.

It wasn't until they were seated on the yellow silk settee in

Trent's parlor and his housekeeper, Amelia, had served them tea that Sage told him exactly what was on her mind.

"You really shouldn't have introduced that woman to Mansard York," she began, stirring a lump of sugar into her tea. "Word about what York did for her will spread. He'll be swamped with darkies wanting to walk right through the front door and demand to put their pennies in his bank." She shook her head back and forth as if flinging such an image out of her mind. "That will never do. Mansard will be sorry." She sighed as she lifted her teacup to her lips. After taking a sip, she sent Trent a knowing glance, as if trying to make nice after scolding a child. "Trent, you still have so much to learn about how we do things here in Charleston," she chided, leaning over the table to grace him with a generous view of creamy breasts bursting from her daring décolletage. "We may have lost the war, but we still have our principals and our traditions to uphold."

Before replying, Trent finished off one of Amelia's cinnamon teacakes and wiped his lips with his white linen napkin. He certainly didn't want to offend Sage, but he wasn't about to let her southern values affect what he felt was right and true. He and Sage had become close, and she had been an excellent resource while helping him renovate and decorate his new home. Her connections within Charleston's elite society, as well as those of her father, had helped Trent gain entrance into exclusive social and business circles where he made several lucrative real estate deals. She introduced him to the men of importance in the city's financial sector, helped him navigate the rules of their regimented social scene, and had practically lived at his house during the extensive renovation of his gardens and interiors, demonstrating excellent taste in her selection of flowers, shrubs, and trees, as wells as drapery fabric and china patterns.

She was not pushy, but she was direct, expressing her opinions in frank conversation that often left Trent without a rebuff. Most of the time her intuitions and opinions turned out to be on point, yet she could be extremely insensitive in her dealings with those of the lower class. She distrusted his housekeeper, Amelia, who in his opinion was an efficient, competent woman whom he trusted to manage his home. Yet Sage often went behind him, giving Amelia instructions of her own, creating a situation where they butted heads. At those times, Trent walked a fine line between placating his housekeeper and remaining in Sage's good graces.

Since meeting Sage, Trent had developed an intense awareness of his physical attraction to her, and he was having a hard time suppressing the reservoir of manly emotions that kept him entranced by her beauty and her wit. He knew he had allowed her to seep more deeply into his personal space than he had first anticipated, but truth be told, he did not mind. He rather enjoyed the shivers of delight that coursed through him whenever they went out in public together. When she took his arm, looked up into his eyes, and pressed herself lightly into his side, his heart turned over in desire. She was exquisitely attractive, cultured to a fault, witty, and possessed of a quick but bold tongue. However, for all of her talk about traditions and southern standards, her kisses and caresses led him to believe that she was just as eager as he was to toss all niceties aside and propel their relationship to a more intimate level.

While discussing their pasts, Sage had admitted to Trent that, after her mother's death, her father had encouraged her to become a more independent woman. The judge allowed his daughter to come and go as she pleased, without the company of a socially acceptable chaperone, as was the custom for unmarried women who spent time in the company of unmarried men. During dinner table conversations, the judge encouraged Sage to freely speak her mind on any subject she chose, never censoring the topics of discussion that arose.

Privately, Trent applauded Judge Turner for encouraging Sage's unconventional approach to the strict rules governing male/female relationships. Her kisses were freely given to Trent, and their caresses, so far, had veered as close to complete consummation as Trent had dared allow them to go. There were times when, at a social affair, he would look at Sage and imagine she was Rebecca sitting across from him at table or holding onto his arm as they waltzed. When his lips covered Sage's, he often found himself imagining that he was tasting Rebecca's sweetness on his mouth. And once, when Sage allowed him a glimpse of her naked breasts while changing her paint-stained shirt, his mind was immediately filled with an image of Rebecca standing in his brother's wagon, her bodice undone, her rosy nipples taunting him. At that moment, all thoughts of bedding Sage evaporated like the river fog that vanished with the rising sun, and his anger over losing Rebecca returned.

However, now, he gave Sage a playful squint from beneath startled brown eyes, as if to dismiss her concerns about York's bank becoming overrun by former slaves demanding to make deposits. "Oh, I doubt York would ever refuse hard cash from anyone who wants to put it in his bank. The only color he appreciates is green. You must understand he's a businessman first, and ..."

"But a *Southern* businessman," Sage interrupted with a huff, expelling her frustration in a whoosh.

"Yes, he is," Trent agreed. "And I am a *Northern* businessman. We're working together to rebuild the city. Money is money when it comes right down to it. Why allow race or class or social trappings to interfere with progress and delay what needs to be done to rebuild South Carolina?"

"Trent, don't be fooled. Mansard York allowed that Negro woman to open an account because he wanted to impress you. He was simply showing off for his important Northern investor. He wants to make you believe he's fine with coloreds banking at his establishment, but you can be sure he won't do it again."

Trent scratched his chin, pondering her remark. "I hope you're wrong," he replied, realizing how much he trusted York and looked forward to working with him.

"In time, you'll see," Sage decided, getting up from the table to stand behind Trent's chair. She swept a hand across his back, as if brushing away a scattering of lint. "No more talk about money or business," she declared, sliding her fingers up onto the nape of his neck, entangling his hair in her hand. She placed her chin on his shoulder, and whispering huskily into his ear, she closed the gap between north and south when she said, "I'd love to see how those new drapes that I selected for your bedroom look."

"And you will," he promised. "Later. After we return from the races. Right now, we must hurry. Your father expects us to be at the racetrack by noon. His new gray filly, Sweet Candy, is running today. He thinks this horse is going to be a true champion."

"And after the races," Sage added in a soft, inviting tone, "we'll have dinner here?"

"Of course," Trent agreed. "Alone."

Mr. York was most accommodating, Eva decided as she headed to the hitching post where she'd left Luvena's horse-drawn buggy while shopping in the market place. *And that lawyer, Mr. Harwell was very helpful as well*, she mused, deciding that Southern white men were not so difficult to work with after all. During her conversation with Mr. York, she'd told him why she had come to South Carolina, and after hearing about Chester's death, he had not only allowed Eva to open a bank account, but had also promised to do what he could to expedite the widow's pension and back pay that she was due. She had given him Luvena's address as her place of residence as a temporary solution, but was thinking it might be best to get a post office box as soon as possible. Feeling optimistic about the future, she climbed into the buggy, slapped the reins against the horse's back, and started down Broad Street to the post office, only ten blocks west of the bank. Eva rode along the brick paved street, holding her head high, thinking how nice it was of Luvena to loan her the wagon and how useful it would be to have one of her own. To move around the city while searching for her mother. To be in control of her circumstances.

Ten minutes later, Eva entered the post office, anxious to post the letter she had written to Aunt Tully. She approached the postal window and handed her letter to the clerk.

"That'll be five cents, Ma'am," the young man told Eva as he adjusted the visor atop his unruly red-blond curls.

"When will the letter arrive in Boston?" Eva asked as she placed a coin on the counter.

"I can't guarantee, but it ought to get there in ten days or so if the train runs on time and the tracks hold up," he replied, placing her coin in his drawer. With a sigh, he tilted his head to one side and went on, "Transportation is hit and miss these days. But things are getting better."

"Thank you," Eva said. She started to walk away from the window, then paused, turned back to ask the clerk, "Do you have postal boxes to let?"

"You mean a *private* mail box?" the young man asked.

"Yes."

"For how long?"

"I'm not sure," Eva hedged, realizing she had no idea how long her stay in the south would be. Locating her mother was not going to be an easy task, but no matter how long it took, she was prepared to keep searching, prodding, and questioning every possible source for information about Mayree from Mr. Cantrell's Stillwater Plantation. Perhaps she had not fully considered the difficulty of locating a former slave in the chaotic circumstances of post-war South Carolina, but now that she was here, nothing was going to deter her from doing what she'd come to do.

"How much does a private box for one year cost?" she asked, deciding to allow herself ample time to complete her search.

"It's five dollars for a year," he replied, a undertone of regret in his voice, as if certain this unimposing black woman could ill afford the price. "But if that is too much, you can do general delivery for free."

Without hesitating, Eva reached into her reticle and removed a five-dollar-bill. "No, I'd like to let a private box for one year please."

The man smiled, then picked up his pen and held it poised above a small white card. "Your name, ma'am?"

"Mrs. Eva Simson Phillips."

And without further discussion, the clerk quickly finalized the transaction.

Their afternoon at the Charleston Race Track proved to be both enjoyable and profitable for Sage and Trent. He wagered generously on Sweet Candy and won an impressive amount of money. She played hostess at a private celebration at the racetrack club to honor Judge Turner's winning horse. As her father's hostess, Sage entertained his guests until very late into the day, with everyone remaining at the party until the last drop of champagne had been drunk and all wagers had been won or lost.

Trent was flush with cash and tipsy from consuming so much champagne when he and Sage returned home to enjoy Amelia's delicious meal of pork roast and new potatoes. After a final glass of brandy to cap off the long day, Trent set aside his linen napkin and pushed away from the table. He turned to Sage, gave her a seductive grin, then said, "Didn't I promise to show you the new draperies in my bedroom?"

"You did," Sage agreed in a husky voice, eyes at half-mast.

"Come then, let's go take a look."

He led her up the stairs and into the handsome room above the parlor that served as his manly retreat. The walls, covered in burgundy and gray paisley-patterned wallpaper, sent a message of quiet, elegant serenity. Two large oil paintings of rural landscape scenes set in thick gilded frames occupied wall-space on either side of a stately four-poster bed draped with gauzy white netting. Opposite the bed, three tall casement windows topped with ornate iron rods showcased the rich brown and gold draperies that Sage had personally selected. The low flame of a squat globe lamp sitting atop a round bedside table cast a spray of golden shadows about the room.

After closing the door, Trent gathered Sage close, bent down, and pressed his lips against her neck, allowing her perfumed scent to set his heart racing, unleashing a rebellious agitation he had no desire to control.

Leaning back, she twisted her head to survey the window coverings. "Very nice," she complimented. "The color and the fabric are perfect."

"As are you," Trent complimented, pulling her attention back to himself as he placed his lips to hers and wrapped his hands around her tiny waist. He deepened their kiss, sending an urgent jolt of unfulfilled desire through him that he felt mesh with her. She melted into his embrace, molding her slim frame against his, making contact with the bulge in his trousers that he did not try to hide. Pulling back, he peered hungrily at her, his heart hammering with a shocking mix of gratitude and longing. How desperately he wanted her in his bed! How intensely he craved the touch of her naked skin against his! He wanted to feel their bodies joined in exquisite pleasure. And even though he knew relinquishing all control and submitting to his aching male urge would require an immediate proposal of marriage, he was willing to take such a chance, even though he was not fully prepared for the consequences of his actions.

While fingering the lacey edge of Sage's low-cut neckline, he studied the violet-hued fabric, his manly ache surging for release, rising swiftly to the surface. "You are a very lovely woman," he told her, sliding his fingers back and forth across her creamy flesh. When she did not resist his probing fingers, he realized she was not going to play their usual game of tease and torture as they had done before. He could tell that she was primed to succumb completely to the electrified pull that was bringing them together. Chancing the correctness of his assumption, he touched the first pearl button on the front of her bodice and easily undid it with his thumb. Then he moved to the second button and hesitated, waiting for her to tell him to stop. When she made no protest, he crushed his lips over hers, shattering all pretense of holding back from the course they had chosen, her tongue flicking over his in a swirl of anxious acceptance as the remainder of the pearl buttons quickly came undone.

It took only moments for him to strip away the rest of her clothing. After her bodice fell to the floor, she gracefully stepped out of her skirt and tossed her unmentionables aside to stand elegantly naked before him. With lashes lowered to avoid his brazen gaze, she let him drink in the sight of her, as if daring him to take the final step.

Trent quickly accepted her challenge and shed his clothing. Taking her by the hand, he led her to his massive bed and eased her down atop the thick velvet coverlet that she had selected for him. Lying side by side, Sage rubbed her nipples across Trent's bare chest while making a soft purring sound in her throat, forcing a groan from him that sounded like a cross between a murmur of contentment and a growl of aching expectation. When Sage closed her eyes, he noticed that her lashes created dark half-moon shaped shadows on her cheeks, which were flushed as pink as her moist lips, making him even more intent on making love to her, of satisfying her needs as well as his, of honoring what she expected from him.

Trent urged Sage to lie down on her back and then placed his hard body flush over hers. He allowed the feel of her skin against his to fill him up as wave after wave of intense pleasure undulated through his body. Gently, he moved one hand down to the silken patch of hair between her thighs to seek the pearly core of her womanhood. As his fingers massaged her slick, ripe bud, he felt her open up to him, offering herself with complete abandon as she begged for more of him, all of him at once.

With a soft nudge, he moved her hips more fully beneath him and urged his swollen member into place, making her gasp in sweet agony as he spread her legs and pushed completely into her. Thrusting with as much restraint as he could manage, he sank into the waves of exquisite release that had been building for too long.

"Oh, Trent," Sage whispered, gripping his shoulders to raise her face closer to his, her breath sweet and hot as it brushed his chin. "Oh, please, please, don't ever stop."

Trent didn't stop. He swept his slick, wet tongue along the side of her neck. "Delicious," he admired, stroking her even harder, riding her until both he and Sage climaxed in a crash of quivering light-filled shudders that left them panting, moaning, their slick bodies entwined.

Afterward, his heart pounding, his seed spent, Trent wondered if marriage to a woman like Sage might actually be possible. He was a Yankee. She, a Southern belle. Her distain for anyone not of her social class or of a different race was as ingrained in her as was her southern accent. Would it be fair to her, or to him, to even try to make such a union work? He had to admit that he did have a strong attraction to Sage, but he knew it was not love. How could he continue to take her to his bed if his intentions were not declared? But how could he propose marriage to a woman he did not love?

Trent's frustrating thoughts were interrupted by a moan of satisfaction from Sage as she spiraled down from her rollicking climax. Relaxing into his own delicious eruption, he sighed, rolled off of Sage to lie next to her, his mind filled with conflicted worry. As his breathing slowed, he turned onto his side, his face dotted with perspiration, aware that he needed to clarify his intentions and set some kind boundary to this sudden expansion of their relationship.

"I care deeply for you, Sage. You know that, don't you?"

"I do," she whispered. "And I care deeply for you as well. Just promise me that what we have now will last a long, long time." She paused, making a slight lift of her bare shoulder as she spoke. "Permanent, I do hope?"

Trent lay quiet for a moment, then said, "We are together now, that's all that matters. We have differences that could make moving too fast the wrong way to proceed."

"I know, I know," Sage admitted. "We come from different parts of the country, and we look at some things in different ways, but our feelings are the same, aren't they?"

"Yes. I agree with you on that," Trent replied. "But still, we need time, Sage. Time to fully examine and appreciate the differences that remain."

"Time? Why? You're *everything* I need, Trent. You are exactly the kind of man I have dreamed of marrying. When you entered my life, everything changed." She nuzzled his chest with her nose.

"I understand. But let's not talk about marriage just yet," he gently stated, turning her away from what was on her mind. "In time, it will all come together as it should."

"Perhaps, you're right." She sat up and swung her legs over the side of the bed, keeping her back to Trent. "I must get dressed and hurry home now. I'm sure father is there, wanting to talk about every detail of the race." She leaned down and picked up her bloomers from the floor, glanced over her shoulder at Trent, and then added, "God, I hate to leave."

Impulsively, Trent rose onto his knees, pressed his bare chest against her back. A slow heat began to build inside of him, making him heavy with need again. The sensation intensified his realization of how sexually unfulfilled he had been when Sage came into his life, and how deeply she had satisfied him. Making love to her had sucked all the breath from his body, erasing his deep-seated loneliness, reviving him completely. He reached around, caressed a taut nipple, and held on to her, aware that perspiration was dripping off her chest and running through his fingers. It was taking all of his will power to keep from easing his hands down to the patch of hair below his hand as his second erection, rigid and swollen, was begging for her to touch it.

CHAPTER 16

After a long, heartfelt hug, Eva stepped away from Luvena and said goodbye to her new friend. She climbed into Zack's mule-driven wagon, which was loaded with kegs of bacon, bags of cornmeal, sacks of grain and rice, along with her small trunk tucked among the cargo. She settled onto the driver's bench beside Zack and they moved out of the city on a well-defined road running parallel to the railroad tracks. Moving slowly at first, Zack urged his mule through the city, passing throngs of desperate freedmen, displaced farmers, soldiers, and anxious citizens that continuously clogged the streets. Most of the people were carrying their meager possessions in burlap bags, canvas sacks, or straw baskets atop their heads.

In time, Zack moved farther away from Charleston and deeper into the countryside where the crowds began to thin and a land-scape ravished by war came into view. They passed fields stripped bare of crops, burned-out plantation houses resembling charred skeletons, an emaciated countryside of once-fertile land that now lay fallow and deserted. Outbuildings on farms resembled piles of rubble, and what livestock remained was bone-riddled and sickly.

As if reading Eva's thoughts, Zack lifted an arm and pointed across a field where a handful of men, both black and white, were scavenging for kernels of corn left behind after the last harvest. "Most everything got taken by the Army. Even the wild turkeys that used to be runnin' all through these woods done just disappeared. Food's real scarce now. If not for the Army, lots of folks wouldn't eat nothin' at all. Thank God, the government's doing what it can to help those that are hungry, 'cause everybody done suffered enough."

After traveling steadily for several hours, Zack decided to stop. While he watered the mules, Eva set out the basket of food that Luvena had packed for them. While eating slices of ham and warm cornbread, Zack described the route to Moncks Corner.

"Up ahead, we gonna come to a spot where two roads come together. Probably be close to dark by then. We'll be goin' east … toward the Cooper River. Won't be too far from Benton Langdon's place. You can stay there while I go deliver the goods to the Bureau. Won't do much good for you to go see Captain Liedtke 'til tomorrow anyway."

After their meal was finished and the afternoon was waning, Zack took a hand-lettered sign from the wagon and nailed it to a tree. "Vote Republican!" Eva read from the sign, and then questioned him about it.

He defiantly replied, "I done pledged to vote Republican and I want all black folks to do the same. I know there's some people don't like the idea of a black man having a say 'bout the government, and all. There been threats, some beatings, and a few burnings … just to keep colored men away. Them angry rebels be determined to keep us in our place. They the ones behind a lot of the trouble brewing in the county."

Without making a comment, Eva silently applauded Zack's brave remarks, knowing how dangerous it was for him to publicly support this newly awarded privilege for black men. She could sense his pride, as well as his determination to play a part in the formation of his county's new government.

As the sun moved steadily across the sky, Zack veered onto a narrow, less travel-worn path, but after going only a few miles, he encountered a lost load of lumber lying in the road. The huge pine logs that completely blocked the trail appeared to have been recently harvested, their pale ends still oozing sap. After studying the situation, Zack turned to Eva. "Gonna lose some time but I guess we got no choice but to go 'round all this mess." And muttering under his breath, he began urging the mules onto a shady path leading off the main road.

The lush tree-canopy that capped the new trail provided relief from the bright white sunlight. Eva took an interest in the exotic-looking ferns, bushes, and wild flowering vines that hugged the trunks of tall pine trees and climbed into their branches, feeling oddly secure in the closeness of the overgrown forest.

"What is that?" Eva asked, pointing to a stout plant with wrinkled, hairy leaves and a spray of tiny white flowers.

"Boneset," Zack replied. "Dry the leaves and the flowers, then brew it in a tea. Makes a good general tonic, and some say it's 'specially good for malaria fever."

"Really? Can you stop the wagon for a moment? I'd like to pick some."

"If you like," Zack agreed as he halted the mules and motioned for Eva to stay put. "Don't you get down. Awful muddy over there. I'll get some for you real quick." He got down, stepped off the path, and went to gather a handful of the boneset.

Just when he returned to the wagon and was handing the bouquet of wild herbs to Eva, a rifle-toting man wearing a Confederate uniform emerged from the shadowy depths of the forest. He had a red kerchief tied around his face, with only his eyes visible beneath the brim of a large black hat pulled low over his forehead.

"Get away from the wagon," the man gruffly ordered Zack.

When Zack hesitated, he shouted, "I said leave the wagon!"

Hurriedly, Zack, eyes wide and mouth agape, stepped off the path and into a stand of thorny bushes.

"You stay over there!" the intruder ordered. "You're not gonna take this food to those sorry blacks, not as long as white people are starving."

When Zack started to move, the man lifted his rifle and pointed the long gun at Zack. "I'll shoot you right where you stand if you don't get the hell outta here! Run, nigger, run!"

Zack eased backwards, moving away slowly while keeping his eyes on Eva, who was biting her bottom lip in fear. "Get on," the man ordered. "Get on back to Charleston! If you tell anyone what you seen here I'll track you down and kill you!" Then he took aim at a spot above Zack's head and fired off a blast that made Eva scream and cover her ears.

Turning his back on Eva and the wagon, Zack fled into the woods.

"You get down!" the man shouted at Eva, who in her fright, could not move.

"Get down or I'll shoot you," he threatened, waving the long rifle in her face.

Scrambling to get out of the wagon, she grabbed her soft valise and obeyed his command, but as soon as her feet touched the ground, he used the butt of his gun to strike her down, slamming her headfirst into the trunk of a tree.

"No, No!" she screamed, placing a hand to her head, her fingers sliding into the trickle of blood running down the side of her face. "Leave me alone! Please. Leave me alone!" Fearing his attack, she scrambled onto her knees and began to crawl away, but he grabbed her by her foot and yanked her back to the base of the rough cypress tree. "Please, please, don't hurt me," she begged, clutching her skirt around her ankles, staring at him with terror in her eyes.

Scoffing a laugh, he snapped, "Don't flatter yourself! Why do you think this white man would want you? I'd rather stick my white prick into the back end of a cow than a monkey-whore like you."

Cowering against the tree trunk, Eva took no comfort in his rebuff as she warily watched him shoving the contents of the wagon around. He examined each box, barrel, and parcel, and after rummaging through the cargo, he came upon Eva's small trunk, which he tossed to the ground and pried open. He pawed through its contents, snatched out her toiletries, discarded her gloves and scarves, and threw two of her three dresses into the brush.

"Nothing of value here," he decided, yanking out her quilt.

Eva shot to her feet and rushed to grab the coverlet, pulling so hard on it that it tore, leaving the man holding a piece of the tattered bed quilt. More angry than frightened, Eva wrenched it from his hands, clutched it to her chest, and glared at him. He laughed at her and spit a stream of tobacco juice at her feet. Eva jumped back to escape the slimy spittle as her attacker climbed up into the wagon, slapped the reins to alert the mule, and then careened off into the forest, leaving Eva watching in despair.

Zack was right, she mentally groaned, recalling his words of caution about the level of hatred and violence that still existed in the South. *Luvena was right, as well*, she admitted with a choke of a sob. The only thought that summoned a bit of relief was the fact that the bulk of her money was safely stored in The Bank of Charleston, and the small amount on her person remained tucked into the corset that Aunt Tully had made for her.

Eva scrambled to gather her toiletries and the clothing that he had scattered all over the ground. Quickly, she shoved everything back into her trunk, fearful that another marauder might show up to rob or assault her. With no idea of which way to go or how to find help, she grabbed the leather strap attached to her trunk, plunged into the forest, and pushed her way through tangled brush until the sun slipped below the tops of the trees and daylight began to fade.

This is of my own doing, Eva reminded herself, refusing to give in to her fear. *I came here to find my mother, and I will not be frightened away*. However, the idea of spending the night in the forest initiated a flash of panic that brought her up short and forced her to assess her surroundings. After locating a sheltered spot between two gigantic oaks trees with low-spreading limbs, she covered herself with her tattered quilt, tucked her soft satchel under her head, and within a very short time, fell asleep.

Eva awoke to the scratching sound of a squirrel scampering in the branches of the tree under which she had spent the night. Her head was pounding in pain and her mouth was parched. Dried blood clung to the side of her face. Scanning the area, she focused on the shafts of morning sunlight radiating through the canopy of leaves as she tried to determine the angle of the rising sun. She recalled Zack's description of the route he had planned to take, recalling he had said they would come to a place where two major roads intersected and that Benton's place would not be far from there. But where exactly? she worried, feeling confused and alarmed at this turn of events she told herself to calm down, to think. And soon, a possible solution came to her.

"The map I drew from Aunt Tully's recollections!" she said aloud, opening her satchel to extract the rumpled piece of paper. After consulting the map and the rising sun, she decided to travel northward, and hopefully be headed toward Moncks Corner. Standing, she shook out her skirt and stretched to relieve the aches in her back from sleeping on the ground. She gathered her things, and while keeping the emerging sunrise to her right, started walking, plowing her way through thick underbrush and tough twisting vines that fought her every step.

The bright yellow sun inched its way higher as Eva continued walking, and by the time it had reached the center of the sky she came to a fork in the road, just as Zack had described. Turning eastward, Eva pushed ahead until arriving at a wide expanse of water, which she hoped was the Cooper River. She consulted her map, then stepped close to the craggy riverbank, where she discovered a narrow footpath of hard packed earth tracing along the river's edge. She was heartened to see that it showed signs of recent use initiating a flutter of hope that swept through Eva as she gritted her teeth and pressed on.

After walking only for a matter of minutes, the footpath suddenly ended, placing Eva on the outer edge of what appeared to be a fallow cotton field. Broken stalks and crushed bushes lay rotting on the ground, evidence that no farmer had tended the land for some time. In the distance, facing the river, stood a boxy wood frame house with peeling white paint, situated in a tangle of over-grown gardens that seemed to anchor the house to the land. The two and a half story house, rectangular in shape with twin brick chimneys and a gabled roof had a wide upper veranda running the length of the structure. Dark green shutters flanked four dormer windows, as if keeping watch over the river.

Though cautious, and alarmingly afraid of what she might be walking into, Eva started up the slope toward the house. She stopped at a gate that opened onto a weed-choked yard, and just as she lifted the latch, a man dressed in a white ruffled shirt, tan riding pants, and knee-high brown boots emerged from behind the house and started across the yard. From his expression, Eva sensed that he was surprised, even anxious, to see a strange woman on the property.

"Hello there," he called out, striding toward Eva. "Do you need help?"

"Hello," Eva managed in a voice strained and weary. Using a briar-scratched hand, she pushed hair from her face and wiped perspiration from her neck. "Yes, yes, I do need help," she admitted, taking a moment to more fully assess the man whose skin was so light he might have passed for white. However, his pale complexion and clear gray eyes did not conceal the roots of his African heritage, evident in the fullness of his lips and the loose curl in his wavy black hair. He stood a full head and shoulders taller than Eva, with a slender frame that he held erect in a prideful, confident manner that bordered on haughtiness. "I was robbed ... I mean, the wagon I was riding in was robbed." She paused to take a deep breath, then plunged ahead. "I was traveling with a man named Zack. He was taking supplies to the Freedmen's Bureau. You might know him, he said ..."

"Zack?" the man repeated. "Zack Foster?"

"Yes, that's right. You do know him!"

"Yes, I do." He paused, inclined his head slightly, and told Eva, "Excuse my manners, ma'am. My name is Benton Langdon."

"Oh! Mr. Langdon! I'm Eva Phillips. Mr. Foster told me about you. We were on our way here…" She stopped talking and glanced around. "Am I in Moncks Corner?"

"No. This is Cordesville. But you're not so far from where you were headed."

"Oh, thank God. Mr. Langdon. It was absolutely awful. A man came upon us on the road."

"Where is Zack?"

"That's what I was saying. A man with a gun ran Zack off. He threatened to shoot me! He …"

"Oh, my. How awful," Benton said as he unlatched the gate and motioned Eva into the weed-filled garden. "That can wait. Now, take your time, Miss Phillips," Benton cautioned as he peered down into Eva's face.

"It's *Mrs.* Phillips," she informed.

"Fine, fine," he replied, and then, making a tisk-tisk sound with his tongue, he commented, "I see you've been injured."

Eva touched the cut on her head. "Yes, the man who robbed us pushed me into a tree. He shot at Zack, ran him off, leaving me alone. I …"

"Oh, my," Benton remarked again, examining Eva's blood-streaked forehead. "Better come inside. You can tell me what happened while we tend that cut. Looks like you've had a pretty hard time of it," he said, taking up her trunk as he took her by the arm.

Exhausted and in pain, Eva let the tears that she had been holding back burst forth as she walked with Benton, a strange man who seemed genuinely eager to help her.

"Now, now. Don't cry. We will get to the bottom of this," he comforted, taking her by the elbow.

Eva leaned on him for support, too tired, upset, and hungry to turn down any offer of assistance. *He is a friend of Zack's. Who else can I turn to?* she fretted, wiping her eyes with the back of her hand. *He's very polite. Well dressed and mannerly, too. Certainly I can trust him to be a real gentleman.*

Walking with Benton across the yard, Eva entered the back door of the decrepit mansion and found herself standing in what looked like a common eating area. Two long wooden tables were stationed in the center of the room, while baskets of food, large kettles and cooking pots, and a variety of utensils filled shelves along the walls. A lazy hound dog, sleeping at the edge of the fireplace, stirred, got up, and ambled out of the room.

"Come right on in. Let me see…. Now, where's Bina?" Benton questioned, looking around. He frowned, then shouted, "Bina! Bina! Come to the kitchen. I need your help."

Within seconds, an elderly woman wearing a white scarf to keep gray-streaked hair from her coffee-hued face appeared in the door, fanning her white apron as she approached Eva. "Well, well who do we have here?"

"This is Mrs. Phillips," Benton replied as he helped Eva into a chair, then waved a hand at the woman. "This is Bina, my house-keeper and cook," he told Eva, then asked, "Are you in pain?"

"No, not much," Eva said, offering the woman a weak smile before introducing herself.

"What you doin' out here, all alone, child?" Bina asked, scruti-nizing Eva's stained shoes and torn clothing. "You look awful beat down. What happened?"

"I was riding with Mr. Foster. On our way to Moncks Corner when a man robbed us. He shot at Zack, took off with the wagon. Left me stranded. I slept in the woods. I walked …"

"My goodness, let's see about that cut on your head," Bina inter-rupted. She removed a clean piece of cloth from a drawer, and after pulling a chair close to Eva, told Benton, "Hand me that pail of water so I can clean off all this blood and see how bad this is." Bina dipped the cloth into the water and began to gently wipe the blood off Eva's face.

While Bina cleaned and bandaged her wound, Eva finished telling Benton and Bina about her journey to South Carolina, and why she had been riding on the government supply wagon headed to Moncks Corner.

"Did you see the man's face?" Benton asked, squinting at Eva, his lips tight. "Was he a white man? Black? Would you recognize him if you saw him again?"

Eva shrugged, seemingly apologetic. "I saw his hands, his blue eyes. He was a white man," she began. "He was thin, but I couldn't see his face at all. He had a red bandanna over his nose and a big black hat on his head. He was dressed in a Confederate soldier's uniform."

"I hate to admit it but I am not surprised," Benton said, handing Eva a tin cup of water. "These kinds of things are getting to be real common. Travelling the roads can be dangerous nowadays, and the lack of law enforcement in the area encourages such thievery. You are lucky you got away with only a scratch on your head. But, I caution you, Miss Eva ... don't go 'round talking about what happened. Let it go. There are people who will not believe you and some folks might even take offense."

"Offense?" Eva was shocked by Benton's suggestion that she should keep quiet. "I was assaulted. A government wagon driver was robbed of his cargo! I must report this to the authorities."

Benton scratched his chin and shook his head. "That won't do you, or anybody living around here, any good. If you take this issue to Sheriff Cholett...you being from the North and all. Well, let me just say, he doesn't take to Northerners who start trouble."

"Start trouble? What do you mean?"

"Zack's been speakin' out. Supportin' the Republicans, telling everybody he meets that black men got the right to vote. That may be true, but he's been warned more'n once not to go around talking about votin', or nailin' signs to trees."

"I see," Eva murmured, grappling with the seriousness of the struggle that blacks were facing in the post-war South. They were in constant fear of being threatened or jailed for any number of reasons due to the presence of whites who refused to obey the new government's laws and who hated the Freedman's Bureau for assisting the newly freed slaves.

"Well," Benton went on. "It was just a load of government

159

supplies. Food that some hungry soul is going to be mighty glad to get."

"But the supplies are meant for the Freedmen, the destitute," Eva insisted.

"Who knows? Those supplies might just as well end up in the hands of folks who need them, but they'll get there by a different route."

"Oh, so stealing from the government is not a crime?"

"It's a crime all right, but as you'll soon find out, there're different kinds of crimes down here. Some bad, some we just have to tolerate ... if we want to avoid problems."

Realizing it would be useless to press her point, Eva clamped her lips shut and stopped talking.

After Bina had finished treating the cut on Eva's head, Benton told her to prepare a room for Eva to spend the night, and then he left the two women alone. Bina placed a bowl of broth and a chunk of cornbread in front of Eva, and agreeably answered all of Eva's questions about her host, Benton Langdon.

"He was a slave here on this property. Fair Oaks it's called. Belonged to the Jutland family for generations. Master Jutland got killed in the war. His widow packed up and left Fair Oaks the same day she got news her husband was dead. Just rode off in a wagon. Said she didn't want nothin' to do with South Carolina any more. Left Benton standing in the yard, alone. All the other slaves ran off real fast. You see, Benton said Widow Jutland had already told him the house was gonna be his 'cause he been so faithful while her husband was at war. So he stayed. It's a fine house, been through a lot, but it's got a roof and it's more'n enough for Benton. He lets out rooms to a couple of men who pay him a few coins for a room and a meal."

"Who else lives here?" Eva wanted to know.

"Oh, right now, there's Roby Green, a young man what works at the lumber mill. You won't see much of him. He stays down at the mill workers' camp most all week and just sleeps here at Fair Oaks when he get a day off. The other boarder is Oscar Singleton ... a real gentleman, he is. He's in charge of building us a Freedman's School in Cordesville. Right ambitious man, he is. Born and raised in Saint John's Berkeley. Went off to Charleston and studied. He's wantin' to be a part of the votin' to get in the state convention. I sure hope he gets elected ... but you know white folks ain't gonna let that happen."

"Zack was telling me about that."

"Oh, yes, we need some kind o' real government cause we shore can't let the Army be running everything forever."

"I understand what you mean."

"Yeah, I think Oscar would make a good representative. He's smart, fair-minded, and he knows everybody 'round these parts. He wants to get rid of old Pate Cholett. The sheriff. Cholett's been in charge of things 'round here too long. Turns a blind eye to all the hurt the freedmen be sufferin'."

"I look forward to meeting Oscar," Eva decided.

"You will, don't worry. Right now, you need to get some rest. Come on," Bina urged, taking Eva by the elbow to help her stand.

Following Bina, Eva passed through several empty rooms on the lower floor, all of them dim and dusty and littered with broken furniture. Cracked mirrors hung at crooked angles among once-grand portraits in splintered gilded frames that showcased the former owner's ancestors. She and Bina ascended a creaking staircase to the second floor and entered a spacious, adequately furnished room on the riverside section of the second floor landing.

"Got a bed, a dresser, a lamp, and a wash stand," Bina said. "A good view of the river, too. Benton put your trunk over there by the window. You go on. Lie down. Everything gonna be fine."

"Thank you," Eva told Bina, exhausted and grateful for the kindness of these strangers. After Bina left, Eva sat on the edge of the bed, unbuttoned her shoes, kicked them off, and was about to sink into the cornhusk mattress when there was a tap at the door.

"Come in," she called out.

Benton cracked the door wide enough to stick his head and shoulders into the room. "Everything all right?" he asked.

"Yes, thank you so much." Recalling what Bina had told her, and with no place to live, Eva decided to put her trust in Mr. Langdon. "I understand you take boarders. Would you be willing to rent me a room? I do need a safe place to stay as I make inquiries in the area."

"Of course, of course," Benton quickly agreed. "I'd be happy to have you here. "

"How much would it be? I don't know how long I'll be here."

"Would fifty cents a week be agreeable with you?"

"More than agreeable," Eva told him, overcome by a sense of relief as he retreated from the room.

Outside in the hallway, Benton pulled the door to Eva's room nearly closed, leaving it cracked open just enough for him to watch as she removed a tattered quilt from her satchel and spread it over the bed, then pulled a bundle of money from her corset and placed it under her pillow.

CHAPTER 17

After a restful night's sleep, Eva awoke feeling less anxious about her circumstances, but still concerned about Zack Foster's fate, especially after learning from Benton that such assaults had become fairly routine in the area. Where had Zack fled after running off into the woods? Did the stranger go after him? Hurt him? Eva replayed the incident over and over in her mind as she washed, dressed, and then went downstairs to find Bina.

Entering the kitchen, she greeted the elderly housekeeper, who was squatting in front of the fireplace, a black skillet in her hand.

Bina raised her head and glanced at Eva. "You look a might bit better this morning," she remarked, standing, tilting her head to the side as she assessed Eva. "You sit down now, have a bite to eat and a cup of tea," Bina urged, just as a slender man carrying a stack of papers entered the kitchen and introduced himself.

"Hello, Mrs. Phillips, I'm Oscar Singleton, Ma'am," he said, nodding respectfully. "Bina already told me all about you and your terrible ordeal. We're glad to have you here."

"Thank you. I appreciate Mr. Langdon's hospitality," Eva replied, taking in Oscar's scholarly appearance. He was wearing a rather severe black suit that was slightly too large, a clean white shirt, and a blue and yellow striped tie. The short black boots on his feet were scuffed, yet polished to a decent shine in spite of their worn appearance. His thick dark hair was parted in the middle and swept into two soft peaks on either side of his face, adding several inches to his modest height. The beads of perspiration on his dusky brown forehead quickly disappeared as he mopped his brow with a crumpled handkerchief.

"I understand you're involved in the construction of a new Freedman's School," Eva remarked.

"That's right." Still clutching his papers, Oscar sank into a chair opposite Eva and accepted the tin cup of water that Bina set before him. "It's gonna be one big room, 'bout two miles from here. Large enough to seat thirty students."

"A real school house...somethin' the chil'ren 'round here never had," Bina added. "Getting teachers gonna be the hard part."

"When will it be finished?" Eva wanted to know.

"I'm hoping, by the fall," Oscar said, setting down his stack of papers. "All depends on how long it takes to get the money for the lumber. Then I gotta wait for the men to bring the logs up here from the mill." Draining his cup of water, he cocked his head and told Eva, "I've got it all worked out, just need the money for materials to start building. You might like to come and see it when it's finished, Mrs. Phillips."

"Call me Eva, please."

"All right. Guess that's fine, seeing as how I'll be seeing you around here. But if you will please excuse me, I've got some studying to do on these building plans. I have to present them to Captain Liedtke's land manager for approval before week's end."

"Captain Liedtke? At the Freedman's Bureau?" she inquired, alerted by his mention of the captain's name.

"That's right," Oscar confirmed, straightening his papers, tapping them into a neat stack.

"Might I ride along with you when you go to see the captain?" Eva asked, going on to tell Oscar why she wanted to speak to him.

"Why, of course," Oscar said, seeming impressed with her tale.

"I'll let you know as soon as I'm prepared to make the trip. Let's see, today is Wednesday. Friday, perhaps? Is that acceptable with you?"

"Perfect," Eva answered, relieved to be moving one step closer to meeting the captain who, hopefully, would have some record of Mayree.

On Friday morning, during their ride to the Freedman's Bureau, Eva told Oscar more about her childhood escape from Stillwater.

"I understand your desire to locate your mother, but right now … well it might not be the best time for you to be traveling around these parts alone, asking questions," he calmly observed.

"Too late. I'm here now, and I plan to talk to as many people as I can and visit any place where she might be."

"Yes, yes, but Miss Eva. You must be careful. Going up to the Cantrell place? I don't know about that. Stillwater plantation has been abandoned for years. Not much there but a burned-out house and some old slave cabins that are falling down. I strongly advise you not to go up there."

The Freedman's Bureau at Moncks Corner was located in a well-preserved barn on a large cotton plantation. The first thing Eva noticed when Oscar pulled his wagon onto the property was the crowd of ex-slaves; there were men, women, and children, along with quite a few whites, milling around the yard.

"All of them are waiting for whatever they can get today," Oscar remarked as he helped Eva down from the wagon.

Leaving him to find the appropriate soldier to approve his building plans, Eva crossed the yard and took her place among the people standing in line outside the main building. She was immediately struck by the destitute conditions of the newly freed slaves. Many of them were wearing threadbare rags, torn pieces of cloth that barely covered their bodies. It was clear that many were desperately in need of food and medical attention. She listened as they spoke among themselves. Some were worried about securing transportation to find a family member, others sought someone literate enough to scribble a note to pass along as they tried to find their relatives. Most were hungry, confused, and homeless; they were living in tents or shanties thrown up on the roads.

The freedmen eyed Eva with curiosity. They could see that she was Negro, but she was clean, dressed in nice clothing, appeared healthy, and did not look as if she had ever lived on a plantation. Several of the women in line murmured under their breath and pointed at Eva until an elderly woman with a dour set to her mouth stepped forward to ask Eva where she was from and why she was in St. John's Berkeley.

Eager to answer, Eva told the woman that she had been born on Stillwater, the Cantrell family's plantation, and she was searching for her mother, a slave named Mayree.

The mention of the name Cantrell brought a groan of disgust and a gasp of horror. The woman shook her head and looked at Eva in despair. "I heered a bunch of Cantrell slaves was sold off when Massa Joseph fell sick. After that, the missus let it all go to ruin. She passed away 'bout the time the war ended. Folks say she drank too much laudanum and just went to sleep and never woke up. Freedom scattered them slaves all over. I doubts you could even find ya ma now."

Before Eva could speak, the woman simply walked away and joined a man who emerged from the building carrying a burlap sack. She watched as the couple peered into the bag, nodded, and then started off down the road.

Soon after, a man in a uniform stepped onto the porch and spoke in an animated way with a young soldier who looked to be no more than fifteen. Eva asked a lady standing in line who the older uniformed man was, and learned that he was Captain Liedtke, the commander of the district at the Moncks Corner Freedman's Bureau.

The captain approached the crowd of people milling around outside the bureau and lifted his hand to get their attention.

"I have just learned that the delivery from Charleston did not arrive last night, nor has it been located this morning. Therefore, we have no rations of bacon, corn, or grain today. If you need blankets or shoes, I still have some." Then Captain Liedtke turned around and strode back inside the building as the people, some of whom were visibly upset, began to grumble and drift away.

Eva wasted no time catching up with the captain. She hurried up the steps, entered the building, and immediately introduced herself to him, and despite Benton's warning to keep quiet about the robbery, she told Captain Liedtke what she had witnessed when the wagon was stolen.

"Can you describe the man who took it?" Captain Liedtke asked.

"A tall white man. Rather slim. Blond hair, kind of long. He hid his face beneath a kerchief, but I did see his eyes. Pale blue and very mean. He walked with a sort of limp, favoring his right leg. And he kept saying that the freedmen don't deserve supplies when white people are suffering as well."

"Hum…" Captain Liedtke murmured, as if he'd heard such talk before. "Tell me all that you can, Mrs. Phillips. This is the third wagon we've lost to bandits this month. And last week, the passengers on a train arriving from Atlanta were stripped of all their valuables. The government must find out who is behind this thievery!"

Quickly, Eva went on to provide as many details as she could recall about the encounter while the captain took notes. "I'll file my report with the Army," he told her. "However, I urge you to tell Sheriff Cholett what you witnessed."

"Sheriff Cholett?" Eva repeated, having heard Bina mention the name but having no idea where to find him.

"Pate Cholett …the sheriff of Charleston County. You see, the Army is working with local law enforcement to keep the peace. The robbery occurred on the road just outside the city … within the sheriff's jurisdiction. You go see Cholett and make a report so he can launch an investigation as well."

"I will do that," she promised, and then added, "Where do I find him?"

"In Charleston. On Magazine Street," he told her rather brusquely, as if she ought to know where the sheriff's office was.

"Oh, yes," she remarked. "You see, I'm new to the area, Captain. I've just arrived from Boston."

"I thought as much from the way you speak. Boston?" He scrunched his lips in thought. "So, what are you doing here in Saint John's Berkeley?"

"Looking for someone," she said, filling him in on her search for Mayree.

Captain Liedtke went to his desk, perused the pages of a large ledger, and then shook his head. "Unfortunately, I have no record of any Stillwater slaves having come to this Bureau for assistance."

"Nothing?" Eva queried, deflation flattening her voice.

"No, but new freedmen register here every day. We are keeping very precise records related to our assistance. You check back with me again. Also, try the Freedman's Bureau Hospital. Over toward Whitesville. Not so far from here. She might be there."

"I will," Eva promised, thanking the captain as she exited the building and went to sit in the shade of a sprawling oak tree to wait for Oscar to come for her.

Eva had not been seated for more than a few minutes when a woman approached Eva and handed her a scrap of paper and a stub of charcoal.

"I heard you talkin'... I 'spect you can write?" the woman inquired, her eyes lowered sheepishly, a hand over her lips.

"Yes, I can write, and read," Eva told her.

"Can you write me a note ta pass ta a man goin' to Kingstree? I'm hoping he can help me find ma daughter."

"Of course," Eva said without hesitation, realizing she was far from alone in her search for a loved one.

Eva quickly penned the note, and as soon as she finished it, another former slave asked her to help him draft a claim against his former master over a mule that was stolen from him. Again, unable to refuse, she complied, and by the time Oscar arrived to take her back to Benton's house, she had spent several hours writing notes and helping freedmen file claim for benefits from the government. When she told Oscar about Captain Liedtke's suggestion that she visit the Freedman's Hospital, he quickly agreed to take her there.

The sun was setting when Eva and Oscar left the Freedman's Hospital and started down the road back to Benton's house. She'd had no luck at the hospital, either. The doctor in charge of the small, but adequately equipped medical facility housed in a log cabin, reviewed all of his records but did not find Mayree's name among those he had treated.

As they made their way down the road, Eva told Oscar more about her discussion with Captain Liedtke.

"He's right to say you ought to go to Charleston and talk to Sheriff Cholett, but I doubt it would do any good."

"Why do you say that?"

"Because Pate Cholett has never done anything good for the freedmen. He kinda turns a blind eye on anything that hurts us, but he helps *his* people whenever he can. That's why I'm running for a spot as a convention delegate. I might not win, but if I do, I plan to make folks 'round here see him for who he really is. I wish I could go to the city with you when you talk to the sheriff but I have to leave in the morning for Columbia."

"Oh? You're going to the state capital? How long will you be gone?"

"Don't know for sure. Taking the train. Gotta be there on the first day of June the letter said, if I want to speak with the Freedman School's district supervisor about my plans. While I'm away, feel free to use my buckboard, please."

"That is very generous of you," Eva said. "I appreciate your offer."

"I'm happy to assist. No sense in the wagon just sitting around while I'm gone. But you better handle this old mule carefully. At times he can be quite ornery," Oscar remarked.

With a chuckle Eva said, "I've handled a few cantankerous horses in my time. I think we'll get along fine."

"Good. I'll leave you the wagon. Benton can take me to the train station."

"That would be very helpful. Thank, you," she replied, looking forward to getting around on her own.

The setting sun was streaking the sky orange and blue by the time Eva and Oscar arrived back at Fair Oaks. While he took care of the mule, she went to sit on the weathered veranda with Bina, who was shelling peas harvested from her struggling kitchen garden.

"Is Mr. Langdon around?" Eva inquired of Bina while taking a seat in the wicker chair beside her.

Bina split another pea pod with her thumb before she replied. "No, he's been gone all day. Where he slips off to, I never know." She set the bowl aside and wiped her hands on her apron. "How did your talk with the captain go? Any good news?"

"Unfortunately, no," Eva replied, going on to describe her meeting with Captain Liedtke. She also told Bina what the old woman had told her about Stillwater. "She said a lot of the Cantrell slaves were sold off before the war, when Joseph Cantrell fell ill."

"Probably right. I heard the old man died of lung fever some time back."

"So, there is nothing left for me to do but go there. I have a map that my aunt, who was a slave on a nearby plantation, helped me draw. I think I can find Stillwater. Maybe if I went there…"

"Oh, I guess you might find some folks who could tell you somethin'," Bina murmured.

"I'm sure a lot has changed since my aunt left. It's been more than twenty years, but…" her words drifted off as she considered the possibility that her map might not be as useful as she'd hoped.

"Honey, I done lived in Saint John's Berkeley all my life. Not much changes 'round here," Bina stated. "Stuff gets all tore up or it rots away and falls apart, but things don't really change."

Eva considered Bina's observation, having seen wasted farmland and crumbling brick buildings alongside stately manor houses and marshy swamps that looked as if they had not changed for centuries. "Well, I'm thinking of going to Stillwater tomorrow."

Bina grimaced, a worried look on her face. "All right. I know I can't stop you. Let me see that map of yours."

Eva hurried to her room and returned with the drawing she had made from Tully's remembrance.

Hunching over the map, Bina traced the lines on the paper with her index finger, nodding in approval. "Looks 'bout right. The Cantrell place would be right here," she said, pointing at the spot where the Santee and the Cooper Rivers came together.

"That's where my aunt says she met my mother," Eva added.

"Well, it's a bit of a ride," Bina said. "Yep…right 'round the old Santee Canal. Just one little country road leads into that property… if it ain't overtaken by wild vines by now. Stillwater was always closed off from strangers. A slave-breeding hellhole it was, sittin' all by itself way out in the country. The slaves called it Hell on Earth. Joseph Cantrell was a mean, angry man. The Yankees burned his house and he never got over it. Hope ain't nothing much left of that devil's den by now."

"But I still have to see it for myself," Eva said firmly as she folded her map and bid Bina goodnight, then made her way up the stairs to her room.

The next morning, Eva was in the kitchen when Benton walked through the rear door of the house and acknowledged her with a nod. "Good mornin', Mrs. Phillips," he said.

"Good morning, Mr. Langdon."

"I just put Oscar on the train to Columbia. He told me you spoke to Captain Liedtke about what happened with Zack."

"Yes, I did. And I hope to speak with the sheriff as soon as I can get back to Charleston."

Without commenting, Benton took up the pot of coffee and poured a generous amount into a chipped china cup. "No need," he told her, his tone flat and decisive.

"No need? But I promised Captain Liedtke …"

"I already spoke to Sheriff Cholett 'bout the robbery," Benton calmly interrupted.

"You saw him?"

"Yes. At the train station this morning. He was dealing with some vagrants who've been riding the rails on government runs."

"What did he say?"

"Oh, he'll be investigating, for sure." Benton looked directly into Eva's eyes as he told her, "He was real glad to hear what I had to say, and he promised to get to the bottom of it. Government wagons getting stolen can't continue."

"But…" Eva stammered, slightly puzzled. "Doesn't the sheriff want to talk to *me*? I was there, I saw the man. Maybe I ought to go to the station and see if …"

"Cholett's already on his way back to Charleston by now. Don't worry. I told him *everything* you told me. Spared you the upset of talking to the law."

Relieved that she would not have to face the sheriff, yet slightly annoyed that Benton had assumed a responsibility that was definitely hers, Eva excused herself and, wrapping her shawl around her shoulders, walked outside, crossed the veranda, and stood in the overgrown garden while pondering her next step.

CHAPTER 18

The sound of rain hitting the windows awakened Eva, as it had for the past three days. Lying beneath her torn quilt in the center of the narrow iron bed, she turned her face toward the floor-to-ceiling window that was framed with the remnants of what once had been fine yellow satin draperies. She frowned at the ominous gray sky, mentally cursing the unceasing thunderstorm that had ushered in the fourth day of June as another gloomy day to keep her captive inside Benton Langdon's house. An angry flash of lightning cut through the murky skyline, followed by a deep roar of thunder that sent a coil of disappointment through Eva, making her groan and close her eyes.

She had slept badly, turning from side to side as images of the men and women she'd seen at the Freedman's Bureau flashed into her mind. So many desperate people. So much loss and destruction. Yet, she sensed their hope, coupled with fear, as they struggled to patch together some kind of a life in the aftermath of war. And here she was among them, undertaking her own journey to piece together the remnants of her past. She had been in South Carolina for nearly two weeks, and still had no clue to the fate of her mother. Worried, she opened her eyes and gazed at the droplets of rain sliding down the panes of glass, slipping and dissolving into the sodden earth, as if erasing all traces of Mayree. Giving herself a mental shake, Eva sat up, determined not to sink into a state of despair, resolved to remain optimistic.

"Well, I have letters to write and stockings to mend," she muttered, resigned to the fates of nature as she went to the washstand and poured water in the bowl.

For three more gloomy days, Eva remained confined in the house, growing increasingly anxious about delaying her journey to Stillwater. The swollen Cooper River spilled over its banks and flooded the land surrounding the house, making prisoners of those trapped inside. For the most part, Benton remained closeted in his room, doing what, she did not know. With Oscar still away and only Bina to talk to, Eva welcomed the talkative woman's ramblings about her life in Saint John's Berkeley.

When the epic storm finally weakened and moved on to pummel cities along the eastern shore, it left behind a sun-filled sky that lifted Eva's spirits and solidified her determination to get out on the road and on with her journey.

After stepping into Chester's old trousers, Eva pulled on a loose shirtwaist dress that covered the masculine attire. She stuck her feet into sturdy walking boots and placed a battered straw hat that Bina loaned her on her head. Feeling prepared for whatever conditions she might encounter, Eva packed a lunch of apples and nuts, stuck her map into her straw bag, and climbed into Oscar's buckboard, not at all confident that she would be able to manage his stubborn mule. With a wave to Bina, Eva started off, heading toward the road that ran parallel to the river, sloughing her way through the soggy muck that had turned the area into a sea of rust-red mud.

The going was slow but the air was vibrantly clean and clear, and the warmth of the sun healed her frustrations. Along the route, she encountered streams of people, both black and white, on foot, on mules, on oxen and even a few on horseback. Everyone was heading in different directions. Their rickety big-wheeled wagons and tiny handcrafted carts sinking into the muddy roads. Some of the passersby nodded at Eva in greeting, while others paid her no attention at all, moving on without shifting their eyes from whatever destinations were fixed in their minds. Fires burned along the roads where refugees living in crudely constructed shacks and government-provided tents cooked their meager meals. Half-naked children splashed in puddles of muddy rainwater, their innocent laughter rising in sharp contrast to the shockingly visible absence of any essentials of comfort.

When Eva came across a young mother carrying two small children with a third tied to her apron beside her, she stopped and offered the woman a ride, which was gratefully accepted. Once settled beside Eva, the young woman broke into tears of gratitude and despair, telling Eva that she was on her way to the Freedman's Hospital in hopes that the doctor would be able to heal the infected wounds on her youngest child's legs. The young mother was talkative, bright, and once she had calmed down, began to ask Eva questions about her presence in the area. After listening to Eva's story, the girl promised to make inquiries about Mayree wherever she went. The two women chatted easily for the next hour, until Eva came to the crossroads where the young mother told her to stop. It was time to depart. Eva was a bit reluctant to see her go. The company and the conversation had been a comfort, making Eva feel less like a stranger and more akin to those who were reeling from the after-effects of war.

The crowds along the road thinned as Eva drove the wagon farther to the north where she entered a dense overhang of ancient live oaks that created a tunnel of vibrant green. The air was heavy with water from the recent storm. The nearby swamps were filled to capacity, and the buzz of mosquitoes was as vicious as their sting.

Arriving at a languid creek where waterfowl rested, Eva consulted her map, got her bearings, and turned to the west, crossing over what she decided must be the old Santee Canal. The overgrown path running along the canal was narrow and flush with thorny bushes that whipped the sides of the wagon and angered the testy mule. Pressing on, she travelled the dense pathway for more than hour until the cantankerous mule stopped in front of a tall split rail fence that separated the forested trail from what appeared to be plantation grounds. A painted sign, hanging askew from a rusty nail read, Stillwater Plantation Keep Out.

Peering through the fence, Eva saw abandoned fields thick with shaggy weeds and heavy vines. All of the deserted acreage was surrounded by high wooden fencing that had mostly rotted away.

With great effort, Eva managed to lift the heavy iron bar securing the gate and urged the mule through the rough splintered fence, praying the large wagon wheels would not get stuck in the marshy land. Once she was through the gate, she continued across the near-barren field to a spot where the river, once again, curved close to the land and created a protected spot beneath a stand of tall pine trees at the water's edge. The sight made Eva's heart beat faster. She yanked on the reins, pulled the mule to a stop beneath a gnarled oak tree veiled in low hanging Spanish moss. The gray tendrils floated down from the tree limbs like pieces of silver lace as the wind off the river vibrated the air around her.

I remember this place, she cautiously thought. *The last time I stood on this land I was four years old,* Eva recalled, stepping up to the river's edge to look as far down river as she could. *This is where my mother sang to me, where she gave me to Aunt Tully, where she let a stranger take me away.* Drawing in a calming breath, Eva lifted her face to the sky and let the water-laden breeze swirl across her face, absorbing the memories of that painful time. Standing quietly, she took solace in the fact that at last, she was on the land where she was born.

Once her emotions had settled enough to continue, and the mule's thirst had been sated, Eva moved on, scanning the landscape with interest. In the distance stood a shell of a house, its once-sturdy walls broken and burned, the land around it strewn with debris. The mansion lay in skeletal ruin, depleted and unimportant in the white-hot glare of a scorching rebel sun.

That was my mother's master's house, she mused, a jolt of longing heightening her emotions. It was a house that Eva barely remembered, though she knew it in a vague, foreboding way. Her long-buried memories of entering the back door with her mother, of trying hard to stay out of the mistress's way, of never feeling welcome, came back to her in a rush. She wished she could have returned sooner, wished her mother would walk right up to her now and put her arms around her. But none of that was possible.

Eva thought about all the ghosts that rested among the shadows of the place where she once lived. *So many lifetimes ago*, she sighed, her memories collapsing into that deep, quiet place where she always hoped to see her mother's face and hear the sound of her voice when she sang the "Don't Cry" song.

Eva stepped over a crumbling garden wall and headed toward what had once been the rear entrance to the big house. Now, the door was nothing more than a vine-tangled slab of wood blanketed in wire-tough foliage. Gingerly, she stepped inside to find nothing but waste and ruin. The charred walls and broken bricks held no trace of the lives that had once resided in the house, which was now occupied by a covey of black birds that squawked and pecked at the insects and rodents that had taken up residence in the once-grand mansion. The sight was shocking and discouraging. A casualty of war. With the big house reduced to nothing more than a charred pile of rubble, what clues could possibly remain about the slaves who once served the master of the house?

Turning away, Eva scanned the acreage behind the house where a constricted footpath ran between two rows of ramshackle log cabins, some of them barely standing. Overcome with nervous anticipation, she headed toward the old slave quarters, drawn to the third cabin on the right in the middle of the row. She could almost hear the voices of those who once lived there, smell the wood smoke that rose from their cooking fires, feel their sadness fueled by anger, and see their ghost-like images passing by. When she stopped in front of the cabin, she was certain she had once shared with her mother, her heart turned over in longing.

There was no door. The roof was still intact and the weathered stoop looked as if it would support her. Carefully, Eva stepped up onto the creaky step, then into the entrance and peered into the dark interior. The dirt floor was surprisingly clean and the single window was covered with a piece of white gauze netting. She was about to move deeper into the cabin when she saw something move in the corner. Thinking a raccoon or a possum might have taken up residence, she stepped back, but stopped in her tracks when a voice called out, "What you looking for? Ain't nothing here."

With a gasp, Eva fled outside and remained on the path, standing with a hand to her mouth, her heart pounding. Slowly, an elderly man emerged from the cabin's shadowy interior. He was holding a crudely fashioned cane in one hand as he presented her with a toothless grin.

"Don't be scared," he cautioned, remaining in the doorway. "Ain't nothin' ta be scared 'bout now. Everybody done gone. Nobody 'round here no more. 'Cept me." His grin broadened as he stared at Eva.

"I'm.... I'm not scared. Surprised ... yes, very surprised," Eva stammered, assessing the gray-bearded man who was dressed in a patched long jacket and pants cut off at the knees. His clothing was mud-stained and rumpled, as if he'd worn the same suit of clothes since the first day of freedom. A shocking bush of fuzzy gray hair surrounded his nut-brown face like the frame of a portrait protecting its image.

"So, how'd you come ta find youself here?" he asked, stepping over the stoop with the aid of his cane. With care, he moved close enough for Eva to look directly into his cloudy, aging eyes.

"Well, that's a long story," Eva replied, relaxing a bit. "I *think* I was born in that cabin ... or perhaps ... I lived there at least." The realization that she might have finally encountered someone who could help her brought on a sudden sense of calm. The man wasn't angry or hostile, or even resentful of her arrival. In fact, he seemed pleased about her unexpected intrusion.

"Well, *I* was born here," he told Eva, walking surprisingly fast as he moved past her, his cane tapping the ground with each step. When Eva did not follow, he turned around and narrowed his eyes. "You comin'?" he said, more as a command than an inquiry. "I 'spect you got some questions you want answered."

"Yes, yes, I do," Eva quickly agreed, falling in step beside him as they made their way around the back of the cabins toward a long wooden bench beneath the shady drape of a weeping willow tree. He sat down at one end of the bench, tugged his tattered jacket by the lapels, and pointed with his cane at the opposite end of the bench.

"Sit down. I'm Luke, and I got plenty of time," he told Eva. He cocked his head to the side, both eyes wide open now. "You can tell me all about it ... if you want to, that is."

Eva sat and shared her lunch of apples and nuts with Luke as she told him her story. While patiently listening, he nodded in understanding from time to time, frequently tapping his cane on the grass when she said something that seemed to stir him.

"Your aunt told the truth. Was hard times here at Stillwater." He waved his walking stick back toward the double rows of cabins. "Everybody gone but me. Didn't have no place to go, and with all these empty cabins, I just stayed on. Ain't so bad, living here. I make out all right."

"Did you know my mother?" Eva cautiously ventured.

"Oh, yes... Mayree was one o' Massa Cantrell's favorites. A gal with spirit, I recall."

Eva froze, her heart pounding. She bit her lip, nearly breaking the skin, afraid to make a sound, afraid to interrupt this man who had known Mayree. She had to let him tell his tale in his own way before she bombarded him with the questions that burned on her tongue. "Tell me about her," she urged.

"She weren't a loud gal... had a quiet way 'bout her, but she was strong. I 'member once when Massa got on her 'bout pilin' her hair all high on her head like a twisted crown. He tole her she better cover it up 'fore he cut it all off. She just stared him down and tole him, 'Don't much belong to me but my hair and I gonna do with it as I please.'." Luke cackled with glee at the memory. "That got her a hard smack across the lips, but Massa left her alone after that. She kept that hair piled up like she wanted. Mayree was a good breeder, you see. I think that's why Massa stepped back from real punishment. She was a beauty, that's for sure."

"Did my mother suffer greatly because she sent me away?"

Luke raised his boney shoulders almost to his ears. "When Massa learnt you was missing, Mayree tole him you fell in the river and drowned. He weren't too happy 'bout that, so he whipped ya momma pretty bad, then he tole Ole Stump ... what we called the overseer... to make her lay down with the men a heap more after that." Luke's grimace contorted his deeply wrinkled cheeks. "'Course we all knew she handed you over to that free lady goin' to the North. Keepin' that secret from Massa made all us feel good."

Eva absorbed Luke's words as if she were drinking water to quench a long-standing thirst. To think that her escape from Stillwater had brought a glimmer of joy to others was humbling. Though hesitant to ask, she was eager to learn all that Luke could provide, and so she asked him, "Did my mother have more children after ... after I was gone?"

"Ah, yes. She bore lots more babes for Massa Cantrell. He sold 'em all," Luke said, his voice fading to a whisper, as if speaking too loudly about those old memories might bring them back to life. "You see them two rows o' cabin? That's where we slaves all lived. The men on one side of the road, the wimmen on the other. The wimmen was two to a cabin. The men, well sometimes might be as many as eight or nine of us all crowded up together. Ole Stump forced the wimmen to lay down with the men. Two times a month, at full moon and half-moon, in their cabins. The wimmen suffered something awful. Mated as soon as they were childbearing age, and 'spected to produce a babe every year or so. Iffin she didn't, she be sold."

"How awful," was all Eva dared manage, her eyes tearing, her heart breaking to think of the callous, inhumane treatment her mother and all the women at Stillwater must have suffered.

"Yep. Much as it hurts me to say it, I was here. I was part of it all. Guess I'm papa to more babes than a man ought to claim. But we men … we tried to make it easy on the wimmen 'cause they was the ones who had to carry the chillen then let 'em go when Massa Cantrell took 'em to Charleston and put 'em on the block." Luke stopped talking and sucked in a long breath, his quivering hand at his bearded chin. "You be glad your mamma sent you North. This wasn't no place for a pretty chile like you."

Sensing he had more to say, Eva quietly asked, "Do you know what happened to my mother? Is she alive?"

With a solemn nod, Luke licked his lips and said, "Oh, I reckon she be alive. On freedom day, she walked right out that cabin and started down the road to Charleston. Don't know where she ended up or where she might be now, but I remember she had that hair of hers all twisted up on top of her head like a crown last time I saw her." He smiled again, a much broader one this time. "Don't you stop lookin' for her. Mayree strong. She be out there livin' free somewhere."

CHAPTER 19

On her way back to Fair Oaks, Eva kept repeating Luke's words in her head: *She be out there somewhere living free.* How desperately Eva wished that were true, that she would find Mayree safe, and well, and eager to reunite with her daughter. The trip to Stillwater had been fruitful; at least she now knew her mother was most likely alive, and this made Eva more hopeful and determined than ever to track Mayree down.

The need to stop by a stream to water the mule broke Eva's thoughts about all that Luke had revealed. While standing at the water's edge, she heard a noise that made her freeze. Remaining quiet, she listened closely to identify the sound. It was a mix of muffled voices and low grunts that seemed to be coming from behind a cluster of slender trees downstream. When the tone of the voices suddenly grew harsher and more insistent, it seemed clear that two men were engaged in a disagreement of some kind. The realization caused Eva to become alarmed. Leaving the mule to drink, she crept back toward the wagon, but stopped in her tracks when a terrifying scream cut through the muggy air like an axe striking a log. Moving quickly, she slipped behind the buckboard and trained her eyes on the shadowy forest as two white men emerged and came into view. They were dragging a black man who was shouting for them to let him go.

"I'm a take you to the island if you don't stop all that politicking," a stocky red-haired man threatened. "You better not show your face in town come election day, you hear?" He struck the victim hard, then kicked him in the stomach.

The other man, who was stout and swarthy with a blue rag tied over his nose and mouth, raised a thick piece of wood and struck the black man on the top of his head several times.

Shocked into silence, Eva pressed her lips together to stifle her own screams as the red-haired man beat the victim with a wooden club until his shouts subsided into a whimpering moan for reprieve. After shoving the beaten man into the brush, the assailants ran off.

Eva waited until she was certain the men were long gone, and then crept from behind the buckboard and hurried to check on the injured man.

"Let me help you," she urged, slipping an arm around the bleeding man's shoulders.

With a great deal of difficulty, she managed to get him up and into the back of the wagon.

"They grabbed me right out my house," he mumbled. "Pushed me to the ground. Tied me up. Brung me out here in the woods."

"How awful!" Eva uttered in a voice tight with disgust. "What's your name?" she asked in a much softer tone.

"Little John," he replied, then added, "my pappy called Big John, so I just Little John to all my kin."

"Little John, do you know the men who beat you?"

"The red-headed one … that be Hatch Ambrose. He in with them men terrorizin' the black folks all 'round here. They behind all this mess, threatening black men who talk about showin' up come Election Day. The other man with Hatch … I never seen him before."

Distressed, Eva handed Little John a rag to wipe the blood off his head, then asked him where she should take him.

"I live 'bout a mile up the creek, Miss. I sure do thank you for this help. Jus hope this don't get you in trouble."

"Don't worry about me," she told him. "I can't leave you here, hurt as you are. Are you sure you don't want me to take you to the Freedman's hospital?"

"Oh, naw," Little John was fast to reject. "I been beat worse'n this many a time. I be all right."

Eva slapped the reins hard against the mule's back and the buck-board lurched back onto the road. "How long have these kind of things been going on?" she wanted to know.

"Ever since the Black Codes started."

"Black Codes?" she questioned.

"Laws that them rebel men are usin' against us who used to be slaves. Black people got no power. No way to fight these punish-ment laws. Even though there's more blacks than whites in this county, we can't stop 'em. They gonna do all they can to keep us from livin' like we really free."

"Can't the government help protect you?"

"How? We gotta work or be arrested. Can't go to court against a white man. Ain't nothing much changed from slavery times. We still be put in jail for talking back or if we not in the house by dark."

"What did the man called Hatch mean about taking you to "the island"?

"Oh, there's talk 'bout ghosts livin' in the old prison out there in the harbor. But ain't nothing there. Just talk to make us scared."

At the crossroads, Eva stopped to let Little John get out. But before he walked away, he looked up at her and said, "Best not tell anyone 'bout what you saw or what you did for me. Mighty grate-ful, Ma'am, but I'm fearful for you getting hurt."

Then he disappeared like a ghostly shadow limping down the road.

～

The stench of rotted straw, horseflesh, and manure seeped from the rough-hewn walls of the old brick building and permeated the air inside in spite of a gaping hole in the roof. The stifling heat and the nearly insufferable atmosphere were due, most likely, to the fact that the embrasures that had once allowed for the firing of cannons were now securely bricked over and sealed shut. The horseshoe-shaped structure, located on the southern tip of Shute's Folly in Charleston Harbor was referred to as Pinckney Castle, an imposing structure that had once been fitted with two tiers of guns, a good magazine, and enough quarters to hold two-hundred Confederate officers and enlisted men. Having served as a prison for captured Union soldiers during the war, it had emerged partially intact from the conflict, but was quickly abandoned by the Confederates upon their defeat, leaving the place to rot and decay.

Leon Turner bolted the Castle's door with a heavy piece of lumber, then sat down on an overturned barrel marked *Property of US Government.* Turning his head to the side, he scrunched his lips into a pucker and spat a dark brown stream of tobacco juice onto the matted straw on the floor. His stoic expression conveyed the seriousness of his remark when he told the two men seated on similar barrels in front of him, "We gotta do a better job of rooting out the troublemakers. Make 'em understand we mean business."

"Well, Little John, for one, won't be posting any more of those damned handbills like Zack Foster was handing out," said a man with flaming red hair and a thick red mustache that nearly covered his large white teeth.

"You shoulda dragged Little John's black ass to the castle, Hatch," Leon grumbled. "Leavin' him behind like that ain't good." Leon tugged his Confederate soldier's cap lower onto his forehead and tilted his slim body forward, as if to make sure he had Hatch's attention.

"Vern said he heard somebody in the woods, so we got outta there, fast," Hatch hedged.

"That's right," Vern Thompson, a lanky young man who had

served in the Army with Leon and Hatch, agreed. "I heard a wagon pull off the road, real close. I smacked Little John a few more times, give him a real hard lick, then we ran 'fore somebody saw us."

"Don't matter," Hatch injected. "Little John ain't the problem, it's that smart-ass school teacher we gotta get."

"That's for sure," Leon agreed, rewarding his war buddy and longtime friend with a nod. After pulling his grape shot revolver from the holster at his waist, he took a rag from the pocket of his gray army pants. Leisurely wiping the weapon he had carried into battle and used many times, he told Hatch, "Ain't no way Single-ton's gonna be building that school for those nigger kids when there's white kids don't have a school. Them damn darkies can't learn nothin' noway. It's a big waste of government money. I fought against 'em gettin' freed, and I'll keep on fightin' 'em as long as I breathe. The damn darkies cost me lot," he complained, tapping his injured leg. "I'm not gonna rest til I make 'em pay for what I lost."

"Right," quipped Vern, yanking a blue kerchief from around his neck. "Times might be changin', but that don't mean we gotta accept them changes."

"Damn carpetbaggers buying up our land," Hatch added with a snarl. "That Yankee, Hartwell.... busy trying to be a big shot... bought fifty acres of rice fields that used to belong to my momma's people. Now a Yankee owns what was mine? Ain't right. Yankee Republicans and Nigger Republicans takin' over like that."

"That's so hellfire wrong," Leon agreed, his anger rising with a snap. "But we can't stop trying to get ahold of money and food to keep white families from starving. Robbing trains and government wagons is getting' risky. And ole Langdon don't hardly pay enough for the trinkets I snatch off the ladies and take to him for sale."

"We're not stoppin'," Vern assured Leon. "It'll all work out fine if the whites stick together."

"True," Leon agreed with a shake of his head, as if to clear away the troubling subject. "But right now," he added, holding Hatch's attention with a challenging expression, "we gotta deal with the problem we got here."

Hatch swiveled his chin from side to side, considering Leon's remark, then muttered, "You're right. Don't worry. I know what to do."

The man listening to the voices coming from the front of the crescent-shaped bastion shuddered in despair. Their hate-filled words floated toward him on a wave of troubled air. And yet, he licked his parched lips and swallowed hard, anticipating his captor's arrival. He was desperate for a sip of water, just enough to keep his tongue from sticking to the sides of his mouth. He scooted across the filthy floor of his prison cell and pressed his back against the iron bars that separated him from the freedom he had fought for, from the freedom he deserved. How awful it was to look forward to the visits of the rebel soldiers who hated him so fervently, but he was hungry, thirsty, and willing to smile at the red-haired man, as he knew he had to do, in order to get relief.

With a soft thud, he braced his head against the cell's iron bars and let himself go limp, allowing a wave of despair to flood his soul. He had been imprisoned at the castle for nearly four years, had come to know, and fear, the three men who held him captive. He stared at a cluster of jagged scratches on the crumbling brick wall where he had foolishly begun marking the days of his captivity. Early on, he had been naively hopeful that liberating soldiers of the United States Army would arrive to rescue him and his fellow prisoners. But after scratching the wall with two-hundred marks, he'd stopped, resigning himself to the unknown.

The charge on Battery Wagner had been a fast, furious descent into hell, impossible to forget, and it lingered in his mind like the aftermath of a horrifying dream. When he fell wounded, he had closed his eyes while lying in the sand, bleeding on the beach, certain he would never see daylight again. But he did, only to discover that his wound had been bandaged, his rifle was gone, and chains had been fastened around his hands and feet.

Now, with a stifled moan, he shifted his gaze up the moldy-green walls to the brick-covered casements that had been converted into three tiers of bunks to serve as sleeping quarters for him and his two cellmates. There had been five of them at first: five colored Union infantrymen all from the 54th, each one pulled from their sandy grave and brought to Castle Pinckney. Within the first thirty days of captivity, Stephen and Willie died, leaving only Pickens, Scooter, and himself to linger in the putrid cell.

So far, his health was holding up despite the rat bites on his legs and an infestation of head lice that he could not shake. Twice a year, during their time of imprisonment, the man named Vern shaved their heads and beards and doused them with a foul smelling concoction that provided temporary relief from the ravishes of filth. However, Scooter was growing weaker by the day, and had become so thin and crippled he was barely able to care for himself. Pickens was plagued with a nasty cough that rattled his chest, made him spew blood, and often left him in a near-unconscious state.

We will be freed, Chester Phillips mentally chanted, his optimism arising from some unknown source that greeted him like an unbidden guest he felt compelled to welcome. *Someone will find us. But how? When?* he worried for the thousandth time. *How much longer can we endure this torture?*

A faint image of Eva flitted through Chester's mind, making his heart turn over in pain. How he missed her soft voice, her gentle touch, and the love they had shared so briefly. *At least she is far away from this madness, safe in Boston where she can live the life she deserves,* he repeatedly assured himself. However, as much as he hoped his beautiful bride had moved on with her life without him, a bitter seed of resentment took hold at the thought of some other man winning her heart.

PART IV

... But we vex our own with look and tone
We may never take back again.

Margaret E. Sangster, Poet

CHAPTER 20

August 1867

The late summer dinner party began with frosty glasses of sweet mint juleps and ended with a heavenly dessert of peach cobbler smothered with heavy cream. After the meal, when a heated discussion of the volatile atmosphere surrounding the upcoming elections erupted, Trent, Mansard York, Judge Rowland Turner, and Dixon Gallard retired to the judge's library with cognac and cigars while the women took tea in the parlor.

"The governor has appointed me Commissioner of Elections," Judge Turner informed his guests as he sank down into the oversize leather chair behind his desk. He opened the center desk drawer and removed a printed circular. "These instructions came to me from the Secretary of State. I have studied the rules of the election and have promised to faithfully manage my duties according to law in order for us to regain governance of our state."

"Exactly when is the election?" Dixon wanted to know.

"Mid-November," York stated. "I know that sounds a long way off, but we must move quickly to support delegates who favor the Republican position at the constitutional convention."

"Exactly," Judge Turner agreed. "And as Commissioner of Elections I am charged with selecting Managers to oversee the voting and make sure the rules are followed. I'm hoping you, my friends, will help me spread the word to fellow Republicans that we need all of our citizens to cooperate and, hopefully, we'll have as few problems as possible."

"Count me out," Dixon quickly decided, swirling amber liquid in his crystal snifter. "Never been one to get into politics. Not that I am against the election, it's just that I don't have the stomach for the trouble I see coming. Threats, beatings, and even mutilations are going on right now."

Mansard York nodded. "Unfortunately, some very angry men are physically threatening the coloreds who plan to vote."

"Absolutely ... openly and harshly, the judge agreed. "There have been quite a few ugly incidents." Judge Turner tensed his jaw, demonstrating the well-known display of determination that was part of his character. "The Democrats, and all the angry white Southerners and cash-poor Northerners are responsible for such despicable acts."

"Yes, they are," Dixon affirmed, shifting to the edge of his seat. "I've heard that only blacks who own real estate will be allowed to vote anyway. So, how many of them own land? Not very many I'm sure. If they have to bring land deeds to the ballot box only a few will show up, so their votes won't impact the outcome of the election."

"I've heard as much," Judge Turner interjected. "But it's not true. Democrats are spreading that lie. Any man, black or white, who registers to vote will be given a ballot. Republican, Democrat, landowner or not. However, gentlemen, let's face facts. The North won the war. Now, the people of South Carolina must resign themselves to the fact that *all* men deserve the opportunity to participate in local elections. The federal government has spoken and we must follow the law."

"Seems like you have a pretty heavy burden, Judge. I'd like to help you out, but I don't think I'd better push my luck by getting involved in the election," York finished.

Dixon Gallard nodded his agreement with York's decision, then asked, "Judge, what is happening with your son, Leon? I see him around the city from time to time, still wearing his uniform. Where does he stand in all of this?"

An expression of resignation collapsed the judge's features as he ran a hand across his broad, freckled forehead. "I'm afraid my son has thrown in with the Democrats," he replied, eyes trained on the inkwell on his desk. "I've tried to talk some sense into him. Tried to make him understand that the Democrats want nothing more than to see Reconstruction fail. And if that happens, we could be at war once again. More fighting and destruction. Haven't we suffered enough? It's time we moved on and put hatefulness aside. I've done my best to change Leon's mind, but he refuses to listen to me. In his opinion, the freedmen deserve no liberties at all."

"He'd do well to remember that Congress passed the civil rights bill allowing black men to vote. Like it or not, it's the law." York took a long puff on his cigar, taking care to keep his attention on the judge. "Are you going to post a deputy at the polling place to make sure there's no trouble?"

"That's what I plan to do," Judge Turner confirmed. "The outcome of this election will have a long-lasting impact on the future of South Carolina."

Dixon puffed on his cigar, then added, "Let's hope it all works out as we hope. I'm getting extremely tired of the Army running our city."

Trent murmured his understanding as Judge Turner said, "A successful election will not only speed the rebuilding of the South, but it will also restructure the political landscape. The constitution delegation must represent all of our citizens." He let a short space of silence settle over his guests before turning to Trent to say, "Hartwell, I would like for you to consider running for a spot as a delegate."

With a jerk, Trent tilted forward in his seat, eyes narrowed in surprise, clearly caught off guard. "Well..." he hesitated, "I don't know about that. I hadn't considered such a move."

"Well, please consider it," Judge Turner prodded, and then turning to Dixon, asked him, "What do you think?"

"Hum...I agree ... Hartwell should definitely run for a delegate spot. Why not?" Dixon replied. "Let's see, our Yankee friend is a white man, a lawyer, and now a South Carolina landowner. His sympathies lie with the freedmen, who do deserve their full rights. He currently owns hundreds of acres of farmland in St. John's Berkeley and employs a large number of men, both black and white, to plant and harvest his fields. I suspect he is a fair and just employer who pays adequate wages for work done." Dixon grinned as he focused on Trent. "Am I right, Hartwell? You'd be the perfect delegate, I'd say."

"Perfect? I don't know about that. But I will consider the idea," Trent decided, shrugging off Dixon's shower of compliments with a laugh. He was relieved when the discussion moved on to the recent construction of a new hospital near Mill Pond. However, for the rest of the evening, Trent's mind kept straying back to the prospect of throwing his hat in the ring.

While the men talked politics in the library, Sage, Martha, and Coretta sipped tea in the judge's parlor.

"So you and Dixon have definitely decided to sell Bryan Tract?" Sage asked Coretta, who was carefully placing the ornately embellished silver teapot back onto its matching tray.

Coretta held the handle of her porcelain teacup between two fingers as she turned to face Sage, adjusting her ballooning hoop skirt as she shifted back in her chair. "Yes. I can't wait to get rid of the place."

"How much acreage is there now?"

"We recently had the property surveyed. A little over seven-hundred acres. Taxes on the property are due, but I told Dixon we're not paying the tax assessor a dime. Why sink money into a rundown house and fallow land when we need cash to maintain our homes in town."

"Have you approached Trent about buying it?" Sage wanted to know. "I rode with him to view a parcel of land last week in Pimlico ….the old Durey plantation. He plans to rip out the old cotton plants and put in corn and potatoes, food for the people in the area. I feel certain he'd be interested in acquiring a property like Bryan Tract."

Martha flipped open her fan and began waving it back and forth in front of her face as she zeroed in on Sage. "You rode out into the country with Trent Hartwell?"

Sage grinned, eager to divulge more. "Yes, I did. He and I had the most adventurous day."

"Adventurous? You mean to say you went out into the country with him … alone?" Martha pressed, eyes widened more with curiosity than alarm.

"That's right. We were absolutely alone," Sage boldly confirmed, laughing aloud, not even bothering to cover her lips with her gloved fingers. "And, Martha, you will never guess what else happened," Sage teased.

"I can't imagine."

"I let him kiss me when he brought me home."

"Really! On the lips?" Martha spat out, clearly intrigued.

"Really, on the lips," was Sage's smiling response.

Coretta, whose eyes were shining with curiosity, spoke up. "Trent is a very handsome man."

"And quite the gentleman, too," Sage added.

"And such a wealthy, eligible bachelor. He told Mansard he was once engaged to a woman he loved deeply but she broke his heart when she turned to his brother," Martha finished in a conspiratorial tone.

"Trent was betrayed by the woman he loved?" Coretta repeated. "What a tragic situation."

"According to Mansard, Trent was shattered when he found them together," Martha contributed. "He came to South Carolina to get over her."

"That's a lot for a woman to overcome, don't you think, Sage?" Coretta teased.

With a shrug, Sage replied, "I'm willing to bet I can make him forget her, whoever she might have been. Remember ladies, Trent's old love is in Iowa, cuddling up next to his brother. I'm here in Charleston, helping him create a home and make profitable investments. Who do you think he will turn to when he decides to take a wife?"

The women giggled beneath their hands. "Should we start planning the wedding?" Martha excitedly tossed out. "I easily see that Trent is absolutely taken with you, Sage. A marriage proposal might be in your future."

A self-satisfied tilt came to Sage's lips. "Not too far away, I predict. In fact, perhaps, quite soon." She smugly smoothed the folds of her striped hoop shirt as she said, "I just need a bit more time."

"Be careful," Coretta cautioned. "Trent may be good-looking and have a healthy bank account but what do we really know about him? Remember, Sage, he is not one of us."

Making a tisk-tisk sound with her tongue, Sage wagged a finger at Coretta, one eyebrow arched. "Coretta, *you* should talk. Not one of us? Really? I don't think *you* meant to say that, did you?"

A deep red flush crept up Coretta's neck and onto her cheeks as she locked eyes with Sage. With a slight huff, she jutted out her jaw and sat back in her chair, taking in a long, calming breath as she studied Sage through narrowed eyes.

It was close to midnight when Coretta thanked Dixon for the ride home in his carriage, told him goodbye, and entered her townhouse. She went directly up the stairs to her spacious, pink-hued bedroom and immediately noticed that the room was frightfully dark, causing a frown of concern to cloud Coretta's delicate features.

After removing her cloak, she tossed it across the rose-colored, upholstered bench at the foot of her bed and immediately lit two crystal oil lamps on either end of the fireplace mantle. The soft yellow glow of lamplight tempered the dark shadows, engulfing the room with a golden sheen.

"Bessie could have lit the lamps before leaving," Coretta quietly grumbled while silently reprimanding herself for allowing her housekeeper time off to go tend to her sick mother.

"Four days, that's all," Coretta muttered, frustrated that Bessie, who could be obdurate at times, was not there to tend to household chores. Yet, Coretta relished the prospect of being alone in her house. The servant's absence seemed to be a fitting circumstance after such an animated evening at Judge Turner's dinner party. Coretta felt content to be unencumbered by the presence of a servant, and relieved to be far from Sage's gossiping tongue and her annoying insinuations.

Moving to her cedar-lined wardrobe, Coretta removed a rose-patterned dressing gown and began to change out of her silk magenta dress. Sitting at her vanity, she removed the two combs holding her long, dark hair in its upswept style and began to bush her raven locks as she studied her image in the expansive oval mirror.

Not bad for a widow woman of thirty-two, she silently told herself. Her complexion was just as creamy and unblemished as it had been when she was twenty. Her figure had not suffered from four years of eating rice and corn while living in the country, and her pouty red lips and deep blue eyes still managed to draw a man's attention. She placed her hands on either side of her chest and pushed her voluptuous breasts into two soft mounds of pale white flesh that strained against the soft cotton of her dressing gown. "Holding up very well," she murmured, admiring their perky presentation.

With a smile of satisfaction, Coretta resumed brushing her hair, but suddenly paused, her silver-backed hairbrush aloft, when she heard a scratching noise coming from downstairs. Remaining very still, her heart pounding, her breath trapped in her throat, she listened as soft footsteps landed on the carpeted stairs. When her bedroom door creaked open, she whipped around, her mouth tightening into a line as her eyes locked with those of the man who was staring at her.

"Benton!" she managed, a hand at her throat. "I didn't think you would come tonight."

"Yes, you did," he tossed out with a snappy grin. "The key was exactly where you said it would be. You must have known I'd be coming.... or did you place it there for some other secret lover?"

"Don't say such things," Coretta saucily replied with a toss of her long black hair. "It's just that .... it's very late. I didn't think you'd make the trip into town tonight, that's all."

"But I did," Benton softly replied, closing the door as he walked closer to Coretta.

"And I'm glad you did," she huskily admitted, knowing the words she was saying were dangerous, yet so true. She didn't care what others thought about who she had taken as her lover. All she knew was that Benton Langdon was a man who made her feel alive. She was captivated by his handsome face, his gentlemanly manners, and the intelligent air of confidence he projected.

They first met five months ago when he was serving expensive French wine at her friend's birthday party. She made a comment to Benton about the scarcity of good wine, and two days later, he showed up at her house with two bottles of champagne, a gift he said, for a lovely lady.

She invited him in, showed him where to stock the bottles of wine, and conversed with him for half an hour about the scarcity of decent food and drink in the city. He was polite, quite charming, engaging Coretta in a lively discussion about his ability to locate luxury items that had disappeared since the war. And when she told him she was in desperate need of a new pair of black lace gloves, somehow he was able to procure a pair, which he delivered to her within the week.

During his second visit to her town house, she had been feeling lonely, bored, and eager for attention so she let him sit and talk with her. He had not been flirtatious at all. On his third visit he brought her a tin of imported English tea and stayed while she brewed him a cup. Their unconventional friendship easily slipped into something she had never dreamed would happen to her: She fell in love with a man of color. She never asked him personal questions and did not know how he obtained the lavish gifts he brought her. She never knew when he would show up at her back door or where he went when he left, though she had learned, after making casual inquiries, that Benton had been given his former master's rundown plantation house, where he lived with an elderly housekeeper and two male boarders.

Who is spreading gossip that seems to have reached Sage Turner's ears? Coretta wondered, tilting her face up to Benton's to accept the deep kiss that he placed on her lips.

After their first time making love, she had sworn it would never happen again. She resisted his draw with all her power, but lost the battle the next time she was with him. And now, it was happening again.

A shiver of anticipation warmed Coretta. She loved the excitement he brought to her life. It was as if Benton Langdon had simply dropped out of the sky and into her life to brighten her lackluster existence. Now, she allowed him to envelope her in a tight embrace, desperate for the comfort of his arms and the feel of him holding her close. When he kissed her again, the impact of their connection quietly reassured her that she was still desirable, attractive, and worthy of being loved.

"Damn, I've missed you," Benton said as he hugged Coretta around her waist.

"It's only been a short time," she murmured against his starched white shirt. "I've missed you too, and as impossible as it sounds, I wish we never had to be apart."

"Perhaps, one day. Who knows what might happen?" he taunted, playing with a lock of her hair.

"Ever the optimist," Coretta observed, though she knew she had given him every right to feel as he did. How could she have known that she would look forward to sharing a colored man's bed? Anticipate his touch? Or start acting like a teenager in the blush of first love while craving mature sexual intimacy that swept away her loneliness?

"No more talk," Coretta whispered, easing out of his embrace. She padded on bare feet to her massive sleigh bed, turned back the coverlet, and extended her hand.

In two long strides, Benton shed his jacket, moved to her and sank down on the fluffy feather mattress. Reaching up, he traced a finger along the side of her jaw. "You're lovely tonight," he said after a long moment of just looking at her. "Our time is short. Let's not waste a second."

With the ease of a routine they'd rehearsed many times, they undressed. Coretta pulled back the sheets and lay down, inviting Benton's naked body to cover hers, so warm and soft, yet firm and manly. She cuddled close when he slid down beside her, welcoming the feel of his bare skin slipping across hers. When Benton teased her lips with flick of his tongue, and then kissed her hard, she felt a force that made her body jerk in pleasure. Coretta placed one leg over his and rubbed her foot up and down his calf, stroking his tan, muscular form, which was in very good shape for a man not quite thirty. When he rose up and placed his body on top of hers, the bulge in his groin was so prominent and real, it intensified Coretta's craving for him and shut out all of her worries.

"I can't get enough of you, Coretta," he softly murmured into her ear, his voice as soft as a caress.

She didn't respond, refusing to dilute the exquisite moment by talking. She did not want to admit that she was deeply in love with Benton. A colored man. A former slave. Yet, her stomach contracted when he touched the tip of his tongue to her bottom lip and gave it a nibble. Lifting her hips, she guided him into the thick patch of black hair between her thighs, and then, with boldly increasing speed, fell into a rhythm with him, groaning her pleasure aloud.

CHAPTER 21

Roby Green tugged at the front of his sweat-stained shirt, bothered by the fact that yesterday, Mr. Hopson kept all the Negro mill hands laboring at the lumber mill long into the night —punishment for taking too long of a mid-day break. When Roby awakened this morning, Hopson's punitive act still grated on his nerves like sand ground into the open wounds he had on his hands, the result of gripping large metal plates with serrated edges for hours at a time. The Freedman's Bureau contract under which Mr. Hopson employed former slaves to work his mill clearly stated that the men he hired were to receive thirty minutes of rest once a day, but Hopson granted the freedmen only fifteen minutes of rest, while the white men took as long as they wanted.

The workload at the mill was brutal, nearly intolerable in the ninety-degree heat of a low-country September, but still Roby stayed. Where else could he earn eight-dollars a month, with housing, rations, and medical attention thrown in? At least tomorrow was Sunday, a day free of work. He looked forward to returning to Fair Oaks so that Bina could cook him a decent meal.

With great care, Roby untied the laces of his thin leather boots and placed them on the weathered fishing pier that extended far out over the river. Glancing up, he squinted at the orange-gold crest of the rising sun, then slipped out of his overalls, picked up a frayed fishing net, and entered the water. He let his body sink downward, the cool water sluicing over him like a rushing, gushing faucet, a welcoming balm that erased the night's sticky sweat, along with his frustrations. Roby extended his arms, slowing his descent, and then sank low and began to swim. Opening his eyes, he hoped to see a turtle or a few catfish that he could quickly snag with his net, but everything was pitch black, as if the river had been shot through with printer's ink, and he couldn't see a thing. He hadn't expected that.

Kicking his feet, he pushed forward, hoping the water might be less murky in another spot, and quickly found that it was. With increased visibility, he continued to search for a fish to take back to the mill shed to fry for breakfast. However, what he saw was a large object floating toward him that eventually bumped into him, arousing his curiosity. Immediately, Roby rose to the surface and took a deep breath. With two hard jerks of his head, he whipped water from his eyes and then dove down again, reaching out as he tried to grab whatever was floating around. Determined to see what had been thrown into the river, he swam close, grabbed hold of it and immediately knew what he had captured. Pulling it to shore, he gasped, his heart tightening in fear. It was the body of a man. A black man. And Roby knew exactly who it was.

The number of people who showed up at the nearly complete Freedman's school was less than Oscar had hoped for. But as he stood before the agitated group, he was thankful for the attendance of those who'd dared to come out to hear what he had to say. In addition to its role as a classroom for the children, the new school also served as the local meeting place for the black community, creating a much-needed sense of collective protection from those who harassed and threatened the black freedmen.

After letting it be known that his name would be on the ballot to serve as a delegate to the constitutional convention, Oscar had worried that some might not be brave enough to show up. But now, as their stares of anticipation drilled into him, he raised a hand to settle the crowd and began to speak.

"Surely, the most important mission for every colored person in St. John's Berkeley is to educate our children. There was a time not too long ago when we had to teach them to read in secret, hiding books in our homes, meeting in the woods. Folks over in Cherry Hill are talking about establishing their school, and now we here in Cordesville have nearly completed our own, and it will be a wondrous place for our children to come and learn."

"How will we get desks for the children?" a woman in a pink flowered dress asked.

"I'll be heading into Charleston in a few days to pick up a load of desks donated by Emanuel AME Church. Thank God for their support of the freedman's efforts," Oscar said.

"What's the name of our school gonna be?" a man at the back of the room called out.

"I've had plenty of suggestions," Oscar answered. "Dixie School, Freeland School, First Liberty. All good names, but we'll be discussing all of that a bit later," Oscar went on. "Right now, we must talk about the upcoming election. Now, people, you cannot forget that we have the right to vote … it was given to us by the federal government. It's the law. I know there've been terrible incidents happening in our community to frighten you and make you stay away from the polling place. But I urge each and every black man in the county to vote, and vote Republican come Election Day."

The cheers that erupted caught Oscar by surprise, making him pause and take a deep breath before going on. "The senseless ransacking of our homes, the brutal beatings, and the horrible acts of vandalism must not deter us from going to the ballot box. Our community has experienced a rash of evil threats that have created an explosive situation. Unless law enforcement officials and the civil-minded residents of our state join forces to address these problems, racial tensions will continue to grow, along with the number of criminal attacks. Certainly, in order for our community to progress and survive, we need citizens like you ... who do not wish to sit by and watch as these scalawags try to put us back in slavery. I've been told that my name will be on the ballot as a delegate to the convention. If I am elected, one thing I will do is work hard to get us a new sheriff. So I hope I can count on your support. But even if you don't support me.... you gotta turn out...be at the ballot box on Election Day. We have the right to participate, so if anyone ..."

"Remember the attack on Little John!" a farmer wearing a battered straw hat and mud-caked overalls tossed out in a shout that made Oscar stiffen. "Them ole Jonny Rebs beat Little John bad....coulda killed him!"

Immediately, grumbled mutterings denouncing the attack erupted, initiating animated chatter in a chorus of distressed voices.

"Yes, that's true," Oscar affirmed as he tried to calm the people with a raised arm. "Two men bashed in Little John's head with wooden clubs, and they probably would have killed him if Mrs. Phillips, the lady from Boston who's living over at Fair Oaks, hadn't interrupted the attack and rescued him."

More anguished murmurs broke out within the crowd.

Oscar lifted a hand to quiet the people, a steely jut to his jaw. "Little John refuses to say who did that to him," Oscar stated sternly, fueled by the tension rising from the crowd. "But I promise to do everything I can to find out who they were and bring such men to justice." Expelling a long breath, he took a moment to study the faces looking back at him. These were freedmen, men Oscar had known all his life, some he'd labored with in the fields while picking cotton for the same master. He knew the fear in their hearts was deep and the hope in their souls was strong. No matter what happened, he would never stop pushing for their right to live as free, decent men and women in Saint John's Berkeley. Hoping to inject a glimmer of optimism into the meeting, Oscar was about to launch into his report from the Commissioner of Education about the future of their school when Roby Green came bursting through the door, shouting and waving his hands in the air.

"Zack Foster done been killed!" Roby yelled, forcing everyone present to turn and stare at him in shock.

At Fair Oaks, later that afternoon, Eva and Bina were grinding corn in the kitchen when Oscar came in and breathlessly announced, "I have bad news."

"What is it?" Bina asked, setting aside her large pounding pestle, wiping her hands on her apron.

"A real tragedy has happened."

"Tragedy? Mr. Singleton! What has happened?" Eva wanted to know.

"Roby Green, the young man who works at the lumber camp and stays here at Fair Oaks from time to time … well … he found a body floating in the river this morning. Down near the mill, right off Gippy Dike. He pulled the man out and saw it was Zack Foster. Dead. Stabbed in the chest. His hands and feet were tied."

"Oh, no," Eva groaned, a sinking feeling hollowing her out as she gripped the edge of the table. "How horrible!"

"I was holding a meeting at the school house when Roby came running up and told us how he found Zack. Such a tragedy, it is. I'll be leaving tonight to take the body up to his family in Columbia."

"I can't believe it. Zack is dead! Does anyone know who did it?" Eva pressed her hands to her stomach, absorbing the shocking news. "I didn't know him well… but he was such a gentle, helpful man. Very passionate about politics."

"That's probably what did him in," Benton snidely remarked, walking into the room while fastening the buttons on his white tailored shirt.

Eva whirled around to face Benton, disturbed by his accusatory tone. "Mr. Langdon! Are you blaming Zack for his own death?"

Benton shrugged and pulled at the cuffs of his shirt. "No.

However, Mrs. Phillips," he began, pacing closer to her, "you may have been the last person to see Zack Foster alive."

"What are you trying to imply?" Eva snapped.

"Just that the sheriff now has to investigate a murder, not simply the theft of a government supply wagon."

"I don't know anything about his murder! I don't know what happened to Zack after that man ran him off!"

Benton pulled a handkerchief from his pocket and dabbed at his brow as he spoke. "That may be true, but 'round here, it doesn't take much to find yourself inside a jail cell. Remember.... I told you not to go around talking about what happened with the wagon. You didn't listen. You decided to tell all to Captain Liedtke. I already reported the incident to Sheriff Cholett to try and keep you from any involvement. But now, you're stuck in the middle of a murder investigation. Not a good place to be."

"I had no idea ..." Eva tried to defend, then stopped to collect herself.

"That's right! You have no understanding of what black folks here in Saint John's Berkeley have to do to survive! The slightest hint of involvement in a criminal act gives license to the evil haters to do to us whatever they want." He leveled a stern glare of reproach on Eva. "Might be best if you stay here on the property until all this blows over. Don't go wandering around, talking to folks about what you know or what you saw."

Bina, who had been standing quietly while listening to Benton's accusatory rage, finally spoke. "Let it be, Benton. Think of poor ole Zack Foster. I always worried he was gonna pay a price for speaking out and posting handbills on trees and such. I'm so sorry 'bout what's happened, but God forgive me, Eva, I ain't surprised."

Distressed by Benton's threatening attitude, coupled with Bina's hint of support, Eva suddenly felt overwhelmed. What did all of this have to do with her? What had she fallen into by simply accepting a ride on Zack Foster's wagon? Her upset over the news of Zack's death nearly equaled her anger over the fact that Benton was acting as if she were now involved in Zack's murder! After giving Benton a stone-cold stare, Eva turned her back on him and rushed outside. She crossed the veranda and raced across the grounds, stopping among the flowering tomato vines and rows of knee-high okra in Bina's garden. She wrapped her arms around her waist to stop her body from shaking and lifted her face to the sun, considering her situation.

Eva had to admit that, for some time, she been feeling increasingly uneasy about remaining at Benton's house. And now he was trying to prevent her from leaving? Who knew what his real motives were? Though they had been civil to each other since her arrival, she always sensed that he was not the friendly, concerned man she had first thought him to be. He was a well-spoken, good-looking man who knew how to turn on the charm when he was with strangers. But he was also a very secretive, calculating person who spent hours either away from Fair Oaks or closeted in his secluded bedroom, which had once been his master's upstairs sitting room and library.

Bina told Eva that Benton's bedroom was off limits to everyone in the house and that she didn't even go in to clean the room unless he asked her to. Eva once caught a glimpse of Benton's abode when he left the door slightly ajar while preparing to leave. She was surprised to see that the floor-to-ceiling shelves lining three walls were crammed with books, ledgers, and documents, along with a jumble of personal grooming items and clothing. On most days, he emerged from his room at daybreak, ate the meal that Bina always prepared for him, and then hitched his horse to his wagon and disappeared down the road, not to be seen again until late at night. Where he went and what he did with his time, Eva did not know, and neither did Bina, at least that's what the elderly housekeeper said.

Now, Eva felt trapped, isolated, and anxious. Time was slipping away, and clues to her mother's fate were vanishing with each setting of the sun. Luke, the old man at Stillwater, had told Eva that Mayree walked off the plantation on freedom day, but so far, Eva had found no records of Mayree having registered with the Freedman's Bureau. Eva knew it was time to leave Saint John's Berkeley and return to Charleston, where she sensed she might be more successful in discovering leads to assist her search. The wasted hours she had been forced to endure while stuck at Fair Oaks had already cost her dearly.

CHAPTER 22

The next morning, as soon as Eva was certain Benton had left for the day, she opened the back door and stepped out into the garden. A quarrelling pair of blue jays that made their nest in the red maple tree were at it again, making short, razor-sharp, cackling sounds like nails being hammered into wood. The sound of the birds and the soft morning breeze filtering across the yard eased the heavy thoughts that had kept Eva awake all night. Her decision had been made. She was determined to leave Fair Oaks today, while Benton was away. Who was he to tell her where she could or could not go? She would pack whatever she could carry in a plain straw basket and tell Bina she was going to the Freedman's Bureau for supplies. However, she would actually walk to the train station, purchase a ticket, and be on her way to Charleston. She would send for her valise and her trunk later.

Thinking she might find a large basket in Benton's storehouse, Eva tromped across the weed-choked field toward a weathered shed behind the house. She gripped the iron latch that secured the store-house door and was relieved to discover that the heavy pad-lock was not engaged.

After entering, she remained in the door for a few seconds while sunlight flooded the musty building and her eyes adjusted to its dim interior. When she spied a round sweet grass basket sitting on a nearby shelf, she reached up for it and pulled it down. Immediately realized it was not empty. Curious, she glanced into the barrel-shaped hamper and frowned to observe its contents. Nestled inside was a lovely lace scarf in a pale shade of yellow, a pair of handsome gloves of the softest white leather, a beaded velvet reticule with silver link handles, and a leather drawstring pouch.

What in the world are these lovely things doing in here? Eva wondered, lifting the lacy scarf to the light to admire its intricate pattern. The delicate scarf was very similar to the black lace one she had worn for many months after Chester died, and the memory sent a surge of sorrow into her heart, giving her pause for a few solemn moments. Opening the leather pouch, Eva removed a cameo brooch with a woman's ivory silhouette carved into the ebony cabochon, a double string of pearls fit with a golden clasp, and a pair of chande-lier earrings made of burnished silver. Tentatively, she held one of the earrings up to her ear and turned her head to the side. Feeling it gently brush her neck, she wished she had a mirror to see her reflection.

"What are you doing in here?"

Startled, Eva spun around and dropped the earring to the ground.

Without waiting for her answer, Benton approached, his face a stone-cold mask. "You really shouldn't be in here."

"I …I was looking for a basket to carry supplies back from the bureau," she stammered, replacing the other earring into the pouch. Benton's sour expression was alarming. She knew it was wrong of her to be rummaging through his things, but she had not meant any harm. It wasn't as if she planned to steal from him. "I apologize. I wasn't snooping or stealing, I just wanted a basket to …"

"Well there're no empty baskets in here," he grumbled, stooping to pick up the earring Eva had dropped. He took the pouch from her, placed all of the jewelry back into it, and put it back in the basket. With little effort, he heaved the hamper up onto a higher shelf. "Just trinkets that Widow Jutland left behind when she moved out," he offered, as if obliged to provide an explanation. "I just put 'em in here, thinking one day she might come back."

"Oh, I see," Eva began, "but they are very nice items, rather expensive, I believe. Why not keep them in a safe place inside the house?"

Benton made a sniffing sound, dismissing her remark as he thinned his lips and stared at her. "They're safe enough out here," he finally said. And then, narrowing his eyes at Eva, he added, "As long as I keep that lock on the door and nosey people keep out."

"Oh, well…" Eva started, her face burning in shame. "I do apologize for entering your storehouse without permission."

"I *thought* you were someone I could trust," he curtly replied. "Did I really misjudge you?"

"I'd better get back up to the house," she hurried to say, realizing how angry he was, deciding to put her early morning departure on hold.

"That might be best," Benton sternly agreed.

Turning, Eva hurried out the door and back through the garden, more worried than ever that Benton Langdon was not a man she could trust.

That night, lying against her pillow, Eva pushed stray bits of worry around in her mind. She'd spent most of the day struggling to keep her thoughts from converging into a single cohesive statement that would define her anxiety and bring it into focus. Now, she listened as Benton's footsteps thudded on the stairs. Glancing toward the door, she counted each creak as he made his way downstairs. She flinched to hear the whine of the back door's hinges when he opened it, the slam of it when it closed. Then came the rattle of his wagon as he left the property, a sound that made her go limp.

Getting out of bed, she quickly dressed, gathered her few possessions, wrapped them in her tattered quilt, and stuck it into her soft valise. She penned a quick note to Bina to thank her for her kindness and request that she send Eva's trunk to her at Luvena Nesbit's address. Then Eva crept into the hallway, tiptoed to Bina's closed door, and shoved the note beneath it before making her way down the stairs to slip outside.

When the huge iron clock outside the train station struck twelve, Eva was sitting in the Colored section of the South Carolina Railway's midnight train to Charleston.

CHAPTER 23

"We just had Bryan Tract surveyed," Coretta said to Trent after handing him a copy of the land surveyor's report. "A little more than seven-hundred acres. There's a house on the property but it's in need of some repair and the indigo fields have not been worked for years. Neither Dixon nor I have any desire to set foot on Bryan Tract again. It's time to let it go."

"I understand the taxes are somewhat overdue?" Trent ventured, trying to ease discretely into a necessary discussion of the Gallard family's finances.

"Yes, three years overdue to be exact," Coretta confirmed. "The tax assessor has given us thirty days to clear up the arears or the property will go up for auction. We have the money to pay the taxes, but I refuse to put another penny into the place, and Dixon agrees. We've made the hard decision to sell," she sighed, then added, "Such a stressful time for everyone …. all because of that terrible war." She dabbed at one eye with a lace handkerchief, appearing genuinely overcome with emotion. "I know the war was not your fault, Trent. You just happened to live in the North, we, in the South. But if a Yankee is going to take possession of my family's land, I'd rather it be you than a stranger I don't know."

"I understand completely, Coretta, and I appreciate your candor," Trent sympathized. "I'm glad you feel comfortable turning to me in your search for a reliable buyer."

"Who else *would* I turn to," Coretta lamented. "So many of our friends would have been eager to buy my family's property, but they invested heavily in the Confederacy. They're cash-poor, as poor as our famine-murdered land. However," she continued in a whispery voice, "that's all behind us now."

"Yes, it is," Trent agreed. "Now…how much are the taxes?" he inquired, eager to move forward with his most ambitious purchase to date.

"Two-hundred-seventy-five dollars." Coretta said this as she turned from Trent and removed an envelope from the side table, which she handed over to him. "As you can see," she began while he perused the documents, "the deed is in both my and Dixon's names. However, I signed a quit claim to absolve myself of ownership in the property, giving my brother sole rights to handle all the transactions."

"It appears that everything is in order," Trent decided, re-inserting the documents into the heavy envelope. "Bryan Tract is in a very promising location and I'm extremely interested in making an offer."

Coretta sat back in her chair with a slump, as if relieved of a burden she did not want to carry. "It would be a great relief to me if you negotiate the terms with my brother right away," she began. "Go and speak to Dixon now so we can settle all of this."

Dixon Gallard's houseman opened the door before Trent could raise the brass knocker to announce his arrival.

"Saw your carriage through the window, Sir," the polite young man with copper-toned skin and curly black hair told Trent. "May I inquire who is calling?"

"Mr. Hartwell calling on Mr. Gallard," Trent informed the servant, who stepped back to provide Trent a clear view of the dim foyer. "Is Mr. Gallard available?" he inquired glancing around the entry hall, feeling slightly unsettled by the sight that greeted him. The Italian marble floor was cracked and dull and the oval-shaped space was totally void of furniture. A frayed wing chair, a spindly side table, and a slender oil lamp with a glass shade in need of a good cleaning could be seen in the adjacent sitting room, which was dark and uninviting. Trent recognized that the interior of Dixon Gallard's home stood in great contrast to its polished exterior, and was not at all what one would expect of a man with such high social standing. However, Trent had heard the rumors of Dixon's penchant for playing cards and rolling dice as he wagered money he often did not have. Clearly, the absence of a fashionable décor and the lack of quality furnishings in his home were the result of too many losses at the gaming tables, coupled with an excess of bourbon at the bar.

"Sorry Sir, but Mr. Gallard is not at home."

"Do you know where I may find him?"

"I believe he's over to the Luckey Star having lunch with some gentlemen."

"The Luckey Star …" Trent repeated, nodding. "Fine, fine I'll catch up with him there."

Trent found Dixon in the hotel dining room, sitting alone, devouring a plate of the hotel's highly celebrated shrimp and grits.

Dixon smiled and stood as Trent approached, and after a quick handshake, he settled down to finish his meal. "Join me?" he asked, forking a shrimp, which he lifted high, admired, and then popped into his mouth.

"No, no thanks," Trent replied, settling in his chair before turning to the server and requesting a glass of wine. "I spoke to Coretta this morning," he said to Dixon, ready to talk business. "I understand you'll handle all transactions related to the sale of Bryan Tract."

"That's right."

"I'd like to make an offer."

"And?" Dixon mumbled around a mouthful of shrimp. "What do you say?"

"I'll pay eight-hundred dollars for the property..."

Making a leisurely lift of his wine glass to his lips, Dixon took a sip, then glanced at the ceiling for a long moment as if thinking about Trent's offer. "Humm, I don't know, Hartwell... more than seven-hundred acres ..." Dixon hedged, clearly fishing for Trent's bottom line.

"All right. Eight-fifty," Trent tossed out. "I reviewed all the pertinent documents ... I know how much the back taxes are." Trent delivered this in a business-like tone while watching for Dixon's reaction as the server placed a crystal wine glass in front of him. He twirled his glass by its stem as he waited for Dixon's answer.

Dixon shrugged, motioned for the server, and ordered a decadent dessert of bread pudding and heavy cream before replying. "Eight-fifty? I don't think that would put much in my pocket once the transfer expenses are figured in. You know, I *could* get a higher bid if I made it known that I'm willing to sell. Coretta and I just thought we'd keep this transaction quiet, entertain your interests first, but if eight-fifty is the best you can offer, ..."

"All right, one-thousand," Trent calmly stated. "Final offer, I'm afraid."

Dixon patted his lips with his linen napkin, picked up his wine glass, and touched it to Trent's. "You have a deal, Hartwell. Draw up the papers and Bryan Tract is all yours."

After settling on the terms, the men shook hands, and just as Trent was about to leave, he noticed a man walking toward Dixon's table. He was dressed in a long black duster coat that reached the tops of his tall black boots and he had a wide brim black hat in his hands. His long blond hair was pushed back behind his ears and his eyes remained trained on Dixon as he drew near.

"The men at the table waitin' on you, Gallard. You still gonna play?" he asked, without introducing himself or making eye contact with Trent.

Dixon whirled around, grinned, and then pushed the last of his dessert into his mouth. "Hey, Leon. I'm coming. Just give me a minute." Then he waved a hand at Trent and added, "You know Trent Hartwell, don't you?"

"I know *of* him," Leon replied in a sullen tone, making no move to offer a hand of greeting. "You're the carpetbagger that's been spending so much time with my sister, huh?"

Shocked by Leon's rude remark, Trent slowly rose to his feet and calmly answered, "That's right. Obviously, your sister seems to find this Yankee's company a lot more pleasing than that of her brother's. I always wondered when I'd finally meet you." Then he bowed slightly at Dixon, gave Leon a look of dismissal, and walked out of the dining room.

CHAPTER 24

Using the key to her new postal box, Eva opened the small square door and was excited to see a single letter inside with an October 2, Boston postmark on the envelope. She sighed with contentment, her spirits lifted immediately. At last, a letter from Aunt Tully.

Eva had been in Charleston, living with Luvena, for the past three weeks, spending most of her time seeking information about her mother. She visited hospitals and churches, went to the local Freedman's Bureau every day to speak to former slaves who arrived at the location for assistance. She walked the streets, questioned merchants, made inquiries of shopkeepers, and even approached soldiers and strangers at the railway station to unearth clues to Mayree's fate.

The only real luck she'd had was three days earlier when she received a glimmer of hope that her attempt to uncover the fate of her mother might not be in vain. While shopping in the market-place, she heard a woman singing, *Ka a fo, ka a fo, Kaa;* the same lullaby her mother used to sing. Eva quickly sought the source of the song, only to come upon a young woman sitting in the alley behind the market stalls, cradling a baby in her arms while crooning to the child. Her hair was braided and piled high atop her head. When Eva asked the woman if she knew of a former slave named Mayree from the Cantrell plantation who spoke the same language, the young mother shook her head and pointed to her mouth, indicating that she did not speak Eva's language. When Eva raised her hands to her head and made the motion of piling her hair atop her head, the woman broke into a wide smile and nodded, as if she understood what Eva meant.

Excited by this affirmation, Eva scanned the alley for someone who might help her communicate with the woman, praying someone in the market might speak the same language. Spying an elderly lady who was sitting on a blanket and weaving a basket at the back entrance of the market, she ran to her for help.

"Do you know the language that the woman was singing? Do you know her? " Eva pressed.

"No, I do not know her," was the answer. "I think she just come here from Africa."

"Africa? Where in Africa?" Eva wanted to know.

"Don't know, but I hear other women sound like that sometime. I can't tell you nothin' more."

Eva turned back, anxious to question the young mother further, but saw that she and the baby had vanished. Distraught, she spent the remainder of that afternoon looking for her, but to no avail.

Though discouraged, Eva did not give up hope. She remained focused on her search while enjoying her stay with Luvena, whose company was welcome after her dismal time at Fair Oaks. Bina had sent Eva's trunk to the city with Oscar, who arrived in Charleston to collect a load of desks for his school that had been donated by a church in support of the Freedman's School. She had been delighted to see him and to learn that his name would be placed on the ballot as a Republican delegate to the constitutional convention.

Eva had been eager to receive her trunk, which contained her few dresses, Chester's trousers, and her red velvet hat, which she removed right away to examine. The sight of the items stirred memories of her brief marriage, of the love she had lost too soon. However, when Luvena saw the meager wardrobe that Eva pulled from her trunk, she insisted they soon pay a visit to her dressmaker to order new dresses, hats, and shawls.

Now, though tempted to tear open her letter from Aunt Tully and read it right there in the post office, Eva tucked it into her purse for later, and then headed toward the door. As soon as she placed her hand on the doorknob, the door flew open and a man rushed past her, nearly knocking her down. Catching onto the doorjamb to regain her footing, she glared at the back of the man's head as he made his way across the lobby, noticing a slight limp to his stride. A chill of recognition bore down on Eva as she carefully studied his appearance and his gait. He was white, tall, with straggly blond hair that hung down from beneath the brim of a wide black hat. He had a red kerchief tied around his neck, and he was wearing a black shirt with the trousers of a Confederate soldier's uniform.

Panic exploded inside of Eva. She was certain this was the man who had stolen the wagon from Zack. The man who pushed her to the ground and injured her head. Easing to the side to allow a rotund woman to enter the post office, she cautiously watched the man exchange greetings with the postal clerk.

"Well, hello Leon. Haven't seen you around for a while," she heard the clerk say.

"Been avoiding my old man," was the blond-haired man's reply.

Eva gasped softly when she heard him speak. His voice made her stomach turn over in dread. It was the same voice that forced Zack to run away, that threatened to kill her if she did not comply with his demands.

"The Judge been puttin' the pressure on you, huh?" the clerk said.

"Yes, he has ... but I ain't listening to what my father's got to say. Anyway, Tobey, I need to talk to you. Let's go in the back."

Eva bit her bottom lip so hard she flinched, but her eyes remained trained on the men as they walked to the rear of the post office and disappeared from sight.

Moving out onto the sidewalk, she struggled to remain calm. Everyone had told her it would do no good to go to the sheriff. Even Luvena had warned her to keep her distance from Pate Cholett and stay out of the whole nasty affair related to Zack Foster's murder. But now, after recognizing the man who robbed the wagon, she knew she had to do something. Racing along the street, she stopped a laundress who was carrying a basket of fresh linen on her arm.

"Excuse me. Where can I find the sheriff?" Eva breathlessly inquired, struggling to maintain her composure.

"You mean ole Pate Cholett?" the startled woman replied, shifting the basket onto her hip.

"Yes. Yes. Sheriff Cholett."

"Head down Magazine," the laundress offered, pointing toward the street behind her. "Cross over Logan and you gonna see the jail. He be there most o' the time."

"Thank you," Eva hurried to say, then set off across the street.

It took Eva less than ten minutes to arrive at the jail, where a deputy named Willis put her in a small room that held only two chairs and a table. He told her to wait there until the sheriff could see her. After a short wait, a tall gangly man with distrustful eyes and a scraggly salt and pepper beard that brushed the top button of his dingy white shirt entered. Wide blue suspenders hung across boney shoulders that also supported the wide leather strap of a holstered gun.

"I'm Sheriff Cholett. What can I do for you, Miss?"

"My name is Eva Phillips. I believe Benton Langdon already spoke to you about an incident I was involved in."

Cholett studied Eva with suspicion, as if puzzled by her remark, and then shook his nearly bald head back and forth. "Langdon, you say?" He tugged the end of his wispy, thin beard. "Haven't seen Benton Langdon for months. You say he told you he spoke to me?"

"Yes."

"Not true. But … what's this all about?"

"A government wagon that was stolen," Eva began, proceeding to tell the sheriff about the robbery, the discovery of Zack's body, and her sighting of the man called Leon, whom she recognized at the post office.

"First I heard of a wagon gettin' stolen," he said. "Musta happened outa my jurisdiction."

"Oh, no," Eva protested. "It happened not too far outside of Charleston. Before we got to Benton's place in Cordesville." She looked at the sheriff with pleading eyes, as if begging him to believe what she was telling him.

"Well, I do know Zack Foster. Has a livery stable in town. You say he was killed?"

"That's right."

"You see his body?"

"Well... no. But I was told that he was stabbed, bound, then drowned."

"How do you know all that is true if you didn't see his body?"

"Roby Green found Zack's body in the river. Why would he lie about something like that?"

The sheriff simply shrugged his boney shoulders as the corners of his mouth turned down.

"Oscar Singleton, the schoolmaster, took Zack's body to his family in Columbia. Ask him about it if you don't believe me!"

"You not from around here, are you?" Cholett tossed the question at Eva as if throwing a dart at her.

Exasperation colored the sigh that slipped from her lips. "No. I'm from Boston."

"Oh well. You probably don't know too much about how the law works 'round here. Tell you what, young lady, you run along. Don't bother your head 'bout this. I'll send a telegraph up to Columbia and let the sheriff up there handle the investigation. That's where Zack's family lives, as I understand." Then he tilted back his chair, balancing it on two legs as he looped his fingers through his blue suspender straps and stared evenly at Eva.

Frustrated, knowing he was not going to take action on what she had come to tell him, Eva stood, whirled from the room without a word of goodbye, and stomped out of the jail. Oscar had been right! Cholett was not concerned with doing his job! He cared nothing about enforcing the law!

Out on the street once more, she reached into her purse and removed the card that the white lawyer had given to her at the bank. "Trent Hartwell," she read, fingering the card, deciding it might be best to pay him a visit.

Trent Hartwell's office was located on the first floor of his home on Wentworth Street. When Amelia ushered Eva into his office, he immediately rose to greet her with genuine warmth.

"Mrs. Phillips," he said, standing from his seat behind his desk "It is good to see you. Is all well at the bank?"

"Very well," she told him, taking the seat he indicated, settling across from him. "My thanks again for your assistance. Mr. York has been most accommodating."

"Good, good," Trent replied, sitting down. He placed his arms flat on his desk and looked at Eva for a long time, then said, "What can I do for you? A legal matter of some kind?"

Eva firmed her lips, inhaled through her nose, and steeled herself for whatever reaction this man might have to what she'd come to say.

"I think so," she started. "I saw a man at the post office today. I know he is the man who assaulted me some weeks ago, and he also stole a wagon filled with government supplies." A moment passed while she assessed Trent's reaction, and seeing an inquisitive set to his features, she pushed ahead with her story. Taking her time, she filled him in on why she had come to Charleston, her reason for going to Moncks Corner, the robbery of the wagon, as well as Zack's murder. Though tempted to tell him about Little John's beating and her suspicions about Benton Langdon's secret stash of luxury items, she held back, not wanting to go into that.

"That's quite a story," Trent replied after listening to everything

Eva had to say. "I am sorry to hear about your husband's death at Battery Wagner. You should be proud of him."

"I am ... I miss him so very much," Eva added. "At least I was able to see where he was laid to rest, thanks to Zack Foster taking me there. And it is a comfort to know Chester is not too far away."

"Let's hope you have good luck finding your mother," Trent offered. "It's regrettable that you experienced so much trouble on the road."

"Yes, but I won't be deterred. I'll be fine. It's what happened to Zack that haunts me. He was stabbed. His hands and feet bound. Drowned. It's all so, so cruel," she finished.

"So, you spoke to Sheriff Cholett?"

"Yes, though I was advised by more than a few people not to go to the sheriff because I have no proof of anything. However, after seeing that man named Leon at the post office this morning, well I knew I had to do something."

"You said his name was Leon?" Trent repeated.

"Yes, that's what the postal clerk called him. Made a remark that seemed to indicate that Leon's father is a judge."

"Leon. Yes, the judge's son," Trent murmured. He leaned back in his chair, a frown on his face as he narrowed his eyes and tapped the desk with his forefinger. "I'm glad you came to see me, Mrs. Phillips. The atmosphere in the city is quite tense right now.... the upcoming election and all. If you trust me, I'll do what I can to help you sort this out."

"I do trust you." She said this while pulling the drawstring on her purse, and reaching inside, asked, "How much will your services cost?"

Trent waved his hand in a dismissive manner. "Don't worry about that. I think I can help you sort this out. First, we should pay a visit to the District Assistant Commissioner. I could go with you tomorrow. Would that be convenient?"

"Yes," Eva agreed.

"Where are you staying?"

"With a good friend. At thirty-seven Judith Street."

"I will pick you up in my carriage at eight o'clock tomorrow morning."

"Thank you," Eva told him, relieved to have the support of a man whom she prayed could untangle her from this awful set of circumstances that threatened to turn ugly.

CHAPTER 25

General R.K. Scott, Assistant Commissioner of the Freedman's Bureau for the military districts of South Carolina, maintained his headquarters in Charleston. Standing at a commanding six-feet-eight, he had a full head of coal black hair and the ruddy complexion of a man accustomed to spending long hours with his men in the field. His military posture, blunt square chin, and hawk-like nose created a fitting representation of the strength of the United States Army. His statewide responsibilities included the supervision and management of all matters related to refugees and freedmen. In addition to overseeing the disposition of lands abandoned or seized during the Civil War, he was charged with the issuance of rations, providing medical relief to both freedmen and white refugees, the enforcement of labor contracts between planters and freedmen, and the administration of justice.

General Scott listened to Eva without interruption, seemingly immersed in her tale as she recounted what happened to her and Zack while they were en-route to Moncks Corner. His attention perked up when she said that she reported the incident to Captain Liedtke at the Moncks Corner Bureau many weeks ago. And when she told him Zack Foster's body had been pulled from the river near the lumber mill at Gippy Dike, he tilted his bulky body toward her and peered into her eyes with genuine concern.

"This man, Foster was working as an Army contract driver, assigned to deliver government supplies?"

"Yes, that's what he told me."

"Were you provided a valid transport pass by Captain George to travel on the supply wagon with him?"

"Yes, that's correct. In fact," she paused and extracted a slip of paper from her purse. "I have it here."

General Scott took the paper, read it, and set it aside, his demeanor hardening as he lifted his square chin, firmed his lips into a grimace, and spoke through clenched teeth. "I have been extremely concerned about this increasing loss of supplies due to theft and carelessness. Another passenger train fell victim to bandits this week, and now this news of a murder. Such violence must be stopped." A pained expression claimed the general's pinched features as he focused on a tower of papers heaped on his desk. "Captain Liedtke's report may very well be among this unending stream of papers that lands on my desk every day," he stated with a wave of his hand toward stacks of documents and reports surrounding him. "I'll find it, review it, and you may be certain I will take all appropriate action." A beat of silence passed while he let his words sink in. Turning to Trent, he continued.

"Mr. Hartwell, I believe Mrs. Phillips' description of the man who stole the wagon, coupled with what she overhead between the two men at the post office afford sufficient reason to bring Leon Turner in for questioning."

"I agree," Trent said. "This may all be a misunderstanding, and he deserves the opportunity to clear himself of any hint of involvement. I don't know Leon well. I've met him only once, but I am a close acquaintance of his sister, Sage. She's told me that her brother is a Confederate veteran who served valiantly and was wounded. I sincerely hope he is not involved in any of this violence against the military government and the residents of this area."

"Yes, yes. Unfortunately, there are many young men like him

roaming the streets of Charleston," the general said as a scowl constricted his craggy features, projecting his discomfort with the situation. "It may turn out that Leon Turner is not the culprit at all. But I cannot ignore the seriousness of what you both have told me, so I will definitely have a talk with him."

Trent shook his head slowly up and down, accepting the truth of the matter. "I know Judge Turner well," he started. "The last thing I would ever want to do is bring trouble to the Turner family, but …. and this is difficult, the matter requires attention."

"Yes, it does," General Scott promptly agreed. "Thank you, Mr. Hartwell for bringing Mrs. Phillips to me with this information. Keeping the peace and administering justice during these trying times is not an easy task."

"I understand," Trent stated.

The general nodded at Trent, inclined his head at Eva, and then stood, clearly signaling that the meeting was over.

After Trent's carriage driver, Gus, helped Eva into her seat, she sank back against the tan leather cushions and allowed the tension that had been holding her body rigid for the past hour to ease. However, the sense of relief she had hoped to experience after finally telling all she knew about the robbery in the woods, did not materialize. Instead, she felt oddly troubled. The man she had seen in the post office was, according to Mr. Hartwell, the son of an important judge as well as the brother of the woman named Sage, who had spoken so sharply to Trent at the bank. A thread of worry tightened inside of Eva, pushing her to consider what her interference might mean. A member of the Turner family was now the target of a criminal investigation. By implicating the son of a well-respected citizen of Charleston, she had initiated a series of events over which she had no control. And the woman whom Trent obviously cared for deeply might be humiliated and brought to shame. What would this mean for Eva? Now that Negroes had been given the right to testify in court, would she be summoned to speak before a judge? Would doing so make her a target of those who supported Leon Turner's efforts to resist the sweeping changes occurring in the city? The whole sordid mess was wearing Eva down.

"Mr. Hartwell," she started, turning to him. "I'm feeling awfully anxious over what may happen next. Do you think…?"

"Please," he quietly interrupted. "I assure you, Mrs. Phillips, you did the right thing by coming to me, and I was correct to take you to see the general. The situation is out of our hands now. Please don't worry yourself. Let the soldiers do their jobs. You have nothing to worry about."

"Are you sure?" Eva probed, her stomach still in knots.

"Yes, put it all behind you. Don't waste time fretting over the despicable actions of a misguided young man. Unfortunately, war often leaves deep scars on men, and for some, those scars may become permanent."

Eva nodded, unable to reply, though she sensed that Trent was disturbed as well, just unwilling to let his uneasiness show.

When Gus stopped the carriage in front of the Trent's home, Eva offered her gloved hand to Trent, thanking him once again for his assistance. When he took it, he clasped his free hand on top of hers, as if sealing their mission for justice with a gesture of true friendship.

How strange, Eva thought as she relaxed her grip on his fingers, *that this white man would extend his assistance to me, twice, and with what seems to be a genuine sense of caring.*

"What are your plans now?' Trent asked, releasing her hands, pressing his broad shoulders back against his seat, making no move to depart the carriage.

"Well, I'm spending every moment I can, searching for my mother," she said, going on to tell him about the African woman she'd encountered at the market. "If I can locate that young mother, I am hopeful she might lead me to other women who speak the same language. Perhaps one of them might have known, or crossed paths with Mayree. It's a long shot, I know, but what else do I have?"

"I hope you are successful," Trent said, placing a finger on her arm. "Please be careful. A lady as attractive as you are, alone in the city, going around asking questions of strangers....well, it's best to take care in who you approach."

"I understand, and I will use caution," Eva promised, looking into Trent's eyes, realizing how openly sympathetic he seemed to be. "And," she added, "my friend Luvena has been most accommodating. However, now that I have decided to stay in Charleston a bit longer than I had anticipated, I'm thinking of finding a place of my own. But to do that, I need funds, so I must find work in the city."

Trent's thoughtful nod removed his eyes from Eva's face as he glanced toward his house. With a lift of a finger, he asked, "Are you seeking employment with a mapmaker?"

"That would be ideal. However, any type of work that I might be suited for will suffice. I can sew, cook a decent meal, even clean house if I have to, but I'd much rather work for a merchant or a tradesman."

A fine black carriage outfitted with gold trim rolled past, creating a loud clatter that momentarily interrupted their conversation. Once the carriage had rolled on, Eva noticed that Trent was toying with the sleeve of his navy blue jacket while staring at the ornate wrought iron fence surrounding his home. When he looked back at her, he spoke rather quickly, as if trying to say what needed to be said before he changed his mind. "I am a very busy man. Consumed with arranging purchase of lands and I am swamped with paperwork. I could certainly use your help."

"Really?"

"Yes. That is, if you would consider working for me when I am in need of a mapmaker's skills."

"Well, of course, I'd consider it. What do you need?"

Trent's honey-brown eyes grew widener, seeming to be lit with enthusiasm as he explained, "I am about to conclude a most important negotiation for a large piece of property in Saint John's Berkeley. I have the surveyor's report, along with a rather small map...it's just an outline of the property lines. Do you think you could create a larger, more detailed map to include the surveyor's marks?"

Eva thought for a moment, then replied, "I'm sure I could manage that."

"Fine, fine," Trent said.

"When would you need it?" she asked.

With a devilish grin, Trent told her, "As soon as possible. I plan to tour the property tomorrow morning, and a larger map would be extremely helpful."

Chuckling, Eva cocked her head to the side, and said, "Then I guess we'd better get started."

"Now?"

"Yes."

"Oh, yes, please, let's go into my office right now," Trent hurriedly agreed.

Trent stepped out of the carriage, and then offered his hand to help Eva descend. Holding onto her elbow, they walked up the red brick path to his front door. Once inside, they handed their outerwear to Amelia, then went into his office.

"Let me show you the surveyor's report," he told Eva, who settled into a chair across from Trent at his desk. He handed her a stack of papers and remained quiet as she looked them over. After she had reviewed the report, he unrolled a blank sheet of parchment paper onto the desk and placed an inkwell and a quill pen in front of Eva. While she studied the small boundary map, he described the parcel of land that he planned to buy from Coretta Gallard Saveneau.

"It's been in the Gallard family for over a hundred years, but now it's abandoned … been so for quite some time. I see great potential there for farming. With the lack of food affecting so many people, I plan to grow corn, potatoes, vegetables, wheat. The kinds of staples that will yield profusely and quickly help alleviate this dire shortage of food in the city."

Taking up the quill pen, Eva dipped it into the inkwell and sketched with practiced ease while Trent talked excitedly about his plans for the property. Eva murmured her approval as she worked, her fingers holding the quill pen at just the right angle to achieve the fine lines that swirled across the paper. Stopping for a moment, she addressed Trent's remarks.

"When I was staying at Fair Oaks, out in the country, I saw so much abandoned land. So many farms left to ruin. Fair Oaks was like that. I'm sure it was once a beautiful, productive farm, but now it's in shambles. Benton Langdon, who owns the property, isn't at all interested in farming the land. I think his interests lie in a different direction."

"I'm not surprised. Large-scale farming can be quite expensive and all consuming. The collapse of the plantation system has left white planters without a labor force, and blacks without a way to survive. However, the agricultural economy of South Carolina might survive with the government's help."

"How would that work?" Eva asked as she continued with her task.

"Persistent crop failures have forced the federal government to adopt a crop-lien system so planters, black or white, can receive rations for their farm workers. A lien is placed against the planter's crops as collateral for repayment for the value of the rations."

"And these farm workers are the freedmen?" Eva queried.

"In most cases, yes. The former slaves enter into written labor agreements between themselves and the planters. Under the terms of the contracts, freedmen are entitled to housing, rations, medical attention, fuel, and at least half of the farmer's crop. So far, I understand some 8,000 contracts have been signed and thousands of freedmen are now working under federal labor contracts."

"That's good to know. How much are the freedmen paid?" Eva wanted to know.

"Ah, generally eight, maybe twelve dollars a month. Sharecropping makes use of the available black labor. The landowners provide the seed and equipment, like hoes and plows. Freedmen want to work, and in exchange for a share of the crop they have access to food and some control over their lives."

Interrupting her work, Eva glanced up at Trent. "I'm sure your effort to make these abandoned lands productive once more will pay off. For the freedmen as well as yourself."

"That's my plan," Trent said, getting up from his seat to circle his desk to stand behind Eva.

"What do you think?" she asked, looking over her shoulder at him.

"Perfect," he said, leaning down to pick up the map. "You are hired, Mrs. Phillips," he stated, then added, "Is twenty dollars acceptable for your effort?"

Wide-eyed and pleased, Eva did not hesitate to say, "More than acceptable, Mr. Hartwell."

While he wrote out her check at his desk, he continued to speak. "I'd be so grateful if you would accompany me to the property tomorrow to see the lay of the land and make any necessary adjustments to the map." He approached, check in hand. "That is if you deem any adjustments are necessary."

The rich smell of Trent's woodsy cologne rose in front of Eva's face, filling her head with his presence, making her heart beat faster than she'd ever imagined it could. Pulling in a calming breath, she accepted the payment that Trent placed in her hand, and without hesitation, replied, "I'd be very happy to accompany you, Mr. Hartwell."

He returned to his high-back chair behind his desk, nodded, and folded his hands at his waist. "Good. But please, I think it would be better if you called me Trent."

"All right, but only if you refer to me as, Eva," she countered with an ease that surprised her, that made her wonder why she was feeling so delightfully comfortable in the company of a white man she had only recently met. Was it because she sensed his appreciation of her mapmaking skills? Was it because he made her feel useful and valued? Or was it because it had been such a long time since a man had looked at her in the way Trent Hartwell was looking at her at that very moment?

CHAPTER 26

Sage set aside the book of poetry she was reading and hurried to respond to the knock on the front door, her heart thudding in anticipation of receiving Trent while her father and brother were not at home. He had promised to come by after he had settled his business with Coretta and Dixon on the purchase of their property, and she was hopeful that he would invite her to accompany him when he drove out to view Bryan Tract. She was looking forward to another long, private excursion into the countryside with Trent, an excellent opportunity for them to grow even closer. They had been intimate three times, and she had loved every moment of their lust-filled encounters, feeling no shame or remorse for having succumbed completely to his charm. Surely, within the month, he'd be asking her father for her hand in marriage, and Sage had no reason to think that the judge would refuse her suitor's request despite the fact that Trent was a Northerner. She never would have dreamed that one day she would be the wife of a Yankee, but she had never dreamed of meeting a man as handsome, thoughtful, and wealthy as Trent Hartwell, either.

Sage smoothed her hands over the lace-trimmed bodice of her deep rose-tinted linen dress and gracefully opened the door, a seductive smile on her face, her head tilted back in preparation to offer Trent a most heartfelt welcome. However, her sultry demeanor immediately shifted into a squint of confusion when she saw two uniformed soldiers standing at her door.

"Yes?" was all she could manage as she glanced from one stern-faced officer to the other.

"Good afternoon ma'am," the shorter of the two men said. "I'm Captain Miller, agent for the second district." He turned to his companion standing stiffly at his side. "This is Captain Whittier. We'd like to speak to Leon Turner. Is he at home?"

"Leon? Well …. no, he is not here," Sage stammered, clearly puzzled. "Why? What is it that you want?"

"We have an order from General Scott," Whittier began as he pulled an official-looking document from his jacket pocket. "We're here to escort Mr. Turner to General Scott for questioning."

"Questioning about what?" Sage snapped, her earlier sense of confusion quickly turning into resentment. Hadn't these damned Yankee soldiers bothered her family enough? Why were they always poking their noses into people's private lives? Why didn't they just leave everyone alone?

The two officers exchanged glances before Captain Miller asked Sage, "May we step inside?"

Drawing up her shoulders, Sage arched her back and sucked in a short gasp of resignation in an effort to calm down. The last thing she wanted was trouble with the military government. She had no choice but to cooperate. "Yes, yes. Of course. Please come in."

Once inside, Captain Whittier pointedly glanced around the house while Miller spoke to Sage. "What is your relationship to Leon Turner?"

"I'm his sister."

"He lives here with you and your father, Judge Turner, is that correct?"

"Yes, that is true. This is my brother's home, though he's often away for long periods of time."

"Your brother served in the Confederate Army?"

"He did," she sniffed. "It certainly seems that you already know quite a lot about Leon."

"Do you know where he is now?"

"No, I don't."

"Will you allow us to search the house?"

"Search our home?" Sage shot back in disgust. "Do you have a warrant to do so?"

"I do," Miller replied, handing her the document.

As Sage's eyes traced over the words on the paper her lips tightened and her face flushed red. With trembling hands, she pulled the document closer, unable to believe what she was reading: *Based on testimony provided by Mrs. Eva Phillips, who was brought to my office by Mr. Trent Hartwell, it is determined that Leon Turner should be questioned in regards to the theft of a military supply wagon driven by US contract driver, Zack Foster. Orders to search the Turner home for any...*

"This is preposterous! Get out of my home! Now!" Sage shouted, crushing the paper into her fist.

"Ma'am," Whittier started, "we have orders to conduct a search of the premises before we can leave."

"Orders! To hell with your orders! You'd think we were still at war!" she snarled.

"Please ma'am. Don't make this more difficult than it has to be."

"Well go on then! Search the house!" she relented through clenched teeth while flinging the warrant back at the officer. "How much more misery can you awful soldiers inflict upon us? My brother is not here, and you can be sure that my father will make you sorry you ever invaded our home!"

Captains Whittier and Miller moved carefully from room to room, opening and slamming doors, searching the house from the attic to the cellar, looking into storerooms, closets, and even checking the gardens before concluding that Sage had told the truth. Leon was not there.

"If your brother returns, please advise him to report to General Scott immediately," Whittier told Sage, and then the two men left.

As soon as the soldiers walked off the property, Sage ran into her bedroom, flung herself across her bed, and burst into tears. What had Leon gotten himself into? And how could Trent be involved in this accusation of theft? Furious, she sat up, grabbed the antique vase of pale pink roses off the bedside table and hurled it across the room, seething with anger as she watched water and petals and shards of glass shatter against the wall. Chest heaving, tears flowing, she sobbed aloud, not so much for Leon's troubles, but for the absolute destruction of her life. She had put a great deal of effort into nurturing her relationship with Trent, pulling him so close that she could hear the wedding bells ringing, taste the icing on her three-tier wedding cake. But now, all she could see were his true colors… he was a traitor in disguise. She'd given him her trust, her affection … even her body! And he'd turned on her family as if they were the enemy. How dare he work with the government in their effort to question her brother about a crime that he could not have possibly committed? And who in holy hell was this woman Eva Phillips who was obviously his accomplice in this false accusation?

Sitting up, Sage swiped her eyes with the back of her hand and bit down hard on her bottom lip. Furious. Rising, she went to the washstand and splashed cool water on her face. While sitting at her dressing table, brushing her hair, she rehearsed the words she planned to fling at Trent when she paid him a visit to get the answers she deserved.

Sage's unannounced entrance into Trent's office brought him to his feet in an instant and caused him to overturn the inkwell that Eva had used to create his new map.

"Sage! What are you doing here?" he stuttered, righting the spilled inkbottle while Eva hurried to dab at the blue stain with a dark red blotter.

"I came here to talk to you about the lies you are telling about my brother!" she stated, her voice deep and level in an obvious tone of controlled anger.

"Oh…Yes, Leon," Trent repeated, quickly discerning the origin of her fury. "I think we had better talk about this in the parlor," he said, walking toward her.

Sage did not move to accompany him. Instead, she remained standing in the entry. "Why is that colored woman here in your office? What is going on?"

Stopping mid-way toward Sage, Trent looked back at Eva, who was staring wide-eyed at his unexpected guest, the ink blotter in her hand. "Sage, this is Mrs. Eva Phillips. She …"

"I know *who* she is. She's your accomplice in the lies you are telling about my brother!"

"That's not true. Let me explain," Trent began, taking Sage by the arm to maneuver her out of the room and into the hallway.

"Soldiers came to our house! Looking to arrest Leon!"

"Calm down. Let me explain. I believe General Scott only wants to question Leon, not arrest him," Trent clarified as he tried to ease Sage farther down the hallway.

She snatched her arm from Trent's grasp, spun away from him, and stepped back inside his office. She rushed to stand in front of Eva. "I'm not going anywhere!" she shouted at Eva before spinning around to face Trent. "Why did you do this? You have made a huge mistake and you *will* be sorry!" She glanced back at Eva as she spat, "Why is this Negra woman even in your house? Who is she to you? Your nigger bed-warmer, perhaps?"

"That's enough Sage," Trent said in a commanding voice. "If you calm down I will tell you exactly what happened and why I took Mrs. Phillips to see General Scott this morning so she could tell him what she suspected!"

"Suspected! Ha! So she has no proof of anything."

"That's right, I do not have proof," Eva spoke up, standing to face Sage. "But your brother closely resembles the man who robbed a government supply wagon full of food and medicine destined for the Freedman's Bureau. I was on the wagon, I saw him."

"Lots of people are hungry. Everyone is desperate. People steal government food every day!" Sage raged. She turned blazing eyes on Trent. "How dare you take this nigger's word and inculpate my family in this awful matter?"

Trent moved to stand beside Eva and place one hand on her shoulder in a very protective manner. "Sage, if you insist with these insults of Mrs. Phillips, I must insist that you leave my home."

"Oh, I'll leave," she shot back. "But mark my words, Trent. You will pay dearly for treating me and my family so shabbily. And I thought you were a gentleman!"

With a lift of his chin, Trent replied, "I *am* a gentleman, but I am also a lawyer. As an officer of the court I am bound by law to report my knowledge of any suspected criminal activity to the proper authorities."

"Well, all your legal knowledge doesn't make up for your lack of decent manners and common sense. You are no more than a crude, self-centered Yankee. You are not a Southern gentleman, Trent Hartwell, and I was gravely mistaken to think that I could turn you into one!" Then, with a swish of her voluminous skirts, Sage fled from the room, slamming the door behind her.

When Trent summoned Gus and told him to take Eva home in his carriage, she quietly gathered her things and left, departing with a promise to ride with him to see the Gallard property the next morning. Trent was grateful to Eva for not asking any questions or making an attempt to ease his anger over the awful encounter she had witnessed.

Now, standing at the large bay window that faced the street, Trent forced his fury at Sage, as well as himself, to subside. He had been foolish to think he could have become the man Sage expected him to be. He had tried to overlook her high-handed manner and the hurtful, often racist, remarks she made about those whom she deemed not worthy of her respect. She was beautiful, spoiled, and desperate to be loved, and Trent was ashamed to admit that he had taken advantage of her neediness, had welcomed her spirited attempt to seduce him. As much as he enjoyed dining with her, escorting her to social affairs, conversing with her about intellectual affairs, and making love to her in his bed, he now saw that their worlds were too far apart to ever meld into a loving relationship. He now realized that his acceptance into Sage's world would always be due to his success as an investor and his solid financial standing, and not to his tolerant view of the world and all the people in it.

He'd been wrong to engage in intimate encounters with Sage, but he reminded himself, she had been the initiator, kissing him on the first night they met, pushing her way into his life with such force that he felt obligated to go along with whatever she desired. He could not use the excuse that he'd been lonely, vulnerable, and susceptible to flattery because of Rebecca's betrayal. Too much time had passed for him to keep dwelling on what could have been with Rebecca. She was simply a part of his past, as his affair with Sage was now. He had to forget Sage, as he had forgotten Rebecca. But he had to forever remember that he would always be an outsider in the South, a man forging a new life in a strange new land.

Turning from the window, Trent slumped into the wingback chair where Eva had been sitting, overcome by a surge of relief tinged with guilt. As his eyes traced over the map Eva had drawn, his despair began to lift. He smiled a wry grin. He'd paid her twice as much as the map was worth but had no regrets. He liked her. He wanted to help her. She was so very different from Sage. He'd never met a woman quite so independent and brave as the widow Phillips. She had purpose to her life and a deep sense of pride in what she was doing, while all that had seemed to matter to Sage was his attendance at the next gala affair where she could flaunt her relationship with her wealthy Yankee acquisition. Trent pushed up from the chair, extinguished the lamp on his desk, and made his way to the staircase. Walking slowly up the stairs, he prodded his mental focus toward tomorrow, when he would see Eva once more, when they would spend the entire day together, alone.

∼

Sage rushed past her father without a word of greeting and raced up the stairs, breathless, tearful, and angry. After entering her bedroom, she went straight to the antique armoire that had once been her mother's and flung open its heavily carved double-doors with a loud bang. She pulled out the dresses, petticoats, skirts, and cloaks stored within the oak armoire and tossed them onto her bed. Then she got down on her knees, and with a hard yank, managed to pull out an oversize traveling valise that she kept beneath her bed. In a frantic whirlwind of fury and nervous rage, she began to pack her clothing into the bag.

"What is going on? What's all the noise?" Judge Turner asked his daughter after entering her room without knocking. "Where have you been? What's happened?" he probed, his attention trained on the valise that Sage continued to fill.

"Trent Hartwell! That's what happened," she flung at her father as she slammed a feathered hat into its round box. "He is such a disgrace! He is not who you think he is, Father. He is a crude, selfish man whom I hope to never see again!"

Judge Turner approached Sage and placed an arm around her shoulders. "Calm down, Sage. Come, sit down, tell me what happened."

Sage sat on the bed next to her father, and through tear-fueled sobs, related all that had transpired while her father had been at the courthouse. "I cannot stay in Charleston now," she finished. "How can I face my friends? Martha, Coretta, even Bessie will be laughing at me behind my back. I'm going to Savannah to stay with Cousin Hazel."

"Oh? For how long?"

"Maybe forever. Who knows? Who cares?" she sniffled. "Hazel has been begging me to come for ages, now I plan to accept her invitation."

"I think that might be a good idea," the judge mused, clearly distressed over this turn of events. "If that is what you need to do, then I support you fully. Take your time packing. I'll go with you to the train station in the morning."

"But what about Leon, Father? Do you think he's in a lot of trouble?"

"Leave Leon to me. And Mr. Hartwell, as well. I'll get to the bottom of these accusations. I'm just praying they are not true. But, I understand your disappointment, Sage, and I'm so sorry you've been hurt like this," Judge Turner comforted, patting his daughter on the arm. "But don't let this situation spoil your visit with Hazel. You go on. Try to forget about Trent. Who knows who you might meet in Savannah?"

Eva found herself alone in the house, which suited her just fine after experiencing such an exhausting day: A frantic whirlwind, starting with her interview with General Scott, ending with Sage's shocking scene in Trent's office. The emotional drain of the stressful encounters had left Eva totally devoid of energy. And now, as long shadows slipped through her bedroom windows, Eva sat in her bed with the lamp pulled close as she opened the letter she received from Aunt Tully. Just the sight of her aunt's carefully scripted handwriting brought a flush of calm to Eva's anxious disposition as she eagerly read, once again, news from Boston.

The news that Lawyer Daniels was representing a wealthy white woman accused of stealing a jade necklace from a local jeweler brought a smile to Eva's lips. She could almost hear the outcry from the woman's friends over such a scandalous situation.

Minister Pennworth had left Grove Street AME church to establish a congregation among freedmen who were settling in Canada. *Not a surprising turn of events*, Eva mused, recalling the preacher's passionate persistence during the abolitionist movement.

The house next door to Tully's had burned to the ground on the 4th of July, the apparent result of fireworks gone astray. Lawyer Daniels was encouraging Tully to buy the now-vacant lot at a very low price, as property values were steadily rising all over Boston.

If you was to tell me your coming back to Boston, Eva continued to read, *I'd buy that piece of land and get Mr. Lewis, that lazy carpenter what lives down the street, to build a house on it for you. With Chester now dead and you being so young, I hope you come back home and find yourself another husband before long. It'd be so nice to have you here again. But mostly I want you to start over, be it here in Boston or where you are now. Eva, I don't want you to give up on lookin for your mother, but don't give up on getting married again, you hear? There's a man out there somewhere who needs you and wants to love you, I'm sure. Stay sweet. Love to you, Aunt Tully*

After extinguishing the lamp, Eva lay in the dark with Tully's letter still gripped in her hand, unable to stop thinking of her aunt's closing words. Eva had not given much thought to ever marrying again, of being loved by a man once more, or of having a family of her own. But as she stared into the inky blackness enveloping the room, she allowed herself to wonder if such things were even possible for her.

CHAPTER 27

Eva was struck by the vulnerability in Trent's voice as he passionately spoke about the land, as well as his plans for the property. They arrived at Bryan Tract while the sun was creeping over the horizon and fog still hovered above the fields in misty veils that resembled clouds of smoke. They set out to travel the perimeter of the plantation, with Trent driving the wagon he had hired while Eva made notes and markings for the oversize map. They started off at the western boundary of the Cooper River, headed east on Umbria Road, turned northward to trace the old Santee Canal, and now, with the heat of late morning descending upon them, Trent stopped the wagon at the edge of Wadboo Creek, a swampy listless stream that created the plantation's northernmost boundary.

Eva moved into the shade of a leafy willow and sat on the trunk of a tree long-ago fallen as Trent bent down and scooped up a handful of red dirt.

"The only thing of any real value in the South now is this," he told Eva, letting the crumbled earth slip through his fingers. "As it stands, there is no government, very little money, and barely any order here. There is only land." A beat of quiet passed before he added, "And the people, of course."

Pushing at a clump of blooming clover with the toe of her boot, Eva considered Trent's remark. "I am beginning to understand what you mean," she said, taking in the beauty of the old Gallard plantation. Spreading oak trees, their long limbs hung with Spanish moss formed a graceful border along the water's edge. As far as she could see, rows and rows of fallow farmland waited to be tilled, planted, and harvested once more. Even the main house in the distance, made of red brick and in need of a new roof, still retained its shabby beauty.

"This red dirt is the real reason the Civil War was fought," Trent went on, moving to stand beside Eva as he looked out over the land.

"I thought it was a war to free the slaves," she countered, raising inquisitive eyes at Trent.

"It became one," he clarified. "It was actually a war to hold onto land, land that brought riches to a small number of white men who planned to rule the South forever with vast numbers of enslaved people. The entire economy of the southern states depended on the wealth of those men lasting forever, and that could only happen if they owned land and slaves. And now, so much of this beautiful, abandoned land is up for grabs by the highest bidder, and that's one of the reasons I'm here in St. John's Berkeley and not back home in Iowa."

"You say the land is *one* reason you came to the South," Eva began. "What other reasons forced you to settle here?"

A long span of silence followed before Trent moved to sit down beside Eva. He reached out and broke off a piece of tall grass, stripped away the leaves, and let them fall at his feet as he seemed to take a moment to gather himself. Leaning forward, he placed his elbows on his knees and stared straight ahead.

"What else? A woman's betrayal," he finally confessed, "and a brother's betrayal, as well." He tented his fingers and placed them beneath his chin before divulging more. "Her name was Rebecca, his was Robert. Back home in Iowa, I went away to study at the university. You see, my mother wanted me to become a lawyer, so I did it for her. It was a decision that I do not regret, as the legal profession has stood me well. While I was away, Rebecca turned to Robert for the love I was not there to give her.....and so, I lost her."

"I'm sorry," Eva murmured, not sure what else she might say.

"Even though I did practice law, I have never really wanted to do anything but farm. My family's farm at Strawberry Point was the whole world for me, and I never dreamed that one day I'd be forced to sell my inheritance to my brother in order to wipe away the pain of what he took from me."

In an almost spontaneous motion, Eva moved her hand to the cuff of Trent's gray cotton shirt and let it remain there as she spoke. "We mustn't look back and dwell on what we've lost. I think about my husband, Chester, every day, but I've stopped trying to imagine what my life would be if he had not died. All I can hope for is the strength to move forward," she said, recalling Aunt Tully's words. "I'm sure losing your land, the woman you loved, and your brother as well, must have been extremely hurtful for you. But you can't let that pain interfere with the joys that await your future."

Trent nodded, his eyes trained on the ground. "You're right, I know. I've been living through a painful period, as have you. We both are strangers in this peculiar, hauntingly beautiful place. I have no regrets about leaving Iowa. I came into the South to buy land and bring it back to life, to farm it and help people rebuild their lives. All of this," he said, sweeping his arm in an arc, "is what makes the isolation and the sense of not belonging, which I admit to experiencing from time to time, worthwhile."

Eva absorbed his words as he went on to tell her about his arrival in Charleston and how eager he had been to be accepted into the cloistered circle of Charleston society. It became clear to Eva that Trent turned to Sage in hopes of blotting out memories of Rebecca. Eva saw how driven he was, how ambitious yet fair-mined he could be, and because of him, she better understood so many things about the South, among them, the value of owning land. Glancing over at him, she took her time assessing his expression, which was etched with a combination of sadness over his past and excitement over the prospects of bringing the Gallard plantation back to life. When he shifted and met her gaze she was stunned to feel a lurch in her stomach, a strong pull of attraction that stopped her breath and made her wonder why she was feeling this way over a white man whom she really did not know.

Breaking their connection, Trent pulled his watch from the pocket of his vest and sighed. "We'd better get back," he decided, offering Eva his hand as she rose. He led the way through tall winding grass to the wagon parked in the road. Once they were seated, Trent took Eva's hand and squeezed it firmly, more like a handshake than a caress.

"Thank you for coming out with me today. Your company provided a most welcome distraction from matters that seem to plague me at this time."

"It was my pleasure," Eva replied, sensing his discomfort at having divulged the most personal aspects of his life.

The ride back into Charleston unfolded in silence until Trent stopped the wagon in front of Luvena's house. "May I call on you, Eva?" he finally spoke.

"Do you want me to draw another map for you?" she prompted. "I'm available to work whenever you require ...."

"No, I mean ... not to work, but just to share your company," he blurted out in a stammer. "I do enjoy talking with you, and you're such a good listener. Right now that seems to be what I can use most. I hope I'm not being too forward."

"You are not," she declared with confidence.

"Good. I feel at ease when I'm with you, and I'm hopeful you feel the same way. It seems we're both rather alone here in Charleston, trying to forget hurtful pasts. Perhaps we can be friends as well as have a working relationship."

"Of course we can. You may call on me if you wish," she told him shocked by the deep connection she felt for him, surprised by her reluctance to tell him goodbye, and fully aware that they both could be courting serious trouble.

CHAPTER 28

A ring of burning candles atop a rough trestle table chased shadows from the main hall of Castle Pinckney. The vaulted stone walls, hung with spider webs and blotted with patches of mold, captured the silhouetted profiles of two men seated across from one another. Spread out on the table, shimmering in the blazing candlelight, were a necklace of three strands of pearls, six chains of silver, and a small pile of ladies' rings set with colored gemstones.

"I want one hundred dollars for the lot," Leon stated, lips pressed together as he nodded his head up and down, affirming his decision. "All of this would bring three times as much in New Orleans. You could go there, Benton, sell everything for at least three, maybe four, hundred dollars. I hear money is flowing in New Orleans and there're lots of rich men and fancy ladies who love this kind of stuff."

Benton picked up a ring with a large blue stone set on a filigree silver band. "I dunno, Leon," he hesitated. "Don't think I can go that far ... not with all of this. Too dangerous." He tossed the ring back onto the pile. "Broches, hats, purses. All right. I don't have a problem moving stuff like that. But this kind of jewelry? I dunno. Too chancy, I think."

"Take the pearls, then. You know you can sell them in town. How much will you give me for them?"

Benton shrugged. "I don't have any money. I didn't come here to buy, I came here to tell you I'm out."

"Out?"

"Yeah. That's right. I'm through."

"You can't quit on me now. I expected you to bring me some money tonight for these things. You know what the deal is. I take all the risks securing stuff for you to buy from me so you can sell it at any price you can get."

"I told you, I got no money on me now."

"What happened? What's got you so spooked?"

"Me spooked?" Benton tossed back in a gruff laugh. "You're the one been hiding out for weeks. Everybody in town knows the soldiers are looking for you. They searched your house again. You know that, don't you? I hear things, Leon. If you're smart, you'll get out of Charleston, disappear for good."

"I need money for that!" Leon shouted. "I got plans. I'm going to Florida, but I need money for passage on a ship. Money I thought you were bringing me tonight."

Benton shrugged, as if he could care less. "Just can't do this no more, sorry. That lady from up north … Mrs. Phillips … the one who was in the wagon with Zack…. Well she was spying on me when she was living at my place."

"Spying? I never even knew she was living at Fair Oaks! Why was she even there?"

"She seemed all right … and she paid me for the room."

"Stupid move, Benton. Taking in a Yankee like that."

"Yeah, well, she got into my storehouse. Saw some things. Now your sister is telling everyone that the Phillips lady is the one who went to the law about you. I gotta be careful, lay low. I want out."

With a snap, Leon reached across the table, grabbed Benton by the front of his shirt, and dragged him closer. The fury on Leon's face matched the growl in his voice. "You ain't getting' out now. I need money and you're gonna bring it to me, or…"

"Or what?" Benton spat, challenging Leon's threat. "You're not gonna go to the sheriff. Not to General Scott either. You can't say a word about me without tellin' on yourself. Better worry 'bout yourself, not me."

Leon laughed, his accusing eyes riveted on Benton's face. "I ain't worried none. But you better get me some money or …. well, just wait and see what I can do to you."

"Do to me? What's that mean?" Benton managed as soon as Leon let go of his shirt. He rubbed his throat and glared at the man he had foolishly gotten involved with. At first, Leon had simply brought food to Benton that he'd stolen from government transport wagons, and it had been easy for Benton to sell the bacon and flour and cornmeal to people who were starving. But when Leon began showing up with fancy ladies' hats and stylish accessories, Benton knew his friend was robbing more than government wagons. But he'd gone along with Leon's scheme, anxious for the items he could turn into easy cash.

Leon leered at Benton. "I could put you right in the middle of Zack Foster's murder, you know that, don't you?"

"How? I had nothing to do with that, but I know you did. Hatch told me he was there. He hid in the woods watching when you hit Zack over the head, tied his hands and feet, stabbed him, and pushed him in the river."

"You believe Hatch?" He laughed. "You got no proof!" Leon shouted, enraged. But then, as if wanting to lay claim to the killing of a Negro, he added in a braggadocio manner, "Okay, I did it. I got rid of the nasty troublemaker. But you, Benton Langdon, as my partner, are just as guilty. We been in this together from the beginning. You better keep quiet and keep both of us out of prison."

"All right," Benton relented. "Gimme the pearls. I'll sell 'em and bring you some cash. I know a lady who's comin' into some money who might like to have the necklace. But, after this deal, don't come to me again. No more."

"Don't take less than a hundred because I need fifty to book passage on the ship. But if you turn on me, Benton, you will pay dearly," Leon threatened as he bundled the pearl necklace into a cloth bag and handed it over to Benton.

"You just get outta town after this deal is done, you hear?" Benton pocketed the bag of jewels inside his jacket. "Now, what about the black Yankee soldiers? You gonna run off and leave 'em locked up in here? Don't expect me to tend to them!"

"Oh hell no," Leon snapped with disgust in his voice. "Only two of 'em left. They're gonna get what they deserve. I been keepin' 'em alive for a reason. Just leave it to me. It's all gonna end soon. I got it all planned out."

Chester lifted his ear from the musty stone wall and sat back on his heels, his heart pounding, his mouth dry. What he'd just heard was frightening. The man named Leon had confessed to murdering a man named Zack! Surely, he wouldn't hesitate to kill again. Chester's stomach convulsed into a hard knot, one that would not be eased with cornmeal mush and water. His despairing, self-pitying mood suddenly shifted into one of rage and fury, fueling his determination to survive. Standing, he eased over to the bunk bed beneath the barred window and shook his lone cellmate by the shoulder, urging him awake.

"Scooter," he hissed into the man's ear. "They arguin'. They gonna do something to us real soon. I heard 'em talking. Come on, man, get up…we gotta do somethin'…"

With a grunt, Scooter turned onto his back and fluttered his sunken eyes open, then stared at the ceiling with a blank expression on his skeletal face. "What kin they do they ain't already done? Pickens is dead, just you and me left. Ain't nuthun to do but wait."

"Wait for what? For them to kill us?" Chester countered.

"Probably, so," Pickens murmured, shifting his thin body onto his side to face the wall, clearly resigned to his fate at the hand of his captors.

Turning away, Chester moved to the rusted bars at the entry of the musty cell and scanned the dark tunnel leading to the main room of the castle. A dim light glowed at the end of the tunnel and muffled voices filtered through the heavy dank air. Pressing his forehead against the crusty iron bars, Chester shuddered, his frail body shaking in despair as a single tear ran down his cheek.

PART V

"The Yankees told us we could go down and vote in the 'lections and our color was good enough to run for anything. It was a long time after the War before I went down to vote and everything quiet by that time, but I hears people talk about the fights at the schoolhouse when they had the first election."

Anthony Dawson enslaved in North Carolina. Interviewed at Tulsa, Ok. at age 105. *Voices from Slavery* (New York: Holt, Rinehart and Winston, 1970)

CHAPTER 29

"That's a tidy sum of money, Mrs. Phillips," Mansard York said to Eva as he handed her the government check. "There is no recompense for the loss of your loved one, but I believe your deceased husband's back pay and your widow's pension will prove helpful in your future plans. It all amounts to three-hundred-fifty dollars." He made a note on a piece of paper and then looked up at her with an expectant smile. "If you'll please endorse the check, I'll draft a deposit slip for your signature so we can put this into your account. I've made arrangements for your annual widow's pension to be sent directly to the bank, and I will be more than happy to facilitate its deposit for you."

Eva examined the check with sadness in her heart. The back pay represented Chester's service to his country, but the annual widow's payment would serve as a recurring reminder of his death and her status as a widow. How final, and sterile, the transaction seemed to her, as if money could fill the void in her heart and bridge the chasm that Chester's death had created in her life. She almost did not want to accept the payments. However, she had to be practical. This payment, along with what Trent was paying her for drawing his maps, made her financial situation secure enough to consider moving out of Luvena's house and into a place of her own. With a sigh of acceptance, she signed the back of the check, tucked the deposit slip into her purse, rose, and offered the banker her hand, which he shook with enthusiastic gratitude.

"Thank you, Mr. York, for all of your help."

"That's what The Bank of Charleston is here for, ma'am... to serve its customers by taking on the burden of managing financial matters such as these."

Leaving the bank, Eva made her way down Broad Street, then turned left onto Orange, where the dressmaker's shop, *Virginia's House of Style,* faced the stately courthouse. The courthouse clock struck three as she entered the shop, where she had promised to meet Luvena after completing her business at the bank. For weeks, Luvena had been prodding Eva to invest in a new wardrobe, and now that her finances had improved significantly and the cool November weather had arrived, she decided it was time.

Virginia greeted Eva with a warm welcome and escorted her into the side room where Luvena was strolling among bolts of cloth. The rainbow of colorful fabrics piled high on long tables washed away Eva's somber mood. For the past four years, she had been wearing muted shades of brown or gray, instead of black, as was the custom for most widows. However, it was time for her to set aside such somber attire, not to mention the fact that the hems of the modest dresses she'd brought with her from Boston were beginning to show their wear. It was time to brighten up her clothing, as well as the new life she was now leading in Charleston.

"At last. I was beginning to think you'd changed your mind," Luvena huffed in a teasing manner while unrolling a length of jade green wool, which she held up to the light streaming through the large bay windows. "I thought you'd never get here."

"It took a while longer than I expected to get everything settled," Eva replied, her eyes darting among the bolts of silk, satin, cotton, and velvet that Virginia had arranged for her customers to peruse. Eva had never before seen such a wide assortment of exquisite cloth.

"Well now that you're here, let's get you fitted for the latest fashions. You really do need to pay more attention to your appearance, Eva," Luvena lectured, crooking a finger at Virginia. "She needs everything. From pantaloons to evening clothes. And most importantly, hats and gloves to match each dress, as well as appropriate crinolines and corsets." She turned to Eva and said, "And, my dear, I'm getting awfully tired of seeing you in that tired red hat. It has to go."

"But," Eva started, eager to defend her favorite chapeaux. "I love this hat. It was my wedding gift from Chester."

"Then put it in a box to preserve it," Luvena said, as she gently untied the ribbon beneath her friend's chin. "You can take it out and admire it from time to time, but … Eva…it's old fashioned, dating you terribly. Time to let it go, don't you think?"

As Eva slowly removed the hat that Chester had so lovingly placed on her head after their wedding, she nodded in agreement. "You are right. It's a sad reminder of my past. I'm ready to try something new."

After spending two hours selecting fabrics and deciding on clothing patterns, Eva ordered three stylish dresses from *Virginia's House of Style*. Luvena was pleased with her lone purchase, a pale peach frock made of exquisite imported lace, adorned with white silk rosettes which she asked the dressmaker to put in a box so she could take it with her, as she planned to wear it at the hotel that evening. After thanking Virginia profusely for her assistance, the two ladies left the dressmaker's shop and headed to the open-air market to continue their day of shopping.

"Why were you so insistent that the pockets in my dresses be so deep?" Eva asked her friend as they strolled along the street.

Instead of answering, Luvena reached into the skirt-pocket of her forest green dress and pulled out a tiny silver pistol with a gleaming mother-of-pearl handle.

"Oh my!" Eva remarked, stopping in her tracks. Her mouth

dropped open in surprise as she stared at the shiny weapon. "I had no idea..."

"Most people don't," Luvena interrupted, sliding the tiny Derringer pistol back into the folds of her voluminous skirt. "These are dangerous times, Eva. I deal cards at the hotel casino. Foolishness happens when whiskey and money make friends. I've been grabbed, pushed around, slapped, and threatened with harm more times than I care to admit. A few days ago, Mr. Luckey gave me the pistol. He calls it a Philadelphia derringer." She shrugged. "I don't know much about guns except how to fire one, and Mr. Luckey told me he'd have no problem if I had to use it."

"But ... would you really ever shoot someone?" Eva wanted to know.

"Absolutely. If I had good cause." Luvena broke her stride long enough to give Eva a touch on her arm and level a serious look on her friend. "A woman alone in Charleston has to take care of herself. More ladies than you suspect are packing a pistol or carrying a knife. I darn sure don't plan to be the victim of some angry gambler's fit of rage. And, yes, I sure as hell will use it if I have to." Luvena tilted her head upward and started walking again, as Eva hurried to catch up.

Continuing into the busy market, Eva and Luvena took their time selecting the best they could find among the fruit and vegetables offered by the vendors. As they were considering the purchase of a rather skinny, but much desired, rabbit to cook for dinner, Eva glanced across the table and saw something that surprised her. The eye-catching woman standing opposite her was fashionably dressed in a burnt orange frock with matching hat and gloves, and was carrying an intricately tooled leather bag in a lighter hue of orange. However, it was the lovely cameo brooch at her throat that drew Eva's attention, reminding her of the one she had seen in Benton's storehouse. The sight jolted Eva back to the odd encounter she'd had with Benton, peaking her curiosity even more.

Turning to Luvena, Eva whispered, while making an imperceptible nod toward the lady, "Do you know who she is?"

Leaning past Eva, Luvena assessed the woman, nodded, and then put a finger to her lips. Once the woman had moved on, Eva asked Luvena again, if she knew who the woman was.

"Oh, yes. That was Coretta Gallard Saveneau. Sister of Dixon Gallard. Old Charleston royalty, they're called."

"Really?' Eva remarked. "That's the family that owns the property Trent plans to buy."

"Exactly," Luvena confirmed.

"Well, she is very striking. Lovely dress… and beautiful jewelry, too."

"Well," Luvena began in a hushed tone, "Coretta is a widow. Her husband was killed in the war. She's rumored to have taken a black man as her lover, but no one has ever seen him."

"A Negro lover? Here in Charleston?"

"Um, hum. Honey, there are more mixed affairs going on in this city than you would think. Dangerous, but it happens."

"Is that so?" Eva remarked, her mind shifting to Trent and how complicated everything was becoming.

"It's a fact," Luvena insisted. "And don't think I'm blind to how Trent Hartwell looks at you when he comes around to pick you up. Honey, that man is smitten."

"Luvena! How dare you say such a thing?"

"Because it's true. He definitely has eyes for you."

"I don't believe so," Eva retorted, unsure if she was telling the truth. Trent did act as if he wanted to get closer to her in a personal manner, but Eva was not at all certain about his intentions. Was his unexpected interest in spending time with her a result of his rebuff by Sage Turner? Did Trent Hartwell really want only her friendship? Eva worried. Or did he have other expectations in mind?

"Be careful, Eva," Luvena warned. "What might seem innocent to you in daylight can turn dark in a moment, and you don't want to be caught up in the kind of darkness that mixing with a white man will surely bring."

Luvena's words hung in the back of Eva's mind as they continued strolling the market and filling their hand basket. When they'd completed their shopping, they emerged from the shade of the covered market stalls and stepped out into the fading sunshine on Church Street.

"I must leave you now," Luvena said. "It's after six, and I promised Mr. Luckey I'd come in early to help set things up for some high rollers due in from Atlanta. They want to play Faro, and the boss has selected me to be their dealer. I'm afraid it's going to be a long night, but it could also be a very profitable one if the betting goes my way. You take the basket and run along to the house. See you later tonight ... or maybe in the morning."

"That's fine," Eva said. "I'll go ahead and prepare the red beans and rice anyway. You'll probably be hungry when you get home."

"You're such a dear," Luvena gushed, giving Eva a quick hug before disappearing into the crowded street.

Eva turned onto East Bay and made her way north, cutting through the smelly, chaotic wharf as she dodged pushcarts overflowing with shrimp and barrels filled with tea and coffee. At the corner of East Bay and Vernon, she paused to let a mule-drawn wagon loaded with corn husks pass by before crossing. While waiting, she glanced toward the opposite side of the street. "Oh, my," Eva murmured, immediately recognizing the woman strolling past the butcher's shop. It was the young mother who had been singing to her baby in the market. The child was not in her arms now, and she seemed to be in a hurry to get wherever she was going.

Eager not to lose her again, Eva moved quickly across the street, her eyes trained on the girl, having made up her mind to follow her and find out exactly who she was.

By walking in the shadows of the shops, shacks, and makeshift vendor stalls that lined the streets along the wharf, Eva managed to remain far enough behind the woman not to be noticed. After a volley of twists and turns among narrow streets and alleyways, the woman finally stopped in front of a weathered gray shed with a palm-thatched roof that was squeezed between a tavern and a tobacco shop. Eva watched from the shadows as the woman pulled open the door and disappeared inside.

Hesitating, apprehension rising, Eva's determination wavered. She considered turning around and leaving, but was unable to move. Her legs felt heavy, her breath expelled in short, audible bursts, and a spiral of fear tied her to the sidewalk. Even so, she knew she *had* to knock on that door, go inside, and seek answers to the questions that had plagued her for so long. Knowing there was no time to waste, she stepped up to the door and pounded hard on it, as if to prove to herself that she could do this.

Within seconds a rotund woman dressed in a colorful African-print dress pulled open the door and leaned forward, shoving her broad, dark face so near to Eva's that it made her take a quick step back.

"What you want?" the woman demanded in a thick patois that defined her African origin.

Gathering her nerve, Eva stared at the woman, her eyes shifting upward, drawn to the impressive crown of twisted braids rising atop her head. Eva opened her mouth, sucked in a long breath, and then plunged ahead.

"My name is Eva Phillips. I'm ... looking for someone."

"What you look for?" the African snapped, eyes narrowed in suspicion.

"Mayree," Eva stated, lifting her hand to point at the crown of hair on the woman's head.

"Mayree?"

"Yes."

Immediately a wide smile spread across the African woman's smooth round face, softening her demeanor. She squinted her round dark eyes at Eva, then nodded. "Ah, yes, yes, Moree." She pointed at her chest and said, "I am Oda. You, Moree?"

"No, no ... I am looking for a woman whose name is Mayree," Eva repeated, her anticipation shifting to disappointment. Apparently, the woman did not speak much English and didn't understand what Eva wanted. "Can you tell me ... do you know ..."

However, before Eva could complete her question, Oda spun

around, marched back inside the shack, and then motioned with a hand held behind her back for Eva to follow.

The interior of the shack was dim, smelled of boiled meat, and was lit by a single oil lamp set atop a low round table that held a generous platter of steaming brown meat. As Eva's eyes adjusted to the faint lamplight, she saw four more women sitting on the floor, among them, the young mother from the market. Their dresses resembled the clothing of Eva's greeter, and all of them wore braided hair, twisted into the same impressive style.

"Moree," Oda proudly stated as she waved her arm across the heads of all the ladies.

Puzzled, Eva shook her head. It was clear that Oda did not understand why Eva had come or what she wanted. "I think there has been a misunderstanding," Eva began. "I'm looking for a woman named Mayree. She was a slave on the Cantrell plantation. It was called Stillwater. I thought perhaps, because of your hair style that ... oh well," she breathed, letting her words fall away, frustrated by the blank stares peering back at her. "I don't want to intrude on your meal. Perhaps, I'd better leave," she decided, turning toward the door.

"No, please stay," a small voice said, stopping Eva.

A frail woman draped in vibrant red and green fabric rose from the low table and slowly made her way toward Eva. "I think I can help you," she said. "My name is Elmina and I 'spect my English is much better than Oda's. Come sit with us. Tell us, again, who are you? Who do you look for? I will tell you what I know."

The other women shifted around to make space for Eva to sit with them, and once she was seated, Elmina began to speak. "First, we introduce ourselves."

Sitting on the floor, Eva looked from one woman to the other as each spoke her name and bowed slightly at her. The young mother said her name was Kalaju.

"I am pleased to meet all of you. My name is Eva," she began, going on to tell them about her journey, and why she followed Kalaju to this place. "I heard Kalaju singing in the market. I recognized the song. It is one my mother sang to me, so I hoped Kalaju might lead me to someone who could help me." Heart pounding, and praying she might be close to the end of her search, Eva pointed to the twisted crowns atop the women's heads and said, "I was told my mother wore her hair in the same way."

Elmina nodded vigorously, seeming pleased with Eva's story. "Yes, she did. This is our custom."

Eva tensed, then tentatively asked, "So you did know Mayree at Stillwater plantation?"

With a somber nod, Elmina answered, "Yes, I know her. Long time ago."

Impulsively, Eva took hold of Elmina's arm, as if touching her would make their encounter more real. "Oh, please, tell me what you know."

"I will try," Elmina replied.

All of Eva's tension drained from her body as she went limp, anxious to hear what Elmina had to say. Swallowing dryly, she waited, tears filling her eyes.

"Your mama … and all us here… we come from the village of Moree, in Ghana. In our village, the women wear hair like this. Always we do it this way."

Eva glanced from woman to woman as each one patted her hair-do and beamed in agreement.

"At Stillwater, Masa Cantrell give all his slaves a name he liked," Elmina continued. "He named your mamma Betty, but she kept tellin' him, no, no, she was Moree. Pretty soon old man Cantrell give in and started calling her Mayree. He don't understand she is telling everyone she is from the village of Moree. Massa don't much care what any slaves had to say. At Stillwater, just the two of us from my village. Me and Mayree. She be my only friend. A great comfort when Massa take my chillen away."

Eva's mouth opened slightly as it dawned on her that Mayree had never been her mother's real name, but a convoluted pronunci-ation of the name of the village where she was born.

"Your mamma, a brave woman," Elmina went on, as if proud to

be the one to tell Eva about her mother. "I be there when Massa whip her real bad for letting her little girl drown in the river. 'Course, all us slaves know she gave you away. I watched Mayree take the lash, and I cried, but she never did. She said Massa could kill her if he wanted. She didn't care 'cause she knew her baby girl was gone to the North. When freedom come, we walked off that place together."

"Where is my mother now? Do you know?" Eva asked, almost afraid to hear the answer.

"Home. In Africa. If God be with her, she be back in her village."

"How? When?" Eva wondered, stunned by this news.

"After freedom come, me and Mayree come to Charleston. We just two starving, pitiful souls with no place to go. No family to care for us. We be livin' on the street, eatin' what we beg from strangers or find in the trash in the alleys. One day, a white man post a sign at the wharf, said he be sailing back to Africa and he take all who want to go. Mayree got it in her head she was goin' home. Carrying nothin' but a raggedy shawl wrapped around her arms, she walked right up that plank and got on the ship and sailed away."

"And you stayed here? Why?"

"I don't go 'cause I be lookin' for my baby girl. Massa sold her away from me long ago and I heard she still 'round here in Charleston." Elmina glanced over at Kalaju and added, "Thank the Good Lord, I find her."

Eva slumped back on her heels to absorb Elmina's story, elated to know her mother was alive, yet disheartened to learn she was so far away. "What about the ship's captain? Did he ever return to Charleston?"

"No, least I never saw him or his ship in the harbor again. Guess he done with taking slaves back to Africa."

The weight of Eva's disappointment made her physically nauseous. Unexpected tears flowed from her eyes and she struggled to keep from becoming sick. She had convinced herself that simply knowing what happened to her mother would be enough, that it would satisfy her craving to know the truth. But now she realized that was not true. She had desperately hoped to look into her mother's face once again, to feel her arms around her, and to hear her soft voice singing the song that was embedded in Eva's heart. Overcome with emotion, Eva's low sobs grew more intense, forcing her to bury her face in her hands as the tension and hope and expectation she had been living with for so long burst forth in an unchecked rush. As her body heaved and her crying continued, Elmina softly comforted Eva.

"You go on. Cry, my child," she gently urged, sliding closer to Eva, placing an arm around her waist. "Now you know your mamma is back with her people, not wandering the roads, starvin' like a beggar. Mayree left this place, where she suffered so much. I think she happy now, back home in Moree, sittin' in the sunshine, eatin' a sweet mango."

CHAPTER 30

The décor of the Luckey Star Hotel reflected the finest furnishings available to the wealthy residents of Charleston. Authentic oil paintings, imported rugs, jewel-like chandeliers, and exquisite accoutrements from European markets created an interior that rivaled the finest homes in the city. However, in spite of its grand ambiance and implied exclusivity, the Luckey Star was the only hotel that permitted Union soldiers, ex-Confederates, Blacks, Creoles, outlaws, Indians, and lawmen to mount the stairs to the private gaming tables to try their luck at cards, dice, Roulette, Faro, and Poker. The only rule that Mr. Luckey enforced was that the men had to wear clean boots, jackets, and ties, which led to a most eclectic assortment of outfits among those who entered his establishment.

According to many of the men who spent time and money at the hotel's boisterous casino, Luvena Nesbit was the reason they showed up early and stayed late at the gaming tables, wagering until they either exhausted their funds or played a winning hand. For many of the visitors, Luvena was the first lady gambler they'd ever come across, and she made losing a much more tolerable an experience. She possessed stunning good looks, which helped disarm aggressive opponents. Her striking appearance also gave them something pretty to look at as they lost money, watches, horses, and even gold wedding bands taken from their fingers to settle a debt.

Now, Luvena hurried into her dressing room behind the hotel's kitchen to change into the new lace dress she'd just purchased at *Virginia's*. A flicker of excitement ignited her thoughts as she stripped off her day-dress and opened the dressmaker's box. The sight of the frothy creation fueled her confidence and roused her determination to win. She was keenly aware of the power that her appearance possessed, and she planned to use it tonight.

The image reflected back to her in the gilt-edged, full-length mirror met her expectations. Luvena was not ignorant of the fact that her looks and her profession made her the target of ugly gossip and hateful remarks among the snooty elite of Charleston society. But she paid such talk no attention, considering herself a business-woman with a talent for dealing cards, and not an entertainer with loose morals. Such nasty barbs should be targeted at the skimpily attired dancers who escorted men to private rooms, and the buxom vocalists who performed for the men on the variety stage down-stairs. Luvena interacted on a professional level with all: gentlemen, as well as thieves, homewreckers, shady strangers, and those living on the fringes of the law. Her job was not to judge, but to lure players to the gaming tables and build their betting confidence.

Tonight's important game of Faro with the men from Atlanta meant that she, as the banker, had to sell them ten-dollar chips and deal the cards. If the house won, she split the cash winnings with the hotel, but if something other than cash was wagered and lost, the hotel manager was the one to decide if the item belonged to him or to Luvena.

At exactly nine-thirty, she sat down at the casino's most visible Faro table, a flat oval surface covered with green baize cloth with a semi-circle cutout for the banker's chair. She adjusted her chair, straightened the stacks of chips that the players would use to place their bets, and checked the layout board to make sure the entire suit of spades was intact.

"May we join you?" a deep voice inquired.

Eva raised her eyes to see four well-dressed gentlemen standing at her table, smiling broadly at her, clearly eager to get into a game. "Of course," she sweetly answered.

"We're the Dumont brothers," the taller of the quartet announced, then added with pride as he took a seat, "We're the Dumonts of Dumont Carriages of Atlanta."

"Oh, yes, of course," she acknowledged, knowing their company made the finest carriages money could buy. "Welcome to Charleston, gentlemen," Luvena offered in a voice very close to a purr. "Please, sit down," she invited, fanning the deck of cards in her hands.

With great swiftness and expressions of anticipation on their faces, they arranged themselves around Luvena, beaming their pleasure at her. She was just about to shuffle the cards when a fifth player walked over and quietly slipped into an empty chair at her side. Luvena nodded at him in recognition but did not speak, having dealt Faro with Dixon Gallard too many times to count. Tonight, she could tell by the scarlet patches on his face and the traces of red in his eyes that he was more heavily under the influence of his favorite spirits than usual.

You better not mess up my game, she thought, eyeing him suspiciously. She'd been planning on dealing for the Dumont brothers exclusively, and now she had to contend with Dixon Gallard, who was known to be an unpredictable sore loser when the cards did not fall his way.

With all of the men settled into their seats, whiskey at their elbows, the play began. Eva shuffled the deck and placed the cards inside the dealing box, a mechanical device often called the "shoe". With the efficient ease of a professional dealer, she burned off the first card, leaving fifty-one cards in play. Then she drew two more— one for the "banker", which she placed on the right side of the dealing box, and one for the "player" which she set to the left.

Once all bets had been placed on the layout, the play began, with hundreds of dollars passing through Luvena's hands over the next three hours. The men from Atlanta talked among themselves as they discussed their many financial ventures. They talked about the hotels they were building, their new management of a freight line from Atlanta to New Orleans, and the latest styles of carriages. Luvena's nerves of steel and calculating mind were tested with each hand they played as chips were placed and cards were turned and the winnings mounted up, rather equally on each side.

At exactly twelve o'clock, the Dumonts gave up, laughing and thanking Luvena for a delightful evening, even handing her a generous tip. But once they had departed, Dixon Gallard remained. He tipped back the last of the whiskey in his cut glass tumbler and squinted inquiringly at Luvena.

"One more hand for me," he slurred, hitching his body forward, pushing his face close to hers. "I feel like my luck's gonna change right now."

"All right," she agreed, though she was rather tired and had been hoping to leave the casino after finishing with the men from Atlanta. "Ten dollars a chip," she reminded Dixon. When he failed to place his money on the table, she told him again. "Only ten dollar bets at my table."

"That so?" he mumbled, scratching his chin.

The side curl to his lip told Luvena that he was broke, having wagered and lost his cash to the house. She made no comment. Only stared blankly at him while waiting for his money to be placed on the table.

"What about givin' me some credit? Just this once," he proposed, ending his request with a hiccup.

"Not tonight, Dixon," Luvena countered. "Mr. Luckey says no more credit for you."

"Damn!" He scowled, then he stuck two fingers into the inside pocket of his suit jacket and fumbled around until he produced a folded piece of paper. "What about this?" he struggled to say as he tossed the paper at Luvena.

Taking it up, she scanned the deed to a piece of property in Saint John's Berkeley, properly registered to Dixon Gallard. It was the deed to Bryan Tract. The land Trent Hartwell was planning to buy. *Seven-hundred acres ... not too bad,* she decided.

"Sure you want to do this?" she queried, giving him a chance to withdraw from the play.

"Why not? The taxes are more than the place is worth. Might be better to lose it to you than sell it to a Yankee," he laughed, tipping back his head.

Luvena signaled to her boss, urging Mr. Luckey to hurry over to see what was going on. And when he learned how much the taxes would be on the property, he told Luvena, "If you win the play, Luvena, it's yours. I been burned too many times with these kind of deals. I don't want any part of it. " Then he threw up his hands and left her to carry on.

"Fine with the boss, fine with me," Luvena said as she set up the play and pulled the first card.

It did not take long for curious observers to gather around as the play unfolded. Keeping an impassive set to her face, Luvena watched as every bet Dixon placed on the layout's card was lost by him and won by the bank.

When only three cards remained in the dealing box, Luvena called the Turn, which meant if Dixon predicted the exact order of the three remaining cards, he would win, and maintain ownership of Bryan Tract. She knew that the Turn provided the dealer one of the few advantages in Faro, but she was not certain how well Dixon had been counting the cards tonight.

"Five, seven, three," Dixon boldly stated, pronouncing each number carefully.

Those watching held their breaths as Luvena turned over the first card. A five of hearts. Dixon grinned and hunched his shoulders in relief. The second card that she revealed was a seven of diamonds.

"I told you my luck was changing," Dixon shouted to the crowd while grinning at the people who were staring at the green cloth table in anticipation of the finale.

When Luvena turned over the third card and saw that it was a four of clubs, she could not help but smile at this lucky turn of events. Shaking her head, she looked at Dixon through lowered lashes and told him, "Guess your luck didn't hold, now, did it?" She picked up the deed and waved it in the air as those around her clapped and shouted their approval of the play. She turned to the man standing next to her and said, "Would you please bring me a quill and some ink? Mr. Gallard has something he needs to sign and I want witnesses to watch as he does it."

CHAPTER 31

"It was very late when you got home last night," Eva observed as she poured coffee into Luvena's china cup. "I'm surprised you're up so early."

"You heard me come in? It must have been close to three in the morning. Why were you awake?"

Eva bit her lip, pausing, not sure where to begin. The mystery of what happened to her mother had been solved, but the knowledge brought Eva little comfort. The empty ache in her heart remained, and her sense of loss seemed to have grown even more intense. She spent the better part of the night tossing and turning, reliving her encounter with the women from Moree until finally lulling herself to sleep by filling her mind with the African song her mother used to sing. Brushing a stray lock of hair from her face, Eva took a deep breath and told Luvena how she had followed the girl from the market and what she had learned about her mother from the woman named Elmina.

"And all women are from the same village?" Luvena remarked, setting her coffee cup aside.

"Yes, and they all were wearing the same crown of braids. They seemed so proud of their hair styles, too."

"My, my," Luvena murmured. "What a lucky break for you to see that girl again … but following her to that shack on the wharf. Well, that was a dangerous thing to do."

"I had to," Eva countered. "It was the only lead I had."

"Well, thank God things turned out as well they did." She reached over and took Eva's hand. "How do you feel about all of this? Are you all right?"

Eva nodded. "I'm fine. Luvena, I told you I came to South Carolina to visit my husband's grave and find my mother… or learn what happened to her. I've done both. Now, I have to decide if I will go back to Boston or stay here. I just don't know what I should do."

Luvena patted Eva's hand, got up from the breakfast table and went into the parlor. She returned with a piece of paper and took her seat across from Eva. "I have an idea," she started, quickly filling Eva in on her night at the Faro table, and how Dixon Gallard had wagered and lost his title to Bryan Tract.

"I'm stunned to hear this," Eva said after hearing Luvena's recounting of the evening's events. "Trent was promised that land. He's all set to close the deal."

"Not anymore," Luvena said, fanning her face with the deed to the land. "I won it fair and square. Gallard signed it over to me in front of a whole lot of witnesses, including Sam Scott, and he's the county clerk."

"Trent is going to be furious!" Eva exclaimed.

Luvena slammed the deed onto the table and glared at Eva. "Would you please stop worrying about what Trent Hartwell wants! He already owns half of Saint John's Berkeley. He doesn't need another rundown plantation to add to his list of acquisitions." She licked her lips and gave Eva a stern, studious look. "I hope you decide to stay in South Carolina. And if you do, well, I think you should have a home of your own. I don't need a rundown planta-tion. I have all the house I need right here. But just think, Eva. Now that you have money in the bank, why don't you buy Bryan Tract? I'd love to sell it to you."

Shocked, Eva pushed back from the table to take a long look at her friend. "You want to sell it to me? Luvena, you couldn't do that … I can't undercut Trent. He's a good friend. He's been so helpful and kind to me. He deserves the truth, don't you agree?"

Luvena lifted both shoulders in a dismissive manner, her lips curving into a half-hearted grin. "The *truth*? I guess so. But does he deserve to own my newly acquired plantation? No, I don't think he deserves to own it any more than you do. I own *this* house. I live three blocks from the hotel where I plan to work until I'm too old or too unattractive to sit at the Faro table and deal cards. I don't need or want a rotting plantation and seven-hundred acres of farmland to care for. But you… Eva…you could have a place of your own. A home you could build up. Buy it. Hold onto it. If you don't want to live on it, you can use the property as collateral to secure a house in town. I'm sure your banker friend, Mr. York, would be happy to help you with that. Land is more important than money right now and one day you'll be glad you bought it." She unfolded the document and smoothed out the creases in the brittle cream-colored paper. "Now, there is one thing you need to know about this deal."

"What?" Eva cautiously asked.

"The back taxes are due in less than thirty days."

"How much?"

"Two-hundred-seventy-five dollars."

"Oh," Eva flinched.

"You have that much in the bank, right?"

"Yes, but it would take nearly everything I have."

"But, you're working for Trent, making your own money, and your widow's benefit will continue to come in," Luvena calculated, becoming increasingly animated as she plotted Eva's future. "Fifty dollars. That's my price to you for the deed. Then, all you have to do is pay the back taxes, and Bryan Tract is yours."

Biting her lip, Eva looked away, still uneasy with the prospect of undercutting Trent. "I am so grateful for your offer and your friendship, Luvena, and I wish I could accept, but I can't. The land is yours. Trent made plans to buy it. For me to do as you suggest would be like stealing from him."

Luvena cleared her throat and shifted in her seat as if seeking a plausible excuse for Eva to go against Trent. "All right. Go to Mr. Hartwell. Tell him what Dixon Gallard has done. Tell him I plan to let the property go up for auction for back taxes if you don't buy it. Then he can try to rectify the situation by bidding on it like anyone else. Believe me, he does not want to do that. The elite of Charleston will come out in droves to support the Gallards. They'll be bidding against the Yankee from the courthouse steps and they'll band together to drive the price sky high, forcing your carpetbagger investor to pay triple what he planned to spend, if he gets it at all."

By mid-morning, Eva was standing at Trent's door, anxious to tell him what had happened. As she followed Amelia to his office she mentally rehearsed what she wanted to say. When she entered the room, he rose from his desk and hurried to greet her.

"I'm so glad you decided to come early today," he said. "I have a new surveyor's drawing I'd like you to see."

"I didn't come to draw a map," she said rather flatly, and then moved to sit down. She noticed the frown of concern that pulled his brows together.

"I have disturbing news," she started, tilting her head to the side, observing his features as they shifted into a mode of worry.

"Disturbing?" he repeated. "That sounds somewhat ominous."

"It is," she sighed, deciding to plunge directly into what Luvena had told her, leaving him to deal with the mess that Dixon had created.

"He put up the deed to Bryan Tract in a Faro game?" Trent thundered, jumping up from his chair to pace the space behind his desk. His earlier frown turned into a scowl that brought a red flush to his face. "How dare he? Coretta and her brother made a deal with me!"

"I know they did, and I told Luvena as much."

"How much does she want for the property?" Trent asked. "I'll settle with her right away."

Eva swallowed hard and glanced at the floor, searching for

275

words to further explain the situation. "She will not sell it to you, Trent," Eva stated in a voice that drifted into a softer tone.

"Why not!" he demanded in an angry retort.

"Because she wants to sell it to me. If I don't buy it, she says she'll let it go on the auction block for back taxes."

"Sell to you?" he leaned over his desk and locked eyes with Eva. "What did you tell her?"

"That I will not buy it, that you have been wronged, and I refuse to interfere with your agreement with the Gallards."

Trent sank back into his leather chair and rubbed his chin in frustration. "Eva," he started, regret imbedded in his tone. "Excuse my behavior. It's just such a shock to learn that Dixon foolishly wagered and lost Bryan Tract in a game of Faro."

Eva could feel the defeat that she saw in Trent's eyes and hear the ring of anguish in his voice. Pressing her hands together in her lap, she tried to ease the sting of his reaction. "I see how upset you are at this turn of events. You have every right to be angry. Dixon violated your agreement with him and his sister and I know how much you want the property. I walked Bryan Tract with you, I saw how beautiful it is, and how much potential it has for furthering your plans."

Trent's face suddenly relaxed. He drew in a calming breath and closed his eyes for a moment, gathering his composure. "Yes, I want that piece of land, it's an amazing investment, but there are many more parcels that I can pursue. Your friend has every right to sell to whomever she pleases, and if you want to buy Bryan Tract, you should. But please, I will not allow you to exhaust your funds to get a clear title to the property. Let me settle the back taxes for you so the deal can go through quickly. You may repay me over time, but I am not asking you to do so."

Eva sat quietly for a long time, her fingers entwined, a pensive furrow creasing her brow. In an uncertain voice, she asked rather timidly, "Should I?"

"Do you want to stay in South Carolina?"

With a slow nod, she searched his face, then stated with certainty, "Yes, I do."

Without hesitation, he answered her question, "Then absolutely, you should buy it." And then, circling his desk he came to her side and urged her to stand, facing him. "Think of the future, Eva. You are young, attractive, and I must say, very brave. You deserve every chance to build a new life and be happy. Owning property goes a long way in affording the kind of freedom and security you deserve, and need." He leaned closer and gently placed a finger on her cheek. "You can count on me to help you complete the transaction with Luvena. And I'll try to teach you everything you need to know about being a landowner."

With a chuckle, she told him, "I hope you will be a very patient teacher, because I have a lot to learn." Lowering her eyes, she ran her fingers up to the spot here he had touched her cheek, where her skin still burned from his tender gesture.

CHAPTER 32

Coretta moved quickly, like a spider scurrying after its prey—all arms and legs and sticky tongue as she stripped off Benton's clothing, wrapped her limbs tightly around his torso, and covered his mouth with hers. Clinging to him, she molded her body over his and fit his erection between her thighs without using her hands to guide him.

Thrusting upward, Benton obliged her greedy eagerness, clenching his teeth as he probed the silky insides of this delightful creature while exploring her backside with both of his hands. He squeezed her buttocks, squeezed his eyes shut, and squeezed everything out of his mind except holding onto this ride forever. He wanted to give Coretta something that she would remember, something she'd be dreaming about, begging for tomorrow.

Afterwards, while lying in bed, totally spent, Coretta eyed Benton with interest when he reached down to pick up his jacket from the bedroom floor. He removed a cloth bag from its pocket.

"What's in the bag?" Coretta asked in a cool tone.

"A trinket I think you'll like," he told her, spilling ropes of pearls onto the flowered bedspread.

Sitting up, Coretta picked up the pearl necklace and stroked the shiny jewels. "Lovely," she murmured, holding the piece up to her neck. Slipping out of bed, she pulled on a sheer robe and walked over to the mirror at her vanity. She sat down to admire the luminous globes, and when Benton came up behind her she let him fasten the clasp, then ran her hand over his as he stroked the side of her neck.

"Not another string of pearls like this in all of Charleston, you can be sure," he said.

Smiling, Coretta titled her head to the side, watching Benton in the mirror. "How much?" she asked, eyebrows raised. "Unless they are a gift?"

"Unfortunately, my circumstances don't allow me to gift them to you, but I can surely let them go for a very attractive price."

"How much?" Coretta asked for the second time, not hiding her desire to own the lovely jewels.

"For you, two-hundred," Benton stated, watching her closely, assessing her interest in bargaining with him. But when her blank expression told him that he had to do better, he added, "They'd cost three times that much from a jeweler, if you could even find a piece as beautiful as this."

"One hundred. That's all I can spare. I guess by now you've heard about the Faro debacle at the Luckey Star. That floosie who deals cards at the casino took advantage of my brother, stole our property. I had hoped to sell it for a decent amount of cash."

"Humm," Benton murmured, not liking what she told him. "You can have the necklace for one-twenty-five."

"You drive a hard bargain, my love."

He stooped to kiss the side of Coretta's face and whispered in her ear, "And you, my love, can't get enough of my *hard* bargains, can you?"

Giggling, Coretta lifted her lips to his and sank into a deep kiss, her hand at her throat as she slid her fingers over the silky jewels.

Breaking the kiss, she went to the stately highboy chest across the room, opened the top drawer, and removed a leather pouch. After extracting several bills she handed the money to Benton, then locked her arms around his neck and told him, "I believe I deserve a big thank you for taking those pearls off your hands."

"Indeed you do," Benton agreed, pulling her down on the bed.

The clock on Coretta's mantle struck eleven as Benton finished buttoning his jacket. He patted his pants pocket where he'd stashed the money he received from Coretta, wishing he'd been able to get the full two-hundred, but satisfied with what she paid. After giving Leon his cut, Benton would still clear a tidy sum, and then he'd be done with Leon and their business arrangement for good. With Leon hiding from the soldiers at Castle Pinckney, and that Phillips woman running around telling everyone what she knew, Benton knew it was time to distance himself from Leon's criminal activities and straighten out his life.

However, there was one thing Benton knew he would never give up, and that was Coretta. Sighing, he went to the bed and stared down at her. Their affair had started as a daring adventure. However, fooling around with a classy, beautiful white woman, had quickly shifted into an emotional entanglement that filled him with joy. He knew that he loved her, and he was beginning to believe that she loved him as well. Bending down, Benton kissed Coretta on the forehead, smiling when she reached up and wrapped a warm arm around his neck.

"I'll see you again soon," he promised, untangling himself from her sleepy embrace before making his way down the staircase and out the secluded side door that opened onto the densely planted courtyard.

A sultry moon peeped from behind a bank of clouds as soon as he stepped onto the brick path leading to the gate. With a jolt, he stopped walking when he saw a shadowy figure emerge from behind a giant sago palm. Before he could discern who it was, the man struck him with a metal stick and pushed him up against the iron fencing with such force that he fell to the ground. Trapped against the fence, he could not escape the man's repeated blows. Afraid that his screams would draw attention to his presence in Coretta Saveneau's courtyard and involve her in quite a scandal, Benton grunted and buried his head against his chest as the assailant repeatedly struck him across his back, his neck, and even across the calves of his legs. The taste of blood filled Benton's mouth as he heard the crack of a bone in his cheek. A bolt of pain shot through his skull and down his spine, nearly causing him to black out. Collapsing onto the brick pavers, he lay there as his assailant ripped open Benton's jacket, grabbed the money that Coretta had paid him, and then fled toward the side door of her house.

Moaning low in his throat, Benton managed to raise his head from the ground in time to see the man slip inside Coretta's house; a shadowy figure that he immediately recognized. Unsure if he should follow the man or leave, he opted for the latter, limping off into the shadows as he made his way to the carriage he had left waiting three blocks away.

Slowly, cautiously, like a cat approaching its prey, Leon entered Coretta's bedroom to find it bathed in faint moonlight filtering in through gauzy lace curtains at her tall windows. He was immediately and thoroughly disgusted by what he saw. Coretta was lying naked among the rumpled sheets, sleeping like a baby, the pearl necklace on the bedside table. Leon sniffed the air, certain he could smell the stench of her sexual tryst with Benton. Though she was resting peacefully, with an angelic calm to her face, he knew her to be the devil that she was. What kind of a decent white woman would lower herself to sleeping with a nigger? Leon had suspected for some time that something illicit was going on between Benton and Coretta because she often turned up wearing items that Leon had stolen from one of the unwelcome Yankee women invading his hometown. Benton had betrayed him. He'd told Leon that his transactions with Coretta were strictly confined to the exchange of money. That they did not involve the kinds of perverted sex acts that Leon had witnessed while watching them from the courtyard. Parading around naked with the drapes open and lamplight burning! *A nigger-loving whore, that's what you are, Coretta Saveneau. You'll pay for your degrading acts, for soiling every white woman's reputation in Charleston.*

Moving with care across the thick woolen carpet, Leon crept to Coretta's chest of drawers and rifled its contents, hoping to find anything of value that he might use as barter for passage on a ship going south. He was pleased to find a leather bag filled with cash. *An unexpected bonus,* he mused, sticking it into the front of his shirt. With a satisfied smile on his lips, he moved to the bedside table, pocketed the pearl necklace, and stood there, watching Coretta breathing evenly in her sleep. Stealthily, he moved his hand to the waistband of his trousers and slowly extracted the small knife he had carried into war, the dagger he had plunged into the hearts and stomachs of many of the enemy. With a quick, controlled movement, Leon slid the tip of the knife along the side of Coretta's pale white face, deliberately waking her, forcing her to look at him, wanting to make sure she knew who was standing there, eyeing her with disgust.

Coretta's eyes flipped open, and she pushed forward in alarm. "What are you doing here? What do you want!" she called out in shock, pulling the bed quilt up to her neck. "Get out!"

"I'll leave when I'm good and ready Mrs. Saveneau," Leon growled. "But first I'm gonna make you pay for taking a nigger into your bed!" he promised, taunting her as he brandished the knife back and forth in front of her face.

"Get out! Get out of here!" she screamed again, eyes now wide and filled with terror. Frantically, Coretta rolled to the side of the bed and tried to scramble away from Leon, but he clasped her roughly by the arm and forced her back onto her pile of satin pillows.

Coretta screamed again. Louder this time. But Leon slapped a hand across her lips and pressed down hard, grinning as she jerked back and forth in a futile struggle to get free.

"You whore!" he snarled. "Mine is the last face you will ever see!" With a derisive laugh, he shoved the knife into her chest and pressed down firmly. Leaning low over her body, he stared into her eyes, taking pleasure in the wild expression of fear and horror that claimed her delicate features, yet annoyed that it was taking longer than he had hoped for her to succumb to his assault. When she went limp and her breathing stopped, he stepped away, leaving his weapon protruding from her chest as rivulets of blood drained from her body and stained her white satin sheets.

Like a phantom ghost, Leon fled the bedroom, descended Coretta's staircase, and went out into the street with a smug curve to his lips and a triumphant gleam in his eyes.

She'll never show her face in Charleston again, Leon gleefully thought as he ducked into the nearest tavern and ordered a glass of beer.

Groping his way along the wrought iron fence, Benton took slow, careful steps, barely able to stand. He was more incensed over Leon's spiteful attack than the loss of the money he'd been able to secure for the pearls. Crippled by pain, he slumped to the pavement and lay there, cursing himself for believing he could trust Leon to release him from their illicit arrangement without getting hurt. Now, the money was gone. Coretta was involved. Everything was in a real mess.

I'm gonna go see Sheriff Cholett, Benton decided. *I'll tell him where Leon is hiding and tell him about those black soldiers in the castle, too. He'll be glad to know Leon killed Zack Foster. If Cholett agrees to keep me out of this, he can take all the credit for capturing Leon and releasing those soldiers. The government will be grateful for his help,* Benton calculated, hoping his plan would work.

CHAPTER 33

"It's all yours now, Eva. Free and clear," Trent said as he stood in the doorway of Luvena's parlor and handed Eva the deed to Bryan Tract. It had taken a week to complete the transaction but now the property was duly registered in Eva's name.

"Please, sit down," she said, motioning him toward the burgundy chair that faced a small oval table. She was glad Luvena had decided to take the train to Columbia to visit Zack's widow, and would be gone for several days. Eva needed this time to be alone, to think, to make plans for her future. She sat down opposite Trent and accepted the two-page document, which she read slowly, carefully absorbing every word.

"I can't believe I own a plantation house and so many acres of land," she murmured.

"This deed is for five hundred-fifty acres of Bryan Tract," Trent clarified. "There remains one-hundred seventy-eight acres that must be surveyed. Seems there's a dispute over the boundary lines of the property facing the river."

"Well, five hundred-fifty acres is more than I ever dreamed of owning."

"That may be, but it all belongs to you and I plan to pursue the matter until all of Bryan Tract is yours. You deserve to own what you paid for. Leave it to me."

"Such an unexpected turn of events! I never would have believed that one day I would be living in South Carolina with the burden, and the blessing, of owning such a large tract of land. Where do I start?"

"By allowing me to help you with the plans to renovate the house and return the land to a useful state."

"Oh…there's so much to do."

"You can do it," Trent assured her. "But I understand how you must feel. During these fast-changing times, a man's … or a woman's … circumstances can be altered in a moment."

"So true. My life was changed by the turn of a card in a Faro game," Eva mused, grateful for Luvena's insistence that she buy the land from her. "But, surprisingly, I feel at peace with what has happened." A beat passed as she locked eyes with Trent, and it occurred to her that since her arrival in South Carolina she had never been completely on her own, that it was time for her to leave the comfort of her friend's house and begin her new life as a true South Carolinian. She was eager to write to Aunt Tully and tell her all about her purchase, and in time, after Eva fixed up the place, she would invite Tully for a nice, long visit.

"How can I thank you for all you have done?" she asked Trent, placing the deed on the table.

"By allowing me to take you to dinner."

"Dinner? Tonight?" she repeated, caught off guard by the sincerity in his voice.

"Yes, tonight."

"But Trent… do you think it would be proper to be seen with me socially? The election is only days away. You are on the ballot as a delegate to the state convention. Drawing maps for you is one thing, but dining with you in a public setting? I'm not so sure."

"Being a delegate to the convention does not mean I can't have a social life."

"But your political foes could turn our friendship into something ugly, for no reason."

"Let me worry about politics. All I am asking is that we have dinner to celebrate your first land purchase. We'll go to Justine's. It's a small café across the street from my house. Justine's cooking is wonderful, and I'd love for you to meet her. I'm afraid I dine at her place more often than I do at home, though Amelia is a fine cook." He took Eva's hand in his. "You won't feel uncomfortable there, I promise." He studied her with expectation, giving Eva a moment to consider his invitation. "You know I would never put you in a position to be embarrassed, don't you?"

Without hesitation, Eva replied, "I know you wouldn't." She rose, picked up the deed, and gave him a smile. "All right. Let's celebrate." She started toward the staircase, then turned around. "Let me put this away, get my hat and my shawl, and I'll be ready to go."

She quickly managed the stairs and rushed into her bedroom. When she caught a glimpse of herself in the mirror of her vanity, she stopped and gazed at her reflection. Her cheeks were flushed, her eyes were wide and bright, and the smile on her face was one she had not seen in a very long time. Was this change in her appearance due to the pride she felt in becoming a landowner or to her excitement over going to dinner with Trent? With a mental shake, she laughed under her breath, realizing it didn't matter. Her life was changing. She could envision a future in this new homeland. And no matter what lay ahead, she was ready for the challenge.

Moments later, as soon as Eva and Trent walked out of the house, the skies opened up and an unexpected lashing of rain erupted, pummeling the earth like volleys of sharp arrows. To escape the gusty thunderstorm they hurried to climb inside his carriage, shaking water from their clothing as they settled onto the soft leather seats. Trent pulled out his handkerchief and began to wipe moisture from Eva's cheek, allowing his hand to linger beneath her chin. Eva, tensing under Trent's flirtatious gesture, locked eyes with him.

Why am I so afraid of opening up to this man? she worried. *I have shed my widow's clothing and I'm ready to be loved again.* But would loving Trent bring more pain than pleasure? she questioned, watching him closely, realizing he was so different from the man who accosted her in the woods and the rude men who treated her as if she had to keep to her place. However, Trent *was* white, and this *was* South Carolina, where mixing of the races could be dangerous.

When Trent leaned over to kiss her, she did not protest, allowing their lips to briefly meet. However, when Trent pulled her flush against his chest in a fierce embrace and deepened the kiss, she stiffened, recalling Leon Turner's harsh rebuke. *Why would this successful white man want me?* she fretted. *Is he honestly attracted to me? Can I trust him?* she worried. However, determined not to let fear destroy the blissful moment, she decided to take a chance. Eva relaxed in Trent's arms and let him kiss her again, and again as the sound of rain thundered in her ears.

~

After listening to Benton's proposal, Sheriff Pate Cholett laid out his terms for protecting Benton from prosecution for his part in the government robbery scheme.

"You say Leon Turner confessed to you that he killed Zack Foster and stole that wagon?"

"Yes, he did," Benton confirmed.

"When's the last time you saw Leon?" Cholett wanted to know.

"Been a week since he did this," Benton replied, touching a cluster of scrapes and bruises staining his pale face and neck.

"How do you know he's still on the island?"

"Where else can he be? He's got no other place to hide. He knows the Army is looking for him. Trust me, he feels safe there, and if he'd left town, I'd of heard about it. Hatch Ambrose or Vern Thompson would've told me."

"So Vern and Hatch are in on this as well?" Cholett rubbed his chin in thought, eyes gleaming with interest.

"Not in the killing, but they been helping Leon keep those soldiers alive."

"Tell you what, Langdon. I'm gonna act on what you're telling me, but it's gonna cost you."

"How much?"

"Not how much. You got something I want."

"What?"

"Fair Oaks. Sign it over to me, and if I get Leon, I'll make sure you don't spend one night in jail."

"Yes, Yes, I'll give it to you. The place is nothing but a headache anyway. You can have it."

"Time to get that plantation back in white folks' hands anyway," Cholett muttered, giving Benton the kind of look that dared him to reply. "We're gonna make it legal right now," Cholett said, shoving a pen and paper at Benton. "Write what I tell you," he ordered as he began to dictate the terms of the transfer. "But if you are lying about any of this, you go to jail, understand?"

"Fine," Benton tossed out rather casually as he signed the document with a flourish and passed it to the sheriff.

Cholett read the words that Benton had hastily written and smiled. "All right. We got us a deal, let's get going." Cholett slammed a dirty gray hat onto his head, checked the chambers in his Griswold revolver, and ordered Benton to take him to Castle Pinckney.

Their short boat ride to the island was made on rough, choppy waters due to the violent rainstorm that had just swept through the area. When Benton and the sheriff arrived at the castle, shivering and soaking wet, they lit flaming torches and crept through the moldy building, searching for Leon. However, they found no one. The place was deserted. Leon had fled, and the prison cell that once held the Union soldiers was empty, though evidence of their presence remained.

"If you expect me to protect you now, you'd better deliver Leon and those black soldiers to me! Fast!" Cholett shouted, outraged that Benton had wasted his time, had not produced what he promised. Stomping out of the deserted castle, he shouted, "Get back in the boat! We're going back to the city! I'm giving you one hour to find out where Leon and those soldiers are hiding or I'm going to have a talk with General Scott. Tonight. So if you don't want to rot in a federal prison for your part in this fiasco, you will bring Leon Turner to me immediately!"

As soon as the boat docked at the harbor, Benton jumped out and fled, eager to get to Coretta's house. He'd heard that she had been attacked, but had survived, and he was desperate to see how she was doing. He entered through her courtyard, eased in through the side door as usual, and found her alone, sobbing in her bedroom. Benton was horrified to see how pale and drawn she appeared. Her usually coiffed hair was in disarray and the large bandage that the doctor had placed on her chest wound was visible beneath the shawl she had wrapped around her shoulders.

"Leon did this to you! I'll find him and kill him!" Benton raged, pacing in front of Coretta.

"No, Benton. Don't go after him. What good would that do? Just be thankful that his aim was so poor, that his knife did not pierce my heart. I played dead. I fooled him into thinking I was dead. Just take me away from here. Please. That is all I want."

"Yes, yes, we will go away," Benton agreed, trying to comfort her.

"Doc Thomas says it's not a deep wound and I should heal in time. I'm a bit weak but I can travel. Oh, Benton, I don't ever want to set foot outside my house again," Coretta complained between sobs, touching the bandage the doctor had put over the wound. "It's not too painful, but I will have a nasty scar in a place where a lady would never want one," she sniffed as she wiped her nose on a lace-edged handkerchief.

"Don't cry, Coretta. Don't cry anymore," Benton comforted. "I hate this happened to you, and I will make it up to you, but first… there's some things you oughta know." Releasing her, he paced the room once more as he confessed to his role in Leon's robberies, as well as his meeting with the sheriff.

"I suspected the pretty things you brought to me might not have been obtained in the most legal of manner. But," she paused and wiped away a tear, "I knew you wanted me to have nice things and I knew you needed the money. But I don't want you to go to prison! Where is Leon?"

"I don't know."

"What can you do to keep Cholett from arresting you?"

"Nothing but leave town. We have to go, Coretta. We can't stay here any longer. We'll leave Charleston tonight."

Lifting a tear-streaked face at him, she squinted at Benton. "I'm already packed," she confessed. "There's nothing here for me now. My brother is a drunken gambler. His house is mortgaged to the bank. I'm land poor and nearly cash poor. Leon stole my savings… stole my money as well as my beauty. I'm ruined. I have nothing!"

"You have me, Coretta. You always will."

With a shudder, Coretta nodded, sucking back her sorrow. "I know, I know. And you mean everything to me. But Benton, what about Fair Oaks? Are you willing to walk away from that?"

With a derisive cackle, Benton tilted back his head, laughter spilling from his lips. "I signed the place over to Pate Cholett, but," he paused, then erupted into another guttural chuckle, "Fair Oaks was never mine. Old Lady Jutland didn't deed that place to me. In fact, her last words to me were, 'You can get off my land now, you lazy, black bastard. You might of been my *husband*'s son, but you were never mine'."

"Oh, Benton. How awful for you."

Shrugging, he went on, "Wasn't so bad. When Widow Jutland left, I just hid in the woods until she was gone, then I moved into the house and told everybody it was mine. So what? Nobody cared. Everybody in Saint John's Berkeley knew ole man Jutland was my daddy."

Coretta caressed Benton's bruised face and then told him, "If we're leaving Charleston, let's go right now! We can take the night train to Charlotte, then travel up the coast to Virginia. You can pass for white … we'll sit together on the train. We'll find a place to settle where no one knows us and no one cares who we are."

CHAPTER 34

Looking out the window, Josephine Ruby saw that the train station at Charleston was much busier than she had expected it to be at midnight. However, she should have known it would be clogged with travelers now that the war was over and so many people were coming into and moving out of the city. The sight of uniformed soldiers standing at the depot gave her some sense of comfort: The government was making a visible effort to maintain order in the nearly chaotic scene as travelers, both black and white, made their way onto and off of their designated cars.

Firming her grip on her small portmanteau, she got up from her seat and made her way down the center aisle of the train toward the open door of the Whites Only car she had dared to sit in during the last leg of her trip from Chicago. With her hair firmly covered by a subdued navy hat and light powder covering her myriad of freckles, no one had questioned her right to sit among those who, otherwise, would have ejected her. Lifting her chin to assess the crowd, she stepped onto the platform, just as a man and a woman moved to enter, bumping into her, making her drop her bag.

"Oh, excuse me, ma'am," the man rushed to say, bending to

recover her bag. He pulled his hat low on his forehead as he eased to the side and handed her bag to her.

"Oh, no need to apologize," Ruby replied, taking her portmanteau from him. "I wasn't paying attention," she added, shifting her gaze from the man to the woman, who wore a rather sad expression on her face and a large bandage high on her shoulder. A slight smile came to Ruby's lips as she nodded at the couple and moved deeper into the crowded depot. *He'll pass just fine*, she mused. *Just as I did. I wonder where they're going.*

After locating a bench in a quiet spot on the far edge of the platform where she could remain beneath the depot's roof and out of the hustle and bustle of the station's foot traffic, Ruby pulled up the collar of her warm woolen cloak and settled in for a long wait. She had no intention of going into the city to look for a room to spend the night, as she had been told that the lawyer's office was only three blocks away from the depot, and she planned to be there first thing in the morning. Still curiously anxious about the reason she had been summoned to meet the attorney, she opened her purse and took out the letter from Waterway Improvement Corporation that had brought her back to South Carolina, back to the place she had vowed never to return.

The corporation's office on Cannon Street was only three blocks from the railroad depot, right across the street from Mill Pond. When Ruby opened the door, the tinkle of a bell summoned a man from behind a closed door at the end of a narrow hallway. He approached with his right hand extended, clearly eager to greet her, and when she looked into his face, she offered him a genuine smile of relief. He was a colored man with neatly trimmed black hair and a pointed goatee that gave him a professorial appearance. His gray pinstripe suit was impeccably tailored to fit his slender frame, and the wire-rim glasses perched on his nose twinkled when they caught the light.

"Josephine Ruby, I presume?" he asked.

"Yes," she replied, releasing his hand.

"I'm Dirk Moultry, assistant manager. I hope your journey wasn't too arduous."

"Not at all," Ruby responded, feeling very self-satisfied, yet a tad guilty, to have ridden in more comfort than she would have if she had obeyed the law.

"I guess you are eager to hear what I recently learned about your father."

"Very curious. It wasn't an easy decision for me to come to Charleston, but your letter was so insistent that it made me curious enough to undertake the journey."

"I understand. Please, come into my office and sit so we can talk."

Ruby followed Mr. Moultry into a spacious room at the back of the building. The interior was shabby but clean, and the air was scented with the smell of lavender soap. She took a seat at the side of his desk where he had placed an open folder of papers.

"This all came to light upon the recent death of Elmer Ashford, for whom, I understand you worked for many years."

"That's right. He took me to Chicago with his family when I was just a girl and I lived with the Ashfords until I was grown."

"Mr. Ashford and your father, Jonathan Ruby, were shareholders in the Santee Canal Company, which has long been out of business. Upon Mr. Ashford's death, his widow discovered a packet of materials that indicated her husband had converted both his, and your father's Santee Canal shares into Waterway Improvement bonds."

"What does that mean, exactly?"

"It means that your financial future is secure, Miss Ruby. However, it'll take a while to settle everything. Our headquarters is in Columbia, so you will have to make a trip to the capital to sign the final papers. But, for now, you should remain here in Charleston. And don't worry about a thing. My wife has already prepared a room for you at our home so you can stay with us until you are ready to return to Chicago."

As Ruby reviewed the documents that Mr. Moultry had prepared for her, she began to wonder if returning to Chicago was what she really wanted to do.

CHAPTER 35

Night before Election Day

The sound of breaking glass shocked Judge Rowland Turner awake. Shaken by the abrupt interruption of his sleep, he sat up in bed, looked around, and then pulled back the quilt. Just as he stood, the thud of a brick landing at the foot of his bed propelled him to the shattered window. Fumbling to settle his eyeglasses on his nose, he searched the street below and found a knot of white men dressed in Confederate uniforms carrying lighted torches and yelling obscenities up at him while shaking their fists in the air. The judge held his breath, eyes flitting over each face, exhaling only when he was certain that his son, Leon, was not among them. The fact that he suspected his son might be involved in such hateful violence brought a deep swell of sadness to him. Angrily, he raised his own fist and shook it back at the men, letting them know he was watching, that he recognized many of them.

"Niggers will never vote!" one man shouted.

"Stop the blacks at the ballot box!" another chimed in.

"Traitor! Cancel the election! White men will rule this city!"

Stepping back from the gaping hole in his bedroom wall, Judge

Turner sank onto the edge of his bed and lowered his white-haired head into his hands. "We've come to this," he muttered. "All of my hope for an orderly, uneventful election is ruined." More disappointed at this turn of events than fearful of the rioters below, he clasped his hands in frustration. He'd done as good a job as he could as the local Commissioner of Elections. He had followed the federal laws and appointed three Negroes to serve as election observers. He had encouraged all men to register and exercise their right to vote. He could not let a gaggle of disgruntled, angry ex-Confederates interfere with the most important election ever to be held in South Carolina. The only thought that gave him relief was the knowledge that Sage was safely out of Charleston and living in Savannah with his wife's cousin.

Raising his head, Judge Turner stared into the sullen night as his body quivered with a great sense of loss. He knew there were many men and women living in Charleston who believed in justice and equality for the Negroes, as did he. But would they show up tomorrow to support his efforts to ensure a fair election? Or would the vigilantes and vandals like those standing in the street frighten them so much that they would stay away?

When a flash of orange erupted in the distance, the sight initiated a flood of concern. Fires were alarming occurrences in Charleston, with winds from the harbor sweeping through neighborhoods, carrying flames from building to building. An entire town could be turned into a simmering pile of ashes in just a matter of minutes. Turner watched as the specter of a massive blaze intensified on the horizon and the acrid scent of charred wood wafted into his bedroom. Placing both hands on the window sill, he leaned out into the night, focusing on the source of the fire as he shook his head in sorrow – the Freedman's Bureau and the military headquarters of Major General R. K. Scott were going up in flames.

Leon peered through a ragged hole in the wall of the musty hayloft.

His second-floor hiding place in the long-abandoned barn on the western edge of Charleston had served him well so far, and now that flames were illuminating the night sky above the city, his fear of capture shifted into a twisted sense of satisfaction. A crooked smile slid across his face. He had successfully eluded the sheriff. He'd brutally punished that traitor Benton for his sinful relations with Coretta, whom Leon had easily put out of her self-created misery. Zack Foster was no longer running around telling black men to vote, and now, that hellhole called the Freedman's Bureau was little more than a burned out shell. Leon chuckled under his breath. His plans were working out just as he knew they would. Now he had everything in place: The black soldiers remained bound and gagged in the bed of the wagon he'd stashed inside a smelly horse stall below, even though Hatch had urged Leon to let the black soldiers go and leave Charleston with him.

"Why you keepin' 'em alive?" Hatch had questioned. "Why're you worryin' about these nigger soldiers when *our* families don't even have food?"

"I know, I know," Leon agreed. "Keeping 'em alive means I can use 'em for leverage. It's time to demand what we deserve from the government. Don't worry. I know what I'm doing. They're valuable hostages. I've been waiting for the right time to cash in. Anyway, they're not eating nuthin'. They done had enough to make sure they don't die." Leon examined the barrel of his gun, spit on it, and then rubbed it with a rag.

"I hope your plan works but I'm outta here," Hatch had told Leon before disappearing into the night.

Leon had simply grunted, glad to see Hatch go. He didn't need him anymore. He had big plans that he was determined to see through to the end. He was not about to panic: A Confederate soldier would never turn tail and run away from a fight with the enemy.

CHAPTER 36

Election Day

Instead of cancelling the election, as the midnight marauders had demanded Judge Turner do, he asked General Scott to post military guards at the ballot boxes, arm his men with guns, and order them to ensure that black men could safely vote.

As soon as the ballot boxes had been placed on a table at the foot of the courthouse steps, men, both black and white, formed a line, eager to move up to mark their ballots and place them in either of two boxes: One box with a large red R painted on the side, the other with a D. An impressive crowd of observers, including women and children of both races, turned out to witness the historic event, and the festive air of Election Day was heightened by music from a brass quartet, even though the celebratory mood was tempered by the news of the burning and looting that had occurred overnight.

Eva stood with Luvena among the crowd, watching as Judge Turner mounted the courthouse steps, turned to face the people, and began to speak. "What happened last night was a tragedy, Charlestonians.

We are better than this! The war is over! We must learn to live together, respect the law, and follow it. These recent acts of violence, threats, and arson by a small number of our citizens cannot and do not reflect the values and beliefs of all of us. Participation in today's election is open to all men, both black and white, Republican and Democrat. As the Commissioner of Elections, with General Scotts' help, I now invite all eligible voters to cast their votes!"

There were loud cheers of support from the Republicans as they vocally praised the judge's words, as well as an outbreak of boos and hoots of rejection from the Democrats, making it clear that the public remained divided on the issue of black men casting a vote, and this divide created a most volatile atmosphere.

Eva waved at Trent and Oscar, who were standing in the long line of men waiting their turn to vote. After following Luvena to a shady spot beneath a canvas awning, they chatted and observed the election's progress as the crowd continued to grow.

"Let's pray these people listen to Judge Turner," Luvena grumbled. "I never believed I'd see the day when colored men would be allowed to vote and white men would be standing in line with them!"

"I find it all very exciting," Eva said, rising on tiptoes to see above the heads of those standing in front of her. "Just think. If Trent and Oscar win seats as delegates they will be involved in the formation of the new government."

"That may be true, but don't think for a minute they'll have an easy path. Just look at what happened last night. The Freedman's Bureau burned to the ground. A warehouse full of food and medical supplies gone up in flames. The Army headquarters was totally destroyed. And this is just the beginning."

"I know," Eva sadly agreed, "but for today, let's try to take heart in the good that is happening."

"I'll try, but it doesn't help that, from what I understand, Sheriff Cholett hasn't done a damn thing about tracking down those vandals who caused so much destruction overnight."

"I'm not surprised," Eva commented, recalling her less-than

satisfactory chat with him. "Oscar said, if he wins a spot on the dele-gation, the first thing he plans to bring up is the removal of Cholett as sheriff."

"If the Republicans kick out Cholett let's hope they put a decent man in that job."

As the women continued to chat, they watched the voting line inch along. The brass band entertained the crowd with a variety of patriotic numbers and children played in the street, dancing to the music and chasing one another while their fathers voted and their mothers looked on. Everyone was so involved in the historic, unusual event of black men voting alongside whites, that no one paid any attention to the flat-bottom wagon that rattled up to the courthouse steps and stopped directly in front of the table holding the ballot boxes.

Leon Turner stood up in the center of the bed of his wagon, his Brunswick rifle pointed toward the sky. When he fired a warning shot above the crowd, he immediately got everyone's attention. The unexpected eruption of gunfire initiated screams from the women, who ran to grab their children, and shouts from the men, who scat-tered and crouched down behind whatever protective barrier they could find. Many took cover among the horses and carriages lining the street or raced to cower beneath the overhangs of shopkeepers' doorways. In the rush of confusion, Eva and Luvena found them-selves pushed to the rear of the crowd, unable to see what was actu-ally going on. Within seconds, the band stopped playing, all conversation stopped, and a sinister hush claimed the once-clam-orous atmosphere.

At Leon's feet sat two Negro soldiers, their hands tied, their mouths bound with rags, their blue Union uniforms filthy and tattered. As the people stared at Leon in horrified silence, he tilted back his head and laughed at the sky.

"Won't be any more blacks voting today!" he shouted, bran-dishing his weapon at the crowd. "If one more nigger casts a vote,

I'll put a bullet in *this* man's brain," Leon threatened as he yanked Scooter up onto his feet. The emaciated man teetered, stumbled close to the edge of the wagon, then slumped back against Leon, his head wedged beneath Leon's chin. With a shove, Leon flung Scooter away, pushed him down onto the wagon floor, and jammed the barrel of his rifle against Scoter's forehead. "Listen up, you darkies! Get on home! Now! Clear outta here or there's gonna be a dead nigger messing up my daddy's courthouse steps."

As if frozen by fear, at first, no one moved. No one spoke. All eyes swiveled to Judge Turner, who was walking calmly toward his son.

"Put the gun down, Leon," the judge ordered in a commanding, yet gentle tone. "You know what you are doing is wrong. Put the gun down and let those men go."

With great effort, Eva and Luvena managed to push through the frightened crowd. "I've got to see what's going on," Eva said, inching closer toward the front. And when she finally stepped from behind a matronly woman sporting a tall, feathered hat, she stopped, both terrified and shocked by what she saw.

It can't be! It isn't! How can that be Chester sitting at that man's feet? But it *was* her husband. He was thin, haggard, with a head full of matted hair and a beard that grazed his chest, but she knew it was the man she had married staring back at her!

"Chester!" Eva shouted, shoving aside Luvena's grasp of warning. "Chester!" she screamed once more, rushing forward without thought of harm, closing the space between herself and the man in the wagon holding a rifle.

The crack of a gunshot exploded. Scooter's head burst open and his body rolled off the wagon and onto the ground, leaving a bloody trail behind.

Horrified, shocked, but unwilling to retreat, Eva plunged ahead.

"Get back, lady!" Leon ordered, leveling his gun on her. "You better stop where you are or I'll pull this trigger and shoot you too."

Eva stopped. She lifted her chin and stared at Leon Turner, the man who had pushed her to the ground and threatened to kill her once before. She hoped the disgust in her eyes was seeping into his soul, filling him with her hatred for what he was doing, for what he had done to her husband, and for what he had probably done to Zack Foster, as well. Unafraid, she locked eyes with Chester, whose pleading expression cut straight into her heart, searing it with his pain.

"You blacks got no vote here today!" Leon bellowed again, keeping his gun trained on Eva. "If ya'll don't scatter outta here right now, this lady's gonna be the next dead nigger in the street."

Taking a chance, Eva jerked forward and raced toward Chester, startling Leon, who swiveled his attention back to his hostage. When Eva threw herself down onto the ground near the back of the wagon, her movement initiated a wild shot from Leon that luckily passed over her head. Before he could take aim again, she shoved her hand into her skirt pocket, pulled out a tiny pearl-handled pistol, looked up, and fired at Leon, praying she would not miss her mark.

CHAPTER 37

An empty conference room at City Hall had been converted into General Scott's temporary headquarters in the wake of the fire that burned his office to the ground. Located only a block from the Court House, the general deemed the City Hall conference room a convenient space for the meeting he had called. Soon after he and the country clerk were seated at the head of the conference table, Trent arrived, followed by Judge Turner, and his colleague at court, Judge Edwin Vickers.

"Judge Vickers, Judge Turner, Mr. Hartwell, let's make this meeting a short one," General Scott stated in a terse manner. He opened a folder and removed two sheets of paper, which he scanned while he spoke. "Hatch Ambrose and Vern Thompson have been apprehended and are currently incarcerated. They have been charged as co-conspirators in the illegal incarceration of Union soldiers and the theft of government property. A man named Benton Langdon, who was peripherally involved in this horrible scheme of kidnapping and robbery, remains at large. We have not been able to locate him." General Scott shuffled through the papers in the folder, took out one, placed it on the table, and then continued. "Now, we must address the situation with Mrs. Phillips."

"Absolutely," Trent agreed. "I am here to request the immediate release of my client, Eva Phillips. She cannot be held on a false charge of murder. It is true, she shot Leon Turner, but as her attorney, I plead self-defense on her behalf." He paused to address Judge Turner. "I am very sorry for the death of your son, but … you were there, as was I. We saw what happened. She defended herself, that's all there is to it."

With a solemn nod, Judge Turner agreed. "As grieved as I am by this tragic event, I hold no malice toward your client, Hartwell. And I want you to know, Mr. Vickers, that I have recused myself from this case, as I should. However, I have to agree that Mrs. Phillips shot my son in self-defense and should be released from jail immediately. I hope you see it as I do."

"I'm not sure that I do," Vickers shot back.

Trent folded his arms across his chest as he, too, addressed Judge Vickers. "If you put Eva Phillips on trial there will be riots in the streets. There were many witnesses to the incident who will agree that she was in the right to shoot Leon."

"That's easy for you to say," Judge Vickers scowled, his small dark eyes flashing. "I can't simply let a black woman go free after she has killed a white man. There must be a trial. We must let a jury decide her fate. And if the jury says she's to go free, so be it." He huffed a short breath and fingered the bushy sideburns on his puffy cheeks. "Leon told her to stay back. She taunted him by running forward, as if she were going to attack him. I don't think everyone feels as you do, Mr. Hartwell."

General Scott coughed into his hand, lifted an eyebrow in question, and leveled a stern gaze on all three men seated at the table. "As the final arbiter of legal matters in the Second District of South Carolina, I order the immediate release of Mrs. Eva Phillips. No charges will be filed." Then without inviting any comment on his decision, he signed the formal order, handed it to the clerk, and said, "Please take this to the Court House and file it, then go tell Sheriff Cholett to release Mrs. Phillips at once."

"Sorry, Luvena, can't let you bring that in," Pate Cholett said as he lifted his rib cage and thrust out his chest as if to ensure that the black woman glaring back at him took notice of the silver badge on his shirt.

In a dismissive move, Luvena took a step forward, trying to push past Cholett, who was stationed just inside the jailhouse entry.

"You ain't goin' in," he growled.

"Please step aside and allow me to pass," Luvena said in a surprisingly even tone. "I brought Eva her lunch, 'cause I know you don't feed anyone decent food in this jail. She's been here for two days now."

"Sorry, but no one brings food or drink into the jail." Cholett tilted back his head and rolled his eyes to the side.

"Well, I am not going to toss out this perfectly good soup. All I want to do is give this to her. There's no harm in making sure she has food to eat!" Luvena's words flew at Cholett in a blast of irritation. "Why are you being so rude!"

"Rude? Don't get loud, now," the sheriff cautioned, adopting the take-charge attitude he had been using on troublesome people for years. With eyes at half-mast, he sized up the carefully-put-together woman who was sending evil thoughts his way. "I'm the law in here. You really don't want to mess with me. So quiet down."

"I am not being loud," Luvena insisted in a voice that rose from deep within her throat. "I just want you to let me see Eva."

"Sorry, can't make exceptions, even for you. Why don't you just give me the food and I'll make sure someone *deserving* gets it," Cholett chuckled, obviously amused with himself. He placed both hands at his waist, pushed his lips together, and waited for Luvena's response, clearly determined to remain in control of the situation.

"You don't frighten me, Cholett. I came here to personally deliver this to my friend and you are not …." Luvena stopped in mid-sentence and lifted her nose, focusing over Cholett's right shoulder, causing him to turn around to see what she was looking at.

The County Clerk strode over to the sheriff and stood next to him, casually observing the scene. Cholett shifted his shoulders back in tiny movements, as if proud of himself for enforcing his rules.

"Hello, Ma'am," the clerk said to Luvena before nodding at Cholett. "What's going on here?"

Luvena immediately launched into a recap of her request.

"Well, ma'am, you go on and take the food to Mrs. Phillips so she can eat," he stated. Then he faced Cholett while holding out a piece of paper. "Here's General Scott's order for Mrs. Phillips' release."

"Release? When did this happen?"

"Half an hour ago. All charges have been dropped. You can let her go now."

"But she's a murderer," Cholett protested.

"Not according to General Scott. The general says she killed Leon Turner in self-defense."

Against Eva's protests, Luvena urged Eva to eat a portion of the soup she had prepared, and then helped her change into the fresh clothing Luvena had brought to the jail.

"Where is Chester?" Eva fretted. "I didn't even get a chance to touch him, to speak to him before Cholett hauled me away! I must go to him. Now!"

"In time, Eva," Luvena assured her friend, resting a calming hand on Eva's trembling arm. "He's at the Freedman's Hospital. I went to see him yesterday."

"How is he?"

"According to the doctor, he's dehydrated. Malnourished, but in fair shape for what he's been through."

"Did you tell him everything?" Eva asked in a tentative voice.

"Not *everything*. He knows why you are here in Charleston and that you are staying with me. But, other than that, well, I thought it better left for you to tell him, don't you think?"

"Oh, yes, I guess, but," Eva whispered, "what am I to do?"

"Go to your husband, take him in your arms, and tell him that you love him... you do love him, don't you?"

"With all my heart."

"Then that's all there is to it. Nothing more needs to be said. Ever."

Eva nodded in agreement.

"Now," Luvena began, "I want you to look your best when you see your husband." She removed a hairbrush from her bag and began brushing Eva's dark curls, sweeping them into a lovely cascade at the back of her head. Dipping a cloth into a basin of water, she wiped dirt from her friend's mud-streaked face and applied a touch of rouge to her cheeks.

"Oh, Luvena, this is all such a shock!" Eva said, turning to grab hold of Luvena's hand. "Chester is really alive! I can hardly believe it. But he's suffered so much. My heart breaks to think of what he must have endured."

"But endure he did," Luvena replied.

"Yes, that's true. I'm so proud of him for holding on, for coming back to me! It was such a shock to see him in that wagon, with Leon Turner waving a gun around, and on Election Day, too!" She paused, reflecting on the incident before suddenly asking, "The election! What happened?"

"When the vote was counted, Berkeley County elected eight Republican representatives to the constitutional convention, including Trent Hartwell, and one Negro, Oscar Singleton."

"Oh," Eva sighed, relieved. "Good. They won. That makes up for a lot."

"Yes, it does," Luvena remarked while finishing with Eva's hair and then dabbing a touch of perfume behind each of Eva's ears. She placed both hands on her friend's shoulders and turned Eva to face her. "You certainly surprised me! You? Packing a pistol! When on earth did you get it?"

"Soon after Trent completed the paperwork for my purchase of Bryan Tract. I began thinking about living out in the country, all alone. With so much violence going on, I thought, why not purchase a gun, just for protection? So, I went to the gunsmith one afternoon and bought a pistol just like yours."

"Thank God you listened to me," Luvena laughed, shaking her head. "Eva, you are not like any woman I ever met. And I love you for being who you are."

The hug that they shared was long and firm and filled with the love of their friendship, and when Luvena pulled away, she was wiping tears from her eyes. "All right. Time to go. Trent sent his carriage to take you to the hospital."

"Oh, my. He did?" Eva remarked with concern. "He has been so good to me. How can I ever thank him for all he has done?"

"By remaining his friend while you build a wonderful life with your husband, I would think," Luvena supplied.

"I certainly plan to do just that," Eva promised.

Luvena smiled, then gave Eva a final hug. "I think you look presentable enough. Are you ready to greet your husband now?"

"Absolutely," Eva replied, holding back tears she knew were going to fall as soon as she set eyes on the only man she had ever loved.

When Eva stepped outside the jail, she was surprised, and pleased to find Trent standing beside his carriage, waiting for her. She had been worried about seeing him, now that her circumstances had so dramatically changed, but when he removed his hat and smiled at her, she saw acceptance in his eyes and knew their friendship would last, that their uneventful flirtation would fade into memories of a time when they both had needed comfort more than love.

Once she was seated inside Trent's carriage, she turned to him with a grateful heart, eager to thank him for believing in her, for encouraging her to remain in South Carolina.

"If you had not pushed me to buy Bryan Tract I might have returned to Boston, and things would have turned out very differently," she told him.

"That's true," he agreed. "But remember, because you attended the election, you were there to save your husband's life."

"Yes, I was," she acknowledged. "And I didn't even know what I was doing. I just took out the gun and pulled the trigger." A pause as she pondered, once more, what had actually happened. "What if I had shot you! Or a child? Or a man standing in the voting line?" She shifted to the side to look into Trent's honey brown eyes. "I couldn't live with myself if I had accidentally killed an innocent bystander. It's hard enough to live with what I did to the Turner family."

"Don't dwell on that, Eva. You have so much to look forward to."

"I know," she agreed.

"Life tests us in many ways... personally, financially, and even romantically. I'd like to believe that you and I have passed such tests and we'll remain good friends as our separate journeys unfold."

"I'd like that very much," Eva agreed, giving Trent's hand a firm squeeze.

Trent inclined his head, took a deep breath, and then spoke to his driver. "Gus, I'll walk home from here. You take Mrs. Phillips to the Freedman's Hospital. Her husband is waiting for her."

Trent remained on the sidewalk, his hat in his hand, watching his carriage until it disappeared around a corner. An odd sense of defla- tion suddenly collapsed inside of him, dissolving the tension he'd been harboring since the day Eva was arrested. It pleased him to know she was now free to unite with her husband and build a future with him, a future he hoped would be peaceful, and long lasting. As for himself, he had no regrets about having acted on his feelings for Eva. She was a captivating, smart, and very brave young woman. Why wouldn't he have been attracted to her?

With a nod to her departure, Trent placed his tall beaver skin hat on his head and started northward on Meeting Street, anxious to get home and sit quietly on his veranda to contemplate his own, rather muddled, future. He'd had rather bad luck with women so far. Betrayed by Rebecca, spurned by Sage, replaced by Eva's brave husband. He sighed. *Everything happens for a reason*, he told himself as he lifted his chin and continued on his way.

Moments later, while standing at the corner of Meeting and Cumberland, he was looking toward the old Powder Magazine, which had safely stored tons of gunpowder during the American Revolution, when he saw a woman hurrying toward him and calling out, "Trent! Trent Hartwell!"

Curious, he did not readily recognize the woman, who was wearing a floppy blue hat with a profusion of multi-colored feathers springing from the crown and veil that covered half of her face. He stopped and stared at the woman as she came closer.

"Trent! I knew it was you!" She lifted her chin and pushed back the veil.

"Ruby! Josephine Ruby," Trent exclaimed, matching her grin as he took her extended hand and squeezed it in genuine pleasure to see his lovely friend once more.

"What are you doing in Charleston?" he asked.

"I was about to ask you the same thing. I had no idea where you went when you left Chicago, but I wasn't surprised that you left."

"Well…it's a long story." He pressed his lips together in thought. "I should have told you I was leaving Chicago and going to South Carolina, but…"

No," she interrupted. "You owed me no explanation."

"I know. But you … you said you would never return to the South."

"Yes, I did say that," she agreed, "but I am here to claim an inheritance I never knew existed."

"How nice. I hope it's a big inheritance and I hope that means you'll be staying in Charleston for a while," Trent replied, taking in Ruby's stunning appearance. He'd never seen her wearing anything but plain, drab barmaid's clothing, and certainly no rouge on her lips and cheeks. But now, she was fashionably dressed in a tailored blue dress with matching gloves and her once-unruly red curls had been partially tamed and coiffed to perfection.

Ruby smiled when she told him, "Perhaps I'll stick around," as her eyes traveled to his left hand and back up to his face. "Looks like you're still playing the role of the lonely bachelor?" she said, more like a question than a statement of fact.

A slight shrug of his shoulders accompanied Trent's answer. "Looks that way, doesn't it?"

With a lift of a perfectly arched brow, Ruby hooked her arm through his. "So, when can we catch up?"

"Now. Right now," he replied. "There's a nice café a few blocks from here. We'll have coffee ... or," he chuckled, "would you prefer beer?"

Ruby gave up a throaty laugh and shook her head, bobbing the red curls that escaped her hat and framed her face. "Coffee will do just fine."

"Good. I want to hear all about this inheritance of yours." He held her by the elbow as they made their way across the busy the street, and once they were safely on the other side, he looked over at Ruby and let his eye take her in. She looked different outwardly, but she was just as he remembered. Open, honest, easy to be talk to and fun to be with. She had become, perhaps, even more attractive than he remembered, as if the years since he'd last seen her had enhanced her beauty and matured her demeanor. "Do you have a lawyer to assist with your legal affairs?" he inquired.

"As of this morning, I don't."

"Well, now you do," he told her, offering her his arm as they continued on their way.

CHAPTER 38

For a long time, Eva and Chester simply held onto each other, as if regaining lost touches, recapturing lost time, their cheeks pressed together, their eyes closed in blissful remembrance. The doctor placed a tall folding screen around Chester's hospital bed, providing the couple a modicum of privacy, for which Eva was very grateful. As she traced a finger along her husband's recently shaved jaw and drank in the sight of him, she was shaken by the truth of his presence. Sorrow, swift and raw, suddenly engulfed her at the sight of his near-skeletal appearance, the dark circles under his eyes, the scar on his face where a bullet that failed to kill him had torn his flesh away.

How strange, she thought. *I came to South Carolina to find my mother, but found my wonderful Chester instead. What forces of nature were working in my favor for such a thing to happen?*

"Do you want to talk about it?" she tested, not wanting to tire him or revive memories that he most likely wanted to forget.

"I don't mind," Chester answered, reaching out to take her hand, sinking back against the hospital pillow. Turning solemn, he went on. "I thought about you every minute of every day I was holed up in that prison," he said in a serious tone. "I got hit in the belly during the first wave of fightin' on the beach at Battery Wagner. I was ready to go to Heaven when I closed my eyes and gave up. But Leon, Hatch, and their gang of thieves pulled me and four other colored soldiers out of the sand after the smoke had cleared and the defeated Union soldiers retreated."

"There were five of you?" Eva remarked.

"At first. All from the 54th… but three died, leaving me and Scooter, the man Leon shot in the head in front of everyone."

"How in the world did Leon think he could get away with such an evil plot?"

"'Cause he was surrounded with men just like him. At first, I heard 'em talking about keeping us black soldiers alive to use us as hostages to rob the Union camps. They wanted to force the officers to trade food and supplies for freein' us. But that fell through, and when the war was over, the Confederates all ran off. They abandoned the Castle, but Leon stayed behind. He kept us at the Castle just to feed his hatred of black men. Then one day, I heard him telling Hatch he was gonna use me and Scooter to make trouble on Election Day."

"And he did."

"But I heard the votin' went on and a black man's gonna be at the convention."

"That's true. His name is Oscar Singleton. A friend of mine. You'll meet him soon enough," Eva said, going on to tell Chester about her encounter with Leon on the road to Moncks Corner and the murder of Zack Foster. "I went to General Scott because I wanted Leon to be punished…. not killed." A sob escaped her throat and she suddenly broke down, shedding raw tears of shame. "I didn't think about killing Leon. I guess I never thought I'd ever really use that gun. I didn't even know how to fire it. I just pointed it and pulled the trigger."

"Good thing you did… you saved both our lives, Eva. Don't you ever feel guilty 'bout that. God was watching out over us, that's all there is to that." Chester gathered her into his arms, pulling her head against his chest as he stroked her hair and kissed the side of her face.

"Leon Turner won't be makin' trouble anymore, for anybody … and you don't have to feel bad about what you did." Chester eased her off his chest, shook his head in amazement and gave her a puzzled look.

"Never in my dreams, and I had plenty of 'em about you, did I ever imagine seeing you in Charleston, and most certainly not toting a gun!"

Eva sniffled, grinned sheepishly, and lifted her chin at Chester. "Guess that shows you how much you still have to learn about your wife."

EPILOGUE

Three months later

After Eva's guests had roamed the expansive gardens and admired the pink oleanders, the white gardenias, and the yellow black-eyed-susans in her carefully tended flowerbeds, everyone retired to the shady upper veranda for refreshments.

Bina, now residing and working at Eva's new home, had been planning and cooking for nearly a week, preparing platters of fried rabbit, bowls of Carolina red rice, heaps of fried green tomatoes, and buckets of spicy Creole shrimp.

The low country menu that Eva offered her guests had been as carefully prepared as her guest list, which included new friends as well as those from long ago.

Luvena arrived with Millie Foster, Zack's lovely widow, who thanked Eva effusively for bringing her husband's killer out of the shadows and to the end he deserved. Oscar brought Roby Green and Little John to the party, as well as news that Pate Cholett was no longer the sheriff, having been replaced by a colored man from Mount Pleasant who was a well-respected lawman with an excellent reputation for keeping order.

Elmina, Oda, Kalaju, and all of the women from the village of Moree came together in a wagon that Chester sent to pick them up. Their colorful African print dresses and tall crowned hair-dos infused a festive spirit to the gathering. Elmina also brought news that stunned Eva into silence: After an exchange of letters with her relatives in the village, Elmina had located Mayree, who was well, and excited to hear news of her daughter, whom she was anxious to see once again.

And of course, Aunt Tully, who had been in South Carolina for nearly a month was there, having made the trip with Lawyer Daniels, bringing news about what was happening in Boston.

"More lemonade, ma'am," Bina asked Tully, leaning over the woman's shoulder with a frosty pitcher of her cool citrus drink.

Tully grinned and extended her glass without remark, smiling at Eva as Bina poured. "You and Chester's home is all so lovely, Eva," she told her niece. "So much more lovely than you described in your letters."

"That's why she insisted we come to see all of this for ourselves," Lawyer Daniels added, polishing off his second mint julep. "Chester!" he called out, signaling his former assistant to his side. "You got an awful lot of rooms to fill up in this house. I understand that the next time I come for a visit I'll see more'n you and Eva living on this place."

Chester laughed and went to stand behind Eva, gently caressing her shoulder. "That's right. In a few more months I 'spect there'll be a little one running around these grounds," he assured Lawyer Daniels, giving him a sly smile as he leaned down and kissed Eva on the neck.

Eva reached up and covered her husband's hand with hers as she looked out across the refurbished property. Her gaze lingered on the metal placard swinging above the tall iron gates at the end of the road where a sign announced to all visitors that they had arrived at her home, *Moree.*

Shifting her attention to her guests on the veranda, she thought about the only person who was missing: Trent, who was in

Columbia helping his lady friend from Chicago with a legal matter. She wished he could have brought Ruby to meet everyone, and to celebrate with her, but there would be other reasons to celebrate and she'd see Trent and Ruby soon enough. However, he had surprised her by sending along a note of congratulations on her successful renovation of the old Gallard place, along with what he referred to as a delayed wedding gift for her and Chester: The deed to the missing one-hundred-seventy-eight acres of adjoining land that faced the Cooper River. As stated in the deed, the land was hers to hold forever for her and Chester's heirs. She and Chester were already making plans: As soon as their first child was old enough to travel, they would make the journey across the ocean to find Mayree and restore the missing link in their family chain.

AFTERWORD FROM THE AUTHOR

ANITA RICHMOND BUNKLEY

The Twisted Crown is a work of fiction, set within the historical framework of America's post-Civil War Reconstruction era. Minor liberties related to the actual timeline of events have been taken in order to create and enhance the dramatic premise of the novel. Though the characters are fictional, the storyline was inspired by the unusual life of my great-grandfather, Adison Carey (A.C.) Richmond, a white man born in Springfield, Vermont in 1833, who moved to Iowa as a young man, and then migrated to Charleston, South Carolina after the Civil War.

The *Charleston City Directory* of 1872 lists A.C. Richmond as residing in a house at 51 Wentworth Street, though he also maintained a residence in Moncks Corner, SC, some thirty miles to the north. There, he met my great-grandmother, Ellen Josephine Singleton, an African-American woman who bore him six children. Even though miscegenation was deemed illegal in most of the South at that time, my great-grandparents listed themselves as "married" on the 1880 Federal Census record.

Though A.C. Richmond referred to himself as a farmer, he invested wisely in large tracts of land and became involved in the political restructuring of the South. He was a member of the Reconstruction Convention of South Carolina at the close of the war and eventually became a State Senator. The earliest record of his political presence in South Carolina is found in an 1868 notice published in *The Journal of Negro History* (Vol.5, No.1, Jan, 1920) which contains the names of the Delegates elected to the South Carolina Constitutional Convention held at Charleston, SC, January 14 to March 18, 1868. The (Saint John's) Berkley delegates were, as stated in the publication:

M.F. Becker, D.H. Chamberlain, Timothy Hurley, Joseph H. Jenks, *A.C. Richmond, white;* William Jervey, Benjamin Byas, W.H. Gray, George Lee, colored.

Between 1876 and 1877, A.C. Richmond formally deeded one-hundred-seventy-six acres of land directly to my great-grand-mother, Josephine Singleton, of which a portion remains in my family today. The property was always referred to as Bryan Tract. A.C. Richmond stated, according to this excerpt from the wording in the original deed, that the land was:

...To have and to hold all ... by the said, Josephine Singleton during her natural life for her support and maintenance and for the support and maintenance of her three (3) children heretofore named. (Mary Rebecca, Benjamin Smalls (my grandfather), *and Frances) And at the death of the said, Josephine Singleton, the said property shall become absolutely the property of the said three children, their heirs and assigns forever.*

The US government's effort to reconstruct the South was not a success. There were not enough white men willing to make the effort to work with blacks, and funds to rebuild the South did not materialize. The cash-strapped Freedman's Bureau never received sufficient money or adequate staff to accomplish the promises envisioned for the program. The Bureau was abolished by an act of Congress approved June 10, 1872 effective June 30, 1872. When the Freedman's Bureau shut down, its banks collapsed, former slaves lost their money, and the reconstruction government could no longer collect sufficient taxes to adequately govern.

At its height, the Freedmen's Bureau in South Carolina established a medical department with several camps, dispensaries, and hospitals, providing care for close to 5,000 whites and more than 40,000 blacks. In the latter part of 1868, Bureau hospitals were either closed or turned over to local officials, and dispensaries were discontinued.

During the 1866-67 school year, the Bureau spent nearly $25,000 on freedmen schools. However, by the end of 1868 waning support from Northern benevolent societies and a steady decrease in freedmen contributions reversed some of the early progress made in the establishment of the freedmen school system. By the summer of 1870, with all funds exhausted, the Bureau's educational program in South Carolina came to a close, and its buildings were turned over to benevolent societies. (Lowcountry Africana: Records of the Field Offices for the State of South Carolina)

By 1876, South Carolina, Louisiana, and Florida were still ruled by black and white Republicans, kept in power by the presence of Federal Troops. Southern Democrats continued to fight for the overthrow of the Reconstruction Governments in the former rebel states. The political rise of the Democrats led to the eventual formation of fear-based groups like the Klu Klux Klan, who blamed the freedoms afforded to the former slaves for the economic and social problems in the South.

When Rutherford B. Hayes, a Republican, was narrowly elected President of the United States, the southern Democrats forced him to agree to the removal of all Federal Troops so they could run their states as they wished.

By 1877, all Federal Troops had been withdrawn from the South, ending the era of Reconstruction.

(PHOTOS FOLLOW)

Author's Great-Grandfather
Adison Carey (A.C.) Richmond 1833-1883

Author's Great-Grandmother
Josephine Singleton Richmond 1854 -1914
With their daughter, Mary Rebecca Richmond

Author's Father
Clifford Oscar Richmond 1909-1997 (second from right). The first
public school for Negroes in Moncks Corner, SC was founded
in 1880.

Photo taken at Dixie Training School, Moncks Corner, SC. Circa 1925
with students and principal, R.A. Ready.
The three-room Dixie Training School was built in 1918.

DISCUSSION QUESTIONS

1. What characteristics initially draw Eva and Chester together? How do these characteristics serve them as their story unfolds?

2. How do you describe Eva's reaction to her young husband's desire to fight for the Union? How does this affect her decision to return to the South?

3. Would you consider Tully a selfish woman? Why? Why not?

4. Why do you think Trent was so racially tolerant? In what ways does his attitude serve him/ harm him when he goes to South Carolina?

5. How does the political atmosphere in South Carolina reflect the changes in the cultural post-war landscape?

6. Why do you think Leon's attitude about life after returning from war is so different from his father's? How does it compare to his sister's?

7. Do you think the establishment of the Freedman's Bureau in the southern states was a valid concept? If so, what could have been done to prevent it from failing?

8. Land ownership was very important after the Civil War. Why do you believe so many black families lost land they once owned?

ABOUT THE AUTHOR

Anita is an NAACP IMAGE AWARD nominee, a member of the TEXAS INSTITUTE OF LETTERS, winner of Favorite Author Award from Go On Girl Book Club, and the recipient of a Career Achievement Award from *Romantic Times* magazine.

Reviewers and fans alike refer to her novels as sweeping sagas that are extremely entertaining—embraced for their historical accuracy, strong romantic themes, and vivid characterizations of people of color in periods of history not widely showcased in literary works.

A native of Columbus, Ohio, Anita lives in Cypress, TX with her husband, Crawford. She holds a Bachelor of Arts Degree from Mount Union College, Alliance, Ohio.

www.anitabunkley.com
arbun@sbcglobal.net
www.rinardpublishing.com

amazon.com/author/anitabunkley

www.ingramcontent.com/pod-product-compliance
Lightning Source LLC
Chambersburg PA
CBHW070210260626
47160CB00002B/513